Come Back Yesterday

Maura Keane

ISBN: 978-1-908477-69-9

A CIP catalogue for this book is available from the National Library.

Published by Original Writing Ltd., Dublin, 2011.

Printed by Clondalkin Group, Clonshaugh, Dublin 17

To my children Filumena Maria and Michael Joseph.

Also my late son-in-law Darragh McGrath.

Contents

Chapter 1

This is 1922 and the roar of the twenties is gaining momentum. The age that produced the flapper, daringly short hemlines and eton- cropped heads.... all epitomised so brilliantly in the sparkling music of the Charleston.

This is the decade I stepped into when my Aunt Cissy took me out of my quiet Wicklow village and brought me to Dublin for a holiday.

My name is Lynette, youngest daughter of a small farmer. There were three of us sisters in the family, Nell, Dora and myself. We were not well off and Da and Mam worked very hard to keep us in modest comfort. In spite of many ups and downs we always had enough plain fare on the table and a good thatched roof over our heads. In winter and summer a blazing fire of turf and pine logs made the old kitchen, with its slanting rafters and flagged floor, a cosy little haven.

Timmy Foley....that's Da, bluff, good-natured and quick-witted....was very popular with the friendly inhabitants of the little village.

My mother, small, dark and shy, was known to everyone for her kind heart and capable help. The local children referred to her affectionately as Mothereen.

When I was twenty, Da's sister, came to visit us. She was a single lady, a dressmaker in Dublin; she was a good deal younger than Da and much prettier too, with large grey eyes and curly black hair. In spite of being so conversant with the rag trade, she never wore anything fashionable herself, but always appeared in non-descript colours, baggy jumpers and over-long skirts.

After remarking what a big girl I had grown and how much I resembled Da (how relations ramble on if they believe you take after their side of the family) she continued.

"How would you like to come to Dublin, Lynn, just for a bit of a hol?"

"Oh Aunt!" I shouted, midway between hysterics and ecstasy.

"Then you'd like to come?"Aunt Cissy pursued with an impish smile.

"Oh yes, I'd love to," I cried, clapping my hands like a child.

Dublin to me was the most wonderful place in the world; indeed it was the world. There amid flashing lights and magical trams....a far cry from our easy-going pony and dilapidated trap....one could enjoy oneself in the most exciting manner, or so I fondly believed.

Fantastic shops would be everywhere....hadn't I seen the advertisements in the Dublin newspapers which Aunt Cissy sent occasionally?

I closed my eyes, as I contemplated the miracle of electric light everywhere, even in the streets! What a change from our candles and smelly paraffin lamps.

My friend, Eileen Keogh, who had visited her married sister in Dublin City and considered herself very well up on all aspects of life there, was delighted when she heard my news.

"Oh Lynn," she said breathlessly to me one evening over a cup of tea, "ye would never have to peel a pratie up there. They have special gadgets for doin' all them things....and playhouses and ballrooms and inside taps with running water...."

"Hold on!" I interrupted, "that's enough to be going on with. I can't take it all in."

I gazed at Eileen with awe and she younger than me too!

When Da and Mam saw how eager I was they agreed to my going, with all sorts of rules and stipulations, of course.

Being the youngest I was treated like a bit of a mat by my sisters Nell and Dora. Bossy Nell would say: "You stay in this evening and help Mam grade the eggs, and next week you and I will go to the concert in the village."

Or Dora would wheedle: "Just this evening, Letty. It won't take you long to help Mam with the baking and I'll lend you the latest book that Josie Moons gave me. It's powerful altogether and with saucer-like, eyes she would whisper the title: "One Desperate Night Of Love."

This was meant as a most beguiling inducement to me to stand in on her jobs.

"Another penny dreadful," I would retort contemptuously, for my taste in books by-passed romantic fiction and was rooted in Irish historical characters and local folklore. But foolishly I fell for a lot of their promises, and by the time I had finished all their jobs and my own too, I was only fit to fall into bed.

But when it came to Nell's promised concert she was adept at excuses. She was always washing her hair, mending her stockings or resting with some frightful home-brewed concoctions on her face.

You can't expect me to go out looking like this," she would mumble between stiff lips, peering out of a hardening face mask of greyish sludge and herbs.

"No," I would have to concede reasonably and then in a fit of anger add:

"Why do you have to make such an onslaught on the local male population, anyway. Heavens! If they saw you now they'd die of shock."

Subdued by the hardened beauty mask, Nell would have no option but to listen to the abuse I gave her "for her own good."

As the argument was so one-sided, I usually gave up after a few rounds and went off to tackle Dora.

With Dora it was always "tomorrow" when everything would be great, and she would disappear into our bedroom with the latest herbal remedy on her face to bleach the hated freckles that powdered her snub little nose. After giving her remedy time to produce results I would return to the attack, only to find her head a tangle of newspaper curls. Words would come tumbling over each other in incoherent excuses while I, seeing with rage that I was beaten, could only threaten retribution at the earliest possible opportunity.

The end of the story was always the same; Lynette Foley did not get to the concert or anywhere else as promised. Foolishly, I always forgave them, especially when some little peace offering exchanged hands. Yet to my chagrin I still fell for their promises.

Chapter 2

I went upstairs to pack my most respectable looking skirt and jumpers with other bits and pieces. I had not much in the way of finery and a neat parcel was soon completed. Nell and Dora bustled about in a mixture of envy and amazement at what they termed "my luck."

"You must have the lend of my amber necklace," offered Nell. I stopped stitching a long tear in a faded pink petticoat to stare at her. Such impulsive generosity was surprising. Those amber beads were a present from her godmother in America and her most treasured possession. No one dared lay a finger on them.

"I couldn't possibly take them," I stammered.

"Of course you can; they'll bring you luck when you're on the look out," said Nell with a knowing wink, as she folded the glowing beads between my two flannel nightdresses.

I hid a smile at Nell's preoccupation with being on "the look-out," wherever she went.

Me on the look – out, I mused and laughed uproariously.

"Well," chimed in Dora archly, "don't you want a man like everyone else?"

I thought that was putting it too baldly, so I only nodded vaguely and went on with my mending.

"Then," said Nell in superior tones, you must look about you. You've a wonderful chance. "Wish I were you...." she trailed off enviously.

"Me too," sighed Dora reflectively, toying with a frizzy strand of tortured hair.

There was a long silence, each of us lost in her own thoughts. It would be the first time we had ever been separated. Tears shone in Nell's eyes and Dora suddenly jumped up.

"Your handbag's too shabby for Dublin," she exclaimed with forced brightness, as she pulled a smart little brown bag out of her drawer.

"It'll do," I said absently, thinking about my family and sick at the thought of leaving them.

Nell eyed me sternly. "Dora's right," she said "take her bag; it's leather anyway."

I felt my eyes burning with unshed tears as I tried to thank them, but there was no time for wavering regrets. Mam's voice drifted cheerfully up the stairs calling us down to tea.

I was advised by all to "bunk" it early, as I had a very exciting day before me.

"You must put your best foot forward tomorrow, girl," advised Da, while Mam fussed about with parcels of eggs and brown bread to sustain me in Dublin.

I obliged by going up to bed, but did myself little good by tossing and turning all night. At cock-crow, I had everyone awake with last minute preparations, amounting to panic, when my only decent blouse was blown off the line and lay inert and soggy in a pool of muck outside the pig house.

Chapter 3

We had to leave early to catch the eight o'clock train. I must confess I cried a little when, with fifty shillings from Mam and Da tucked safely in the leather handbag, and Aunt Cissy dabbing her eyes beside me in the old trap, I clung to each of my family in turn, and wondered what had come over me to ever think of leaving them....

At last we were on our way, waving and crying to the receding figures of family and neighbours, until we turned a bend in the boreen and were lost in a cloud of dust.

Da was driving us to the station, and I was glad he was with us just a little bit longer.

"Enjoy yourself," he bellowed, kissing me heartily, and pushing me onto the train, as my lips trembled on a shaky "good-bye Da."

"Take care of her, Cissy," he whispered with anxious eyes.

"You know I will, Timmy," she said gently, "and thank you for letting her come."

It was my first time on a train. I pinched myself to make sure I was not dreaming. One day to be doing just ordinary things, and the next to be speeding past unfamiliar landmarks in this great black monster, which snaked along its silver rails. Mesmerised I listened, as the train kept singing "diddily-do, diddily-da," while a great panorama of mountains, rivers and fields unfolded, lovelier than I had ever imagined.

"The garden of Ireland," murmured Aunt Cissy, and I saw that she too was spellbound.

Sometimes my heart leapt in terror as we passed another train, which seemed to be shrieking and rampaging through the deserted countryside, enveloping everything in black steam. Little sleepy stations sped past, frost gleaming on roof and hedgerow, for it was early Spring and very cold.

At various stations, red-faced farmers with an assortment of vegetables and livestock, got in or departed, and the carriage was wrapped in a variety of farmyards smells and clouds of tobacco. A fat, merry-eyed woman, lost in a huge shawl, plodded on. She deposited a great basket of eggs on the floor and fell thankfully into the seat opposite us. She was soon regaling everyone around her with all the local gossip, until she reluctantly got out at her stop in Wicklow town.

I felt a bit tired after all the excitement of the journey when the train puffed importantly into Westland Row station.

Aunt Cissy hailed a taxi to her flat in the South Circular Road. I was thrilled to be travelling in such an elegant modern motor. It was square-shaped, black and with beautiful inlaid mahogany fittings.

It's called a "Mathis," Aunt Cissy enlightened me, regarding the make of the car.

We moved serenely through a bewildering maze of streets, amongst horses and carts, trams, motor-bikes and sidecars, motorcars, and even a drove of cattle on their way to market.

Aunt Cissy pointed out various imposing buildings, and told me who lived in them and a bit of their history. I had never seen so many people together in my life, but the thing that remained rooted in my mind about the capital was the hurry everyone seemed to be in. Everything moved with terrifying speed, and I was filled with fear that they would all meet at a certain point in tremendous collision.

It was nearly dinnertime when we reached Aunt Cissy's flat; situated in a terrace of Victorian red brick houses, with stiff lace curtains on the windows, and a patch of garden in front.

Her flat was neat and compact, and consisted of a tiny kitchen with creamy walls and red and white checked curtains. A jug of frilly daffodils on the table glowed in a sudden shaft of sunshine.

A nice young woman from the flat opposite brought us in some milk, bread and butter.

While I laid the table and cut the bread, Aunt Cissy extracted a sort of meaty soup from a tin, and set it to heat on the stove beside a saucepan of potatoes.

Over dinner, she explained the mysteries of gas and electricity. She clicked the light switch several times to demonstrate her point.It was all very exciting, and the tin food a novelty, even if it did taste very far removed from what Mam made at home.

Afterwards, we cleaned up the kitchen, complete with running water. I ran it for some minutes to savour the sheer pleasure of it. At home, every drop of water used for drinking or washing, had to be drawn by bucket from the well-field, or the pond in the cobbled yard.

The rest of the flat was comprised of a spacious living room in which my aunt carried on her dressmaking business. A large Singer sewing machine stood in the middle of the room, a cloud of pink tulle anchored to its needle. All sorts of coloured materials littered everything.

A half finished dress of pink crepe-de-chine, with the fashionable low-slung bodice, hung from a rail which ran the whole length of the wall. Several others in various stages of completion, swung behind it, and over every available chair and table, lay many jumbled bits of sleeves and skirts.

Aunt Cissy had a great love of her job; even it could be termed a vocation with her. Lovingly she ran her fingers over the surface of several materials and showed me the different types, and what sort of design they were most suited for.

"This is a natural shan-tung silk," she explained, "it will wash like new every time, and this is crepe corona, ideal for blouses and underwear," and she held it out for my inspection.

"What's this one?" I asked with interest, gently touching a long piece of matt stuff in a rich plum colour.

"That's crepe morcain and much beloved by the older lady for evening wear," said my aunt, carefully folding it back in its bag.

I wandered around in this Aladdin's cave, repeating the names of the different fabrics as Aunt Cissy rhymed them off.

There was mousse line dress satin, black chiffon taffeta, foulard silk, floral shan-tung, silk stockinette, rich midnight blue velvet, and gorgeous French crepe-de-chine delightfully patterned with flowers. I sighed blissfully picturing myself clad in some of this grandeur.

"Wake up , Lynn," said my Aunt briskly and gently took the silken mound out of my arms.

I followed her into the pretty primrose bedroom, which I was to share with her for the visit. What struck me most about it was the magnificent quilt of intricate patchwork, which Aunt Cissy had made herself, from hundreds of pieces of silks and cottons left over from all sorts of garments.

"I must tell you about it some time," she said noticing my interest in the quilt. "Each patch has its own story," she added with a twinkle.

Lastly, we looked in at her green and white bathroom.... another aspect of modern living which promised me great satisfaction after the tin bath of home, which was arduously fed from the range with pots and kettles of hot water.

I moved about excitedly, fingering every other thing reverently until suddenly glancing up, I saw my face clearly reflected in a large oval mirror. At home our only mirror was peeped into quickly, to see that hair was tidy and hat on straight, but the glass was mottled and dark.

I stared back at myself timidly, surprise reflected in the dark blue eyes, at the clarity and glow of a country complexion. I pulled a face at my too large mouth...cupid's bows were all the rage....and the brown curly hair which, in spite of every restraining effort with clips and pins, crept all around my face in fluffy tendrils. But my clothes were so drab....

I became aware of Aunt Cissy watching me in the mirror and blushed with embarrassment. She did not seem to notice my discomfort, but continued to regard me critically.

"You have great possibilities," she remarked thoughtfully.

I tried to think of something off-hand to say, but nothing smart would come.

"Who'd be looking at me anyway?" I asked lamely.

We went out shopping in the afternoon and my first ride in a tram took us to Westmoreland Street. There we stopped at Bewley's so that I could sample a cup of their delicious coffee. I had never seen any place like it, with its crimson plush seats set in cosy alcoves. Tall stained-glass windows gave a delightful oriental radiance to the cafe. The scent of coffee being ground hung like incense on the air, and I was happy to see Aunt Cissy purchase a quarter pound of Mocha coffee for our delectation at home.

Well fortified we travelled up Sackville Street, past Lemon's sweet shop and crossed over to window-shop for bargains in Clery's drapery emporium.

Then we strolled to the rubbled remains of the General Post Office, destroyed in the 1916 rebellion. Behind this a temporary office operated and enabled us to send a telegram home, informing the family of my safe arrival.

Our next visit was to Woolworth's in Henry Street, which Cissy described as the three penny/sixpenny store. Here were counters of so many assorted products ....jewellery sparkling like real gems, cosmetics, alluring with beguiling scents and colourful packaging, glowing pots and pans in pyramids to the ceiling, and the children's toy counter had me handling every doll and plaything in the shop.

As nothing cost more than sixpence, I ended up with a ruby brooch for three pence and a bottle of pink nail varnish for four pence halfpenny. I made a mental note to come back here to shop for the family when I would be going home. Aunt Cissy insisted on buying me the material for a new dress in Todd Burns of Mary Street. They had a wide variety of fashionable dress fabrics and I chose a pastel crepe-de-chine in a flowery pattern.

We wandered in and out of so many shops that I was quite bewildered, and wondered if I would ever find my was around all the various streets and lanes.

Aunt Cissy always purchased her butter in the Monument Creamery.

This was a most distinctive shop with a white marble counter on which were displayed baskets of "hot buttered" eggs and a great white basin of cream.

The butter came in huge wooden containers which were unpacked to stand in large yellow squares on spotless marble shelves. Butter clappers stood nearby in white bowls of water, and were used to slice down a hunk of butter and beat it to the required weight on a shining weighing scales.

Glass-fronted cases exhibited biscuits which were sold loose, and I became particularly addicted to the yummy, flaky jam puffs, and brown-iced Cafe Noire. Aunt Cissy was talking about getting some fruit and vegetables, and for these we turned into Moore Street. This thoroughfare was flanked with stalls of fruit and flowers and vegetables of every colour and description.

A heavy smell of fish led us to an abundant supply of it at the side of an alleyway, and there was even a rack of unfashionable old clothing being picked over by a keen-eyed crowd of shoppers.

Over the stalls a regiment of plump, red-faced, black-shawled amazons presided. They wore big white aprons, starched to a cardboard-like stiffness.

I thought them very formidable looking and would not have liked to draw them on me.

Papers, battered vegetables and slimy skins, littered the pavement. All the lush produce was built in enticing mounds on every stall. The air was pierced with frenzied cries of "penny each t'apples and or-an-ges," or "lu-vely tamatas, buy lady, owny four pence a pound."

It was an effort at all to move amongst the multitude of prams laden with shopping. Rosy-cheeked babes sat clutching loaves of bread as large as themselves, nibbling messily at the crusty heels. Now and then, a raucous scream arose from the depths of a pram, when a child considered that enough had been piled on top of it. Other infants peered fearfully from amongst a forest of cabbage or leeks and protested indignantly with furious howls.

"Can't ya stop yar ballin'?" roared one mother of such a child. "Wan would think I was killin' ya. Here's yar soother, now quit yar goin's on," and she licked a well-worn dummy before sticking it in to the open mouth.

We moved to a cabbage stall behind which loomed a bouncing woman with flaming red hair. She was engaged in noisy conversation with a younger woman, whose heavily painted face was framed by fuzzy hair of a brassy lemon colour.

The steel curlers, arranged all over her head, bobbed up and down whenever she moved.

"Yes mam?" said the stallholder to Aunt Cissy who was poking every head of cabbage on view.

"There's no heart in any of them," she whispered to me.

I did not understand what she meant and I was suddenly alarmed.

"Are they dangerous?" I hissed back.

Aunt Cissy gave me a queer look.

"Are what dangerous?" she snapped.

I pointed to the dealer poised like a warrior over her stall. Aunt Cissy laughed. "I wasn't talking about them; only the cabbages....heartless the lot of them."

I blushed at my stupidity, and looked up as the dealer affirmed again with brisk thigh-slapping:

"Yes mam.Luv-ely cabbages. Feel the hearts in them, will ya?" and the cabbages visibly wilted under the power of her hand.

Unconvinced, Aunt Cissy prodded again while the dealer's attention was caught by the lemon-haired woman.

"And how did ya get on at the dance last night, Lizzie?" she inquired, pushing a cabbage forcefully into a customer's over-laden basket.

"Oh gorgeous, Aggie. I danced all night with Kickie Brown's friend. Oh such a gorgeous fella you never saw and dia know what he said?" Lizzie paused in the act of slapping a sad-looking fish on her scales.

Not unreasonably the red-headed woman shook her head. I waited breathlessly for more, but Lizzie took her time and patted a curler coyly with a hand glittering in fish scales. "He said I was the best lookin' girl in the room," she said triumphantly, and even the dealer was suitably impressed.

"Will ya go way outa that, Lizzie Mulligan!" she screamed, kicking a bucket of stale cabbage from the side of her stall nearly under the hooves of a horse with a fish-laden cart.

The animal reared and for a terrifying moment I thought he was going to charge backwards into a shop window. But amid great hilarity and helped by many willing hands, the horse regained control and continued on its way with much neighing, head-shaking and roaring abuse from his master. Unperturbed by the commotion, Lizzie was shouting: "He's gorgeous doin' the Charleston, ya know."

The dealer paused to absorb this shattering piece of information, while counting out change from a massive starched pocket. She eyed the belle of the ball fiercely and threw another question.

"Was Pansy Nolan there?"

"Oh yas," came the response. "A common hussy that wan is alright. Ya shoulda seen her and her carry on with the Dixon fella last night. I wonder they look sideways at her."

"Yas mam?" the dealer's little hard eyes were on Aunt Cissy again.

"How much is this head?" queried the aunt holding a cabbage in either hand, while I held on to her handbag and basket for dear life. I expected to be deprived of them at any minute, so I stood as still as the large female behind me, with the spikey hardware sticking out of her basket, would allow.

"Tuppence," growled the dealer.

"That's too much," retorted Aunt Cissy, dropping the cabbage back on the stall.

"Ya want jam on it, lady," snarled the dealer, grabbing the rejected cabbages and flourishing them under my aunt's nose, before handing the smaller of them to a timid little woman who did not dare to argue. She stuffed it under her arm clumsily, dropped her money, thereby causing the excitement of an extensive search of the red-headed woman's territory. The dealer cursed loudly while the little woman wept with fright. I spotted a sixpence in the folded leaves of a cabbage and handed it to its grateful owner, who thanked and blessed me fervently.

The dealer snatched the money, but was still unappeased. She went on shouting to all and sundry about "oul wans who try ta cod ya when yarback's turned."

Some of the watchers sniggered and nodded assent, while the little woman beat a hasty retreat among the dwindling streams of shoppers. We were just about to move on when we got a violent push from behind. I was clutching Aunt Cissy's arm for I had a terror of losing her; she straightened her neat cloche hat, which had fallen over her ear, while I turned cautiously to stare at the woman who had pushed us so roughly aside. Evidently she had reached her destination, and was standing with arms akimbo before the lemon-haired Lizzie.

She was a dark gypsy-looking person with flashing gold earrings, jangling almost to her shoulders. A wide purple belt held together a flaming orange skirt and grubby white blouse.

"There's going to be a row," whispered the knowledgeable aunt, nodding in the woman's direction.

Many other people thought so too, for women with kids, shopping and prams, were surveying the opponents with shameless interest. A few nervously moved away, but we were stuck fast in the crowd.

With startling suddenness the dark woman screamed:

"So dere yar, Lizzie Mulligan. Ya painted divil. How dar ya! How dar ya, ya dirty lookin' sight!" She paused to let the insults find their target before proceeding: "But ya won't get away with it. Oh no ya won't. I'll give ya a clatter that'll knock the smirk off yar dial. Tryin' to pinch me 'usband with yar lipsticked lips and yar plucked eyebrows."

There was a laugh from the audience, and a big gander of a woman yelled:

"Go to it, Magda. Let her have it. Ya can't be expected to take that stalin' of yar 'usband sittin' down," and she smacked her ham-like hands together in delighted anticipation. I was about to give a hearty laugh myself, but a quick glance at the firey Magda made me change my mind.

The red-headed dealer, who up until then had continued to serve her customers as if nothing unusual was happening, now decided to take a turn in the proceedings.

"Oh Lizzie," she cried piously, and the scandalized look on her face brought an audible titter from the crowd.

"Ya never done such a ting now, did ya?"

The yellow-haired Lizzie opened her mouth, but no sound was heard, as Magda could yell louder than any of them.

"'Twas morning' when he walks in ta me. Mornin'! Dancin' the night away and worse with this wan, the forward, shameless hussy," she screamed, her eyes daggers on the erring Lizzie.

Swiftly she leapt on the "shameless hussy" and gave her a sharp slap in the face, but Lizzie recovered rapidly from the surprise attack and with clenched fists she faced the furious Magda.

Dealers in standing white aprons threw off their shawls, and joined the fray with friend and foe fighting each other with total abandonment.

Fruit flew through the air to squash on any target until a shrill cry rent the air.

"The coppers,"

Instantly the fight changed direction. There were curses, yells and kicks as some tried to escape from the vicinity. Apples and oranges rolled, and were eagerly pounced on to be confined to capacious shopping bags. Amid the whirling feet, a respectable-looking woman scuttled, stuffing tomatoes into her pockets until the juice ran down the sides of her coat.

Then the police were swarming everywhere, shouting orders above the din.

Some of the buxom fighters turned to look at them contemptuously, and then with one accord their grievances were forgotten. Magda and Lizzie stood side by side aiming bruised tomatoes at the intruders. All the dealers joined in and Aunt Cissy and I escaped behind an evil-smelling hall door, from whence we were able to view the battle to its conclusion.

A policeman blew his whistle, but still the rebels took no notice. He was a sorry sight; uniform and every visible bit of him covered in a sticky mess of fruit and battered vegetables. A tattered messenger boy with a funny dirty face, threw aside his bicycle and climbed up a lamppost. Every now and then he hollered: "Bravo! Up the rebels! Come on Magda! Come on Lizzie, can't ya?"

He became convulsed with laughter when a blawsy-looking woman fell into an upturned stall and nothing was seen of her but a frantically waving pair of stout buttoned boots and a maze of white petticoat. A shower of tomatoes rained on her.... some short-sighted person must have taken her for a policeman in disguise!

Eventually she was rescued by two policemen, but she seemed convinced that at least one of them was responsible for her undignified collision with the stall, for she beat off their helping hands, and abused them roundly for their "disgustin'" behaviour.

Meantime the dealers had caught hands, making a chain around another policeman, and in a swirl of cotton drawers they galloped around him singing raucously:

"For he's a jolly good fella,
He' a jolly good fella,
He' a jolly good fe....ll....a
And so say all of us."

They had just graduated to "Charlie Is Me Darlin'" and slowed down to as graceful a trot as their large boots and ample curves would allow, when a police lorry , dubbed the Black Maria nosed its way through the crowd.

Rapidly the dancers were scattered, and amid violent threats, and racy language, they were soon hoisted on to the lorry. Legs in black stockings in various stages of disrepair, and long coloured bloomers, swayed in every direction. Newspaper men with cumbersome cameras appeared from nowhere to picture the scene. The lorry was started, its horn blasting a warning, while the dealers still bellowed another chorus of "Charlie." Waving gaily to the astonished onlookers they were driven to Mountjoy Jail for a cooling off period.

For us the incident did not quite end there. I was having a lie in next morning when the aunt rushed in. Excitedly she held a newspaper under my nose.

"Look Lynn, look," she ordered. Sleepily I took the paper and focused on the picture she indicated. Then I was fully awake staring at a print of the dealers fight, but that was not the funniest bit. What caught my attention was the jutting brim of Aunt Cissy's hat, and the smiling face of myself peeping around the shabby hall door in Moore Street.

Chapter 4

The lure of bygone days has always held a fascination for me. I can never pass an old building without stopping to look at it. If possible, I will go inside to investigate further....knock on walls, just in case a secret passage, a crock of gold or a sprawling skeleton, might be revealed. Maybe in a Georgian house I might hear the rustle of silk, catch a whiff of a forgotten scent, or hear the far- off tinkle of an eighteenth century harpsichord.

Since I loved visiting different places, Aunt Cissy took me out to see the new suburbs. These comprised of concrete villas reaching out to what was lately wild country. If you listen you can spot a different class of people in the trams to these destinations. "Posh!" was the aunt's description. The accent is clipped and very grand; the conversation of the men centres on the "guardening" and the lawn. If some of these gentle folk can afford a "guardner," then you certainly will hear a lot about the condition of "the lawn," the golf which is practised on it, and the "dug" who rolls over it, but the most popular topic is the weather. These gents in spats and white shammy gloves, swinging elegant walking sticks, wear "glosses" and not spectacles, though some have these too, including the elegant monocle, "but what they actually mean by glasses," whispered Aunt Cissy, is "Barometers."

These impressive gadgets apparently have the disconcerting habit of going up and down, and no two gentlemen will agree on the outcome.

"I looked at the "gloss" this morning and the indications favoured rain," says the first grandee, "the "gloss" was down."

"Oh I wouldn't think that correct at all," disagrees his companion with a careless puff of a "Players" cigarette. "I'd say we're done with the rain for some time now." He pauses to give a superior smile that brooks no argument. "My "gloss" was up when I was leaving the house."

Shamelessly I listen, even more avidly to the snippets of gossip with which the ladies of these places regale each other.

The problems of trying to "civilise" the maids, of discouraging their "followers," of "finding the right "school" for Elizabeth Alexandra....such a sensitive child....simply couldn't allow her to go to that local place....such common children attend it, my dear."

Not to be outdone, her friend boasts of her new car, the arrival of her telephone, what she had paid Switzers for a new fur coat.... "Dennis simply insisted I bought it before the Russell Martins' come over from London."

Some of the more voluptuous-looking females confined their chat to food, and what luscious dishes their cooks, of varying degrees of competency, succeeded in accomplishing or destroying.

The provision of afternoon tea came high on the list of social obligations, as did the drinking of brandy, whiskey and sundry wines, which seemed to be freely available at Bridge and card parties on a weekly rota.

I noticed that the more stylish ladies, with bobbed hair and powdered faces, were unanimous in their disapproval of a mysterious female, always referred to as "she."

"She had visions of grandeur."

"She was living beyond her means."

"She had lost the run of herself."

"She was only a schoolgirl when he married her."

"She was only a shop girl when he married her."

"She didn't know how to dress herself."

"She was really dirt plain, but the clothes and the good food...."

There were rumours that "she" and Mr. Middleton....here the voice dropped to a scandalized whisper, and try as I would, I could hear no more. Disappointed, I tried to envisage what "she" had done to or with, the unknown Mr Middleton.

One incident sticks in my mind. I was sitting in the tram when a smart young woman got in and seated herself opposite me. She opened her bag and after extracting her fare, drew out a silver cigarette case. After lighting her cigarette, she puffed smoke in all directions, crossing her long legs until her short skirt climbed up alarmingly to reveal pink cami-knickers, lavishly trimmed with lace, and the gartered tops of sheer silk stockings. Blushing, I did not know where to look, and wondered if she was aware that so much of her person was on view to the public gaze.

Yet in spite of myself, my eyes wandered back to the lady, but she never changed her pose, and seemed totally unaware that there was anything unusual about her behaviour. Once our eyes met, hers hard and unsmiling, I looked away quickly, praying that the man beside me would keep his head in his newspaper, at least until I got out.

At last she reached her stop; uncrossing her legs she stamped out the smouldering cigarette, swung to her feet, and nonchalantly tweaked her skirt about her knees. Just before she got off she bent towards me and said sarcastically: "I hope you got a good look."

Mortified, I could think of nothing to say. I was afraid to look in any direction for fear her reprimand had been heard all over the tram. Somehow, she made me feel that it was I who had done something reprehensible.

Chapter 5

In spite of its modern bustle, Dublin is a very old place and the sense of its past permeates everywhere. I always enjoyed Irish history and never missed an opportunity of linking my knowledge to reality in visiting ancient sites connected with people and events.

Aunty Cissy was surprised.

"I thought you'd rather go to a theatre than slogging around dusty old places and tenements," she observed a little frostily. As she was unable to accompany me due to her business commitments, I simply went about the city myself with a historical guide book in my bag.

But Aunt Cissy was all interest when I returned, and told her excitedly where I had been. Secretly I think she was very glad to escape some of the forays I made into dilapidated houses, eerie crypts and lonely ruins.

"I shook hands with the crusader to-day," I greeted her delightedly, referring to a visit to the vault in St. Michan's Church.

"I saw Lord Edward's coffin in Werbugh Street Church; it has his initials scratched on it," and I eagerly gave her a fairly comprehensive report on the district surrounding Christ Church Cathedral. Poor Aunt Cissy would try to share my elation when I launched into long descriptions, and conjectures of controversial events. I discoursed on the probable burial site of Robert Emmet, and the reason why his insurrection had been such a tragic disaster. Sometimes, she was alarmed by my dishevelled appearance, and questioned whether it was "healthy" to be spending so much of my holiday rooting up the past, when I should be out and about enjoying myself.

However, as she had her dressmaking business to look after, I cut down my lone outings a little to help her with pulling out tacking threads, sweeping up the bits and pieces of her trade, and parcelling neatly the finished garments for her customers. She was always protesting about this...."I wasn't a maid and a holiday was a time for resting."

I tried to make her see that I enjoyed working anyway, and could make a clean sweep of her flat in no time. After my own country home where every drop of water had to be bucketed in, and where electricity and gas were yet only fantasies, I could do all her housework in half an hour.

In return, we might go to Charlamont House or Trinity College, where I would try to visualise life in another age that I had only known from books. The shadow of old Dublin falls romantically across the city, on the great Georgian Squares and aging buildings.

Off the main streets, tenements team with poverty-stricken humanity. Frozen-faced women, clad in enveloping black or grey shawls, push broken prams piled with firewood, tattered clothing, or meagre groceries. Bare-footed children run wildly about, kicking balls, playing hopscotch with an empty Nugget tins, or swinging on ropes around lamp posts. Two skinny little girls turn a skipping rope for their small companions who, oblivious to everything else, chant the ancient childish rhymes in strident tones:

"Tinker, tailor, soldier, sailor, Rich man, poor man, beggar man, thief...."

Beggars abound and one may be accosted at every turn for "a little help, Missus." There was a little man with a barrel-organ on Carlisle Bridge in Sackville Street. While he wound a handle to produce plaintive music, a tiny monkey held out an old cap for alms.

Once I heard a great commotion, and a tall, ragged man charged past, brandishing a long key and shouting "Bang! Bang! You're dead." To my amazement and apprehension, a number of staid-looking citizens obligingly "dropped dead," when he aimed his "gun" (alias the key) at them. The play ended when Bang-Bang pocketed his "gun" and disappeared into a convenient public house.

I reflected sadly on the tragic and bitter-sweet humour of to-day against the glories of yesterday, as I walked around Mountjoy Square, destitute and mouldering with its cargo of suffering humanity.

The ghosts of another age were all about me in the Rotunda Gardens, where Grattan's Volunteers had often stood to attention. Here the Lords and Ladies of Dublin enjoyed a promenade, with music by the great composers, played by a military band. Doubtless, many a laddie whispered sweet nothings in a fair maid's ear, as they rambled among the flowers and foliage.

After a visit to Swift's great St. Patrick's Cathedral, and the neighbouring March's Library, Aunt Cissy and I made for the quays through Fishamble Street, darkly winding and oppressive, but of special interest, as it had housed the old music hall. The colourful theatre has long since gone and in its place Keenan's Ironworks, has made a dull substitute.

Echoes of majestic music tantalised my mind, and I remembered that here the first presentation of Handel's "Messiah," had awed a Dublin audience.

I was greatly impressed by the beautiful Parliament House, now the Bank of Ireland, on College Green, but I was especially interested in Trinity College, not only for its age (dating back to Elizabeth I) or the debonair young things who continually streamed through its massive doors, but because of the dreams it evoked of other days, other men....Emmet, Goldsmith, Curran, Tom Moore....

My first Easter in Dublin must be special, said Aunt Cissy; her brow wrinkled in perplexity, as she pondered the problem of where we should go.

But for me, there was no hesitation; I wanted to see Rathfarnham. I was interested in the district because I knew a good deal about it from two sources. The first was Amy Mays, Postmistress of our village. Amy was a middle-aged spinster who had been born and reared in a small farm, which sprawled beneath the slopes of Mount Peliar. This hill was a famous landmark in Rathfarnham, for on its crest brooded the old ruin of the shooting lodge known as the Hell Fire Club.

What dire stories Amy told of this place in a voice quivering with fear, or falling to an eerie whisper. I listened, round-eyed and terrified, never doubting a word of the lurid tales in which phantom horsemen, black cats with burning eyes , headless coaches, and demons disintegrating into balls of fire, went about their wicked business "on certain nights, to this very day," Amy would conclude warningly.

Well, I was not going to see "that" place," I told myself firmly, although Aunt Cissy assured me that many people climbed up to see it and enjoyed the experience, even returning to their city homes unscathed, but I was adamant.

There were other parts of Rathfarnham....places full of romance and history, and my mind swept back to that second source of information contained in a book called "Footsteps Of Emmet," which is still one of my treasured possessions.

Actually it had come to me, or rather Da, in a rather funny way. Mam and Da had gone to an auction in an old manor house nearby, and had returned home with a wheelbarrow full of rusty farm implements....a broken gramophone and an ugly soup tureen....all for I/6.Da had made a beeline for the barrow, and had spent the evening happily sifting through the rust and dirt, while Nell and Dora sank their considerable energy into trying to re-start the gramophone.

I was left with the tureen, and curious to see what designs lay beneath its layers of grime, set about rubbing it gently with a damp cloth. Absorbed in the task, I gingerly lifted the lid and was astonished to find a muddle of books in front of me. Excitedly, I rooted through them; they were mostly about farming and housekeeping. There was a torn first edition of Mrs Beaton's cookery book, and at the very bottom, I lifted out the wonderful "Footsteps Of Robert Emmet," which although very dirty, was undamaged, and also a first edition.

Of course, I did not know how interesting it would prove to be as I leafed through the pages, and stopped to pour over the pictures of Sarah Curran and her home, "The Priory," in Rathfarnham. I was soon lost in the book which traced the life of the ill-fated Emmet and his tragic romance with Sarah

"That's where I want to go," I insisted, "to The Priory."

We got a tram to Rathfarnham village, and hired a pony and trap to take us into the country side. It was a lovely drive;

the Dublin Mountains softly sloping all around us, with little white-washed cottages glowing in a brassy sun, and fields of sheep and lambs ba-ing their contentment.

The dark ruins of the Hell-Fire Club frowned down on us, but I carefully averted my eyes, and concentrated on the splendid herds of Herford cattle on the other side of the hedges.

Eventually we reached "The Priory," with its breathtaking view of Dublin city, and out to the right, the sea shimmering in the sunshine against the dark bulk of Howth.

A winding, overgrown avenue, led from creaking gates to the home of the famous barrister, Philpot Curran, renowned for his ardent defence of the United Irishmen who led the rebellion of 1798. But years of misfortune had soured and disillusioned him, and by 1803, the year of Emmet's revolt, he no longer wanted to be associated with the cause of Irish Republicanism.

It was therefore, an outrage to him when his daughter's love for the patriot Emmet, became known to Dublin Castle, and he never forgave her. All the sadness of their story filled my mind, as Aunt Cissy and I stood by the empty, derelict house.

We clambered over a crumbling window-sill into what may have been the dining room. Silently we crept through the house, past curtains of cobwebs; our footsteps echoing on the broken floorboards. Once I screamed as a rat scurried by in the gloom. In one particular room upstairs, a broken window rattled forlornly in the wind, and the presence of some other entity seemed very close.

Feeling faint, I turned to Aunty Cissy, "take me out, take me out," I moaned.

Wrapping a protective arm around me she helped me carefully out of the desolate house, where I recovered on an old seat in the tangled remains of the garden.

"You gave me a fright, girl," she whispered, her eyes wide with concern.

"I'm sorry, I'll be alright in a minute." I told her.

She sat down beside me on the creaking seat, and my mind wandered to Curran's favourite daughter, Gertrude, who had fallen to her death from an upstairs window, when she was only twelve years old. So overcome was Curran by the tragedy that he would not allow her to be interred outside the grounds of the house. A stone slab had once revealed the site of her grave, but that was long missing, and I could only try to calculate its original position from the pictures in my book.

An eerie thought crept into my mind; could the strange presence I had felt in that upper room be the ghost of that poor little girl crying across the centuries?

Chapter 6

Many people had visited "The Priory." Amongst them Henry Grattan, the parliamentary reformist and leader of the patriots in the House of Commons, who used to sit in the garden of an evening, talking to Curran and gazing down on the city in the fading light. Here, in his declining years, Curran strolled alone with his memories, staring at the far-off dome of the Four Courts, where his great gift of oratory had been spent.

From "The Priory," we could see St. Enda's, the boys school founded by Patrick Pearse in 1909 and which had also been his home. Boyish voices, long past, seemed to echo from its deserted playing fields and mingle in the sudden moaning of the wind.

Aunt Cissy's voice broke into my melancholy thoughts.

"I do declare we have spent enough time in the past for one day. I'm famished; let's go for a nice cup of tea," she finished with some asperity.

Wordlessly I followed her along the winding road, and dusk was falling as we entered a pretty thatched cottage in the shelter of Cruagh mountain.

In answer to Aunt Cissy's knock, a friendly middle-aged woman in a blue-checked apron, brought us to a little table in a small, over-furnished room off the kitchen.

She gave us a delicious tea of fresh boiled eggs, brown bread, curraney cake and raspberry jam, followed by thick slices of a rich cut-and-come-again cake.

After the meal, we sat drowsily by the kitchen range and our friendly hostess, whose name was Mrs Printon, and an old acquaintance of Aunt Cissy's, proved herself very able in the telling of ghost stories.

"Make yourselves aisy," she bade us, "and I'll tell you about the knocking goose, which I can vouch for as I seen it myself." While she spoke, she gazed nervously towards the window, with its white-washed sill and scarlet geraniums. It was nearly dark and she rose to light the paraffin lamp.

"I seen it meself," she emphasized softly, as the gentle light flickered around the kitchen, and the turf sank and crumbled in the range in a flare of red sparks.

I looked anxiously through the window, and was rather disappointed to see only the wooden gate and the green fields beyond, instead of a spectral white goose hissing and flapping his wings at me.

"Where did you see it?" I ventured, as Mrs. Printon pulled the curtains tight.

"Well," she began "it was a long time ago when me poor mother...the Lord be good to her....was dyin,' that I seen it. The doctor had been sayin' that she might pull through, but I felt unaisy as I sat be her side all night. 'Twould be midnight when she asked me for a sup of water, and I went out to the kitchen to get it." she paused and gazed towards the lamp with a far-off look in her eyes.

"I was just fillin' the old yellow mug that me mother always used from the bucket of water be the door, when all of a sudden, the wind that was blowing noisy all night, seemed to quit tearin' the old hawthorns, and the room was filled with a queer silence. I felt frightened, awful frightened be myself, with nothing but the candlelight jumping up the walls. Sibby, she were the old tabby cat, got up from her mat on the hearth. She arched her back and stuck out her tail like a poker, and gave such a long-drawn yowl. All I was seen were her green eyes like marbles staring at me. I felt sweat on the back of me neck. I tried to put the butter muslin over the bucket again, but me hands shook so much I had to give it up. Then the clock struck twelve. I near dropped the mug with the jump I give. There was a sharp peckin' noise at the window, the curtains blew back, and I seen it as plain as I'm seen you now; a big white goose was staring at me with terrible fiery eyes and out-stretched wings. The yellow beak was open and it was hissing like mad. It pecked at the window with such fury that I was sure it was trying to get in .Then it were gone, and the wind started howlin' again, as if 'twere the last day. I knew then that me poor mother would leave me and I cried 'till I remembered she was wanting the water. I went into her and she took a few drops. After that, she got worse, and then sort of quiet, and I was thinking she'd sleep a little, but as I looked at her I knew she was gone."

Mrs. Printon sighed and lay back tiredly in her chair. After some words of consolation from us, and a brief exchange of news concerning some people only known to them both, Aunt Cissy rose, and said we would have to be going, as we had a long journey before us and the pony and trap would be calling for us soon. Mrs. Printon would have none of it until we had partaken of more tea and scones with her special rhubarb jam. This jam was very special; its recipe a family heirloom. She showed us her great grand- mother's pottery bowl, green with faded red poppies, in which the first helping of the jam must be served to be successful . We enjoyed it so much that Mrs Printon insisted on packing a 2lb. pot for us to take home.

Mrs. Printon came as far as the gate with us, as Mr. Black appeared around the bend of the road with his pony and trap. We made our good-byes and promised to come again soon.

We set off at a smart trot, as darkness threw her gossamer veil over the purple mountains and drowsy fields. It was still early spring, and a light frost chilled the air. The night drew on, silent, except for the bleet of a sheep, the moo of a cow or the ghostly flutter of a bat.

Time seemed suspended, and in my dreaming state, I wondered about Sarah Curran, who had known the district so well. Did those gnarled trees and white-washed cottages go back to her time? Were the dusty roads the same, unlit and lonely, as when she and her father had travelled by coach from the city?

Spectres drifted by, and I was startled by the galloping hooves of a horse and cart passing us.

"Good night to ye there," shouted the farmer on his way home.

"Good night," we returned sleepily.

We reached the village of Rathfarnham and transferred ourselves to the tram for Aunt Cissy's flat. She seemed very quiet and lost to her surroundings. I roused her gently.

"A penny for 'em," and gave her arm an affectionate squeeze. She smiled wanly. "I'm not very good company, Lynn dear, am I?"

I assured her she was just a bit tired, and the best aunt in the world, as indeed she always was to me.

Chapter 7

In the following weeks we saw many more places, but Aunt Cissy having been born under a practical star, insisted on combining business with pleasure.

We usually wandered about gathering shopping en route, and she was always apologising for giving me so much to carry. But mostly I did not mind; she had a way of talking so earnestly about bargains that I found myself falling in with her plans.

She never cared what she carried or where. I was horrified one day when she took an ancient kitchen clock across the city to be repaired, with no paper bag to screen it from the public view.

To-day we were making for the millinery shop in Henry Street. I knew that one weakness she was unrepentant of was a fascination with hats. She simply could not pass a hat shop without going in to try on all sorts of head-gear; some of it outrageous, ridiculous or downright funny. I asked her why the cloche hat was so popular, as she patted hers, complete with moulting feathers, placidly on her head, and got the standard reply, "It's the fashion."

"I think it's dreadful," was my uncompromising opinion, but the aunt gave a knowing wink, "you'll learn," she laughed, sailing happily through the door of the "hattery,"

There was great excitement in the shop as a Sale was raging. Hundreds of women were converging on the hat department, and with fanatical determination pouncing on a vast assortment of headgear. They whipped off their own hats and grabbed an array of various styles, which they fingered carefully into place on their untidy looking heads. In desperate efforts to get the most flattering models at the beguiling half price advertised, they jostled each other impatiently to reach the already overcrowded mirrors.

Basically I felt sure that these were ordinary, staid, good-natured women, but I could not imagine what had got in to them, and their manhandling of the hats filled me with surprise. There seemed to be no referee to call them to order, and the rampage went on with Aunt Cissy in the thick of it all, fighting every inch of the way.

When I glimpsed her again she had captured a mirror and was peering critically into it, a little red horror pulled tight to her head, and flaunting a huge jungle-like poppy at her ear. Encouraged by the push and shove antics of the crowd, I managed to reach her.

"Not exactly flattering," I laughed. "In fact it's a fright."

"It's the fashion," Aunt Cissy snapped, and that I understood, explained the riddle of every ugly ensemble with which women draped themselves at regular seasonal intervals.

She suddenly swooped on a yellow creation and slapped it critically on my head; it looked like a bucket.

Undaunted she tried another. It had a weird band of flowers around it, and a handle-like appendage at one side. This I pronounced unsuitable because of its likeness to a chamber pot.

Aunt Cissy was disgusted. "I see you have no fashion sense at all, and you're just not the hat type," she said acidly.

A little annoyed, I ached to ask her why, if she was so fashion conscious, did she wear such drab colours and shapeless garments herself. But good sense and manners prevailed, and I only demurely inquired her reason for never buying one of the daft hats.

She looked at me in amazement.

"I prefer the plain little cloche myself....sure where would I be going with one of those daft yokes on my head?" and she disdainfully cast aside a ghastly monstrosity of black spangles and tulle flowers, and began to search for her own abandoned little cloche in a huge drawer of discarded hats. Suddenly she dived into the centre of it, and emerged triumphantly waving a red hat, which only differed from hers in that it was new and minus the droopy feathers clinging to the crown. Now it dawned on me that I had actually seen Aunt Cissy's old hat, inadvertently sold a few minutes earlier, to a posh looking woman who had disappeared among the shoppers, wearing it.

There was no doubt in my mind on this point; it just had not registered with me at the time; for there was no mistaking her red cloche with its bedraggled feathers.

Shaking between fright and laughter, I made no comment as the aunt sailed out of the shop with the brand new cloche firmly anchored to her head.

Lagging uneasily behind, I gazed at the gaudy merchandise all around me, and tried to imagine myself fighting my way down Moore Street with one such exotic confection nodding uneasily on my head. The image evoked, brought on a splutter of laughter, as I escaped from the shop.

Another time she laced a pair of boots together with twine and asked me if I would mind taking them into the cobblers down the street. Of course I agreed and began searching for a suitable piece of paper to put them in.

"You don't want to waste paper on those," the aunt was disbelieving.

I felt like a footballer carrying the boots by the twine, but when I saw supercilious eyes on me, I tried vainly to conceal them in my handbag.

Aunt Cissy was swinging a mangy old fur tippet, complete with bushy tail and glaring eyes.

"Wherever did you get it," I had asked when she produced it, stinking of mothballs, from her wardrobe.

"One of my customers kindly made me a present of it," she replied with an injured air. "It's real fox."

I did not dare to give my opinion of her customer's generosity, but shuddered when she held it against my cheek so that I might "appreciate the quality of the fur."

This horrid piece of fashionable equipment was on its way to be cleaned and have its raggy lining repaired.

I felt hot with embarrassment until we reached the cobblers and I thankfully disposed of the boots, while Aunty Cissy deposited the dead animal in the fur shop. Now I could look the rest of humanity in the face...at least until the next time!

In the country, folk are a lot more conventional than their townie cousins, especially in the matter of carrying things about in public. At home, we make everything into a neat parcel before venturing abroad, be it a couple of apples or a borrowed tablecloth.

"You don't want everyone knowing your business," is the standard explanation.

As we completed our shopping I was all excitement for our last port of call.

This was to a shop in Abbey Street to collect a photograph of Aunt Cissy and I, which had been "snapped" a few days earlier by a street photographer on Carlisle Bridge.

Eagerly I whipped the picture from its envelope, and the two of us burst out laughing at what it revealed. There was Aunt Cissy, laden with her haul from Moore Street, a look of diminishing hope on her face, as she struggled to hang on to a bag of eggs from the Monument Creamery. And here was I with Aunt Cissy's broken electric kettle in one hand, a "bargain" saucepan in the other, and under my arm a loaf of bread, which threatened to hit the wet pavement at any moment.

But Aunt Cissy had not totally escaped disaster that day, for when we were unloading later in the kitchen, she found a damp yellow hole in the egg bag, and a subsequent sticky mess down the side of her coat. I tried to look suitably concerned when she speculated as to where she had lost the eggs. But she had a great sense of humour; a frame was bought in Woolworth's for the photograph and, giggling like a schoolgirl, I often saw her showing it with great hilarity to her friends.

"Priceless!" she described it smugly.

Chapter 8

Of the many places we visited, St. Stephen's Green, was the one I loved best of all. Sometimes we strolled idly through it, admiring the flowers and feeding the ducks who got to know us so well, that a wild dash was made in our direction whenever we appeared.

On other days we would rest on a seat near a fountain, dislodging the groceries from our persons with relief. Then I could assume the dignified role of historian.

"That was the home of the Emmet family," I informed the aunt, pointing through the trees at the Georgian house overlooking the Green.

"Dr. Emmet had it divided in two, so that his elder son, Addis, could live with his own family in the same house."

Aunt Cissy was always flatteringly impressed by my knowledge.

"You should be a teacher of history, Lynn. You have a real feeling for the past," once she observed reflectively: "I never realised those people in books could be so interesting. It seems strange that I have walked around Dublin all these years completely unaware of so much history everywhere."

Once, in Suffolk Street, she was startled when I told her she was probably walking on the grave of Ester Van Omragh, who was the "other" lady in Dean Swift's life.

"Yes, it's true alright," I smiled, and she jumped aside, as if to avoid tramping on the dead. I pointed to the beautiful Church across the road:

"Here was situated its burial grounds, but they took away the tombstones and built a road over it. That's what they call progress!" Aunt Cissy crossed herself hurriedly, and hauled me off to Robert's Cafe in Grafton Street for a cup of coffee. This was served by a pretty waitress in a dark dress and a frilly white apron. As we enjoyed our coffee and some little iced cakes, three dignified ladies in a palm-filled alcove, played soft music on piano, cello, and violin....tunes from the popular new musical...."The Boyfriend," the aunt informed me.

All too soon it was time to go, Aunt Cissy hoisting a spiky leek under her arm, and I with a sheaf of rhubarb bumping against my knees.

As we stood at the top of the Green waiting to cross the street, I found myself wondering why my aunt had never married. I stole a look at her pink cheeks and lovely long-lashed eyes and thought sadly: "Not much hope of her doing so now. She must be at least thirty."

"Wait, Lynn," her agitated voice broke into my reverie. I had absent- mindedly stepped off the pavement when a huge horse and dray, laden with coal, swept by, and I jumped out of its path just in time.

"Didn't I warn you to concentrate on the traffic when crossing the street," she said angrily. "You could have been killed."

I humbly followed her when a lull occurred, but once safely across, she lost face a little when she had to re-cross to rescue a bunch of onions, which had fallen out of her basket at the other side of the street.

Aunt Cissy was visibly wilting by this time and I was so relieved when we reached home to a warm fire. While she was recovering from her fright, I got our tea of boiled eggs, toasted crumpets dripping in butter, and jammy Swiss-roll.

Chapter 9

Aunt Cissy and I were waiting to see "Nicoletos" at the Tivoli Music Hall in Burgh Quay. There was a long queue and we were near the end of it.

Ragged, bare-foot, children, ran up and down, begging for a copper "to get a bit of food, Missus." An old man with a mouth organ gave a soulful and piercing rendition of "She Is Far From The Land." When he stopped to get his breath and make a collection, a barrel-organ on Carlisle Bridge made a plaintive onslaught on the silence with "Wont You Buy My Pretty Flowers."

Suddenly I became aware of a wiry little man strolling alongside the queue. He was wearing an ancient black overcoat, mottled with stains, and sporting a moth-eaten astrakhan collar. Resting on his cauliflower ears was a battered bowler hat, and from a grimy-gloved hand swung a silver-topped walking stick.

A fat black and white mongrel waddled sedately by his side, a folded newspaper clamped in its jaws.

Cringing here, argumentative there, the little man skipped up and down the double rows of people soliciting "the price of a cupa tae, for God's sake."

"Watch that fella trying to edge himself into the queue instead of going to the back," Aunt Cissy whispered, closing the gap firmly between us and the couple in front. But his efforts were grimly repulsed by the crowd, and with much swearing, he vanished in the gloom, dog and all.

Once again we settled down to await the opening of the theatre, and the old man with the mouth-organ, appeared alongside us, but this time he was singing in a loud tuneless voice.... "Marry me, me darling', I'll die if ya say no."

He was rudely interrupted by a male voice bellowing from the direction of the Liffey.

"Man Overboard!"

My heart jumped. I turned to Aunt Cissy, but to my surprise, that lady was laughing heartily, as were several others around.

I was appalled.

"Someone is drowning," I gasped, as the breath was knocked out of me by a large woman jostling past. I made to follow her, but Aunt Cissy laid a restraining hand on my arm. By now most of the queue had broken from their orderly file, and were rushing towards the Liffey wall. Soon an excited crowd were peering into the water's oily depths.

"That's an old dodge of his," commented a young man with a smile.

"Is there any chance someone would tell me what's going on?" I asked bewildered.

The young man took it upon himself to enlighten me.

"See that oul fella that was here a minute ago trying to jump the queue?"

"Yes," I answered, even more puzzled "Well he does that regularly. The young man gave me a quizzical look. "He shouts "man overboard" and when the crowd rushes off, he nips to the front of the queue. "You mean there's no one in the Liffey?" I asked stupidly. "Not a sinner," the young man laughed.

"Look!" and he pointed in front of him to where the cunning little man stood innocently at the head of the queue.

When I saw him again, the wily old fella was comfortably ensconced in the theatre with the dog on his lap. All through the show, the animal watched the stage as if he were enjoying and understanding, everything that was going on.

Chapter 10

Aunt Cissy looked up from her sewing as I burst into a fit of giggles.

"What's the matter with you?" she asked in surprise. "It must be very funny," she went on crossly, as I tried to suppress the laughter.

"It is indeed," I grinned, shaking the newspaper I was reading. "I didn't know you had different knickers down here for every occasion."

Aunt Cissy looked puzzled.

"I don't follow you..." she began testily.

"Well it's all down here in black and white," I said triumphantly." "Listen to this", and I read the advertisement aloud:

"'At the Henry Street Warehouse....Directoire Knickers, Dancing Knickers, Golf Knickers in great variety,' and if that isn't enough," I shrieked, "here's another:

"Clery's offer Camibokers....Artificial silk, opera top, elastic underarms....'"

"Sch...." Aunt Cissy begged, grinning hugely. "our neighbours will think we've taken leave of our senses, or else that I've got some very funny customers."

I continued to peruse the advertisements in silence until I came to an announcement from Kellets of George's Street.

"So that's what the fashionable woman wears under all the silks and spangles," I exclaimed with the relish of one who has made a great discovery.

"Corsets with master fronts," I quoted, awed by the bone and steel and armour-like contraptions, disguised in different strengths and shades of flowery brocade, in the illustrated advertisement.

"So these dictate the shape of the modern woman," I said in surprise.

"And they're only built for the average figures, they claim. What do the fat ones get into?" I shuddered.

Aunt Cissy laughed outright.

"The rule is the fatter you are, the stronger the corset," she said seriously.

"It's a perpetual battle between the flesh and the steel; you have to be squeezed into them, otherwise there's no point in wearing one."

I shook my head and thought of some of Aunt Cissy's heavier customers, who came creaking and wheezing to fittings. But they too were being catered for as revealed in a following advertisement, which wished to inform their "fuller" customers of "reducing models with rustless and unbreakable steels.'

"So that explains it then," I said in surprise. "I thought they all had bronchitis."

Chapter 11

The days full of happiness and interest, passed all too quickly, and it was nearly time to go home again. Then something happened which changed my life forever.

Aunt Cissy and I had set sail for "another round of the tenaments," as she jokingly described my historical ramblings. She complemented me on my appearance as we were ready to leave.

"Quite stylish," she observed critically, as I twisted and turned for her approval in a fancy pink jumper, and the neat navy-blue skirt she had made for me.

The day was warm and sunny; a frolicking breeze chased bits of paper and cigarette packets in whirling capers around the street. We did our bargain hunt, enjoyed Bewley's coffee and cakes, and left the sophisticated streets for the shabby ones.

As usual, Aunt Cissy made for Moore Street, where we ambled happily among the laden stalls, and piled our baskets with an assortment of dirty-looking vegetables, while the aunt joked and bargained to her heart's content with a variety of street traders.

She was just treating herself to a bunch of daffodils, when we heard shouts further down the street. Curiously we followed the sounds and found ourselves among a crowd of people gathered around a medley of stalls. Aunt Cissy, flushed with excitement, dragged me after her; our bananas and cabbages threatening to scatter in every direction, while it was all too evident that the daffs would never survive the stampede.

A push from a red-faced woman nearly sent me sprawling into a pram full of indignant children, who instantly set up a squalling protest. A dangerous-looking woman flew to their rescue, while the aunt only saved herself from falling on top of me, by swerving violently into a murky drain and bringing an adjacent sack of potatoes down with her. I felt about six inches high, as I floundered after hundreds of potatoes, rolling merrily into the dirty stream of water in the gutter.

Suddenly a very large woman, wrapped in a black shawl, loomed over me, hands on hips.

"Well bad cess ta yis," she roared, "but yar nothin' but a crowd a thieving' badgers. Get ta hell outa here afore I loose ne temper."

Aunt Cissy, realizing she was no match for her opponent in her present condition, picked herself up and both of us tried to retreat out of range of the gimlet eyes.

But it was now the turn of the woman with the pram.

"Yad better mind yarselves, yous," she yelled. "Fitter for ya to take it aisy instead a knockin' down a dacent body's little childer. The bloody cheek a yous!"

We seemed to be running in every direction in our efforts to escape. Aunt Cissy was minus a cabbage and I wondered if she would have the nerve to go back for it. To my utter relief, she hadn't.

At length we found ourselves back where the commotion had started. Crowds jostled excitedly, and the cause of the uproar seemed to emanate from a large woman of powerful build with bulging muscles. A heavy grey shawl was draped slackly around her shoulders, and from its depths a baby balled loudly.

Facing her was a timid little man on crutches.

The woman started jumping about, and the only way I can describe her antics is to say she galloped....galloped like a foaming charger up to the little man.

With an expression of the utmost ferocity, she screamed:

"Strike me now! Strike me now, me brave bowsie, and me with the child in me arms," and the roaring infant was flourished daringly under his nose.

The crowd tittered and a jovial voice shouted:

"Come on Mixer. Don't be backwards in comin' forwards."

"Who is that little man?" I heard Aunt Cissy enquire of a mousey-looking woman beside her.

"Mixer Flanagan, her husband," replied the woman, throwing her eyes skywards, "and the dancing' master in the skuel."

My aunt gasped in disbelief.

"Dancing master!" she exclaimed," but he's on crutches...."

The woman sniggered derisively.

"That fella's not alees on crutches, I can tell ya," she answered with a knowing wink, edging her way expertly through the crowds.

The little man made no movement, as his wife revolved mockingly around him, not even when she stopped abruptly and proceeded to abuse him in very strong language. Unconcernedly, he drew a clay pipe from a ragged pocket, and lit it slowly. He puffed absently, a resigned look in his eyes, as if he had witnessed the same scene many times before.

Infuriated, she commanded him to " get home afore me and don't be makin' an egit of yarself, yar poor down-throden wife and innocent little chisler, in front of the whole blinkin' world."

They disappeared into the crowd, the woman still berating her spouse for "drinkin,' smokin', and gambling'," She hinted at some other part-time occupation of his, but unfortunately, Aunt Cissy chose that moment to distract my attention, so I was unable to decipher the final insult.

The crowd drifted away; Aunt Cissy belatedly remembering her lost cabbage....the flowers had vanished early in the fracas, and the bananas were a write-off....began lamenting the loss of to-morrows dinner.

My feet were aching and wet and I was longing for tea by the fire, when we walked into another fight.

It was as well we had a human wall between us and the contestants, for the weapon employed was slimy, malodorous fish. The combatants were a sailor, a young woman with beautiful auburn hair, and the inevitable brassy blonde.

The latter was dressed in a shabby brown velvet coat, with vivid leopard-like spots, and sprawling raggy fur collar, silk stockings and dirty, white buttoned shoes. I thought her an export from Grafton Street looking for bargains!

The woman with the marvellous red hair, wore a flowing, cotton garment, under a large black shawl to her knees. Her long shapely legs were bare and spattered with mud, and her feet were encased in a shoddy pair of shoes from another era.

The two women eyed each other with deadly animosity; neither moved. Then the auburn-haired one, evidently believing surprise to be the best form of attack, suddenly lurched forward and caught the blonde by the hair. She kept pulling and screaming, until strands of hair remained in her hands like tufts of hay.

The blonde fought her side valiantly, kicking her aggressor and using the coarsest language in the struggle.

"Thar, ya rossy," snarled the red-head. "I'll teach ya to stale me husband and keep him out drinkin' till mornin.' I'll flatten ya! I'll throw ya down the railin's."

The blonde twisted about until she got her head free of the other's nails, then she gave as good as she got.

"How dar ya strike me, Nellie Mullooney. Is that all ya have to do, ya yallow bitch," and she clawed the flaming hair with her scarlet nails.

"How dar ya," mimicked the other woman. "It's me husband yar stalin', ya common-lookin' tart."

This seemed to galvanise "the tart" to greater efforts, and so powerful was her onslaught, that it looked as if the auburn-headed lady must be vanquished.

But here the sailor and cause of all the ructions, intervened on behalf of his wife.

"Can't yous quit it and leave me wife alone," he demanded of the blonde, pushing her roughly aside. However, the wife was unappeased.

She had a big basket of fish beside her, and with hair flying like a red banner, commenced to beat the sailor with armfuls of it. The blonde immediately deflected from her original adversary, and joined her in belting the erring sailor with whatever she could lay her hands on. At length, some of the crowd called a halt and endeavoured to separate the two women from the victim of their fury.

The roving husband, bleeding and covered in fish scales, was half carried off the scene by two stalwart men. The blonde, bedraggled and filthy, disappeared above a midst of her supporters, and the outraged wife followed her husband, shouting:

"Well why were ya out all night with that wan, anyway, ya boozy gouger!"

But the fight had gone out of her, and the men released her husband when they considered him reasonably safe.

"Go wan home with yar wife," one of them admonished him.

The sailor put an arm around his wife and together they advanced up the street. A noisy crowd followed them, led by an elderly woman dressed in a purple jumper, many sizes too small for her ample bosom, and a greasy black skirt. Over this garb was slung an old faded raincoat, reaching to the ankles of her stout buttoned boots. An expectant tremor passed through the crowd at the sight of her "The redhead's ma!" shrieked a young lad gleefully behind me.

The woman, weather-beaten and grim, moved with majestic steps until she reached the tenement where the sailor and his wife apparently resided. We, and a motley collection of onlookers, followed cautiously.

The ma took up her stance in the doorway, and with arms akimbo and legs apart, shouted to the assembled company:

"If that common hussy puts her nose inside this house, she won't live to get outa it again. Murther'll be done this time. Dar ya now!" and she spread her broad person menacingly across the battered hall door.

"Dar ya now, Maggie Mulligan, ta put yar foot thar," and she whisked up her skirt and extended a leg like a tree trunk over the door step, revealing a pair of saggy blue bloomers and torn black stockings.

"Thar!" she thundered, and brought her foot down hard on the step.

Suddenly I was convulsed with laughter, which I had hurriedly to try and smother, at a sharp nudge from Aunt Cissy. The crowd grew intoxicated with merriment; only the children, with mouths hanging open, remained solemnly silent. Then Aunt Cissy got a bad fit of the giggles herself, and could not utter a word, but there was more to come. Stealthily, the titian-haired wife appeared at an upstairs window with a bucket. She leaned out and with evident relish, poured a cascade of water over her mother, no doubt mistaking her for the blonde vamp.

The ma, spluttering wildly, struggled madly with the bucket which followed the water. It wobbled on her head, entangling its handle around her neck like a bonnet. The crowd shrieked useless advice, and after many terrible threats and snorts, the woman eventually freed herself. In a frenzy of rage she rushed into the house "ta bate the hell outa that lazy, good-for-nothin' bitch of a daughter."

The crowd began to move away, when the dishevelled blonde, rising like the Phoenix from the flames, appeared at an upper window in an adjoining house, her hair glinting like brass in a sudden ray of sunshine. She leaned out smiling broadly, and yelled to the crowd:

"Strike up fellas!"

Immediately, a jovial portion of the crowd responded with the chorus of "All the Nice Girls Love a Sailor."

The blonde swung provocatively in time to the tune, joining in the singing in a surprisingly good voice.

By this time, Aunt Cissy considered the show to be over, and picked her way carefully into Henry Street. I followed gingerly with the basket of several potatoes and a lone cabbage, which I had plucked furtively from an overturned stall.

"Is it always like that?" I panted. "Every time we go down that street there's a fight on."

Aunt Cissy laughed heartily.

"Ah sure, it's all very good-humoured in the end," she said, happily waving to a friend.

"I'm sure it is," I said archly, wondering if she would view the escapade with the same indulgence when she took off her coat, and found the stain of squashed fish streaked across the back of it.

Chapter 12

We continued out into Sackville Street, and were gazing through the windows of Clery's drapery shop, when there was a tap on Aunt Cissy's shoulder, and an exclamation of surprise and delight behind us.

She spun around and so did I. In front of us stood a tall, rosy-faced woman in her early fifties, with twinkling blue eyes and a gentle smile. She was beautifully dressed in a creamy coat, and a gorgeous pink hat clustered with flowers and feathers.

But it was her companion who riveted my attention. He was a tall young man in his late twenties, with soft brown eyes, a firm chin and a wide smiling mouth. He looked relaxed and good-humoured in a grey flannel suit.

The lady, who turned out to be the young man's Aunt Clare, was a great friend of Aunt Cissy's.

The two had known each other a long time, and had met through Aunt Cissy's business, for, explained the aunt later, "Clare is a fright for clothes, and her orders alone, are enough to keep me going."

Clare was married to a successful business man named Andy Devlin, and they lived in a lovely old house outside the city in Terenure. They had no children, but were devoted to several nieces and nephews, the favourite being the young man by her side, to whom she was the much-loved godmother.

He was proudly introduced to me as Edward Davis. Taking my hand in a warm, firm clasp he said, "Hello' Lynette," and the brown eyes held mine in a welcoming smile.

A strange, tingling feeling swept through me, as our hands met, and I was afraid he would hear the thumping of my heart. My cheeks grew hot and I was aware of my tousled hair, and the frumpy old coat I wore when an expedition to Moore Street was on the agenda. What must he be thinking of me with all those ungainly vegetables poking out of every where? Worst of all, he was probably struggling to hide his laughter....

I tried to look cool and casual, though I'm sure I only succeeded in looking more stupid. But this wonderful man seemed to understand. He spoke pleasantly of general matters, thereby effectively covering my embarrassment.

Oh, I must see this incredible person again, I found myself thinking with heart-felt longing, gazing into those melting brown eyes as if in a dream.

Clare Devlin was speaking, and Aunt Cissy nudged my basket to capture my attention.

"Cissy and you Lynette, must come and visit me tomorrow evening," she was saying. "Now you must come, Cissy. Your fittings can wait for one evening."

" I wasn't going to say anything about fittings," Aunt Cissy protested.

"Of course we'll be delighted to come and Lynette would love to see your delightful gardens; wouldn't you Lynette?"

I felt myself blushing furiously as all eyes were turned on me, and I wondered if Edward would be there, and how I might tactfully contrive to see him again.

"She doesn't take after her mother like her sisters do," Aunt Cissy was saying.

"She's like her father and our side of the family."

I did not care for all the scrutiny which that observation brought on me, but I was really pleased when Clare pronounced me "very pretty and the image of you, Cissy."

To my relief, speculation was now focused on Edward, but the aunts disagreed over whom he took after. Aunt Cissy opted for Clare, but that lady affirmed he was the "picture of his mother," and produced a photo of her sister to settle the matter.

We would have chatted longer, if Aunt Cissy had not remembered that she had a fitting at half-past five, with Myrabelle Dobson.

"That's the flapper from Rathgar," said Clare with a broad grin.

"'Till to morrow, then," we chorused and went our separate ways, but not before I had stolen one last glance with Edward, who nodded warmly in return.

Aunty Cissy was in a very good humour in the tram going home, and I steered the conversation around to Edward Davis.

"He comes of farming folk in Limerick," returned the aunt in answer to my probing. "He's the youngest of four....two boys and a sister, Peggy, who's a nurse. His father is dead and his mother lives in the family home with her eldest son, Brendan and his wife."

"But what does Edward do?"I inquired casually.

Aunt Cissy gave me a long look and took her time.

"He works in a county council library," she answered with a wicked smile, "and he lives with Clare, not twenty minutes from here as the crow flies. A nice lad," she ended abruptly, as we almost missed our stop.

I spent all afternoon of the next day getting ready for our visit to Clare Devlin's home. I was in a fever of excitement when Aunt Cissy expressed her approval of my new dress.

She had made the dress for me in blue and pink-flowered Crepe-de-Chine.

It had the fashionable dropped waistline and the latest "handkerchief-tipped skirt. Over it went a little coatee of the same material, with sleeves edged in frilly lace. To finish "the look," I wore a long string of crystal beads, which flashed like diamonds in the light, and were a present from Aunt Cissy for "bringing home all those vegetables."

At last we were walking up the drive of Clare's ivy-clad Victorian house, set in an elegant tree-lined road. Clare met us at the door with outstretched arms and kisses; pleasantries over, we were soon sitting around a lavish table in one of the loveliest rooms I had ever seen...all delicate pinks and green, with exquisite white and gold furniture.

I was introduced to Clare's husband, Andy, who was a fine, serious-looking man, with a shy manner and a delightful sense of humour.

"Edward will be in from work any minute now," said Clare happily, and I hoped she had not noticed my disappointment at not seeing him immediately.

A few minutes later, I heard the hall door bang, and my heart jumped.

Then Edward was in the room, his smile warm and friendly for everyone.

He sat beside me at table and during the meal, we had eyes and ears only for each other. I cannot remember what we actually said, but I do recall the laughter and the happiness. The babble of voices seemed very far away, and my heart was trapped in a bubble of sunshine.

After tea, we went into the blue and gold drawing room, just the two of us, to play gramophone records, of which Edward had an impressive collection.

He had a new gramophone, made by a company called "His Master's Voice."

It's trademark was a funny little dog staring inquiringly into the original gramophone horn. There were two little doors on the front of the instrument, which you opened and closed to regulate the sound.

Very soon Edward was playing a medley of the latest dance tunes. How I loved those melodies, and shyness forgotten, my feet were tapping to the "Red Red Robin," "Bye Bye Blackbird," "Charmaine" "Ramona".......

When Edward turned the gramophone handle and "Yes We Have No Bananas," filled the room, he began rolling up the Persian rugs on the polished floor.

Then his whole body took on the magic of the music and he began to foxtrot up and down the room. I watched enchanted; he was such a good dancer, agile and graceful.

Suddenly he leaned forward and caught my hand, "Come on here, Lynette, join me in the dance. Please?" he invited with a bow.

He laughed happily.

"There's nothing to them," he said airily, demonstrating some intricate looking steps. "You'll catch on in a minute."

"I won't, you know," I retorted quickly, making a futile effort to get back to my seat. "It would be like hauling an elephant about."

"Oh come on," he encouraged, gazing at me with a twinkle in his eye. "You look as light as a feather."

He kept a tight hold of my hand, and although I feebly protested, he insisted I follow his steps.

In spite of my doubts, my feet began to twist and turn in harmony with the music, and before I realised it, I was dancing with a certain amount of expertise.

We were laughingly whirling around to the jaunty "Side By Side," when I stumbled against him. Instantly his arms were around me. I lifted my face to his with a thumping heart and a feeling of enchantment.

"Lynette, darling girl," he murmured and our lips met in our first kiss. My arms held him close and an aura of sheer happiness surrounded us.

Lost in our world, we gradually became aware that the gramophone needle was stuck in the groove of the record and needed attention. We broke apart reluctantly, as Clare entered the room with shouts of:

"A cup of tea, my children. Come on now before you dance the house down."

The remainder of the evening was spent with the rest of the party, and I had to concentrate and join in the general conversation. It was not until Aunt Cissy and I were being taken home in Andy's car, that Edward was able to whisper:

"Come with me to the Gaiety to-morrow night. "The Mickado," is on, you'd love it."

"Oh yes please," I replied softly, bemused with joy.

He squeezed my hand. "Pick you up then at half-past seven, sweet girl."

Later, in her flat, Aunt Cissy asked casually if I had enjoyed myself at Clare's.

"I did indeed," I answered too eagerly.

Aunt Cissy paused as she put the milk-jug on the window sill for the morning delivery.

"I think some little lady has fallen in love," she purred, eying me keenly.

I blushed all over my face. "Well, he is rather nice..." I began evasively.

"Don't give me that," snorted the aunt. "I didn't come up in the last shower, you know."

"Oh yes, yes, he's just wonderful," I admitted fervently, knowing it was useless to try and put the aunt off the scent.

Chapter 13

After that, Edward and I met every evening. We went to whatever musical took our fancy, but mostly we strolled around old Dublin, picking out places of historical interest, and ending the evening in a little teashop, laughing and talking.

Our feet danced over the cobbles and our hands clung together as we went back to Aunt Cissy's.

One day we were returning from the Liberties, after visiting St. Patrick's Cathedral and its neighbouring Marches Library. We crossed from Cuff Street, along by the Russell Hotel, past Wesley College and the University Church, until we came to the graceful house of the colourful Buck Whaley....he had been a dare-devil member of the Hell-fire club, and had made a bet that he would play ball against the Walls of Jericho.

"And he did too," said Edward thoughtfully, while I stared at the house, trying to imagine the dynamic Buck striding about the Green in his colourful, eighteenth century clothes.

Suddenly it was real. Men and women in costumes of another age, swept by.

They seemed to float, caught in a haze of iridescent light. I looked at the street, dark-cobbled against the verdant background of the Green. An open carriage, pulled by two black horses was slowly coming towards me. A young man, darkly handsome with cropped hair, held the reins. He was laughing and chatting with a very beautiful young woman beside him. She had short curly hair, a pale complexion and of decided foreign aspect. Her white dress seemed to shimmer as she waved to people passing by.

There was no sound either from the people milling about, or the heavy ornate carriage and high-stepping horses. A voice echoed from a distance, as if the sound had been drifting about for hundreds of years:

"That's Lord Edward and Pamela!"

And so it was, and I could not understand how I came to know that. Then it came to me; only yesterday I had paid a visit to the National Gallery and had seen their portraits side by side....Lord Edward Fitzgerald and his French wife, La Belle Pamela.

Silently the carriage passed, the scene dissolved and melted away, and I felt Edward's arm tight around my waist, and his voice urgent in my ear.

"Lynette, Lynette, what's the matter? Are you alright?"

"Yes, yes, I'm alright," I muttered weakly, and stared blankly about me, but everything was normal again, with horse-drawn carts clip-clopping by, a cheery messenger boy whistling on his over-laden bicycle, and people just going about their twentieth century business. We walked into the Green and Edward found a sheltered seat near the pond. "You look as white as a sheet, sweet girl," he said in a voice full of concern.

I told him what I had seen, holding his hand tightly. As he looked puzzled, I asked anxiously: "Didn't you see it too?"

"No, nothing strange; just what's happening now," he answered gently.

I rubbed my eyes in surprise, what I had seen was so real!

"You're tired out, Lynette darling," he said tenderly. "You've been doing too much walking lately. No more journeys into the past for awhile. It's difficult to distinguish between the real and the unreal when you're exhausted."

I nodded meekly, for it was true that I felt very tired, so arm in arm, we made our way back to Aunt Cissy's for tea.

But the uncanny experience stayed in my mind, and I did not fully accept Edward's explanation of it as the outcome of tiredness alone. Yet, what was it? Were those ghostly people around us all the time; the veil between us lifted for a moment, fusing all ages together in the vast mystery of eternity?

Chapter 14

My wonderful holiday was coming to an end and I pondered, with acute concern, on what would happen to Edward and me when I went home. Was it just a holiday romance to him; would he forget all about me in a few days? The thought brought such pain that I wondered how I would get through the rest of my life without him.

On the day before I was due to leave, we were strolling hand in hand in the Green. A sprightly breeze danced among the flowers and the sunlight rippled the grass in waves of gold. Suddenly Edward swung me around to face him.

"Lynette," he said tensely, "Oh Lynette I love you. Marry me, sweet girl."

I stared at him in bewilderment, unable to believe that Edward really loved me and had asked me to marry him.

With joy pouring through me I reached up and put my lips to his cheek, and my arms wrapped him to my heart.

"I love you too, Edward. I know I've always loved you," I murmured and could say no more, as I struggled to hold back the happy tears.

"Well, I suppose that means you'll marry me then," he said with a smile, which eased the tense emotion between us.

"Yes please," I said primly, but added mischievously, "needs must when the divil drives."

We kissed out there in the middle of the Green, and neither one cared who saw us. Indeed, we could so have occupied ourselves longer, but a big lordly gander, flapped up from the pond, possibly thinking we could have some bread for him, and began smartly poking about in Aunt Cissy's basket of groceries.

We laughed so much we had to reward his antics with a bread roll. He snatched it eagerly and ambled to the pond, where he was besieged by a hungry crowd of feathery girl friends.

After a celebratory coffee and cakes in Bewleys, Edward took me to a jeweller's shop in Wicklow Street, where I was confronted with a battery of engagement rings so beautiful, that choosing one became a problem. I was afraid of picking something wildly expensive, but apparently Edward and the jeweller by some secret code, had that matter in hand.

"What are you worrying about?" Edward laughed. "Just pick the one you like best."

After a lot of heart-felt "ohs" and "ahs," and much trying on and discarding, I ended the search with a superb sapphire and diamond ring. Edward did not turn a hair as he kissed me in front of everyone in the shop, and slipped the ring on my finger.

When eventually we parted and I got home, Aunt Cissy was having a fitting with one of her customers. I stood in the little kitchen and yelled:

"Aunt Cissy! Aunt Cissy. Guess what!"

Aunt Cissy came rushing out. I waved my engaged hand wildly.

What on earth's the matter, Lynn?" she asked, alarmed.

"I'm engaged to Edward," I sang with a couple of excited little twirls.

"Oh my dear, I'm so happy for you," gasped the aunt, hugging and kissing me.

I lifted my face, and looking over Aunt Cissy's shoulder, was surprised to see Myrabelle Dobson, lounging languidly against the open door. She was taking long puffs from her cigarette in its jade holder, and regarding me with narrowed eyes through the smoky haze.

I had already seen her once or twice when she had called to talk clothes with Aunt Cissy. One evening, when Edward and I were saying a fond goodnight in the hall, we had been surprised by her presence, as she was letting herself out after a fitting. I knew when she was around from the smell of her Turkish cigarettes, and the exotic perfume she wore.

Now, I was struck afresh by the classical beauty of her face, which seemed to be chiselled out of marble. Her eyes were like wet violets and her fair hair, styled in the modish Eton Crop.... so unflatteringly harsh on any face I had seen, but on her it was perfect.

I felt awkward under her cool stare, and Aunt Cissy rushed to the rescue.

"Let me introduce you to my niece, Lynette Foley, Myrabelle. She's staying with me for a little holiday."

Myrabelle did not move as I went towards her with an outstretched hand.

"How do," she said carelessly, taking my hand limply.

"So you're engaged," she asked after another uncomfortable pause.

"May I see the ring?" Shyly I held out my left hand, as Aunt Cissy fussed delightedly over it. Myrabelle did not touch my hand, but peered at the ring as if she had difficulty seeing it.

"Pretty, but it's rather small, isn't it?" And she held up her hand gracefully to the light, exposing several flashing diamonds as big as marbles.

I felt anger stab through me at her belittling tone.

"Maybe we don't all want big vulgar rings to flash about," I said coldly, making for the door, but in my haste to get out of the room, I spoiled a grand exit, by tripping over a foot- stool and crashing ignominiously into a rail of half-finished garments.

I heard Myrabelle's tinkling laugh and Aunt Cissy's shout of dismay, as she rushed over to me. "I'm alright! I'm alright!" I retorted shortly, much more angry than hurt.

With poor Aunt Cissy's help, I crawled out of a tangle of spangles, and bales of satins and silks. I got myself into the kitchen, and felt a little relief in banging the door hard behind me.

I went into the bedroom and the fury ebbed out of me, as I tidied the wardrobe and began my packing. I heard the hall door close on Myrabelle's departure, and then Aunt Cissy entered looking very upset.

"I'm so very sorry, Lynn dear," she apologised. "I know Myrabelle can be a bit tactless at times...."

"Tactless,!" I exploded. "How could she be so rude and horrible, as if she hated me, and I don't even know her or want to, come to that."

Aunt Cissy patted my hand and her eyes were sad.

"I know how it sounded, but she didn't really mean it." I opened my mouth to protest, but Aunt Cissy rushed on: "Life wasn't that easy for her. She's had her hopes and disappointments.... probably you reminded her...."But I was deaf to any excuses. Unprovoked rudeness was not to be tolerated, in my book.

" I don't see that she's exactly short of anything," I cried tartly, furiously squeezing an unwilling pair of slippers into my case, "and judging by some of the rumours I've heard, she leads a very liberated lifestyle indeed."

"All the same, Lynn, you can afford to be generous and forgive her," Aunt Cissy's voice was full of pleading. "One day I'll tell you her story, and you'll understand her way. She's really very kind, but unhappiness does queer things to us all."

Aunt Cissy put her arms around me and gave me a hug before going out to the kitchen to make our nightly cup of cocoa. I thought of Edward and my resentment evaporated, and the aunt and I were soon laughing and chatting as usual.

As I kissed her goodnight, I felt secure in my happiness, and Edward's dear face floated through my dreams.

Chapter 15

Next morning Edward took Aunt Cissy and me to the station.

Aunt Cissy was coming home with me for the weekend and I was delighted to have her. I cried as I said goodbye to Edward.

"It's only for a little while, sweet girl," he comforted, as our tears mingled in a last hug.

"Can't Edward go down to meet the family at Whit?" proposed Aunt Cissy wisely.

This suggestion buoyed me up a little, but I held on to him tightly until our hands were torn apart by the movement of the train.

A great welcome awaited us at home. Everyone made a big fuss of me and there was terrific excitement over the engagement. Ma and Da had been previously enlightened about the romance, and on confirmation by Aunt Cissy, that Edward was a "respectable lad with honourable intentions," they expressed themselves happy for me, and willing to accept Edward as the son they never had.

Nell and Dora began beseeching Aunt Cissy with requests for invitations to Dublin. Seeing how well I "had done" they too wanted "a look around."

"The men here are so coarse and common," said Dora affectedly. "Take Dickie Murphy.....he couldn't be romantic in a fit."

I smiled disbelievingly at her, remembering how she had followed Dickie Murphy everywhere... ..since she was ten years old. Everyone predicted that herself and the blue-eyed farmer would make a match of it yet.

"She doesn't always think like that," said Nell petulantly, giving her sister a friendly slap. "You gave everyone plenty to talk about when you danced all night with him at The Farmer's Union Ball last week."

"You mind your own business, Nellie busybody," retorted Dora, crossly tossing her frizzy head.

I lay back dreamily in my chair, idly listening to their banter. I knew I was home again.

Chapter 16

Edward arrived to meet the family at Whit, and was immediately taken to everyone's heart.

"I'm so happy for you, my dear child," said Mam, but there was a little flicker of anxiety in her voice when I told her that Edward and I would like to get married in June.

"Isn't that a bit soon?" she asked, her brow wrinkling worriedly.

"Not really, Mam," I answered firmly. "I'm as sure I love Edward now as I'll ever be. What would we be waiting for with Edward in Dublin and me here?"

"But you have plenty of time," Mam persisted. "You're both so young."

"Yes, but we won't always be young," I argued with all the impatience of youthful love.

Aunt Cissy who had also come down for the weekend, backed me up.

"Let them please themselves, Sarah. After all, Lynn is a mature young woman, and Edward is a fine steady young man with a good job."

Mam still demurred, but seemed more reassured by Da's attitude.

"Let them get on with it, love. Happy the wooing not long a -doing."

The next hurdle was the choice of month. I wanted the end of June," but I was married in September," Mam stated firmly. "It's the nicest month of all for a wedding."

"No it's not," contradicted the aunt. "I agree with Lynn that June is. The fall wouldn't suit her at all; she's a June person." Mam was getting annoyed. "It'll probably be raining in June," she protested.

Aunt Cissy's eyes flashed, "and you may be sure 'twill be raining in September and maybe frosting as well."

Here Da intervened with a twinkle. "And our darling daughter would have to wear leaves instead of all those flowers."

Mam laughed good-humouredly and passed him a cup of tea, and the tension eased.

Dora who was helping Nell to make up some "magical" skin potion with cupfuls of rose petals, suddenly burst out "but she can't change the month now, 'twould be terribly unlucky."

"Looks as if you'll have to go through with it now, Lynn girl," laughed the Da.

I blushed and became so confused that I poured Aunt Cissy's tea into her saucer. Nell, always the practical one, grabbed the tea pot to rescue a cup for herself. Mam was beginning to reminisce about her own wedding, and this brought us on to another debate, as to which colour I should be married in. Mam went for white... "correct for a young bride," while Aunt Cissy wanted pink. "It's a pink month," she explained her preference. "Most flowers are pink. Look at the roses."

No one asked for my opinion. "All frills," sighed Dora dreamily, as she absent-mindedly poured a noxious-looking mixture into a jam jar.

"No dropped waistlines 'round your bottom," grinned Nell, happily sticking a label on the jar of Dora's latest beauty remedy.

Da was watching her with amusement, "Don't forget the health warning," he advised Nell. "Use once for fatal results only." Nell pretended not to hear him and went on with her task while still deploring the present fad for "dropped" waistlines.

"What about mauve?" I managed to break in timidly. This shade, from the range of purple, had become a hot favourite with me and I loved its every variation, but I was instantly routed by them all.

"Whoever thought of getting married in mauve?" came Mam's scandalized voice.

"You're not really serious?" Aunt Cissy asked doubtfully.

I assured her that I was, and that if no one had ever been married in mauve before, it was high time somebody made a start. "Such a gorgeous shade; look at the sweet peas...." I trailed off uneasily at the look of uncompromising disapproval in all their faces, even Da was nonplussed.

Feebly I tried to appeal to Aunt Cissy's justification for every fashion.

"Twould be the latest," I appealed what I thought to be a trump card.

But I got no support; that lady was not concerned with "the latest" in this case.

Pink could be allowed, but mauve.... even Dora was silenced by the combined outrage of the family.

"Pink is the one for you," Aunt Cissy's tone was bossy. "Pink for roses and romance."

I stood my ground a little longer. "The colour should match your eyes," I said stubbornly, "and as I'm not a rabbit mine aren't pink." I had forgotten they were not mauve either.

Mam was adamant for white, and I just sat there wondering which of them would win the battle. As I suspected, Mam did, and it was finally agreed that Aunt Cissy would make the dress and trousseau.

Thankfully Edward and I escaped to the fowl house to feed the newly hatched turkeys, with Mam's indignant voice still ringing in our ears: "You know, Cissy, there's no question about it, but the child could not possibly be married in mauve. What would people say....I do declare, I don't know where she gets some of her ideas from." Edward began to laugh heartily and I turned to him crossly.

"Nice support I got from you with your nose in the newspaper all the time, pretending not to know what was going on...."

He looked at me with his melting brown eyes and cut in softly. "Look, sweet girl, I couldn't care less what colour you wear. I think you'd be delectable in a dishcloth...." and to this piece of outrageous exaggeration I made no demur, especially when it was followed with a loving kiss.

Chapter 17

That night in our bedroom, Nell said thoughtfully, "Would you ever think Aunt Cissy had it in her to drool about pink roses and romance."

Never, agreed Dora, rubbing her face vigorously with their newly-invented face cream. "Maybe, she's in love at last. I wonder why she never married; she's not all that bad-looking," she added condescendingly.

"Far too sensible, I suppose." Nell observed carelessly, and catching sight of me curled up dreamily on the window-seat, pointed an accusing finger.

"Could you just imagine her walking about in the clouds all day like this one here?"

"Still," persisted Dora following her own line of thought, "you'd never know what she'd be up to in Dublin. She could have several lovers...."

She stopped in confusion at where her speculation was taking her.

Nell was instantly on the alert, her attention diverted from me. Soon the two of them were deeply involved in earnest conjecture on the nature of Aunt Cissy's love life.

I remained sitting quietly, idly listening to their wild speculations, and watching the night sky unfolding its canopy of stars, while the coy moon emerged from billowing clouds to glisten on henhouses, stables and fields.

"Come on now, Lynn," Nell's voice seemed to come from a long distance.

"We want the whole story of your great romance and don't leave out any spicy bits either," she warned briskly jumping into bed.

Dora, her face shiny with grease, sat down comfortably on the seat beside me, complete with bag of pipe cleaners, which served the purpose of hair curlers, awaiting heaven knows what revelations.

"Don't be daft. I've told you all I'm going to," I retorted, laughing at their disgruntled faces, and throwing off my dressing gown, leapt into bed.

Chapter 18

Aunt Cissy and I returned to Dublin. I had only a few weeks in which to get my bridal outfit organised, and the wedding arranged. We would be married at home, of course, and have a small reception in the village hall arranged by Mam.

This time there was no ambling around old Dublin, for I was much too excited about the future to contemplate the past. Mostly I window shopped while Edward was at work, only purchasing an item when it really caught my fancy, but every minute we could, we spent planning the path of our future together. Every morning, I organised the flat and did the shopping and cooking, while Aunt Cissy worked against time to have my clothes ready, and still carry on a busy dressmaking business.

As the time before the wedding was so short we agreed to leave the search for a flat until after we came back from our honeymoon. This was Edward's Aunt Clare's idea, and she was going to accommodate us in her large house to give us time to find a suitable place of our own.

So we thankfully postponed the flat hunt, and just concentrated on the joy of being engaged and our coming nuptials.

A couple of days before the wedding I returned home. Aunt Cissy followed later with Edward and his best man, Willie Wright. Then came Aunt Clare with her husband, Andy, Edward's mother, and sister, Peggy.

The great day dawned full of promising sunshine, although a frolicking wind rolled crazily over the countryside.

We were all up at six o'clock....no hardship there, as country folk are always astir by then, and often earlier.

There was much excitement as the important ritual of dressing began, and near panic when my new white shoes could not be found. It was Nell feeding the poultry, who discovered them rolled up in a parcel in the fowl house.

Carefully Mam and Aunt Cissy helped me into the white satin dress. Certainly, the aunt had excelled herself in the making of it. It had a hip-length bodice with strips of delicate lace insertion, the short (and fashionable) gathered skirt, and narrow sleeves, which billowed in a lacy froth at the wrists.

Edward's mother had brought her own veil of Carrickmacross lace for me. This was eventually adjusted on my head after much arguments about its correct position, and everyone in the family had an opinion about that. Eventually, as time was running out, a compromise had to be agreed, and hurriedly adopted, and I managed to sail down the stairs, complete in all my finery, with the veil firmly anchored on my head by a silver Juliet cap, encircled with Lilly-of-the-Valley.

At last I was ready, clutching a sheaf of Lilly-of-the Valley and roses.

Nell, Dora and Peggy, each dressed in romantic pink ....a compromise with Aunt Cissy....all giggling anticipation, set off for the Church in the pony and trap.

Aunt Cissy, in blue crept-de-chine, nodded her approval as she, Mam and Edward's mother, followed in Jonny-Joe's pony and trap from the village. Just before Da and I were to leave, there was a rap at the door, and Billie-the-Post was in the kitchen with a package for me.

"Whatever can it be?" I wondered aloud, tearing the parcel open. A long blue box was revealed, which contained a string of lustrous pearls. A silver and white card said simply: "Be happy, Lynette. Love, Myrabelle Dobson."

I felt tears sting the back of my eyes. I had not seen her since she had hurt me so deeply that day in Aunt Cissy's. Now I felt an inexplicable feeling of pity for her and a surge of friendliness too, as Da fastened the necklace around my neck. The pearls glowed softly against my skin and were the perfect finish to my bridal gown.

Why had Myrabelle remembered me? I had thought her snobbish and ill-mannered and would not have wished to cross her path again. Probably out of compliment to Aunt Cissy, I reckoned, and abandoned the riddle at a shout from Da.

"Come on Lynn, for heaven's sake. They'll think we're not going to turn up at all." I walked down the flowery path of our little front garden on Da's arm and into the rose- decked carriage, which the village blacksmith, Joey Red, hired out for such occasions.

He helped us to our seats with great concern, then seating himself behind Rumpus, his sprightly white mare, he took the reins with a flourish.

"Happy Wedding day, girl," he roared, and cracking his whip enthusiastically, galloped triumphantly to the Church.

We arrived ten minutes late, and I shall always remember the flutter of loving anticipation which greeted our arrival as we walked sedately down the aisle to Mendelson's "Wedding March."

Edward turned to me with such welcoming love in his eyes that my heart felt tight with tears. Then his hand warm and strong closed over mine, and the ceremony proceeded in a haze of happiness.

Chapter 19

After our honeymoon in Connemara, Edward and I returned to Dublin and took up our temporary home with Aunt Clare. But "temporary" was our dictum, and we realised that we had to find a suitable place of our own within a reasonable time.

Aunt Clare was extremely kind to us, making an extended honeymoon out of our visit, but we could not take advantage of that situation indefinitely.

Now we were confronted with the difficulties of flat or house hunting. I lost count of all the house agents we visited. Every evening we set out on a trail of potential properties. We examined houses of every description, from the half-built to the semi-ruin, but all of them were way beyond our means to repair or restore. In the end we decided it would be wiser to concentrate on searching for a flat only.

This meant we had to start the hunt all over again and the results were very discouraging. Foot sore we inspected flats that were too small, too big, too shabby, too inaccessible for Edward's job, or just too plain expensive.

"It looks as if Aunt Clare will have us living with her forever," I opined gloomily.

Then we had a bit of luck. Mrs. Redmond, for whom Aunt Cissy made "sensible" skirts, came in one evening to Aunt Cissy's flat, as I was helping her remove tacking threads from a dance dress.

During a chat over a cup of tea, she happened to remark on how tough it was for the newly-weds to-day, to find a home of their own. Aunt Cissy told her of our plight, and she said she had a small flat to let at the top of her house.

"It's very small," she cautioned. "Only suited to two girls out all day, but sure if you're desperate you can come along and have a look at it. If you think it would suit, you're welcome to it until you find something bigger."

This was the best bit of news yet, and as we climbed the stairs in Mrs. Redmond's house, we were full of hope.

The flat was scrupulously clean and freshly decorated. It had a tiny pink and white bedroom, a kitchen like a big cupboard, and a cosy sitting room with white walls and blue check curtains. There was also a box-room which had been converted into an attractive, yellow-painted bathroom.

The sitting room was nicely furnished with all the necessities, including two large easy chairs with scarlet velvet cushions, matched by a thriving red geranium perched on the windowsill. A gentle breeze from the open window wafted its fragrance towards us, and on the mantelpiece a quaint old clock ticked contentedly; it struck eight o'clock and a striped cuckoo sprang out through a little door and cuckooed the time to us.

That settled it for me. "Oh, Edward it's lovely; do let's take it."

"Are you quite sure," he whispered back. "Bit small maybe...."

I interrupted urgently: "I'm sure; I'm sure. It's only a short ride from your job, and minutes from Aunt Cissy's."

I turned back at the door to gaze into the little room, my eyes drawn to the window and the earthenware pot of red geraniums, luminous in the setting sun.

We arranged with Mrs. Redmond the formalities of taking the flat. She was a very friendly, chatty woman and over a cup of tea, instructed us on the best shops to visit, the times of laundry and milk deliveries, the sharing of the clothes- line in the fairly wild-looking back garden, and one or two other pieces of domestic information.

Of course, I knew all this from my sojourn with Aunt Cissy, which Mrs. Redmond chose to ignore, and continued to regale me with advice until she was satisfied with her own performance and my humble acceptance.

She even offered us the loan of her hoover "to keep the place clean," and she was very particular on this point, with which I was fully in accord anyway.

We moved in a week later with our bits and pieces. Edward had his precious gramophone and record collection, sheet music and violin, not to mention armloads of books. I had our wedding presents and fairly practical items....

china, linen, pots and pans, not to mention our clothes, of course.

By the time we had everything arranged there was not much room for ourselves, but if we were careful and mindful of where we were heading, we might avoid stubbed toes and bumped elbows.

Clare was sad to see us leave, but agreed reluctantly, that we needed to be a self-sufficient team, and set up our own place together, however small. But it was comforting to know we had an open invitation to stay at her home, if the need arose.

We settled down happily to an easy-going domestic routine. I went to Aunt Cissy's every day and helped her with shopping, packing or sewing. In our new home, I experimented with various culinary efforts, some of which were an utter disaster and had to be hidden in the back garden from Edward's unsuspecting gaze. Sometimes he wondered why I produced so meagre a meal, after battling for hours with an exotic dish far beyond my capabilities, and of course, there was always my misinterpretation of the recipe. But he was good natured about what he knew of my efforts, and saved us both from starvation with fish and chips from the local chipper. However, his understanding of the situation was beginning to wear a little around the edges, and I realized there would be a day of reckoning if I did not get my act together pretty fast.

Mrs. Redmond, bless her, who had become a valued friend, got me out of many a tight corner. She showed me how to produce an eatable meal and forget the exotics, so that Edward's diet improved and there was less for the hidden corners of the back garden!

One evening when I went around to Aunt Cissy's, Myrabelle Dobson was there being fitted for her new black satin evening dress. The aunt was kneeling on the floor in front of her adjusting the hem of the skirt, while Myrabelle smoked lazily, and acknowledged my presence with a mocking smile.

The neckline of the dress plunged alarmingly, and there were only crossed straps at the back of the bodice. In the centre of the tightly – fitting decollage sparkled a floppy red rose sprinkled with silver sequins.

I stood spellbound. "It's lovely," I breathed, filled with admiration for the beautiful woman and the exquisite handiwork of my aunt.

"Twas hard work, then," said Aunt Cissy in response to my praise, "but it turned out alright," she added modestly, and bent down again to her task.

Myrabelle looked amused as she puffed a cloud of aromatic smoke in my direction.

"If it isn't Lynette, our little bride,!" she exclaimed with a laugh.

I felt a flare of anger at her tone, but I managed to stay cool, "Good evening Mrs Dobson, how are you?"

Aunt Cissy went to get some sewing silk and Myrabelle moved gracefully towards me and kissed my cheek lightly.

"I wish you every happiness, my dear," she said softly, and when I met her eyes, I could have sworn that they were bright with tears.

Rather disconcerted, I remembered her wedding present.

"I want to thank you, Mrs. Dobson, for the wonderful present you sent me.

The pearls are magnificent. I wore them for my wedding. It was too good of you and I didn't expect anything at all. I never had anything like them and...."

Abruptly her mood changed and she cut in sharply: "Don't keep on about it, will you? It's only a necklace and nothing as valuable as you're trying to make out. Let's forget it, shall we? And now could you please amuse yourself somewhere else while I get this dress fitted?"

She turned her back on me and began examining the hem of her skirt in the long oval mirror.

Aunt Cissy bustled in, and feeling dismissed like a naughty child, I backed awkwardly into the kitchen.

Aunt Cissy's voice broke into my angry thoughts: "There's an apple tart on the table, Lynn. Maybe you'd be an angel and make us a cup of tea."

There was nothing I would refuse Aunt Cissy, so although I had hoped to escape home, I set the tray for two and put the kettle on. One thing I vowed, when Myrabelle Dobson was with the aunt in future, I would take good care to avoid calling when she was there. I would ask Aunt Cissy to tell me when she was expected, for I was not going to be snubbed and belittled again, I assured myself furiously.

I slammed the milk and sugar on the tray and made the tea. When I re-entered the sitting room, Myrabelle was standing by the window in her coat, and Aunt Cissy, oblivious to the "atmosphere," was clearing a portion of the table for the tray.

"I'm just going," Myrabelle was straightening her hat.

"Not 'till you've had a cup of tea, you're not," the aunt said firmly.

I laid the tray on the table and Aunt Cissy immediately spotted that I had not put on a third cup.

"Where's your cup, Lynn," she called as I made for the door.

"I haven't time now," I answered hurriedly. "Edward will be in and I must get the supper."

"Are you sure?" asked the aunt doubtfully, while Myrabelle seated herself at the table and began pouring the tea.

"Leave her be, Cissy," she cut in brusquely. "Can't you see she won't let that new husband of hers out of her sight. This is the lovey-dovey time, let her enjoy it while she can....it's not something that lasts and our little bride...."

But I heard no more. I rushed out, slamming the door and stood angry and shaking on the pavement.

Chapter 20

Everything was indeed lovey-dovey for awhile. Then I began to realise after a few tiffs, progressively getting fiercer, that love and harmony don't automatically go together.

The quarrels started with small silly things. For instance, Edward strongly objected to being given his hot meal on a hot plate. This sounded outrageous to me, for Mam had always insisted that you never served a hot meal on a cold plate. She even scalded the cups before pouring the tea into them. This last always infuriated me, as I hated boiling hot tea, and even considered it a dangerous practise. But nothing would dissuade her, although we rowed about it so often. Heating plates was different and reasonable; I could see a tasty meal becoming a congealed mess on a cold plate.

However, old habits die hard and I blithely ignored all Edward's pleas for cold plates only. Every time there was a heated protest (and how I laughed at the pun) I simply took no notice, stating very reasonably, "What's the use of cooking good food and slapping it up on a cold plate?"

And Edward's reply in rising tones:

"I told you over and over, I don't want food that hot. Do you ever listen to me at all? Cold! Cold! Cold!" and he would snatch up a cup, or other implement off the table, and bang it several times.

Fearing for the safety of our small supply of eating utensils, I would shout back: "Don't you bang cups at me, Edward Davis."

Another bang and a stormy litany of his grievance which, he emphasized, was going to continue until I got the message.

But despite the rows, I continued to try and win the battle of the hot plate. Edward would sit down, feel the plate to gauge its temperature before touching the food, and a furious exchange would result if it climbed above tepid.

One day he just got up, leaving his dinner untouched, and putting on his coat, walked out banging the door behind him.

Then the penny dropped. I rushed out in my grubby apron after him, but he was going so fast I was unable to catch up with him. I shouted for him to stop, but if he heard me, he did not answer, and I saw him leap on a passing tram.

I rushed back, nearly in tears, only to find that the hall door had slammed and I was locked out without a key. Shamefacedly, I knocked on the door, hoping that Mrs. Redmond was in. There was no reply. Desperately, I hammered harder and harder, until it dawned on me that I was not going to get in before someone came along with a key.

Edward! The cause of all the trouble, I sobbed angrily, making me an exhibition in front of everyone.

I gazed about me furtively, conscious of untidy hair, worn-down slippers and, of course, the grubby apron.

But no one was paying me any particular attention. The odd passer-by gave me a curious glance and hurried on. I tried to calm down and think of some other way of gaining admission. I looked closely at the downstairs window of Mrs. Redmond's drawing room and saw, with a leaping heart, that it was open a few inches from the bottom.

Gingerly I shifted myself up on to the unkempt rockery, which bordered the window in the tiny garden. Carefully I eased the heavy window up, fearing that it would crash down and kill me, or worse, break into hundreds of pieces, leaving us liable for its repair.

At last there was enough room for me to squeeze through, and throwing one leg inelegantly over the sill, my foot made contact with the fat, pampered, Redmond cat. He had been luxuriously stretched on the floor enjoying the sunshine.

There was an instant, high-pitched yowl and the startled animal leapt several feet in the air, his white whiskers stiff as wire across his stripey face. He blundered against the gaudy figure of a very masculine-looking china horse, smashing it to smithereens with a loud clatter. Shocked, and fearing the devil was lying in wait for me, I gave a roar and toppled helplessly back into the garden, the cat flying after me.

Next thing I knew I was being hauled up by the milkman, who was going around on his deliveries. Trying to ignore my bruised bottom and conjure a vestige of dignity, I staggered drunkenly to my feet. The milkman was all concern.

"Thank you, thank you, I'm alright now," I gasped, struggling to pull my muddy skirt respectably around me. Then I realised that everything was not alright, my problem was still unresolved. Hurriedly I informed the milkman that I had been cleaning the window when the door slammed and I was locked out.

"No problem, Missus," he said cheerfully, and handing me his milk can, climbed nimbly into Mrs. Redmond's drawing room in his muddy wellingtons.

In a few seconds the hall door was thrown open and the milkman grandly stood aside for me to enter.

When I thanked him profusely for his trouble, he said he hoped he would be handy next time I banged the door, and with a knowing wink, disappeared after his horse up the street.

Just in time, I noticed that he had forgotten to leave us our supply of milk, and putting a chair against the door to prevent another mishap, I tore after him with the milk jug.

Returning to the house with my over-full jug, I was annoyed to find a crowd of chattering children standing at the gate. So I had been observed after all!

Ignoring them, I made for the door to shouts of:

"Are ya alrite, Missus?"

"Missus, are ya a robber?"

"That was a rough tumble with the milkman," a lanky youth jeered.

Another voice shrieked innocently: "Eh, mam, why didn't ya go in be the hall door?"

I slammed the door behind me, feeling bruised, humiliated and furiously angry with Edward. I still had enough presence of mind left to remember the broken china horse scattered on the drawing room floor, and that it needed to be disposed of before Mrs. Redmond came home.

I ran up to our flat for a basin and cloth, And re-entering her drawing room, set about cleaning the milkman's tracks from the drab beige carpet. I gathered together what remained of the horse, priceless for all I knew, and wondered how an animal of its size could have so many jagged pieces.

Leaving the window as I had found it, I crept cautiously upstairs, only to find that in my flight, I had left the kitchen tap running and the whole place was swimming in water. I turned off the tap and slumped into a chair, crying helplessly. After a while, there were no tears left and catching sight of a bottle of cooking sherry, I tumbled the half used contents into a glass and drained the lot.

Feeling decidedly brighter, if somewhat wobbly, I began the task of drying the swamp of a kitchen,....a job which was to occupy the rest of the evening.

I was still hard at it when Edward came home.

"What on earth are you up to?" he asked with no sign of his former bad humour, and gazing at my dishevelled appearance with unflattering interest.

"What do I appear to be up to?" I flung back with a watery flourish of the dripping mop.

"Poor darling," he said worriedly, "you don't have to scrub that hard, but you do seem to be using too much water on the job."

I paused in my vigorous mopping and eyed him suspiciously to see if he was laughing at me, but he seemed all concern, and suddenly I burst into tears.

In a second I was wrapped in his arms and he was soothing me with hugs and kisses.

"Edward, Oh Edward," I wailed. "I thought you'd left me."

"I'd never leave you, sweet girl, he murmured solemnly, but rather spoiled this declaration by lightly adding, "Well not today, love, and certainly not without my dinner."

"Well your dinner's cold enough now" I sighed tiredly, indicating the congealed meal on the plate by the sink.

"I'm sorry for upsetting you, love," he said gently, dropping a kiss on the top of my head. Then with a sudden change of mood he rubbed his hands together briskly and demanded: "Are there any eggs handy, I'm famished?"

"Yes in the cupboard," I told him, knowing that the tender session of reconciliation was over and it was very much back to basic business.

I made no effort to move, and after a brief hesitation he put his arm around me and led me to an armchair. "Don't you worry, darling pet, I'll cook us an omelette, and I' sure the cupboard will reveal something else."

It did, and Edward served them in triumph; omelette with tinned stew and sardines, followed by a tin of our favourite "My Lady Peaches."

Over the meal we discussed the hot plates syndrome, and I promised never to present him with one again.

I went on to give him the sequence of events that followed on his walking off at dinner time. He laughed so much, when I had at least expected a little sympathy, I found myself becoming increasingly annoyed.

"I might have been killed or badly injured." I ventured indignantly.

"No fear of that," laughed my dear one callously, "you're too well upholstered for a bump on the bottom to cause serious damage," and he dismissed the matter with a playful slap on my tender posterior.

I tried to think of something superior and clever to put him in his place, but suddenly I saw a vision of myself on the rockery with the terrified feline flying for his life, and the milk man gallantly rushing to my rescue, and I exploded in fits of uncontrollable laughter.

"This is all very funny," I giggled helplessly, "but what about the horse?"

"Horse! What Horse?" He stared at me in understandable bewilderment.

"Didn't I tell you that the cat broke the horse on Mrs. Redmond's window sill?" I asked impatiently.

"On that little matter," he laughed lazily, "Well, that's between you and the cat, isn't it? I'm sure you can work out some arrangement with him, and anyway, he's not too likely to let the cat out of the bag."

I threw a cushion at his head and told him he could certainly do the washing up for his sins, while I endeavoured to remove the day's grime in a hot bath.

As I was splashing scented water over myself five minutes later, my ear was held by the new record Edward was playing on the gramophone. "What's that lovely music?" I shouted, as I reluctantly rose from the cooling bath.

"Mozart," he answered, whistling in tune with the melody.

As I entered the living room, he turned from a pile of records and stared at me in surprise. "What's all this?" he sang, raising his eyebrows.

"Nothing," I pirouetted provocatively, and leapt into his waiting arms in my bridal nightdress and a cloud of Woolworth's most potent bath salts.

Edward had always brought me a cup of tea in bed before leaving for work, just as I liked it, but next morning I noticed that the tea was unusually hot. I said nothing but left it on the bedside table to cool. The same thing happened the following morning, and the morning after that the cup was so hot I could hardly hold it. Suddenly suspicious, I jumped out of bed and made for the living room where Edward was putting on his coat.

"What have you done to the tea?" I exploded. "The cup is roasting....you must have boiled the tea in it."

He looked at me blankly. "Well darling girl, I think tea should be served really hot and never, but never in a cold cup. I just heated it a little, that's all."

"But you know, you know, I don't like roasted tea," I expostulated.

He laughed uproariously, and the light dawned.

"Why you mean so and so," I shrieked, "and at this bloody hour of the morning...." and grabbing the tea cosy, let fly, but with a quick turn he stepped nimbly out of the door, and whistling cheerfully, ran down the stairs to catch his tram.

Chapter 21

The problem of the china horse was very much on my mind. It was technically true to say that the cat had broken it, yet if it had not been for my untimely intervention, the accident would not have happened. And another thing; what was I to do with all the shattered pieces hiding guiltily in a paper bag, at the back of a cupboard? Maybe I should have left them where they had fallen, and allow Mrs. Redmond to draw her own conclusions.

And, I thought in alarm, supposing the horrid thing was valuable. I tossed and tumbled half the night trying to find a way out of the impasse. At dawn I hit on a course of action.

Next morning around ten o'clock, was our weekly refuse collection. Mrs. Redmond always left the house, on her daily shopping expedition, shortly before this. I would wait until she had left, and then nip down and put the parcel of pieces in the bin. To salve my conscience, I would try and buy, price permitting, a similar-looking horse, and slip it back before it was missed. Pleased with my cleverness, I slept soundly until morning.

But as so often happens, things don't go automatically to plan. During the night, quite a storm blew up and the street was lashed with torrents of rain.

The bin became trapped in a mound of sodden rubbish on the pavement, and depositing my parcel safely in its depths, was no easy task, but eventually I was satisfied with my efforts.

Thinking my problem resolved, I set about my daily chores, singing the latest ditty as I worked to a record on the gramophone.

"The rippling brook goes on and on, on and on and on,
The rippling brook goes on and on all day long forever."
I giggled and scrubbed and warbled the funny bits:
"They asked me what a gooseberry was
And this reply I gave.
A gooseberry is a fruit
That needs a haircut and a shave.

Now skirts are getting shorter
Every year that's fine
I only hope that I shall rise
In nineteen forty nine."

I leapt forward to catch a dripping bar of soap, which shot out of my hand and spiralled in orbit for the ceiling, where it lodged well out of reach behind one of Mrs. Redmond's cherished wall plates. I was about to go in pursuit of it when there was a knock on the door. I dropped the scrubbing brush and rushed to switch off the gramophone, which had graduated to a rather wild version of some Italian Polka. I pulled open the door and was confronted by Mrs. Redmond who, for good reason, I was aiming to avoid until I could ascertain what way the wind was blowing with regard to the demise of her horse. Beside her ambled her cat, plump and disdainful.

"Me....ow, me....ow!" he yowled, arching his back and fixing a malevolent eye on me.

Mrs. Redmond immediately bent down to the animal.

"Boots me old darlin' come to your mammy," and she scooped the cat up in her arms. Then she turned her bright gaze on me. "Mrs. Davis, I just called up to ask if you knew anything about a broken ornament in my dust bin. The bins haven't been emptied yet and the wind has tumbled the rubbish all over the street. The corpo must be late on account of the storm last night....anyway, I found these bits of me china horse scattered everywhere," and she held out a few fragments for my inspection.

I felt the colour flaming in my face. "Oh Mrs. Redmond," I gushed. "I've been meaning to tell you, but...."

"Don't tell me," she interrupted, "but that's the second ornament that Boots has broken in the past week."

"Boots," I murmured stupidly, wondering if I'd heard her right.

"Yes, you know this cuddly old pet," and she patted the scruffy –looking animal, who was busily employed pulling his claws in and out of her second-best coat.

"Let me guess what happened," she went on indulgently, "When Boots knocked over the horse, you heard the crash and went down to see what happened, and you were kind enough to rescue my poor little pussy, and clear away the mess in case he hurt himself on the broken pieces."

She paused, and I felt some observation was called for from me. "Oh not at all," I muttered with heart-felt relief, for I had been afraid we were going to get our walking papers. I actually nerved myself to ask, "Was it a valuable ornament, Mrs. Redmond?"

She laughed derisively and said: "Valuable, how are you! Cost about six pence below in Woolworths. I always hated the thing, but as it was given to me by my neighbour for a birthday present, I was afraid of offending her, so I put it on the window sill where I wouldn't be forever looking at it." She smiled happily and added: "Now I can look her in the eye and tell her how upset I am that it's gone."

Getting a bit more daring I chimed in, "Let's hope she doesn't get you another one."

Just then, Boots shifted his position in her arms and gave me an accusing stare. "Me....ow," he warned, and I thanked heaven we didn't speak the same language.

However, the end of the saga was that another identical china horse appeared on Mrs. Redmond's window sill. She told me that her neighbour had missed the ornament and questioned her on its disappearance. "I told her what happened," said Mrs. Redmond sourly, a fag hanging out of her mouth, as she scrubbed the front door step, "and of course, I had to tell her how much I missed the ugly thing. I thought that was the end of the story," she continued, squeezing her cloth with unnecessary vigour, "but next day in she comes with the very same horse. It seems she had considered them so lovely that she bought two of them at the same time. She bought me one for my birthday and kept the other for herself, but seeing as how cut-up I was at the loss of mine, and seeing as it was a present from herself, she felt the least she could do was give me hers. Well, what do you say to that? All I could do was pretend to be over the moon at her generosity." Poor Mrs. Redmond sat back on her heels and gazed over at the window where the placid-looking china horse stared vacantly back at her. "I shall have to leave it to Boots," she sighed with a certain amount of venom. At this point, I felt it was high time I got out of the line of fire, and hurriedly dodging her bucket, sprinted off to the shops.

Chapter 22

Around this time Edward got tickets for the Gaiety to see the highly acclaimed "Maid Of The Mountains." I arranged to meet him outside Nobletts sweet shop, at the corner of South King Street at 7.45, for he was having tea first with his sister Peggy, in Grafton Street.

I dressed with care for the occasion, in a pretty blue blouse, and after doing my hair, applied a little Ponds Vanishing Cream and powder, which were greatly favoured by society beauties at the time. I thought the face looking back at me from the mirror seemed a little nicer than usual, and was pleased with myself. I was just pulling on my only pair of silk stockings when the coalman banged on the hall door, reminding me that I had agreed to take in Mrs. Redmond's coal for her, as she was out visiting at the time.

I quickly put on my wrap-around overall, and saw the coal safely deposited in her coal house. But the coalman being chatty, the operation had taken more time than I had allowed for. I snatched off the overall and dived into my coat.

Pulling the door after me, I ran for a tram and arrived ten minutes late at the sweet shop.

Edward was there looking anxiously at every passer-by.

"I'm sorry darling." I gasped, as he began to complain about how tired he was waiting for hours in the dust and dirt, after a hard day's work, while I had only to saunter down through the Green and, of course, I couldn't do that on time. He was well into his stride when an old lady with a basket of sweetly-scented violets on her arm, stepped in front of us. "Violets lady, Violets lady," she crooned enticingly. "Not now," snapped the husband impatiently with an off-putting eye.

"Violets for the lovely lady," persisted the woman. I giggled, as Edward looked ready to explode. Then to my surprise and embarrassment, I noticed that the flower seller was staring determinedly at me, and nodding meaningly at the lower half of my body. I thought it some quirk of hers, but her broad Dublin voice fell to a scandalized whisper: "I think the young lady has forgotten something" I felt a rising panic, as I cast an apprehensive eye over myself and was shocked to discover that my coat, which I had left unbuttoned in my haste, had swung open to reveal a pair of bright pink flannelette knickers.....I had forgotten to put on my skirt!

Mortified I stared from the violet lady to Edward, wrapping my coat closely around me.

"Lord! But how did you manage that?" gasped Edward, not long at a loss for words. I found my tongue furiously.

"I managed it only too well, as you can see, and if you say another word, Edward Davis, I shall take my coat right off for all to see," I threatened daringly.

The old woman smiled, and pinning a little bunch of violets on my lapel, assured me that "it could have been worse."

I wondered what exactly she had in mind, as Edward pressed two coppers into her hand, and hauled me into the theatre seconds before the lights went down.

"There's no getting out of it, sweet girl, but you are a card," Edward whispered, all anger evaporated, as we settled ourselves in the grand plush seats. But still aware of my distress, he closed his hand warmly over mine, and laid a box of my favourite chocs on my pink knees. "Don't worry, it could happen to a bishop," he jested cheerfully. "If anyone spots your outfit, they'll think you're one of the high kickers off the stage."

Annoyed, I pretended not to hear him, but as his hand stole into mine, my heart melted and I nestled happily against him.

Lost in music and love, I forgot about my unconventional apparel until I got home, and casually flung off my coat.

There was a roar of laughter behind me.

"I didn't know you'd taken to wearing plus fours, Lynn," said Edward, as I caught sight of myself in the mirror and was appalled at the spectacle I made.

The legs of the pink knickers had sagged unevenly over my knees, and I was irresistibly reminded of the print of Louis XIV of France on Mrs. Redmond's landing, depicting that gentleman dressed in silken, be-ribboned britches; one frilly leg, in pointed velvet slippers, delicately poised in front of the other. Impishly

I eyed Edward, and leaning on a side table, extended my black-buttoned shoe, arranging my pose to mimic the Monarch's.

Chapter 23

About a week later I had an unexpected visitor. It was in the afternoon and I was scrubbing down the sink when there was a knock on the door.

Grabbing a towel and trying to smooth my unruly hair, I opened the door and got quite a start to find Myrabelle Dobson standing in front of me. She was beautifully dressed in a cinnamon-coloured coat and knee length, pink georgette dress. A feathery cloche hat hugged her fair head and her smile was wide and friendly.

"Hello Lynette! Thought I'd give you a call to see what wedded bliss was doing to you. May I come in?"

I stood aside, muttering a greeting and she whirled gracefully past me and into the untidy living room. "I seem to have interrupted something," she laughed playfully. "Are you dismantling the place or have you had a row?"

"Neither," I faltered, swallowing my annoyance and forcing a smile, "just tidying up."

She threw herself into one of the ruffled armchairs, crossing her superb silk-stockinged legs. "There's a little cake for your cup of tea," and she indicated a Fuller's box on the table beside her handbag.

"Oh you shouldn't," I said lamely, as I opened the box to reveal a luscious walnut cake. "It's gorgeous!" I exclaimed, pleased in spite of myself, for Edward and I loved cake, but could not often rise to the luxury of this one.

She glanced at the cake dismissively, and I rushed on: "We'll have a slice now with a cup of tea."

"Not for me," she drawled. "Must think of the old chassy, you know," and she yawned and stretched her slim figure with a satisfied air.

"I suppose you don't bother with that sort of thing," and she eyed my more generous outline critically.

"Well I do try," I began feebly, "but I fare best at the dieting when there are no cakes around."

"Want to watch it then, my dear," she said with a touch of asperity. Then losing interest, she took a gold cigarette case from her bag.

"Mind?" she asked, but before I could answer, she had flicked a diamond-studded lighter and applied its yellow flame to her cigarette. She settled herself more comfortably, exhaling a cloud of smoke, and immediately the distinctive scent of her tobacco was all around us.

"I was dying for that," she remarked complacently. "Well, tell me everything," she demanded as an uneasy silence fell between us. I decided to ignore her request for a cosy chat.

"I'll get that cup of tea," I said hurriedly making for the kitchen.

She held up a pale restraining hand sparkling with jewels. "Not for me, my dear. I never touch tea in the afternoon, but a cup of black coffee would be lovely."

My heart plummeted. Edward and I never took coffee at home, only occasionally in Bewleys, but how could I admit to this elegant woman that we had not a spoon-full in the flat; she would think us primitive. Should I make an excuse and run down to Mrs. Redmond, maybe she would have some?

Then bracing myself, I said casually, "I'm sorry, but I'm right out of coffee, are you sure you wouldn't like a light cup of tea?" and I hopefully put the kettle on to boil. There was a pause behind me and then she said rather reluctantly;

"All right, my dear, just one cup, but make it strong."

She smoked languidly as I got out my best china teacups and arranged them on a white lacy tray cloth, while she kicked off her shoes and lay back with closed eyes.

When the tea was ready I roused her gently and handed her a cup and serviette. She drank the tea slowly, hardly moving from her reclining position.

"Don't cut any for me," she admonished, as I set about slicing the cake. I was greedily anxious for a piece myself, but decided I would not enjoy it under her supercilious gaze. Better wait until this evening and have it with Edward.

Sipping her tea absently, she said, "I've had such a morning of it searching every shop in town for a pair of red shoes. I particularly want them to match a cherry red dress your aunt is making for me. I said to Madge Smithson Elliot.....I'm sure you've heard of her.....he's in Rayham Chemicals, you know."

I had not and did not particularly wish to know, but refrained from exposing my ignorance. Myrabelle's voice droned on, over and away from me, and back again to the onerous task of matching shoes, gloves, bag, hat and jewellery, while rushing for a dinner date with some executive. "And the worst thing about it is making sure that the chauffeur finds parking outside all the shops I have to visit," she lamented.

I grew weary listening to her complaints, which were incomprehensible to me, and the aromatic scent of her cigarette smoke was also making me sleepy. With an effort I sat up and said briskly, "Well I have no such problems, thanks be."

She looked at me with dislike through a haze of smoke. "I didn't think you would," she returned sarcastically.

The clock chimed the hour and I jumped up, and began stacking the china on the tray, hoping to indicate that the "interview" was now at an end. Myrabelle also got up and began rummaging in her handbag. Carefully she drew out a fancy bottle of perfume. "Smell," she ordered, opening the bottle and flourishing it under my nose. I took the bottle and sniffed.

"Delicious!" I breathed, inhaling a rush of exotic flowers and spices. She took a smaller bottle of the same fragrance from her bag.

"For you," she said carelessly. "Use it on that man of yours as the need arises."

"But I just can't take it," I protested, surprised and embarrassed.

"Of course you can," she insisted a little more warmly. "Do take it and please me."

I looked at her face, open and friendly, and tried to understand her changing moods. Why was she so generous, yet so hostile too?

As I was taking another sniff of the perfume, she was saying with a sardonic edge to her voice: "How is the dear Edward? Still the greatest of Adam's sons?"

"Very well at last sighting," I answered shortly, nettled by her tone. Then in an effort to change the conversation I said chattily:

"I hear you're having a great time these days, and that you were the belle of the ball in the Russell hotel last Saturday and," I paused insinuatingly, "got yourself a lot of attention from no less an individual than Lord Alex Pace."

Her eyes narrowed through the smoke of her cigarette. "What exactly did you hear? Something to shock the little bride?"

"Oh just rumours," I returned flippantly.

"I can just guess the sort. That's on the credit side in my circle. They don't talk about you unless you happen to be better looking than most of them, or have a beautifully rich and, therefore, very interesting husband."

"And what way would describe you,"? I inquired curiously.

"Interestingly rich husband," and she absently extended a slender leg encircled by a flowery garter on a silk stocking. "That's why I married him," she went on thoughtfully. "Father had disinherited me, and Alex was mad about me. The idea of poverty did not appeal to me. Alex was rich and we had known each other since childhood. I thought it would work out and I tried very hard at first, but it was no use; I just hadn't the heart for it."

Her eyes were sad and I asked, "Are you not happy then?"

"Happy! What has that to do with anything?" she asked bitterly. "He goes his way, I go mine, and at least, I can spend money all day and be miserable in comfort."

She looked as young and vulnerable as a girl with such stark sorrow in her eyes, that I was aghast, and could think of nothing appropriate to say.

She was the first to break the silence. "Tell me does it work? Is love ever a reality, or just a series of flings?"

I thought of Edward and a great tide of tenderness spread through me.

"Yes, if you have it you're short of nothing, and if you haven't, you've got nothing," I said rather smugly. I sighed happily, sublimely unaware, with the legendary ignorance of youth, of the lack of any room for compromise in my outlook.

There was a lull in the conversation, each lost in her own thoughts. Everyday sounds drifted in through the open window; a bell tolled from a nearby church, a horse clip-clopped in the street below, and the little wooden cuckoo suddenly announced the evening hour.

Myrabelle moved to the door.

"I must go," she said hurriedly, "Alex will be wild if I'm late. Some business dinner and the little wife must play her part. Mind if I use your bathroom?" she asked abruptly, stepping into that apartment before I could answer.

I wondered anxiously what condition the bathroom was in, and if Edward had draped the towel on the rail, or as usual, dumped it dripping on the side of the bath.

Myrabelle emerged several minutes later with richly reddened lips and clouds of the new scent. There was no sign of the troubled woman of a short time ago. Now she was confident and all the sadness replaced with her usual brittle gaiety. "How do I look?" she asked coaxing her hat to its most becoming angle.

"Oh Myrabelle, you look lovely," I sighed enviously, painfully aware of my apron and shiny nose, not to mention all the afternoon chores still undone, and Edward due home shortly.

"Bye darling, see you again, and Oh! thanks for the tea," and Myrabelle was gone before I could thank her for the perfume or cake.

Well, I thought philosophically, at least we have a grand cake for the tea, if not much else. I sliced a generous piece, and sat for five lazy minutes sampling the delights of the delicious confection.

Chapter 24

A few mornings later Edward lost his pin. This was a little gold-coloured bar he wore under his tie to keep the collar of his shirt in place. I found this same pin a never-ending bone of contention between us, and highly likely to cause major disruption first thing in the morning. I had put the kettle on and made the porridge when the shout came from the bedroom:

"Where's my pin?"

"I don't know. Can't you look on the mantelpiece," I said, and followed this suggestion with a litany of probable hiding places.

An indignant splutter and, "I have looked everywhere."

"Try under the bed," I advised calmly.

A grunt and much rummaging. Then, "It's not there and I'm covered in dust."

I felt my temper rising as a cup slithered out of my hand and smashed in pieces on the floor. "Now look what you've made me do," I yelled.

The bedroom door flew open and Edward stood there covered in dust, his hair flopping wildly on his head. "I can't leave that dam pin out of my sight. Someone lifted it. I know they did; I distinctly remember putting it on the mantelpiece last night," he exploded.

He paused, eying me suspiciously. After all, I was fair game, being the only one besides himself using the bedroom.

"It must be somewhere," I groaned with a feeling of defeat. There would be no peace until that pin was found. I put the tea cosy on the pot and went into the bedroom. I looked without much hope on the mantelpiece, dressing table, bedside table, everywhere, even under the bed, but the wretched thing seemed to have disappeared into thin air.

Feeling furious, I gave Edward his breakfast, pointedly ignoring my own in the hopes of winning contrition out of him, while he kept up a running monologue about "someone stealing his pin and being without the decency to admit it."

Actually my conscience was not all that clear. I had pinched the pin whenever the need arose and I could find nothing else, for Edward sometimes wore a polo-necked jumper and then no pin was necessary. Mostly I remembered to put it back in an obvious place before it was missed, but when I forgot, ructions followed. The last time it went astray, it was accidently recovered in the curtains where I had put it to exclude a draught. Now I racked my brain, but still I felt sure I hadn't taken it this time. Edward's voice broke into my futile efforts ordering me to come along now and eat my breakfast. I did not answer and he resumed his tirade about "a man in his own house who daren't leave his own pin on his own mantelpiece....there were hundreds of other pins about, but his had to be the one to be taken...."

The sound of the milkman hammering on the hall door caused a diversion in the battle. I ran up with the jug and the milkman gave me a knowing wink, as he indicated our bedroom with a red fist.

"Himself doesn't sound in the best," he observed chattily, as he poured the milk from his can into the half pint measure. "Morning after is it?"

I held the jug steady, frowning with annoyance, as I tried to think of something cutting to say. Then inspired I said grandly: "Oh, that's just one of our new gramophone records."

"You don't say," he tittered, tossing an extra tilly of milk into my jug. He looked at me solemnly and I thought he believed me. I drew in the jug and wished him a dignified good morning; I was just about to close the door when Edward shouted from the top of the stairs: "Lynn, will you come up here? I'll be late for work and I've no pin." The milkman laughed mockingly. "Some record," he quipped. "Some big ears," I snapped and banged the door. Back upstairs with the angry husband, I searched through my clothes, especially the ones that needed holding together. I even examined Mrs. Redmond's hoover, which I had used yesterday, but no hidden pin was discovered. "You have lost that silly pin yourself, Edward Davis, and you're just using me to look for it because you're too lazy to look for it yourself," was my final verdict.

"That stupid remark doesn't deserve an answer," the husband retaliated coldly. I decided to abandon the subject of the contentious pin and throw in a few grievances of my own. "You're a selfish pig. Every night you pull all the bed clothes over yourself and leave me freezing to death," I accused unjustly. "That's a dam lie....." flamed Edward. "And no matter what I say you always wipe your hands on the tea towel," I pursued relentlessly. "There's never a dry towel in the place," and Edward snatched the offending object from its hook by the sink and waved it around the kitchen triumphantly.

"And," my voice reached its highest pitch as I ducked to avoid the towel, "You leave dripping towels on the edge of the bath for Myrabelle and all the world to see."

The original cause of the dispute was forgotten, as I dealt in detail with Myrabelle's visit to the bathroom, and my utter humiliation when she found the wet towel. He dismissed this accusation with the shocking, "to hell with Myrabelle. What has she got to do with my pin?"

While I floundered about in search of an impressive answer, Edward kept his oar in with: "There isn't a morning you don't leave toothpaste in the wash basin where I have to wash my face. You burn all the saucepans and leave them for me to wash when I come home from a hard day's work." "You offered to wash them last night," I reminded him. "That's the only time you washed a saucepan since you got married. Anything else you have to complain about?"

"Yes!" he shouted, "my pin."

"Is that the lot," I asked icily.

"No!" his anger was unabated. "The last time I was fool enough to take you to the Gaiety, you had to disgrace me by running around the city in your knickers."

At that rather lurid description of my recent exploit, I pulled off my slipper and let fly.

Edward side-stepped neatly and it missed him, striking the jug of milk on the table between us. The jug overturned and a flood of milk cascaded across the floor.

Edward took one horrified glance at me and the mess; in a flash he was through the door and down the stairs.

I stood at the sink with a cup of black tea and had a good weep. Later on, when I started on the washing, I found the pin; It was embedded in a bar of soap on the draining board. Rinsing it under the tap, I remembered that Edward had shaved at the sink last night before going over to Aunt Clare's. He must have absent-mindedly put the pin down and forgotten it. And automatically blamed me, I thought with a rush of rage and self pity.

I rehearsed what I would say to him when he came home this evening . Eat his words for sure he would!

I got cleared up quickly, and when I was dressed and ready for the daily shopping expedition, I met Mrs. Redmond in the hall. She came straight to the point. "A little difference of opinion in the love nest this morning, my dear?"

I blushed and wondered if the whole neighbourhood had heard us fighting.

I nodded, knowing that denial of the uproar was useless; we had been too engrossed in ourselves to keep our voices down.

She put a hand gently on my arm. "Don't worry, Mrs. Davis, I haven't brought up the subject to embarrass you. We've all had our rows and differences the same as yourself, and no one thinks any the less of you for that. I only want to give you a little hint I found useful myself."

"I would indeed be most grateful for any hint that would solve this problem of the pin," I said feelingly.

"Well it's easy then," she said with a chuckle. "Buy a box of tie-pins. They'll only cost you a few pence, and when one goes missing, you discreetly produce another one. The hubby will think it's the same one all the time."

I grinned hugely at her; now why hadn't I come up with that simple solution?

"With me it was the stud," Mrs. Redmond was saying confidentially. "I was persecuted every morning with the same cry, 'where's me stud?' When the idea hit me I was never without a box full, I can tell you. And he always thought it was the same one."

I set off happily and was just crossing the Halfpenny Bridge when I saw an old man selling a card of twelve tie pins for a penny. Delightedly I purchased a card, feeling that one problem had been solved.

That evening Edward came home whistling cheerfully. Wordlessly he held out his arms and I went into them joyfully to be engulfed in many loving kisses. Impishly he whipped a box of chocs, my favourite "Black Magic," out of his pocket. "To sweeten that sharp tongue of yours," he twinkled.

"Do you want any tea at all?" I asked eventually, sniffing the savoury aroma of steak and kidney pudding from the oven, which was his special treat.

"I'm starving," he assured me fervently, "but I have something to show you first." He put his hand in his pocket and drew out a little box of Woolworths tie pins!

Chapter 25

I was gazing into Fullers cake shop, shopping basket laden with mundane groceries, wondering if my money would stretch to one of their luxurious cakes, when I saw Myrabelle Dobson coming towards me.

She was as usual, elegantly dressed in a powder blue coat edged with soft fox fur, over a cream lace dress. On her fair hair she sported a fashionable navy blue hat; its tiny brim almost covering her forehead. She was leaving the shop, laden with cake boxes. I tried to dodge away, but she had seen me.

"Hello' Lynette darling," she gushed, "How very nice to see you."

"Hello'" I responded without enthusiasm, feeling shabby in my old brown coat beside such opulence. "Are you buying out the shop or what?" I added, noting her bulging basket of a variety of expensively boxed cakes.

"It's for my afternoon tea party," she retorted gaily. "Tell you what; you must come along too. You've never seen my house, so what about it?"

"I'm afraid I can't now...." I began evasively.

"Nonsense," she laughed, brushing away my excuses.

Her chauffeur came forward to relieve her of her basket, and she caught my arm and dragged me into the waiting car. On the journey to her home she kept up a running commentary on a dozen different shops, which had stocked, or not stocked, the various articles she wanted.

I listened idly, for apparently no comment was expected from me, and we arrived at her stylish Victorian Villa in Rathgar, with its manicured lawns and formal flower beds. A gardener could be glimpsed in the conservatory arranging pots of exotic flowers.

A trim maid, dressed in black with frilly white apron and matching headband, opened the door into a spacious, tiled hall. Here the sound of laughter and babbled voices drifted from a nearby room, and I shrank at the thought of meeting all those strangers with no preparation. My dress was the pretty crepe-de-chine that Aunt Cissy had made me, but how would it stand up to comparison with Myrabelle's contemporaries?

Myrabelle was leading me into her luxurious cloakroom with its pink basins and gold taps. Gracefully she sank into a pink armchair and proceeded to outline her lips in a wide cupid's bow with a bright red lipstick.

Daringly I dipped a swansdown-puff into one of the crystal powder bowls, arrayed on a white and gold Louis -type dressing table, and tried to prepare myself for the ordeal ahead. The maid hung my shabby, every-day coat on a hanger, as Myrabelle put the finishing touches to her hair.

"Come on Lynette," she called, making for the door, and I reluctantly followed in the direction of the noisy chatter.

This proved to be the dining room. It was a big room with silken walls of red and white striped regency paper. The furniture was gleaming mahogany, the carpet a cool, pinky- beige, and this picture of magnificence was lit by a huge chandelier of dripping crystals. A fire sparkled beneath a marble mantelpiece of exquisite reclining figures, and the long oval table was covered in snowy damask. This was laid with translucent china and shimmering glass. Several maids in the customary black and white afternoon uniform, glided unobtrusively to and fro, heaping the table with a vast assortment of delicious looking eatables.

Among all this grandeur, little groups of elegant men and beautiful ladies stood about, calling and chatting in posh accents to each other. A silence fell when Myrabelle entered the room, and then exclamations of delight broke out, as everyone surged forward to greet their hostess.

Bewildered by this scene of upper class splendour, I cringed behind her, hoping I would be forgotten in the excitement and manage to escape, but Myrabelle turned and drew me forward.

"I want you all to meet my friend, Lynette Davis," she cried, "A young bride of a few months and still madly in love."

I felt my face burn as the roomful of eyes turned curiously on me. Then they were all around me, shaking my hand and making meaningless small talk. I was offered a glass of wine by an elderly maid, and a portly man with gleaming gold fillings in his teeth, held out his cigarette case to me. I politely refused both.

Myrabelle laughed. "She won't touch them Charlie. No bad habits yet...only up from the country, you know," and she helped herself from his cigarette case.

I smiled feebly, wishing I was a thousand miles away from these flashy, worldly-wise people. Eventually, Myrabelle was borne away by a handsome dark-haired man, but before leaving, she designated a formidable, middle-aged woman to "look after me."

This imposing personage was a Mrs Marjorie Gannon-Browne. Her skinny figure was shrouded in layers of grey georgette....not too unlike a spider in a web....and around her stringy neck hung ropes of lustrous pearls.

With majestic mien, Marjorie Gannon-Browne led me to a gilded couch where maid servants were handing out cups of tea or coffee, plates of wafer-thin sandwiches, scones, tarts and an endless variety of cakes and trifles.

How heavenly these would have tasted at home with Edward, I reflected, biting into a delicious cream and apple slice.

As my companions were too busy tucking into the feast to pay any attention to me, I was able to help myself to a fair variety of the delicacies on offer, and as I munched, I noticed one of the maids in particular. She moved unobtrusively among the guests, and appeared to be the person responsible for managing the perfect running of the party. Nothing was left to chance and every detail was carefully planned. Middle-aged, dumpy and be-spectacled, she wore a black dress with a white collar and cuffs, and carried only a tray of champagne. She was very much in command of the domestic fraternity, and appeared to convey her instructions to them by eye contact. Her gimlet eyes were forever darting about, and if a girl failed to interpret the signals correctly, her heavy eyebrows almost disappeared in her hairline. When she turned her back, her dignified bearing was lost, and it was hard not to giggle at her prominent bottom and bandy legs.

Several women around me had settled back in their chairs with cups and well-filled plates, and I became aware that they were earnestly discussing their own domestic servants. Marjorie Gannon-Browne, who evidently considered herself an authority on the subject, joined in the conversation with relish. She soon shattered any illusions one might have of the capabilities of Irish servants.

"I have travelled the world and no where could you find more ignorant and impudent girls than in this country," she pronounced in ringing tones.

Her husband, a mean-looking, bald-headed little man, nodded vigorous agreement to everything she said.

"You must keep them under regular scrutiny," she informed the assembled company, and pompously flopped back in her seat with an angry swing of the pearls. A maid came to her rescue proffering a plate of chicken and ham sandwiches, and there was a pause in the discussion as she eagerly heaped her plate. Satisfied, she held up a commanding hand and the maid withdrew.

Having swallowed two of the sandwiches, she felt free to expound further on the unsatisfactory state of the servant situation.

"I have to make sure myself that all the silver is properly cleaned on a Tuesday," she asserted. "Friday is for the brasses, and the china I have to do myself, of course. The maids smash and break such a lot, and we have some very old, and indeed priceless, dinner and tea sets." Here she sighed nosily and consoled herself with a long draught from her cup. "I know exactly what you mean," sympathized another ample lady, much to the annoyance of Mrs. Gannon-Browne, who wished to peruse her favourite theme at her own pace. Again, she indicated her wishes by raising her much be-ringed hand.

"Do you know, Annabel," she said, fixing that lady with a hard stare, "I had half a Mason tea service knocked off a tray by a stupid girl some years ago, but I tell you this, I stopped every penny for the damage out of that girl's wages.

"Accident, my foot!"

A third lady who was very stout indeed, and evidently armed in heavily creaking corsets, boomed: "What would you say to having a Dresden sugar bowl and milk jug broken beyond repair?"

An appalled silence fell on the little group at this shocking revelation of the destruction it was possible for a servant to achieve. Gradually they recovered their equilibrium, and the silence was filled with the clinking of cups and whispered requests for "a little more "apple strudel, chocolate torte, or just a "tiny" glass of wine."

I held my breath as Mrs. Gannon-Browne took a mouthful of the torte, licking her fingers before she rallied. "Well, I have to lock everything up, even the food cupboards, and I'm not a mean woman, but those lassies would eat you out of house and home."

She raised an imperious hand and a young maid appeared to refill her plate.

While she was thus diverted Annabel seized the chance to air her opinion. In a genteel, but persistent tone, she held forth on the problem of getting her girls to wear their uniform at all times.

"I do not tolerate slip-shod habits," she declared grandly. "I have blue for the morning and black from two o'clock until ten, and that is that, but some of these young ones get notions and think a uniform is beneath them."

I listened with amusement, glad to be free of their perusal while learning quite a bit about the domestic servants lifestyle from their employers point of view. There was indeed another meaning to the title of "general" as applied to women engaged in domestic service. It was the umbrella term for a girl who was parlour maid, char, mother's help, cook, scullery maid and lady's maid.

The booming lady crossed her fat legs and divulged the secret of her success.

"It's all in the method and how you lay down the law at the first interview. Give them a routine and stick to it rigidly. I keep my girls for years and it's all in the method."

There was a pause while the company digested this tried and trusted piece of advice, along with further helpings of the very popular torte. Then another younger woman clad in yards of red lace, who had been concentrating more on her plate than the conversation, suddenly electrified the company with one word: "Followers!" She paused and the others leaned expectantly towards her, even the luscious torts forgotten. "Followers!" she repeated. "Do any of you realise that you know next to nothing about those girls you allow into your house? Now that is a problem, and you don't know either, who they're sneaking into your home while you're out. Last week, I had the decorator in to do my bedroom. I had to go to Eva Smithson's for afternoon tea, and when I returned, there was no sign of Ellen, the new maid. I went upstairs and there was Ellen coming out of my bedroom. I thought she looked quite flustered so I went straight in..." There was another pause, as the woman, Isabel Maitland Roche by name, soldiered on, delighted by the undisputed attention of her audience. "And? Oh! Never!" gasped the women in chorus, holding their cups daintily in mid air with trembling anticipation.

"There was the painter," breathed Isabel dramatically, "stretched out on my bed in his dirty clothes with his big muddy boots on the eiderdown. There he was, propped up on my best lace pillows."

The ladies were speechless, their outraged gentility recoiling from the scandalous picture of a disreputable male, dressed in his working garb, lounging (or maybe worse with the servant girl) on the very bed of the Honourable Isabel Maitland Roche!

"Whatever was he doing?" Marjorie managed at last to give voice for them all, while the booming lady bent closer with protesting creaks of her corset.

"Puffing a cigarette," said Isabel triumphantly.

"Is that all?" Annabel was visibly disappointed.

"What more did you expect?" Isabel's tone was forbidding.

"Well didn't you get rid of the girl?" Annabel persisted.

"I gave her another chance," replied Isabel magnanimously. "I had a round of dinner parties lined up, and she's quite capable really. I just couldn't face all the annoyance of training another one at such short notice."

"I can understand that," said the booming lady sympathetically, and took another forkful of strudel. "You get fed up hiring and firing."

Marjorie Gannon-Browne carefully arranged the yards of grey georgette around her, and allowed the maid to remove her cup. She gave the pearls another swing.

"My problem is getting them up in the morning," she frowned. "I like my morning cup of tea brought up to me sharp at eight o'clock, but it's a job to get Alice to do that. Yesterday morning Jack had to speak to her...."

Jack, the mean looking man huddled at her side, and almost lost in a swath of georgette, stuck out his chest and interrupted, "That's me. But I got her up alright...." he nodded and cast a leering wink at the ladies, "I went straight up to her room and there she was...."

"Yes, yes, that's alright Jack," Mrs Gannon-Browne cut in swiftly, giving her uncouth husband a hefty kick. Jack gave a groan and sank into oblivion among the layers of georgette.

With the attention of everyone focused on Jack, and to offset this, she hurriedly sought distraction. "Annabel dear, I love your dress; it suits you to perfection," and her cold eyes strayed with false admiration, from her friend's violet gown to the purple glow of her pudgy cheeks.

"This old rag!" laughed Annabel, coyly fanning the skirt of the elaborately embroidered dress covering her well upholstered figure. She half rose from her seat to show "the old" rag to better advantage, but her moment of glory was upstaged by a young voice shouting behind her:

"And how are the darling ladies from Rathgar?" and into view bounced a very modern-looking miss, clad in a short puce, frilly dress with floating panels of gold spangles. Around her forehead was a circlet of coloured rhinestones, matched by an armful of slave bangles. Her face was covered in white powder, with eyebrow arches of thinly pencilled lines, over eyelids daubed with black kohl. The look was completed with a startling streak of scarlet lipstick, and long jangling, gold ear rings.

"What are you doing with yourself these days?" inquired the booming lady.

"You don't look well, Marie Rose; you look very pale, doesn't she girls?" Mrs. Gannon-Browne appealed to all within hearing distance.

Isabel Maitland Roche cast a practised eye over the sparkling figure. "Out all night and heavy handed with the paint box.... burning the candle at both ends. What can you expect?" was her contentious opinion.

Annabel chipped in. "I didn't see you at Mabel's party last Saturday. Where were you?"

Marie Rose laughed and shook her head, so that everything shimmered and twinkled on her person. "Ah now, wouldn't you love to know what I've been up to," she countered impudently. "That would be telling, tho' I'll bet you'll find out very soon," she ended mysteriously.

The ladies examined her with renewed interest. Mrs. Gannon-Browne said with apparent indifference: "I couldn't care less what you're up to, my girl; your sins will always find you out anyway."

"That's OK then ladies, I knew you wouldn't be interested in my latest beau," grinned the saucy flapper, with unabashed cheerfulness. "Be seeing you, possibly at the do in the "Sapphire And Gold" Club on Saturday. Bye now," and she was gone in a shower of glitter.

Mrs. Gannon-Browne leaned forward, "A bit fast, that one," and she pursed her lips significantly.

Annabel sniffed disapprovingly, "I must agree with you, Marjorie. I hear she's still knocking around with that Kenny Rivers, and we all know what he's after."

The booming lady was not going to be left out. "A hussy!" she barked, her corset wheezing condemning accord. Her friends lay back more comfortably in their seats, replete with delicious food and congenial company.

Beside me two more elite members of this select group were carrying on a whispered conversation, and I just caught the tail end of it; "What is Marjorie Gannon-Browne going on about; don't we all know she can't keep a girl in the house with that husband of hers," observed a fussy little woman in black velvet with henna -dyed hair and heavy make-up.

Suddenly it seemed the ladies became aware of my presence and to my horror, four pairs of eyes were expertly taking in every aspect of my appearance.

"What did you say your name was," crooned Annabel.

"I didn't," I returned pertly, "but it's Davis, Lynette Davis."

"What a pretty name," said Mrs. Gannon-Browne condescendingly. "Do you live around here, 'tho I can't recollect seeing you anywhere?"

"No," I replied innocently, "I live on the south Circular Road."

The booming lady expelled her breath in a low growl. "Rather a noisy place," she opined cautiously. "Are you not suffocated for air down there?" Before I could answer, Mrs. Gannon-Browne intervened: "Of course, they are fairly big houses, but a lot of it has gone down....not all, mind you," she hastened to add, in a bid to be fair-minded.

"Flats!" said the booming lady gloomily. "Once a place starts going into flats, it's finished. Wouldn't you agree?" and her cold fishy eyes challenged me.

"Well actually I don't have a house yet," I told her sweetly. Wait for it, I thought, and added loudly: "We live in a flat!"

The women were lost for words, wondering no doubt, how such a person, a flat dweller, had got herself invited into the home of Myrabelle Dobson. The awkward silence was broken by the arrival of a tall young man with a narrow moustache, sleek black hair plastered in brilliantine, and insinuating blue eyes. He was dressed in plus fours and puffed clouds of smoke from a cigar.

"My dear girls, how are you all?" he enthused, kissing each hand demurely held out to him. Effusively he inquired about their health and families, his voice caressing, his look intimate, while the middle-aged matrons melted and blossomed.

"Darling boy, you are looking well," gushed Annabel, her bosom heaving under its mound of embroidery.

"And why wouldn't he be," asked Mrs Gannon-Browne indulgently. "Isn't he one of the brightest boys about town."

The booming lady purred:

"You must drop over to see us soon, Dennis. Harry was just saying this morning that we hadn't seen you and Ailsa in ages."

Dennis ignored her and his roving eye landed on me. "Who is this charming lady here?" he asked in a teasing tone.

Mrs. Gannon-Browne looked at me indifferently. "I didn't quite catch your name...."

"Lynette Davis," I repeated as my hand was caught in a vice-like grip and tenderly kissed.

"Dennis Neilson," he laughed with an appreciative wink. "We must get to know each other better."

I smiled uneasily and said as lightly as I could, "I'm afraid my husband wouldn't approve."

"Well, why tell him then?" he asked with a calculating look in his eyes. At that point, a bold-looking, black-eyed flapper, dressed in flaming orange ninon, came forward, and with a proprietary gesture, caught my admirer firmly by the arm. "Come along Dennis," she commanded and led him away without a word to any of us.

"A gay blade!" was the booming lady's final summing up, and her friends nodded complacent agreement, but Mrs Gannon-Browne gave me a warning look as she said: "That was Ailsa, his fiancée, and she has no time for flighty females who might fancy a bit on the side."

I felt my face flame with anger at her unjust implication, and I ached to assure her that I hadn't the least intention of purloining the dandified Dennis. I was just about to make my escape when a tall, slender woman in a shapeless dress and coat of non-descript beige, came over and sat on the arm of my chair.

"I'm Alice Jackson," she introduced herself, "and Myrabelle sent me over to ask if everything's alright."

"How kind of you!" I murmured, shaking her hand. Immediately the four ladies were eager for her attention.

"She's Judge Jackson's daughter, you know," whispered Annabel in a swift aside to me.

"Really! How strange I didn't know that," I smiled, wide-eyed and totally unimpressed with the woman's apparent superiority in the social hierarchy. There was much issuing of invitations to Miss Jackson to attend this function and that, but she seemed uninterested and made firmly polite excuses. It was getting late so I broke into their fawning entreaties, saying that I must go home to get my husband's tea. Mrs. Gannon-Browne gave me a long hard look, clearly affronted by my impertinent interruption, but Miss Jackson turned gently to me and said: "I'll run you home, Mrs. Davis. I pass your way. South Circular isn't it?" I looked at her quickly, but there was not the slightest condescension in her manner. I thanked her fervently, feeling her a kindred spirit, and the two of us, chatting easily, went over to find Myrabelle and say good bye. Myrabelle, the centre of attention at the other end of the room, waved gaily. "Sorry you have to go now, Alice. Mind yourself, little bride," she called with a negligent flash of a heavily-ringed hand.

Laughingly she turned back to the fair-haired man who had his arm tightly around her waist, and they both disappeared into the conservatory.

Miss Jackson caught my arm. "I just must have a word with Andrew Sears," she said. "I won't be five minutes. You wait for me in my car....it's the first blue one outside the gate."

I nodded gratefully and stepped out into the fresh air, but once outside, I was confused as to which car was hers. There was a blue car on either side of the gate; the only difference being that one was a light blue, the other dark. I hummed and hawed, but eventually chose the light blue one. I got into the front seat and pulled the door, glad to be sheltered from the piercing cold wind.

I idly scanned the passers-by and gradually spotted a man on the pavement, hands on hips, grinning at me. It was the debonair Dennis, who had been accosted by the orange-clad flapper, and there was no mistaking the jaunty look in his eyes.

The place had grown quiet; there was no one about and as he strode purposefully towards me, I panicked. Swiftly I locked the doors, but he only laughed and hammered on the window. He seemed to be saying something, but mustering all my dignity, I averted my gaze and stared haughtily in front of me. He continued shouting and beating the window, but feeling secure in the locked car, I glared at him with some ferocity.

I don't know how long this situation would have continued if Alice Jackson and Myrabelle had not come to the gate. They had been talking earnestly, but when they noticed the commotion, they started to laugh heartily, even supporting each other in hilarious abandon.

I felt mortified and wondered what was so comical about a young man trying to break into Miss Jackson's car, terrifying its occupant.

I managed to unlock the door and scramble out with some effort of decorum, but my exit was spoiled by my shoe catching in a piece of threadbare carpet on the floor. I almost fell into the gutter and was only saved from worse indignity by Dennis, who caught me expertly in his arms. Almost in tears, I beat him off with my handbag. Myrabelle joined in the struggle, and I'm not sure to which of us she was giving her support, but I turned furiously on her.

"How dare you make fun of me, Myrabelle Dobson. I'll never enter your house again, just go away and leave me alone."

Dennis released me and rescued my shoe from the car, his beautifully groomed hair standing in greasy peaks all over his head. Still raging I automatically held out my foot to receive the shoe, while abusing him roundly for the fright he had given me.

Alice came over and putting an arm around me said: "We didn't mean to be unkind, Mrs. Davis, and the poor man was not trying to frighten you. She stopped as I stared at her blankly, but it was Myrabelle, trying to control her laughter, who giggled helplessly: "That's Dennis's car you were sitting in. He was only trying to tell you that you were in the wrong car. Poor man! Lord! It's so funny, I'll never forget it," and she was overcome with another fit of laughter. By this time a curious little crowd of by- passers had stopped to see what all the fuss was about, and stayed to enjoy the fun."

Scarlet with humiliation, I leaned against the car, unable to meet the dancing light in Dennis's eyes, but the situation was reversed by the appearance of his orange-clad girlfriend.

"What are you up to now Dennis?" she asked suspiciously.

"Nothing, dear one," he said nonchalantly. "I was just locked out of my car." "Again?" her tone was acid. "So this is your latest diversion. Get in," she commanded, opening the door of the car I had just vacated.

He obeyed with relief and alacrity, and she jumped in beside him. She took the wheel and they drove off with much back-firing and horn blowing.

Alice and Myrabelle had controlled their merriment and were eying me cautiously. Abruptly my rage evaporated, and I saw the funny side of the escapade. I grinned sheepishly. Alice and Myrabelle looked relieved, and like a bunch of conspirators, we all laughed happily together.

Chapter 26

About this time, I had another uncanny experience. It happened at about ten o'clock on a late autumn morning as I was standing at our bedroom window, which faced the back garden. I was shaking out my duster when my attention was caught by a strange little girl playing on the grass.

She was about five or six years old; and she was wearing a long blue dress with a pink ribbon around the waist. Golden curls tumbled from her stiff poke bonnet, and she was pushing a doll's pram, which resembled a baby carriage I had seen illustrated in an old newspaper.

The garden was unlike its usual aspect, which was unkempt, with weeds and a tattered trellis creaking disconsolately in the wind. Now the view before me featured a well-kept lawn, divided by a path of crazy paving, and flanked by borders of flowers. In the distance, the trellis stood upright under a quilt of pink and white roses.

The scene was bathed in a strange haze of silvery light, almost like moonlight.

It was much too late in the year for the riot of roses, and the summer flowers had long faded away. There was an eerie silence, as if time itself hung suspended, and all I could hear was the hurried beating of my heart.

The little girl turned and came down the path towards me. She smiled and raised her hand in a wave. Mechanically I raised an arm, which felt like lead, and the child waved again and seemed to glide back up the path, disappearing beyond the trellis of roses. Then the scene began to dwindle, and once again the broken-down trellis, the rampant weeds and withered flowers, drifted back like a dream. The garden grew dark, rain spluttered in the wind, and a crooked twig tapped forlornly against the window pane. I shivered, aware of an icy chill, and the duster drifted out of my nerveless hand onto the tangled grass below.

I closed the window and sat on the edge of the bed feeling tired and depressed. What was wrong with me? What had I seen, or had I imagined it all? I felt too uneasy and restless to remain alone, so I decided to go down to Mrs Redmond for a chat.

She was in her kitchen baking scones. "Mind if I come in," I greeted her timidly.

She looked up from the oven and indicated a chair, with floury hands. "Sit yourself down Mrs. Davis, child," she said, adding anxiously: "You're looking very pale; are you feeling unwell?"

I nodded dumbly, glad to feel the firmness of the chair under me. Mrs. Redmond bustled about and I felt a nip of whiskey burning my throat, and a warm sensation spreading through me.

Revived, I smiled weakly at the concern in Mrs. Redmond's kindly face.

"What a fright you gave me; you were right out for a few minutes, poor child," and she helped me to the armchair nearer the fire.

Holding my hands to the flames I apologised for the fright I had given her. Mrs. Redmond returned to her scones, buttering their tops and covering them with a fresh tea towel. "Don't worry about that my dear. I've been through it too many times not to recognise the signs."

I stared at her uncomprehendingly as she put the kettle on to boil. "You'll be as right as rain after a cup of tea. How far gone are you?" She asked calmly.

Astonished, it suddenly dawned on me that I might be pregnant, and I could not speak for savouring the realisation to the exclusion of everything else.

I blushed furiously and stammered: "I....I....didn't know.... yet."

She laughed and made the tea. "Well you were bound to find out sometime. Babies have a way of making their presence felt."

The word was out and how magical it sounded. "Baby," I whispered, and thrilled in anticipation of Edward's delight.

Mrs Redmond put a steaming cup of tea, and a plate of hot scones and raspberry jam, invitingly between us. I lay back contentedly to do justice to the delicious repast, stretching my feet blissfully to the fire blazing in the range.

I took a deep breath and said carefully: "Have you a little niece or a granddaughter staying with you, Mrs. Redmond?"

She stared at me in surprise. "No I haven't then. Whatever made you think I have?"

I plunged on nervously: "Well I'm just after seeing a little girl in your garden playing with a doll's pram. She was wearing old-fashioned clothes and...." Her face paled and the cup shook in her hand.

"I'm so sorry. I didn't mean to upset you," I said, laying a hand on her arm.

"What was the child like?" she asked tersely.

"Beautiful, with golden curls and a lovely, laughing little face....about five or six." I answered gently.

Mrs. Redmond was trying to control her agitation. "Little Millie....so long ago...."

Fear clutched my heart. "You're not saying I saw a ghost?" I cried in disbelief.

She took my hand reassuringly. "Don't worry child; no harm could come to anyone through little Millie. There is a belief in our family that when something special is coming to our house, little Millie is seen by the benefactor, and that's why you saw her."

"But who was she?" I was intrigued.

"She would be a great, great aunt of mine," calculated Mrs. Redmond, passing me a second scone. "She was a lovely, happy child. A little angel."

"What happened to her?" I asked.

Mrs. Redmond shook her head sadly: "She was only six years old when she died of consumption."

Silence fell between us as I pondered on the tragedy of that little girl, playing with her doll in the garden, all those years ago. Mrs Redmond sighed as she rose to answer a knock; it was the child from next door whose mother wanted to see Mrs. Redmond for a few minutes.

When they had gone, I got up and let myself into the back garden. As I gazed at the clumps of unwieldy bushes, and the remains of the trellis half submerged in weeds, I wondered if I had dreamed that strange scene of a bygone age. A withered leaf caught in my hair, and shuddering I pulled it away as a sudden gust of wind shook the old trellis, making it rasp against a broken sundial.

I bent to retrieve my sodden duster and, feeling suddenly afraid, dashed into the house banging the door behind me.

Chapter 27

After our tea I went and stood behind Edward's chair, putting my arms around him. "Guess what!" I began shyly.

"What is it now, sweet girl?" he asked, idly turning a page in the evening newspaper.

Laughingly I went to the gramophone and put on the current hit, "My Blue Heaven."

He looked at me indulgently, "Is that a hint for me to do the washing up?"

"Just Molly and me and baby makes three, We're happy in My Blue Heaven." I trilled pointedly.

Edward returned to his paper with his usual, "I'll do them in a minute, pet."

"Oh Edward, you are a fool," I retorted, half annoyed.

"Who's a fool then?" and I was caught in a bear hug.

"It's our blue heaven, or it soon will be," I cried nuzzling his cheek and humming the song again.

At last he got the message and holding me at arm's length, asked disbelievingly: "When? How do you know? Are you sure?"

I realized with a start that I really did not know....at least not for sure. I was only going on what Mrs Redmond had said, and the appearance of a poor little ghost....But as I thought about it, conviction grew that we were about to be a family.

"Well it's not all that surprising, Edward Davis," I retorted, back to my bantering good humour, "unless, of course, you wish to deny playing any part in the proceedings."

I was lovingly hugged again and there were tears in Edward's eyes as he said happily: "Oh Lynn, my sweet girl," and then with a certain amount of agitation he went on: "Sit down, put your feet up, I'll make you a cup of tea."

"Will you stop fussing," I giggled, wriggling out of his reach. "We've just had our tea and besides, it won't be for ages yet."

In the golden glow of happiness, that ghostly episode of the afternoon seemed very far away and I decided not to mention it to Edward. He would most likely, consider it a fantasy produced by my condition.

I went with Aunt Cissy next day to see the doctor, and he confirmed that I was indeed pregnant. We continued as usual with our shopping expeditions, only now they included the baby department of every store. The excitement of Moore Street was excluded from our jaunts, as was the carting of vegetables. Now we went to Liptons in Henry Street, or the Maypole in George's Street for our groceries, and had everything delivered to our doors.

I bought some lovely pastel wools and tried my hand at knitting, but the results were frustrating and funny.

"You can't put a child into that," gasped Aunt Cissy when I showed her a grubby tangled sample of my efforts. "What on earth is it meant to be?"

"A matinee jacket, at least that's what the pattern says," I told her indignantly.

"Oh heaven's, no," and she laughed with abandon as she looked through the pattern. "Did you actually ever learn to knit?"

I held the tatty blue garment up to the light doubtfully. Yes, I had rather a large number of holes and uneven stitches, and the whole thing showed a decided inclination to lurch in one direction; proving beyond a doubt that I had never handled a pair of knitting needles before.

"You know it would be a good idea not to use two odd needles, and avoid having so many knots in the work," the aunt was still smiling, but changed direction at the look on my face. "Let's go down to Bewleys for an airing and a nice cup of coffee; you'll make a better job of the knitting when we get back. We could also go to that baby shop in Nassau Street, and treat the babe to something nice. Safer!" she winked.

To this suggestion I needed little persuading, and five minutes later we were heading happily towards the Green.

Everyone fussed outrageously over me, and I was in real danger of being spoilt. Edward went around with a very serious expression, which he must have considered befitting to his coming status of fatherhood, until I boisterously tickled the smiles back again.

Mam came up and spent three wonderfully happy weeks in Dublin, seeing the sights and giving advice on every aspect of baby care. It would be her first grandchild and her delight knew no bounds.

Nell and Dora wrote regularly, inviting themselves up "nearer the time," and squabbling about the rights of one over the other to be Godmother.

Fortunately, we were able to assure them that if the baby was a girl she would need two Godmothers, but if a boy arrived they would have to cast lots between them, as to which would have the honour.

Da sent me an off-hand message of love and good wishes on the back of an old invoice, but he also included a "few pounds for yourself and the little one."

Chapter 28

I had not seen Myrabelle for ages. Indeed I had practically forgotten about her with all the diversions around me, when answering a knock on the door one day, I found her on the steps.

"Oh hello'" Myrabelle," I cried in surprise, "How nice to see you; do come in."

"Hello' darling child," she gushed, tripping lightly behind me in a cloud of her usual perfume. She entered our bedroom tossing her mink-tipped, cashmere coat carelessly on the bed.

"Cissy told me you are expecting a baby," she said, eying me with bright interest. "How well you are looking, my dear. I am very happy for you, Lynette," and she brushed her lips against my cheek.

"Thank you, Myrabelle. You're not looking too bad yourself," and I grinned at the understatement.

She indicated a box she had left beside her handbag on the dressing table.

"A little of the old walnut cake for yourself and the babe. Let him have a taste of the exotic now and he'll be born demanding the best. No bad thing either; he could very well get it too like his mother."

She seemed suddenly nervous and fumbled in her bag for her cigarette case. She flicked it open, then closed it again with a snap. "I don't think you're that gone on cigarette smoke just now, so I'll curb my longing," she said, fastening her bag, and proceeding me into the dining room where she seated herself comfortably by the fire.

I exclaimed delightedly over the cake, but she dismissed my thanks with a wave of the hand, bored with the subject. "Don't fuss, Lyn," she said tartly.

"It's only a cake, not a diamond."

I put the kettle on and we hopped pleasantly from one subject to another.

She described the pink and gold French wallpaper she was having in her bedroom, and the magnificent eighteenth century dressing chest she had picked up "for a fraction of its value, almost by accident," in the stately mansion of a major General, who was selling up and going to Australia.

She accepted a second cup of tea, but shook her head at further inroads into the cake. "I suppose you read about the wedding of Ailsa Smithson Lowe to Dennis Brown," she asked, as I buttered a cream cracker for her.

I nodded idly and sipped my tea. "I could hardly miss it, and it plastered all over the papers."

I thought of the hard-faced Ailsa of the orangey dress and gaudy jewels, who bore no resemblance to the gentle beauty described in the social columns of the newspapers.

"How do you think she looked?" I ventured. Myrabelle had been a guest at the society wedding and I knew her observations would be astute.

Myrabelle's expression was cynical. "Oh gorgeously turned out as you can imagine. Dress by the London designer Hans Vandell, and of course, the frothy veil softened her a bit. She played the part for all she was worth, acting bashful as a kitten."

Myrabelle leaned towards me confidentially. "Actually there's quite a story behind the whole affair."

"Really! And what is it?" I asked with eager curiosity.

"Well I got it from Dennis's sister, Vivian," Myrabelle began, "but for charity's sake don't let it go beyond you."

"I won't, of course," I promised, agog at the wind of a story.

Myrabelle put her empty cup on the stool beside her and stretched out her silken toes to the fire. "She tricked him into marrying her!" she stated dramatically.

I stared at her in amazement, wondering if she was joking.

"How do you mean....tricked him?"

Myrabelle smoothed her velvet skirt about her knees with deliberate slowness. "The night before the wedding Dennis rang her up to say he couldn't go on with it. He begged her to forgive him and all that. Ailsa appeared to take it very well. Now, either she had reason to suspect that he would try to back out, or else she was gifted with instant inspiration.... and I don't know which applies myself, but anyway, she agreed to call it off. However, she did make one condition."

I held my breath as Myrabelle eyed me playfully. "You'll never believe it, but the bold Ailsa actually cried. Sadly, and no doubt bravely, she asked Dennis to proceed normally with the wedding, and wait for her at the church. He agreed when she promised not to turn up. He assured her he didn't mind being jilted in the least: he quite understood it wouldn't be so nice for Ailsa if she was the injured party....might affect her future prospects," Myrabelle paused with a loud chuckle.

"Now can't you guess the rest." she continued impishly. "There he was at the altar, among the clergy, in a church full of high society guests, presumably wondering how long he should decently wait, when the organ strikes up the majestic "Purcell's Trumpets," and in glides your woman in all her bridal glory."

"What happened then," I whispered impatiently, for Myrabelle liked to take her time.

"Nothing out of the ordinary that anyone could see. The wedding service went on as arranged. In other words , Dennis was firmly hooked before he could recover from the shock, or was brave enough to attempt an escape."

I let out a long breath, bewildered by this astonishing situation. I could see that Myrabelle was enjoying herself on behalf of the suave Dennis and his enforced nuptials, not to mention my incredulous reaction to it.

"Vivian was chief of the six bridesmaids and in her brother's confidence."

Myrabelle drawled on, "She told me she was amazed at the look on Dennis's face when he turned to his bride; he looked so stunned, it was comical. Ailsa simply took his hand firmly, and shyly led him to the priest."

"But I don't understand," I stuttered. "What a risk she took! I mean, how could she...."

Myrabelle laughed, "Don't be such a romantic baby," she reprimanded. "Those two suit each other perfectly. Dennis is the straying kind and she well knows it. They've been together now for years, on and off, and he's embarked on a string of torrid affairs, but she has always managed to haul him back."

"It's a strange set-up," I began doubtfully.

"Our Ailsa is made of stern stuff," Myrabelle commented placidly, "and he'll never escape. Possibly he really doesn't want to, and is secretly glad to have her rescue him from his amorous entanglements."

"Hardly the basis for a happy marriage," I said disapprovingly.

Myrabelle gave me a look of dislike. "Don't be so smug. We all haven't the luck of Lynette Davis," she lashed out bitterly.

I blushed hotly at her words and felt an angry retort on the tip of my tongue, but her mood had swung again and she was saying: "She's no worse than me. I wasn't in love with Alex....I never loved him, tho' I was always very fond of him. Well, I have a comfortable life and what you'd call a good social position."

I gazed at her uncertainly, unable to comprehend such a philosophy.

"You married him without love...." and I could not avoid a censorious tone. She looked at me with some asperity. "Don't be so naive, Lynette; there are other reasons for marrying besides love."

"Are there?" I asked, sad for her. "Are you happy then?"

Her eyes fell under my scrutiny and her lovely pale face was full of pain.

"No," she said simply, "but I manage. I have to now."

A long silence fell between us, emphasized by the slump of the fire falling in on itself, and the far away shouts of the children playing below in the street.

Myrabelle was the first to move. She reached absently for her bag and drawing out her gold cigarette case, flicked it open with trembling fingers.

"Yes," she nodded, "you can marry for all sorts of reasons and I married Alex on the rebound from a great disappointment, and to escape from an overbearing father."

She lit her cigarette in its long jade holder, as I stared at her nonplussed.

She smiled at me with sudden cheerfulness "Don't worry child. I make out alright."

The cuckoo clock "cuckooed" the hour and Myrabelle jumped up, her face assuming its usual expression of indifferent gaiety. "How the time flies!" she exclaimed airily, powdering her nose and re-touching her lipstick. "We have an important dinner date to-night, and Alex expects me to look a bit better than my best", she paused and eyed me warily, "I do try to please him, you know, 'tho' I don't think you believe that." She laughed merrily as she headed for the door, and there was no sign of the unhappy woman of a few minutes earlier.

Chapter 29

The days passed in happy expectation, but one worry loomed on the horizon.

Mrs. Redmond had decided to sell up and go to live with her married daughter in Australia. As she needed vacant possession of our flat, we had to look for another place to live. We had two months to find alternative accommodation, and Edward spent every evening answering ads, and inspecting places which might be suitable.

But nothing any way satisfactory materialised, and as I grew alarmed, Edward's Aunt Clare, came to our rescue again. "Worrying like that is bad for you, Lynette," she said with concern, when I confided our problem to her over a pot of tea in her home, while Edward was out on a flat hunt.

"You haven't to move until June," she calculated, "and by that time the baby will have arrived, so you can come here straight from the nursing home. You know you and Edward are most welcome to stay here with us, for as long as it takes to find what you want."

I was in tears of relief. "But I couldn't really," I babbled. "It's too much inconvenience for you...."

She dismissed my half-hearted protests with a firm, but gentle smile. We have a big house here, Lynette....much too big really for just two people, and I deem it a great pleasure to be able to offer you a little help just now."

"You're too kind altogether," and I was crying helplessly.

Poor Clare grew anxious. "I'm really upset to think you were as worried as that; you should have told me sooner," and her arms were around me consolingly. I wiped my eyes vigorously, feeling a great weight lifted from my shoulders.

Although childless herself, Aunt Clare was delighted by the prospect of having a new baby in the house, and happily set about planning our room, arranging all the paraphernalia associated with a new arrival.

When Edward came to take me home, he was relieved at the immediate solution to our problem, as the flat he had gone to inspect had been snapped up by another couple.

The next happy event was a visit from Edward's mother, Anne. She was kindly, loving and had big brown eyes like her son. She had always been very close to Edward.... "he's like his Ma," she was fond of saying proudly, her eyes always following him affectionately. There was no rivalry between us for Edward's attention; she simply accepted me as a loved daughter and I responded gladly to the contented atmosphere surrounding her.

We spent many restful hours together, talking of Edward's childhood, while we ate toasted muffins by the fire and sorted through piles of miniature garments. Sometimes, Edward laughed at our chatter, but it filled my heart to see how happy he was.

Anne was thrilled at the imminent arrival of another grandchild, and arranged to come up again for the christening. We were sad to see her go, and Clare the younger sister, said it was the happiest family gathering she remembered in years.

In due course, the day dawned wet and windy, when I was taken to hospital.

Edward was pale and fussy, fearing the sudden appearance of the child, without the assistance of a hospital staff. Sixteen hours later our daughter was born, and as I counted her fingers and toes, I marvelled at her perfection, right down to finger and toe nails, and a fine fringe of lustrous eye lashes. She had dark blue eyes and a fluffy quiff of black hair standing straight up on top of her head.

Edward was allowed to see her when she was only minutes old, but his eyes flew straight to me for reassurance that all was well, and as he gathered me close, I felt his tears on my cheek.

I pointed silently to the babe in her cot, and the young nurse lifted her out and into his arms. Yawning widely, and clutching his finger in a tiny fist, our daughter sighed contentedly and slept soundly.

Clare had arranged a christening party in her house, and all the relations and friends were invited. Anne was first up, carrying the family christening robe, which dated back to the eighteen-eighties. The only cloud came from home where Mam and Dora were stricken with 'flu and unable to travel. Nell was having to shoulder the burden of the household and was bitterly disappointed at not being present. This meant we had to find a sponsor for the baby to act as proxy for the two girls, neither of which was willing to relinquish the role of godmother. Our choice fell on Anne, who seemed to have a special affinity with the child.

The christening day dawned warm and sunny and found us still ploughing through hundreds of names for the baby. "Rosemarie," by Franz Lehar, had just hit Dublin, and everyone was humming, whistling, or just plain singing excerpts from it. When Edward bounded into the hospital that morning, he too was crooning :

"Oh Rosemarie I love *you*
I'm always dreaming of you
No matter what I do,
I can't forget you..."

"That's it!" I interrupted excitedly. "We'll call her Rosemarie."

Edward gave me a satisfied look. "That's right," he beamed, and continued singing "The Donkey's Serenade" to his daughter, who was vigorously resisting my inexpert struggles to dress her in the precious robe.

"Rosemarie," murmured Edward thoughtfully, "Rosemarie-Anne, in complement to mother," he said firmly. I nodded agreement and the momentous decision was happily resolved.

The little party set out for the Church, led by Anne and the baby; Edward fussing beside her. Then came dear Aunt Cissy, Clare and Peggy.

"Rosemarie," I shouted after them from my bed, "Not Rosemary."

When they had gone I sank back gratefully under the bed-clothes, feeling a little exhausted. I was just drifting off when a familiar scent enveloped me and a voice said softly:

"Hello Lynette, dear child. How are you?"

I sat up rather bewildered, to see Myrabelle in all her usual elegance, standing by the bed. She threw a bunch of gorgeous roses on the quilt, kissed me lightly, and produced a large parcel from behind her back.

"Oh you shouldn't," I lied ecstatically, burying my face in the flowers.

"And why not, I ask you?" grinned Myrabelle in high good humour. "You're the only person I know who goes bananas when I give her a little gift. I like that."

Fully awake now, I tore open the parcel while Myrabelle sat on the edge of the bed watching indulgently. It contained a glamorous pink silk nightdress with matching bed jacket as light as a spider's web, and a pair of naughty cami-knickers. For the baby there was a fluffy blue rug with a white rabbit on it, and a dainty hand-tucked little dress.

"Oh Myrabelle, I never saw such lovely things," I cried tearfully. "How can I thank you....how can I take all this? Even just one item would have been too much," and I leaned over and kissed her cheek.

"Now don't go on behaving like an old woman," Myrabelle declared bracingly. "You wouldn't have preferred a bag of potatoes or a couple of dusters, by any chance?" and she pulled off her stylish hat and flung it on a chair. Then smiling happily she settled down on the bedside chair, kicking off her shoes, as a nurse entered with tea and biscuits.

"Cissy gave me the news when I went over to see her yesterday. She said the baby was a beauty and yourself in great form, but I thought you weren't due for another week or two. I bit into a jampuff; "Well I suppose it's hard to be exact," I demurred. "Evidently, our little one was anxious to spread her wings and take a look at us."

We chatted away until the quiet was broken by the noisy return of the christening party. Annie handed the sleeping baby to Myrabelle, who cradled her delightedly, and it struck me as sad that she was not a mother herself. There was evidently an emptiness in her life. Maybe a child would have meant joyous fulfilment.

"Guess what?" Edward's voice broke into my reverie. "Didn't the organist play," Oh Rosemarie I love you," after the ceremony, as we walked down the Church.

"And was Rosemarie, good?" I asked, taking a damp baby from Myrabelle, who was grimacing good-naturedly at a watery mark on her dress.

"The best in the world," said Anne tenderly, and the little party set off to celebrate the happy event at Aunt Clare's.

Chapter 30

It was a week later and I was packed and ready to leave the hospital. I sat on the bed, softly humming to Rosemarie-Anne, as I waited for Edward to come and collect us.

Time passed and still he did not come. A nurse insisted I had lunch, and as I reluctantly ate it, a strange sense of foreboding grew in my breast. I felt suffocated and moved to the window to lean heavily against it, in the hope of seeing Edward below in the street. The nurse tried to persuade me to sit down, but I waved her away and prayed for Edward to come.

I do not know how long I waited, strained and frightened, but gradually I became aware that Edward was standing beside me. His face was blank and deathly pale; only his eyes were alive and full of grief.

"Oh what is it," I implored, and moving towards him would have fallen if he had not caught me.

"It's mother, Lynn; she's dead," he said starkly.

I stared at him aghast and unable to voice my shock. He led me to the bed and we both sat down. "She died suddenly....just an hour before lunch....a heart attack, the doctor said."

Wordlessly I took his hand and held it tight. How could this tragic thing be true at such a happy time? Not dear, loving Anne, who had but lately carried her granddaughter to her christening.

Edward roused himself to concentrate on me. "You must stay here until after the funeral. It's a sad house to bring you and the baby home to now."

"I'm coming with you; it's where I want to be," I said with a bravery I did not feel.

He tried to dissuade me, but I was firm, and a little later we left the hospital in silent sorrow. By the time we reached Aunt Clare's, the house was full of family and friends. I crept up to our room to look after the baby, only catching a glimpse of Clare's set face as she shook hands, or handed around cups of tea.

As I nursed the child, I thought what a strange homecoming; a birth upstairs, a wake below. A knock at the door broke in on my musings and Aunt Clare's maid informed Edward that his brother and sister had arrived, and were looking to talk to him. I too, would have to go down and into that room of death to pay my last respects to Anne. I shivered, still weak and unable to take in the finality of it all.

I visited the room where Anne lay next morning, before she was taken to the Church. The same Church, where just a week ago, the happy christening had been held. As my tear-filled eyes rested on the body, so serene and remote, I was apprehensive of I know not what. Maybe the awareness of the awesome presence of eternity, symbolised in the passing of a soul to everlasting life. Yet as I gazed on that pale serene face, I knew that the essence of Anne was not lost; in another dimension she lived, and that more fully. A little consoled, I looked across the room and caught Edward's eyes. He nodded briefly before helping a much distressed Peggy from the room. By the darkened window, Myrabelle and Aunt Cissy were conversing in low tones, and as I moved towards them, I heard Myrabelle saying: "Isn't it strange, Cissy, one Anne going out and another coming in?"

Chapter 31

After the funeral, life settled down to a steady, if subdued routine. Edward took his loss badly, as he was very attached to his mother, and for many a night, I was aware of him crying softly in the darkness.

I did what I could to ease his anguish, yet fully aware of my inability to surmount his pain. Grief is something we have to live through if it is ever to heal; there is no other way.

My days were filled with the demands of the baby. She cried a lot, and sometimes I was at my wits end to quieten her. Edward wearily paced the floor with her at night, in an effort to give me a rest after the non-stop demands of the day. I suppose I could have given her a soother to calm her, but Mam had always insisted that they were dirty things and bad for a child's mouth and teeth.

Edward never complained of the incessant wailing; he spent what spare time he had rocking her in his arms and singing lullabies to her, to give me a break.

These soothed her and she enjoyed them so much that she wanted the same treatment all her waking hours. Sometimes I gained a peaceful interlude by playing records to her, but this did not always work, and it was evident that it was Edward's voice she wanted to hear.

"Maybe she'll be a musician or composer," Edward observed dryly, pausing in his rendition of "Sleepy Valley." Rosemarie, not liking the interruption, gave an indignant scream until the singing was resumed.

Utterly exhausted, as it was three o'clock in the morning, I snapped "maybe, if she stops shouting long enough."

Things were nearly at breaking point when something very strange happened, which brought in its wake a new episode of peace and happiness.

One evening I had hopefully put her to sleep as usual, in the cradle given to us by Anne, which had come down through Edward's family. It was the Moses-type basket with rockers at each end , and you could knit or read while keeping it in motion with your foot.

I left a nightlight burning in front of a large picture of the Sacred Heart, and after making sure she was sleeping peacefully, I crept silently down to the breakfast room, which was directly underneath our bedroom. Gratefully Edward and I had enjoyed our evening meal while chatting in low tones for fear of waking her.

We were alone in the house, as Clare and Andy had gone out to visit friends.

The wind sighed mournfully and a spray of purple clematis peeped in shyly through the open window. I asked Edward something and when he did not answer I saw that he had fallen asleep. Wearily I lay back in my chair and prepared to do likewise. I must have been just nodding off when suddenly I tensed. From upstairs came a wail, which gradually gained in volume....Rosemarie was preparing for action. She was just hitting a very respectable high "c" when clearly came the unmistakable sounds of the cradle rocking rhythmically to and fro. Someone was rocking the child in the bedroom!

Now it certainly could not be the three weeks-old infant operating those heavy rockers, and there was no one else in the house.

Almost rigid with fright, I leapt out of the chair and bounded up the stairs. I stopped at our bedroom door, listening, but the rocking went on and there was no sound from the child.

Taking a shuddering breath, I flung the door open. The cradle was rocking as if some unseen foot guided it and then, in the gentle glow of the nightlight, I saw the figure of a woman sitting beside the cradle; she had one foot on the rocker keeping it in motion. Her back was towards me.

I tried to say something, to clear my throat, but no sound came. I tried again:

"Who are you?" I quavered.

At the sound of my voice, she turned slowly and I was startled to see the face of Anne. She smiled with such reassurance that the fear ebbed out of me.

Gradually the image faded away and the rocking stopped. I was alone with my daughter.

I rushed to the cradle and bent anxiously over the child, but she was sleeping tranquilly. That was the first night of her little life that she slept right through until morning. She became a contented baby and the consequent calm brought a new era of peace and thankfulness into our lives.

"Where's my little weasel?" Edward had often greeted her screams, but now it was, "Fluffykins, where's my little Fluffykins."

Chapter 32

As I grew stronger and more confident in handling a quieter baby, I began accompanying Edward in the search for another flat. There was always some willing soul to keep an eye on Rosemarie....Aunt Cissy, Clare and, strangely enough, Myrabelle.

It was a daunting business searching for a new home; some of the flats were out for a number of reasons...cold, damp, dirt and distance, not to mention price. We were banned from the more hopeful ones by exorbitant rents, or the landlady would not consider us when it was revealed that we had a child.

One evening we rushed down to Hatch Street to find another couple had beaten us to a really nice flat, offered at a fair price. Cold and dispirited, we wandered into Leeson Street, and despite my weariness, I could not help admiring this fine wide street with its terraces of elegant eighteenth century, Georgian houses.

"I'm sure I saw a flat to let somewhere here," said Edward, rummaging in his pocket for the advertisement section of the "Evening Mail."

My interest quickened as we ran through the advertisements; identifying one referring to a "newly converted" flat in Lower Leeson Street.

We found the house without difficulty; it was situated half-way up the street, and from its granite steps, one could look up to the graceful curve of Leeson Street Bridge, or down to the massive iron gates of St. Stephen's Green.

"I wonder is it worth following up," asked Edward doubtfully, "Probably the price will be way beyond us."

But a sudden drenching shower decided us. A smart young maid in afternoon uniform, opened the door to our knock, and on hearing our business, left us to await her mistress in the hall.

There was the sound of movement and a side door opened to reveal an elderly lady. She was tall and thin and dressed in a long black, high-necked gown, which rustled faintly as she came towards us. The delicate fragrance of Eau-de-Cologne wafted gently around her and seemed part of her personality.

She was fingering a necklace of several strands of jet beads with a heavily-ringed hand.

"How do you do!" she greeted us in a surprisingly young voice, shaking our hands. "I am the owner of this house and my name is Maria Gandon. Now will you please follow me," and she led the way through a lamp-lit inner hall, up a lovely curving staircase, past two landings hung with shelves of Eastern china ornaments, marble statues of artistic and biblical characters, and into the drawing room.

This was a beautifully proportioned room with three large windows, from which hung stiffly starched lace curtains. The furniture of ornate mahogany with designs of fruit and birds, had the sheen of age and much polishing. Lovely china glinted from within several glass cabinets, and over a marble mantelpiece embossed with playful cherubs, a gilt pier glass reflected the room in the flickering firelight. A homely touch was the faded walls covered with family photographs and portraits.

Mrs Gandon bade us sit down. We obeyed gingerly, perching on the edge of a huge blue and gold couch. Shyly I told her why we had come, and awkwardly produce the paper with the advertisement.

"Oh yes," she answered. "I have a flat to let at the top of the house. It's nice and light and airy. There is a bedroom, kitchen, living-room, a new bathroom I've had put in, and there's a tiny extra room."

She paused and looked at us closely. "I've never done this sort of thing before and it's all very new to me. There are no other tenants in the house, so it's very quiet and you understand, that is something an old lady like me greatly values."

I nodded dumbly and Edward said quickly: "Could we see it please, Mrs. Gandon?"

She rose and beckoned us to follow her to the top of the house. I was amazed at how bright and modern the flat appeared after the shadowy gloom of the rest of the house. The rooms were all freshly papered in flowery pastels, and although there were a few pieces of ponderous antique furniture, the bed, chairs, table and kitchen fittings, were all new. I exclaimed delightedly over the electric cooker and a fine Welsh dresser, which I mentally stocked with my only tea set, and more modest odds and ends of Woolworths colourful crockery.

"I can see you like it here, dear," Mrs. Gandon was watching our reaction from the door.

"Oh yes," I enthused, "you have made it so lovely and comfortable."

"How much is it Mrs. Gandon?" put in Edward practically.

She named a very reasonable price and my heart leapt and then plummeted. Wait until she heard we had a child, and that would be the end of our hopes. Sadly I knew it must be faced.

"We have a baby," I said baldly, not meeting her eyes and automatically pulling on my wooly gloves preparatory to leaving.

Her reaction astonished me, "That's very nice, dear," she said placidly. "Is it your first?"

"Yes," I answered dismally, forcing myself to meet her gaze. There was a pause. She looked at Edward inquiringly and he said bravely: "It's like this, Mrs. Gandon, we'd love the flat. The price suits us, but have you any objection to child?"

She looked surprised. "Why should I? The poor baby must live somewhere too."

I drew a quivering breath of relief. "You are very kind .Most people don't want to know when you mention children."

"But that is shocking and unchristian. You know what the good Lord said?

"'Suffer the little children to come unto Me....'"

Mrs Gandon sent us down to the drawing room saying that she would follow shortly .As we awaited her arrival, I was caught in the almost tangible atmosphere of happiness in this lovely old house. A strange affinity with it stole over me. Had a house a heart? This one surely had, for a loving welcome seemed to emanate from some vital part of it. Here we surely would have safe anchorage.

"Oh I would so much love to live here," I said fervently. Edward too was taken with the house. He looked relaxed as we spoke in whispers, so that we would not disturb the gentle silence.

An Ormolu clock, with a Grecian lady playing a harp, enclosed in a glass dome, chimed the hour. Edward paused in his examination of an early gramophone with a big horn; there was a foot step in the hall, the door slid open and Mrs Gandon entered with a couple of documents.

Gladly we accepted the terms of the tenancy, the agreement was finalised and we were given our key.

Business completed, we settled down for a chat with our landlady. She asked about Rosemarie, and I took the opportunity of giving a most flattering resume of that young lady's life style, and how astonishingly "quiet" she was. As I rambled on, there was a loud scratching at the door and Mrs. Gandon rose to open it.

"Meet Ginger," she said, proud animation in her voice. I had no idea of who was about to come in. Certainly someone of human aspect, and not the magnificent tortoiseshell cat who swept in, threw a supercilious glance in our direction and leapt nimbly on to one of the regal-looking armchairs. He arched his back and stretched a striped paw slowly, before slumping down on the cushioned seat, his bushy tail carefully coiled around him.

"How are you, Ginger," I said, feeling foolish, but thinking Mrs. Gandon expected the gesture.

The cat opened one eye and yawned contemptuously. Mrs. Gandon pulled a bell by the mantelpiece and shortly after, the little maid entered with a tray of tea and fairy cakes.

After serving us from a silver teapot, Mrs. Gandon began to talk about herself. She was the widow of the late Major Henry Gandon, who had served with the British army in India. They had been stationed in Bombay for several years and all her four children had been born there. She had enjoyed her time out there; life was very easy and sociable for an army officer's wife. Wistfully she spoke of her children, with a far-away look in her eyes, and I felt she was lonely and glad to have someone listen to her memories.

My gaze wandered dreamily around the room, straying from the lustre of a Spode teapot and the crystal chandelier, dripping with gems of opalescent light, to the hand-carved display in rich gilt, of an Indian tableau, complete with jewel-encrusted elephants and brilliantly-costumed ladies.

Mrs. Gandon caught my rapt expression. "This is my favourite room," she said softly. "I just like to sit here of an evening and remember."

I understood what she meant; the peace and beauty of the room had seeped into my heart; its essence was in its harmony with this gentle old lady. They had mellowed together over the years, and the timeless quality of one had complemented the gracious aging of the other.

A discreet knock by the maid, brought her conversation to an end.

We rose to go. "I'm looking forward to seeing you both here next Friday," she smiled, as we said good-bye in the hall. "Baby too," she added hurriedly with a twinkle.

We took our leave with singing hearts. We had a roof over our heads again in a beautiful old house with a lovable landlady, and hand in hand, we danced all the way back to Aunt Clare's.

Chapter 33

We moved into our new home on the following Friday evening, assisted by Clare and Andy. They were sorry to see us go, but understood our need for self-sufficiency.

"It's been lovely staying with you, Clare," I said gratefully, as we chatted over a cup of tea. "I'll never forget your help when we needed it so badly, but it's only right that we stand on our own feet now. A helping hand in need is one thing, but...."

She nodded her understanding. "Always remember we're here if you need us. Never hesitate; as long as I'm alive, Edward's little family are very dear to Andy and me."

A lump rose in my throat and I hugged her wordlessly.

Now she was helping to arrange our humble belongings in our new abode, and had surreptitiously filled a basket with goodies for our kitchen cupboard, the extent of which I only discovered next morning when I went to get the breakfast.

We had a last cup of tea while I waited for Aunt Cissy to appear with Rosemarie, whom she was minding while we got the flat straight.

Feeling tired, but very pleased with ourselves, Edward and I went down to the hall to see Clare and Andy off. As we reached the hall, Mrs. Gandon came out of the morning room and invited us all in for more tea. Clare and Andy accepted, but we had to decline when Aunt Cissy came in pushing a fractious Rosemarie in her pram.

Next day, I had a visit from Myrabelle. She had been visiting Alice Jackson, who ran a kindergarten school across the street.

"So this is where you are!" she laughed, breezing in on the usual drift of perfume. "It's certainly a cosy little nest," and she gazed about her appreciatively.

I grinned ruefully as I struggled to dress the baby, who was strenuously objecting to wearing any clothes at all after her morning bath.

"In a way I don't blame her," said Myrabelle, tickling a pink foot, and watching Rosemarie wriggle easily out of her vest as fast as I got it on.

"The poor little mite is enjoying the freedom of her birthday suit; and after all, it's the one she came in," Myrabelle laughed, and the child kicked and chuckled in vigorous accord.

I was inclined to agree, as I continued the battle with the vest. The number and weight of the garments for so small a person, seemed literally overwhelming.

First there was the said vest in pure wool; then a length of flannel rolled around the tummy and pinned at both ends, called a binder. Next came the napkin, over which went a triangular piece of flannelette, known as a pilch.

After all this, on went the long-skirted barra, which was folded over the feet and secured with two more safety pins. Still the baby was not fully dressed; her day gown followed, and then lastly, a wooly matinee jacket. But for good measure and carrying purposes, the infant was securely wrapped in a fleecy shawl.

By the time this routine was accomplished, Rosemarie was screaming with abandon for her bottle. I was sweating with fear in case she bounced off my knee, or disappeared into all the clothes, or smothered....

"You'll get used to it," Myrabelle encouraged, as full of false courage, she offered to feed the baby, while I cleared the aftermath of the battle.

I handed her the child, and went into the kitchen to heat the prepared bottle.

Rosemarie eyed Myrabelle with unblinking suspicion, as she trust the bottle teat hopefully into the open mouth, and there was blessed silence at last. Evidently the hungry infant was of the opinion that it's only the bottle, and this one can't do much damage with that!

She fastened her lips more tightly around the teat and settled back contentedly to work her way through the almost full bottle of Glaxo feed.

The baby took over our lives and everything revolved around her.

As she grew, she decided to do most of her sleeping in the day time, the night's were dedicated to play and the considerable exercising of her lungs.

While chortling good humouredly in her pram during the day, friends would bend over her in cooing admiration of her auburn hair, and dreamy blue-grey eyes, prompting Edward to say feelingly: "Oh yes, a lovely little darling in the day time, but you should be around for the fireworks at night!"

Before his evening meal every evening, Edward took on the task of getting her to sleep. When she was fed, topped and tailed and ready for the night, he would take up the little bundle and sing her to sleep. I would have his meal ready, and sneaking into the bedroom, find Edward with the child cuddled snugly against his breast, singing a wide variety of songs to her.

If she was not fully asleep....and I believe she fought it off as long as she could....and Edward dared to lower his tone, she would set up a howl of protest, until he hurriedly restarted the singing again. So good timing was of the essence!

The type of song was important too. At night she favoured "Sonny Boy," "Sleepy Valley," "Braham's Lullaby," and oddly, "Me And My Shadow."During the weekend when Edward was at home, he bounced her gently to a foxtrot up and down the living room floor to "The Red Red Robin," and "Black Bottom," and she positively chuckled with joy when he got on to "Bye Bye Blackbird."

Edward had to keep correct time to the tune, by patting her with both hands on the back. Then, after a decent interval, when she appeared to be angelically asleep, he would rise, still singing and patting, while throwing me a meaning glance not to make a sound. Stealthily, he would creep to the cot and tuck her carefully among the blankets, while his old slippers, walked flat at the backs, kept up a flapping sort of rhythm.

"Quite a cliff-hanger getting our angel to sleep," he observed jauntily, belatedly attacking his well-earned meal.

These were the golden days, spent learning and loving together, and that delightful tune of the twenties epitomized it all for us. "My Blue Heaven" was indeed our signature tune.

Chapter 34

It is now three years later and life has been meandering along at a happy pace. Rosemary-Anne has grown into a pretty little girl with a cloud of dark curls, huge blue-grey eyes and a peachy complexion.

But a change in our circumstances is about to occur. Mrs. Gandon, with whom we had an unfailingly good relationship, was found dead in her bed one morning.

Sometime after the funeral, we got a letter from our solicitor, informing us that there were still several years of her tenancy left, and that it had been her wish to have it made available to us in the event of her death.

I drew a long breath of nervous anticipation, as Edward and I discussed it over our breakfast. It would be a big undertaking for us, with no experience, to take on the tenancy of such a big old house, but I loved it dearly, so refusal was not among my options. The rent was very reasonable....not much more than we were already paying for the top floor flat.

Edward had come in to a small sum of money on the death of an uncle in Australia, and we had put it away for a rainy day. Bur why wait for a rainy day?

Why not enjoy it on a sunny day, like today, and put it to work for us?

What would we do with the huge rooms? Why not let them, of course, I thought in a fit of inspiration. After all, it would bring us in a steady income, so we would be able to live rent free. We could not possibly use all the rooms ourselves, and they would only grow damp from disuse.

There was a lot of coming and going and legalities, before we got vacant possession. Mrs. Gandon left us an exquisite pair of Indian lamps and the gilt clock, in its glass dome, on the drawing room mantelpiece. Her son had everything else in the house auctioned, except for a few personal and choice pieces he kept for himself.

From this sale we acquired two fine oak tallboys, some kitchen ware, a couple of Victorian landscapes and the pier glass in the drawing room; all of which went very cheaply. Spurred on by this, I decided to attend some auctions, and pick up all sorts of treasures at bargain prices.

Myrabelle, who knew a great deal about good furniture and where it could be got reasonably, entered into my schemes with enthusiasm.

She was very helpful in a practical way, and began by lending us her charlady to wash the place down thoroughly. To supervise this, and other alterations, she insisted that I must have the assistance of her "general's" expertise. This turned out to be the middle- aged housekeeper of the prominent bottom and intimidating eye, who had caught my attention some years ago in the Dobson household, on the day of that memorable party.

Aunt Clare cleared the decks for us by undertaking the minding of Rosemarie, and Myrabelle and I attended every auction going. Very soon I developed a canny nose for a bargain, and we often came home with several good looking and useful articles. But the day I got a magnificent old oak cupboard, on which rested a matching bookcase, was the most spectacular buy of all.

The cupboard/ bookcase, was beautifully carved with heads and flowers, and the doors panelled with heavy bevelled glass. Each shelf was neatly grooved and scalloped....not a nail anywhere. The whole thing must have weighed a tonne, and for this perfection, I paid five pounds! It looked its best when placed at the opposite end of the drawing room from the marble mantle piece, where its rich ornamentation was reflected in the big pier glass.

Myrabelle recommended her favourite shop to make the Nottingham lace curtains for the numerous windows, which they did, for a very moderate price. The second hand dealers supplied us with floor coverings, including two fairly good carpets for the drawing room, and the ground floor room we were going to use as our own dining room.

Some smaller rooms we managed to re-paper ourselves, but money was running out, so we had to put many of our ideas on the long finger, until some cash came in from our prospective tenants.

We had one surprising find. Down in the basement, in which the old un-used kitchen, cellars and pantries, were located, we came across two buckets of a dismantled chandelier. They were covered in cobwebby dirt and grime, but the contents appeared to be in good condition otherwise.

We hauled the buckets upstairs, and after hours of patient washing, were able to assemble the shimmering, diamond-like droplets, into a glorious centre- piece for the drawing room, to replace the one sold at the auction.

When it was safely up and lighting with the help of an electrician friend, the results were stunning. Every facet caught the light and reflected a kaleidoscope of colours. It riveted everyone's attention, particularly when seen sparkling in the pier glass. It was quite disconcerting talking to a person, whose head was thrown back in absorption of the glittering spectacle.

When everything was ready, we put an advertisement in the "Evening Mail." and awaited, with some trepidation, for our first tenant.

We had a fair number of replies, but in our inexperience, found it no easy job sorting through them. Eventually, we selected, who we considered suitable, and nervously made an appointment with our first paying guest.

One cold night, there was a knock at the door, and a small, fat, elderly man with a flowing beard, stood on the door step. He was a retired seaman named Captain James Rodgers, who proved to be courteous, good-humoured, and a very likable character. In no time he had persuaded us that he was the ideal tenant. He came to settle in next day and take possession of the large room at the back of the house. As he entered the hall he was panting with exertion, and no wonder. He was carrying most of his possessions in a big, dolly-type bag, stained a sludgy brown from long use, and slung heavily over his shoulder. On each arm hung ungainly parcels tied with bits of rope, and in one hand, swung a bird cage, with a bit of red rag flung over it.

"Oul Pol," he muttered in explanation to my surprised stare at the vision that confronted me. Carefully he put the cage on the floor, and began to shift all his accoutrements to more controllable levels.

There was a loud squawk, as the rag fell off the cage, to reveal a green parrot with piercing eyes and tattered feathers. Rosemarie, clinging to my skirt, lost her shyness at the sight of the bird and bent down to examine him.

The bird fixed her with a beady eye and shrieked: "Get ta hell! get ta hell!"

Terrified, she leapt back, while the Captain smiled as he apologised for the bird's language, which, I later discovered, could have been a lot worse.

"Oul Pol," was only quietened by the re-adjustment of the rag, and I breathed a sigh of relief, as the Captain gathered up all his goods and chattels for the grand entry in to his new domain.

"Me and oul Pol goes everywhere together," he said, as I left him at the door of his room.

"I understand," I answered uneasily, wondering what I could have done to prevent oul Pol's inclusion in the tenancy, anyway.

A couple of days later, a long, coffin-shaped parcel, was delivered for Captain Rodgers. Wishing that Edward was at home, I led the delivery men to our guest's room, pondering nervously on whether the heavy object contained dynamite, a body....there were a lot of murders going on at the time....or black- market liquor.

The Captain opened the door to my knock, took in the parcel with a grave nod to the two men, and closed the door firmly on the three of us.

Trying to look nonchalant, I made small talk with them in an effort to cool my unease.

"Are you a friend of Captain Rodgers?" I inquired chattily.

"Not a tal," shrugged one of them "Dia know 'im, Jemser?"

"Never seen him in me life afore," said the other man, scratching his head with a worried frown. "That were a quare weight tho,' Mickey," he added.

"Hope we're not accompanin' after the fact," joked Jemser, blowing his nose hard on a dirty handkerchief, which evidently doubled as an all-purpose cleaning rag.

"Funny oul sod," grinned Mixer, and the two of them automatically rested their buttocks against the hall table. Each one produced a butt of a cigarette and lit up cheerfully, while continuing a bantering exchange of opinions concerning the contents of the Captain's parcel, which were no more outrageous than my own.

"Guns," affirmed Jemiser.

"Naw. I'm oney tellin' ya 'tis the money stolt from the bank this mornin'," argued Mickey.

But Jemser was adamant. "It's a cannon. I could feel it. He could put it threw wan a these windas. That oul joxer's up to somethin.'"

But Mickey was not listening and set off on his own track. "Supposin' he's a smugalar....he'd know all about that classa ting, been a seaman. Supposin' there were a body in that parcel...." He stopped, appalled at where his suppositions were leading.

Feeling decidedly queasy by this time, I jumped with fright at a sudden commotion in the dining room, and Ginger the cat dashed into the hall, sliding and slithering on the polished lino. With tapping claws he careered crazily down the stairs to the safety of the kitchen.

Just then, Rosemarie gave a scream, and as I hurriedly closed the door behind the curious men, I turned to find the child crying on the floor. She was liberally spattered with black ink, the empty bottle of which was swinging wildly on her thumb, where it was stuck fast.

"Take it away," she shrieked.

"Come here," I yelled above the din, angry at the cut of her. She jumped up, dancing about and howling, as I tried desperately to extract her finger from the bottle. "How did you do that?" I asked in growing panic at my fruitless efforts.

"I didn't I didn't!" she screamed. "Ginger stuck my finger in the bockle."

While blame was being apportioned, there was a roar from the back of the hall, and the Captain rolled in, demanding:

"What's to do! What's to do!" Shrewdly he took in the situation, as I babbled helplessly through the shouts of my daughter. Ignoring me, he said firmly, "Come here, little one."

The roars stopped like magic and the child rushed over to him. He lifted her in his arms and inspected the imprisoned finger.

"The Captain will fix that for the little one," he said calmly, and nodding to me, led the way in to his room.

There he seated her on the coffin-shaped parcel, which still lay unopened on the floor. I tried to maintain a casual exterior as I lifted the child cautiously and sat her on a nearby chair. The Captain turned from a cupboard with a butter dish in his hand, and gently anointed her finger with dollops of butter, easing it slowly out of the bottle. A bull's eye sweet, and a look at a ship in a bottle, completed the treatment.

All smiles now, Rosemarie demanded the ship to take to bed. An argument ensued, with alternatives offered by the Captain, entreaties from the child and divertive strategies proffered by the mammy.

The situation was getting out of hand when, with blessed relief, I heard Edward in the hall, and his cheery call for tea and family, in that order.

On hearing his voice, the bid for the coveted ship was withdrawn; out she rushed and into his waiting arms.

"Dadda, Dadda," she yelled. "Ginger put ink spots on me and the nice baldy man took it out and gave me a sweet with stripes on it. Will you buy me a sweet with stripes, Dadda?"

The bossy little voice droned on, while the Captain and I grinned at each other, conspirators in relief.

Chapter 35

Our second tenants came to us a week after the Captain had settled in. They were two middle-aged sisters named Ida and Adelaide Lister. The younger one, Ida, had been a school teacher, but was now retired. Adelaide appeared to be a sort of lady-of-leisure.

When they arrived one frosty afternoon, I took them into the drawing room, where I had a fire going and a welcoming cup of tea at the ready.

Adelaide introduced herself. She was tall, thin and pinched looking; very much the dominant one. In a high pitched formal voice, she told me that she looked after the affairs of both of them. Not once did she consult her sister about anything, and only mentioned "Miss Ida Lister," casually when I tried to draw the younger sister into the conversation.

For her part, Ida remained withdrawn and made little attempt, beyond the bare necessities of politeness. Adelaide leaned on a silver-topped stick and wore a built-up boot on her left foot. "When I was a child, I broke my leg in two places. I fell off a friend's swing," she explained in a cold voice, stretching the shorter leg awkwardly in front of her.

I commiserated nervously, but she seemed indifferent to my sympathy and turned her head away. I hurriedly poured out fresh cups of tea and steered the conversation into safer channels.

As they drank their tea and sampled my hot scones, Adelaide, poker-straight in her chair and Ida slumped tiredly in hers, I noted that both ladies were dressed in nondescript, beige-coloured coats of a fashion popular about ten years earlier. A rabbity- type of fur rambled around their necks, and the head of some fox-like animal stared balefully over each shoulder. Inside her coat Ida, who was tiny and round, sported a multi-coloured dress sprayed with extraordinary-looking flowers. They both wore straw hats, which nearly hid their faces; Adelaide's black and austere; Ida's faded blue and encircled with wilted silk flowers.I was just about to take them up to see their prospective flat....our old one at the top of the house....when Rosemarie, who at last sighting, had been sleeping peacefully on the living room couch, started up the stairs after us shouting, "Mamma, Mamma."

Yes Lambkin," I answered with a sinking heart. "I want Meggy," she persisted, beginning to whinge.

"Alright pet," I responded placidly.

"Now! I want Meggy now," and the sharp little voice rose threateningly.

"Go into the bathroom then," I whispered urgently, as Adelaide turned with a look, which demanded that I get on with the business of showing her the flat.

But Rosemarie continued to wail doggedly for "Meggy." Quietly, Ida bent towards her to ask kindly:

"A little friend of yours, dearie?"

Rosemarie paused in her wailing to eye her scathingly.

"Meggy, my pot," she yelled.

I caught her arm, and excusing myself to the ladies, escorted her to the bathroom.

"You could have done that yourself," I admonished her crossly when she was regally seated on her chamber pot.

I waited until she was ready, pausing impatiently while she scampered back for her teddy bear. The ladies were talking on the landing; Adelaide's back stiff with disapproval.

"I don't like that big lady, Mamma," said the child, pointing at Adelaide for good measure. I knew from the angry glance of Adelaide that she had heard, but Ida gave a sudden twinkling smile, and Rosemarie skipped over to her and took the offered hand trustingly.

"I like you; you come again," she said happily, and my heart jumped in case she passed judgement on Adelaide. But tactfully, Ida distracted her, while I showed Adelaide over the flat.

Grudgingly, and after much humming and hawing, Adelaide expressed herself satisfied with the accommodation, although making sure I understood it was "not the sort of place," she was used to. Imperiously, she demanded some alterations in the placing of the furniture, and the removal of certain pieces, as she intended bringing in some valuable items of her own. To these conditions I agreed; after all, it was a small price to pay for having two genteel ladies as tenants who would add "tone" to my establishment.

While the terms of the tenancy were being hammered out, Rosemarie took Ida down to our kitchen to meet her toy "wabbit."

Chapter 36

Our third and last tenant was a rather eccentric character named Alan Floy. He was smallish, paunchy and "dressed to kill," as Edward described him.

Clad in cream trousers, impeccably creased, a claret-coloured velvet jacket, a pink shirt and scarlet dicky bow, brown spats and matching suede gloves, and a white carnation, completed the gaudy ensemble.

His hair was sleek, like black leather, his eyes shifty and his nose the reddest I had ever seen. In one hand he held a silver-topped walking stick, while the other nonchalantly swung a monocle from a gold chain around his neck.

We had been interviewing him for the large room on the third floor, and after he had gone, I expressed my doubts to Edward.

"You can't take the book by the cover, sweet girl," he laughed merrily, and I felt he was amused and intrigued by our exotic candidate for our last apartment.

"I'd say he's a decent skin under all that raffish splendour, tho' I admit you'd have to dig deep to find it. Anyway, we can't afford to turn people away because we don't like their fancy dress"

I still hesitated, but Edward was not to be dissuaded. "Let's just give him a try anyway. If we don't like him we can always kick him out."

The picture that statement evoked of my gentle husband, manfully flinging the elegant bird-of-paradise into the street, gave me a fit of the giggles, and Alan Floy's appointment to the bedsitter was duly honoured.

A week later, I opened the hall door to find him on the doorstep. He bowed effusively, brushing my Zebra- blackened hand with his lips....I had been cleaning the living room grate when he knocked.

"Mrs. Davis, how very nice," he murmured huskily. "Floy.... Alan Floy. Surely you haven't forgotten?"

Disconcerted, I stared blankly at him, conscious of the unswept hall behind me, the duster on my head, and Rosemarie mesmerised beside me in her nightdress ,with half her breakfast on her bib.

I tried to rise above it all, and mustering a vestige of dignity, I said primly. "Perhaps you could call back later, Mr. Floy. You were not expected until this evening."

He shook his head ruefully, "I am most awfully sorry, Mrs Davis, but this is the only time I could fit you into my diary. I am extremely busy just now."

He gave me a calculating stare. "Perhaps you are not all that interested....perhaps you are booked out...." he left the sentence hang on the air, and I thought of the money we owed the bank, and the un-fought battle was lost.

"Come in," I said, with as much dignity as I could muster, my mind on Rosemarie, and how she would behave in the presence of such an unusual- looking individual.

"Go and play with teddy, pet" I whispered hopefully, but she was fascinated by the appearance of Alan Floy. The only moment she left us, was to rush off for teddy, and with him tucked safely under her arm, she dived up the stairs after us to the drawing room.

Alan Floy settled himself comfortably in an armchair opposite me, and crossed his legs to display a neat ankle and part of a hairy leg. With eyes darting around the room, he searched his pockets for his cigarette case, and flipping it open, offered me one.

I shook my head. "I don't smoke, thank you," I said pointedly, hoping he would take the hint, but he drew a cigarette for himself and lit it ostentatiously.

"I'm sure you'd like to know a bit about your latest recruit to the letting business?" he asked, drawing deeply on his cigarette, but without waiting for an answer, he went on grandly, "Well, I'm a poet by inclination and talent, but by profession, I'm a writer, and a regular contributor to "The Dublin Scholar's Journal"....I'm sure you've heard of me....? Celtic Studies, astronomical calculations, scientific predictions for the next fifty years...." he paused to look at me inquiringly, and threw out an arm to expose the gold watch and chain, stretched tautly across the embroidered velvet of his waistcoat.

I certainly had never heard of him in connection with any, not to mention all, of these grandiose subjects, but felt guilty and ignorant at the omission.

"I'm sorry, but...."I faltered.

He dismissed my lack of knowledge as of little importance, and most likely to be expected, and a good opportunity for him to give me the benefit of his superior intellect. He began with Lindberg, who was headline news at the time, and lectured like a professor, on the significance of the historic flight for the future of aviation.

Eventually, he drifted back to earth, while the cigarette smouldered un-smoked, and I hoped it would burn his fingers, but carried away by his own eloquence, he set off on an analysis of Government policy, and how it could benefit from his advice.

I listened bemused, trying to get a word in, and glancing desperately at the clock.

"Didn't you express a wish to read my latest poem before publication?" I heard him say from a great distance.

I had no such recollection. I surfaced from the depths of boredom or ignorance, to see him stub his cigarette on an old ornamental plate. Inspecting his watch, as if to remind me of all the time he had wasted trying to enlighten me, he drew a pink piece of paper from his pocket, and handed it to me. I took it reluctantly, hoping that Rosemarie would rise to the occasion and cause some sort of distraction.

But contrary to general practice, she was sitting comfortably on the floor, sucking her thumb contentedly, and staring at Floy, goggle-eyed; quiet as a mouse, clasping teddy, and with little dirty bare feet stretched stiffly in front of her.

I felt an urgent desire to laugh hysterically, as our prospective guest went on now to expound on the merits and demerits, of modern art.

"I dabble a bit," he said casually. "Oh yes, several exhibitions....nothing too heavy, you understand? Must let you see one or two from my present collection." He lowered his eyes modestly before adding generously, "Might be able to let you have one reasonably."

I let this pass, as he gazed around the room with evident disapproval at our cheap copies of renowned masterpieces. He visibly shuddered, when his gaze fell on some Woolworth's ornaments, depicting three lurid ducks, flying across the wall, which had been given to us by Myrabelle's "general," when she was "doing" for us and discovered it was our wedding anniversary.

"About the room," I cut in determinedly, angry at the amount of time he had wasted, and still not touched on the matter of business.

"About the room," I repeated loudly, breaking in on the comparison of the brush strokes of Van Gough with those of Monnet.

He halted in mid sentence, staring at me in pained surprise, and swinging the monocle even more furiously.

"Yes," I leapt in before he could get going again. "The room; I take it you're here to let me know whether you want it or not."

"Oh yes, that's right," he drawled absently. "I do tend to forget mundane matters."

I could not see anything mundane about finding yourself a suitable place to live, but forbore from saying so; better not draw him on me again about something else, stick to the point.

He stared at me with narrowed eyes as if he was seeing me for the first time, and not liking what he saw. I felt an overwhelming distaste for him, and wondered wildly how I could get rid of him. I felt sure I did not want him in the house.

Half-heartedly, I discussed terms with him, adding that I did not think the room would suit him.

"Show it to me, dear lady," he purred, "and let me be the judge of that."

Reluctantly, I took him up to the vacant room, clean and sparsely furnished. I felt by the way he looked and spoke, that a room in a first class hotel was more in keeping with his aspirations.

"I'll take it," he nodded, as if he were doing me a favour. I mentioned the price, adding on another pound to put him off. He was quick to notice the discrepancy.

"I thought you said it was...." naming the original rent. Embarrassed, but sticking to my guns, I said I had made a mistake the first time.

"That's alright then, dear lady. It's easy to get confused," and he smiled tolerantly, revealing a band of gold -studded teeth beneath his narrow black moustache.

"That's alright then, dear lady," he smirked again, as if to reassure me that he had forgiven my error. He took out a cheque book and fountain pen from an inner pocket, and murmuring the original sum as he wrote, he filled in the amount for a month's rent and handed it carelessly to me.

Then his mood changed and wrapping the astrakhan collar of his overcoat about his ears, he strode to the door and ran down the stairs, loudly bewailing the lateness of the hour.

Rosemarie and I followed more slowly, and for the first time that morning, my daughter found her tongue. With her usual disregard for the carrying power of her voice, she asked:

"Mamma, if that funny man comes to live here will Dadda throw him into the street?"

Floy heard alright. He turned from the hall table where he had just picked up his hat, and gave me a sour look.

Confused, I struggled to cover the disconcerting situation with empty banalities, as I hurried him through the door.

Rosemarie, still unprepared to have her question ignored, demanded angrily,

"Mamma, when will Dadda throw that funny man into the street?"

Chapter 37

A month later I began calling on my tenants to collect the rent. I started with the Lister sisters, already referred to by us as "the ladies."

Ida opened the door to my knock, her white hair a mass of rag curlers.

"Come in, Mrs Davis," she greeted me cheerily in her gentle voice.

I stepped into the room to find myself looking into the cold eyes of Adelaide, who was rocking herself in an old fashioned chair by the fire, a book on her lap.

"I hope I'm not intruding," I began nervously.

"Oh, not at all," said Ida eagerly, but Adelaide cut in briskly:

"You want your rent....that's why you're here," her tone was scathing.

"If it's not convenient...." but a look from Adelaide silenced me. Ida opened a drawer and produced the rent book. Clicking her teeth impatiently, Adelaide reached into a capacious pocket and withdrew a shabby purse. She counted out the money carefully, and put it with a bang on the table beside her. Then she returned to her book.

Ida insisted I sit down for a few minutes, which I did reluctantly, while she disappeared into the tiny kitchen.

Left alone with Adelaide, I felt intimidated by her silence, and uneasily my eyes wandered around the room. It was very different to the way we had arranged it when first we came to the house. Then it was all bright colours, pine furniture, and rather untidy. Now it looked shadowy and rather depressing, with Adelaide's heavy mahogany book case, ornate china cabinets, and a couple of ponderous portraits of grim-faced ancestors, which I supposed to be forebears of the sisters.

Yet on closer survey, the atmosphere was enlivened by the beautiful needlework on chair backs, fire screen, and the table cover of intricate Irish crochet. The wall behind me seemed to float in a seascape of multi-coloured tapestry, and cushions abounded with rich collages of flowers, and old-world cottages.

What a strange amalgamation of light and shade, the past with all its baggage of mystery and dejection, the present exuberant in a profusion of glorious flowers.

My musings were broken by a step at the door, and Ida came in with a tea tray.

"You have such beautiful things," I said enviously, as she put a knitted tea cosy, shaped like a cottage, over the teapot.

Ida smiled deprecatingly, but I could see she was pleased. She poured the tea into three delicate china cups. Adelaide accepted hers without a word, and I tried to relax, as Ida added milk and sugar to mine.

Awkwardly, we exchanged general chat on the weather, the rise in the price of coal, and Rosemarie's latest (and most respectable) escapade, while Adelaide blatantly ignored us.

I had not meant to stay longer than it took to transact my business. In fact, I wanted to get well out of the way of the un-gracious Adelaide, but it would have been churlish to risk offending Ida, who was so friendly and anxious for the bit of company and, surreptitiously eying Adelaide, I could understand why.

To fill an uncomfortable pause, I remarked on the perfect drawn thread work on the white linen table cloth.

"It was made by my mother," said Ida sadly.

I pointed to all the excellent hand work and asked whose was the magic needle. Adelaide made no comment, and only grunted as she helped herself to another slice of lemon shortbread.

Idea said softly: "It fills in the time for me. I have always loved making things; I used to teach handcrafts at a girl's school."

She went on to show me various examples of her work, and after admiring an elaborately embroidered tablecloth, my gaze was held by a long low cupboard at the other end of the room. It had glass doors, and I was rather perturbed to see a collection of dolls staring fixedly at me from its dark interior.

Adelaide must have been watching me for she got up, and going to the cupboard, took a key from a bunch in her pocket, and unlocked one of the doors.

Almost reverently, she took out a selection of dolls, and one at a time, she brought them to me, telling me each one's history and how she had come by it.

I was amazed by the change in the woman; animated, warm, almost friendly, she certainly loved her dolls. They were all beautiful; hand made in wax, china and polished wood. Their clothes were bright with jewels, lace and embroidery. Some had rich heads of curly hair; others waist-length ringlets, and I wondered in sudden alarm, what would happen if Rosemarie saw them, but thankfully, she was having her afternoon nap.

I put out a tentative hand to touch a charming doll in a pink crinoline. Instantly, Adelaide snatched her out of my reach.

"You cannot touch," she said sharply. "They are very valuable."

I said nothing, and to cover my embarrassment, took a sip of my cold tea, while Adelaide replaced the last doll, locked the cupboard and pocketed the key. I felt that as far as Adelaide was concerned, I had long over-stayed my welcome. I rose to leave, but on my way out, I noticed another glass-fronted cupboard beside me. Unable to stop myself, I paused and peered inside.

Here was another assortment of dolls; their hypnotic glass eyes seemed to fasten on me. Some smiled, some looked blank, others sad. They were all gorgeously gowned, except for one little wooden doll in a corner by itself.

He was the only male doll, and dressed in the uniform of an eighteenth century soldier. The remarkable thing about him was that he looked so dishevelled and tatty beside his splendid companions. Across his chest, a dark stain spread to his knees; it looked as if he had actually been wounded.

Adelaide was jingling the keys in her pocket; her eyes watching me speculatively. Then she seemed to make up her mind, and selecting a key, went to a small cupboard and unlocked it. From this she took a big doll of a swarthy colour, with gleaming eyes and black hair wound in coils about its head. It was dressed in a flowered skirt and richly embroidered blouse. Gold earrings flashed in its ears, but it was the full, red mouth that filled me with a strange repugnance.

I stared at it fascinated, and the opening smiling lips, revealing tiny, needle sharp teeth, seemed to tremble and change until the face was distorted by a long leer.

I shook myself, thinking the light was playing tricks, and dragged my eyes from the doll, but when I dared to look again, the same dire expression repulsed me.

"You may hold her for a moment," Adelaide was saying, pushing the doll towards me.

Involuntary, I stepped back. "No, thank you," I cried, "I might damage it."

"But you must," insisted Adelaide with glittering eyes.

Ida laid a restraining hand on her arm.

"Not now, dear," she said mildly. "Mrs. Davis must go down to prepare her husband's tea."

"Not yet," hissed Adelaide fiercely. "She must take time to speak to Reza."

The two sisters were locked in conflict; Adelaide wild and unyielding; Ida calmly compelling.

I was desperately wondering if I should intervene and offer to hold the repulsive doll, and so mollify Adelaide, but then her mood changed and she eyed her sister mockingly.

"You take her," and she held the doll out to Ida.

Ida recoiled and her voice grew agitated. "No, no, Adelaide. Not now please.

The doll looks tired; put her back to sleep in her cupboard."

That seemed to distract Adelaide. She looked at the doll closely and must have concluded that Ida was right. Silently, the ugly doll was restored to the cupboard, but when she returned, she caught my arm in a hard grip and explained, "Reza sleeps by herself because she fights with the other dolls.

She threw a shepherdess out of the cupboard and her face is all cracked....Ida found her; didn't you, Ida?"

Ida winced, and reluctantly admitted finding the doll on the floor next morning.

"Maybe she just fell out...." she began soothingly.

"You know very well she did not," Adelaide turned on her furiously. "Reza and she were always fighting, and you know yourself, how frightening Reza can be. Remember that night on the avenue...." and her voice faded, taut with mysterious implication.

"You have a wonderful collection of dolls, Miss Lister," I broke in, in an effort to change the subject. "I never saw so many splendid dolls in my life; you should have an exhibition...." I gabbled on.

Somewhat appeased, Adelaide interrupted me. "There was a larger collection.

They had a special room all to themselves at home in Heatherfield Hall."

She gave a heavy sigh, and her voice rose again, edged with anger.

"Those were the days of civilized living. Plenty of well-trained servants who knew their place, and we gave balls and at-homes where the best in the land were proud to be invited."

She seemed lost in the past, and anxious to escape. I picked up the rent from the table. Immediately she noted my action with a look of distaste, and Ida said quickly:

"It's all gone now, and we cannot live in the past. There was a lot wrong with those days too."

Adelaide turned on her stormily: "How can you talk like that? It is but fitting that people of class and breeding should be at the head of affairs. Look at the country now since the bogtrotters took over!"

"It's no longer the classes but the masses," persisted Ida bravely. "Money and power do not automatically make great or good men. This class thing never did me any good," she ended with a despondent shake of the head.

Adelaide drew herself up to her full height with the aid of her stick. "I do not know where our family got you from," she responded crushingly. "You never behaved like a lady, or looked like one either."

She paused, as if gathering all her strength, and in a rising voice, accused her sister of the ultimate faux-pas...."talking to any and every common person....no self respect. How could you expect people to have any value on you, when you have never kept at the front of your mind the memory of our family, our dignity, and how people looked up to us."

"I don't want people to look up to me," cried Ida stubbornly, "I only want to be friendly with them."

"Friendly!" Adelaide spat the word.

I got quickly through the door, closing it quietly behind me, as Adelaide loudly denounced and Ida doggedly stood her ground.

Feeling both shaken and relieved, I hastened thankfully down the stairs to give Rosemarie her glass of milk and jampuff. I could hear her moving about in the living room, and a sudden scream of, "Mamma! Mamma!" brought her into my arms in the hall.

Chapter 38

Around this time, Edward decided I needed some help in the house, and it would be a good idea to have a maid, as we could just about afford one now.

I had not long recovered from a bad dose of flu, which I had struggled to put over on my feet. It had left me pale and listless, so I was very grateful at the prospect of some domestic help, if a little uneasy, when I realised it would mean working with a stranger.

We went to a domestic servant's agency, and a girl with impeccable references, was recommended to us. The "girl" turned to be a tall, gaunt woman of indeterminate age, named Agnes Smith. Her greying hair was pulled into an uncompromising bun at the back of her head, and her eyes were blue and bulbous. When you were talking to her, she had the habit of fixing them on a spot beyond the top of your head, so that you never knew whether she was looking at you, or watching something else.

Her clothes were ill-fitting and too young for her; the short skirt of her flowery dress displaying a most un-shapely pair of skinny legs. Around her thin neck hung several strands of large, coloured beads, and her yellow cloche hat was stabbed with a long red feather, which looked as sharp as a razor.

I left her to unpack a battered suitcase in her room, while Rosemarie obligingly napped in the living-room.

Feeling free for the moment, I made my way to the Captain's room with the rent book. After knocking, he gruffly bade me enter. He was sitting at the table pouring over an ancient stamp album, heavy spectacles perched on his nose.

"Come in, me dear and sit yourself down," he bid me graciously. I explained my errand shyly, for I was not yet blasé about the business of rent collecting. He nodded good humouredly and pulled an old beaded purse from his pocket. He counted the rent out slowly and I signed the book.

We chatted amiably and I was just about to leave, when I noticed a tall stand bearing a fine plaster bust of a bearded man.

The whole thing was life size....my intriguing, coffin-shaped parcel of a few weeks ago!

The Captain noticed my interest and pulled reflectively at his white beard. "Know who it is?" he queried.

"Yes, it's Charles Stuart Parnell," I said smugly, pleased to air a little knowledge.

"A fine model," he observed, and laid his hand lovingly on the white plaster.

There was a sudden diversion, as the parrot flapped about in his cage.

"Go to hell," he shrieked.

"Go to hell yarself," shouted his master, flinging an old cloth expertly over the cage.

"Oul bastard!" screamed the out-raged bird.

"That's a most derogaterry fowl," complained the Captain, looking abashed, and speaking loudly in the hope of masking further abuse from his feathered friend. After an indignant fit of squawking, the bird settled down and peace reigned.

"See that nose," observed the Captain, pointing to the said appendage, or lack of it, on the plaster face of Parnell. I looked closely and noted that most of the nose was badly damaged.

"Julia did that," he said with an angry frown.

I waited bewildered, and he went on. "I had three wives, ya know,...Oh not all together, heaven forbid." He leaned confidently towards me, adding: "Would you believe it, I buried them all."

I shivered a little at his phrasing; surely he had not murdered them all?

The Captain painstakingly stuffed his pipe with tobacco. "There's a quare wan for ya," he said boastfully, striking a match.

"Anyways, Julia were the last wan and a proper targer she were too. I didn't know 'til the knot were tied that she hated Parnell." He paused to see how I was taking this sensational piece of news, but he evidently considered that I was suitably impressed, for he waved his pipe in the air and continued.

"Now all me family were devoted, devoted missus, to Charles Stuart, and would fight to the death any wan who would say a word agin him. Up comes this wan, after we were wed, mind you, and tells me to get rid of Parnell.

"I'm a Healyite," she tells me, "and I have no use for that oul statsha gatherin' dust in the hall."

He stopped and dramatically tapped the head of the plaster statue gently with his pipe.

"I won't soil yar ears, missus," he resumed, "with her language, but yon bird there soon copped on to it, and beggin' yar pardon, missus, geta hell, were the cleanest part of it."

There was silence as he concentrated on re-lighting his pipe. Puffing to his satisfaction, he went on with his tale: "I needn't tell ya, I made it very clear that if Parnell went, I'd go with him. To cut a long story short, we fought mornin', noon and night, over that there statsha.

"I'm Healyite," she'd yell for all to hear, and she'd be on about Kitty O'Shea, and what she wouldn't do to that trollop. That used to get me rag out fine and proper, I can tell ya, and she'd get a bit more back than she could chew."

He gazed back over the years reflectively, puffing hard on the pipe.

"Anyways, she grabbed up the poker wan day, and rushed at Parnell. I couldn't believe that she would actually injure the statsha, and I wern't quick enough for her, but all of a suddent, she brings the poker down hard on it and a chunk flies up in the air....his nose were gone with that wallop....bandjaxed forever."

He blew his own nose absently, depriving the parrot of his cloth for the job. The bird instantly set up an uproar, and the Captain swiftly restored the rag to its rightful position.

I was lost for words, appalled at the battlefield his married life had been over politics.

"But couldn't yourself and Julia have come to some compromise," I ventured, but stopped at the fanatical fire in his eyes.

"Yar not sugestin' I shoulda got rid of Parnell?" he asked in amazement. Seeing the utter uselessness of arguing with him, I retreated quickly, and asked what had transpired after Julia's attack on the bust.

"I just tolt her I were goin' off to sea, but this time, I wouldn't be back."

"And how did she take that?" I responded curiously.

"She begged me to stay; that she would never touch "The Chief" again, but it were too late; I'd had enough. Two of me mates carried Parnell to the boat for me, and I never seen her again."

"Where is she now?" I was hoping there might be still a chance of reconciliation, unpardonably forgetting that he had numbered her amongst his departed wives.

"I heard she died three year ago askin' for me," he said in a non- committal tone, "but I were in the far east at the time. She were buried and gone when I got wind of it."

I looked at him sadly, and Shakespeare's apt words flashed through my mind...."What fools these mortals be...."

The Captain turned from me in the fading light, and gazed through the window at the dark chimneypots of the huddled Georgian houses. His lips moved mutely over the dead pipe; was he offering a little prayer for his last bride, or asking forgiveness for his part in their mutual folly?

A knock at the door made me jump; it was Agnes, dressed in a skimpy black frock and frilly apron.

"Beggin' your pardon, ma-am; would you like me to bake some scones for tea?"

"I would indeed, Agnes, thank you," I responded, as I rose to leave.

Bidding a polite "good evening," to the Captain, to which there was no response. I left his room quietly, and followed our new maid thoughtfully into the kitchen, where Rosemarie was happily absorbed in making a "goosebuyee" pie of raspberry jam and several fresh eggs. The fact that she was unable to reach the flour bin cost her no problem at all; she simply improvised with a large tin of talcum powder heavily scented with "Ashes of Roses."

Chapter 39

After a storm of protest, I managed to distract the child and clean her up, but the pungent scent of "Ashes of Roses," haunted the house for days.

I felt very tired after that set-to, and decided to allow Agnes (whose references proclaimed her undoubted ability to handle children with "every competence") to have sole charge of her in the evenings.

Rosemarie loved her bedtime bath, but was a little fiend when it came to having her hair washed. She screamed when I got ready to administer the shampoo, and I dreaded the ordeal, which left me soaked and limp.

Now it was the turn of Agnes, and I awaited her efforts with some trepidation, but she fared no better than I had. Evening after evening, I would try to close my ears to the battles in the bathroom. Sometimes I felt a wild urge to go up and do something....I never knew exactly what, since I had already used every means of appeasement I could think of, but Edward always stopped me, firmly closing the door on the uproar.

"There's no use in keeping a dog and barking yourself," was his oblique comment.

Agnes would eventually emerge, wet and with heightened colour, from these encounters. Many times I felt she was going to hand in her notice, but she proved stubborn against being ousted by so small an aggressor.

She tried again with a different approach; I did not interfere, knowing that if I did, Rosemarie would be triumphant and unmanageable, resulting in my never being able to keep a maid. Sometimes she would try to distract the child with animal or fairy stories, complete with actions. This might work for a while, and I could restore bottles and glasses to the bathroom shelves, but it never lasted.

Agnes seemed to have endless patience, but one evening she had a bad headache, and as the bath proceeded, with the yellow duck bumping about in the soapsuds, she endeavoured to come up with an amusing story before reaching the hated hair-wash.

She did, but my young daughter disapproved of it, and began her usual kicking and splashing protest. In the ensuing battle, Agnes lost her temper, and gave the little pink bottom a well-earned slap.

Bursting with indignation, Rosemarie leapt up, and as Agnes reached for the shampoo, the child grabbed the dripping sponge and squeezed it dry over her opponent's head.

Agnes downed tools and rushed down the stairs to the kitchen, where I was baking, and Edward reading me the newspaper. She strode in, and without preamble, stated that she was leaving; the child was impossible and she could not cope with her any longer. I wasn't exactly surprised at this, but I was on tender hooks, wondering how long it would take to get to this point.

Upstairs, Rosemarie could be heard shouting for Agnes, and getting no response, got straight out of the bath and headed for the kitchen. There she landed, dripping in her birthday suit, and hoping to intimidate her, I brandished the wooden spoon I was using to make a cake. This threat she blithely ignored, and wrapping a towel around her, Edward carried her back to the bathroom where I dried her and put on her nightdress.

Agnes had fled to her room; whether to dry herself, pack, evaluate her situation, or all three, I had not the energy to contemplate.

Meantime, I tried to reason with Rosemarie who had plenty of spirit, and showed a defiant inclination to give me some of the treatment she had meted out to Agnes. However, tiredness was wearing the fight out of her, and the stormy tears gradually faded to gentle sobs. I tucked her up cosily in her cot beside our bed with teddy, and went down to get her supper of jam puffs and milk.

After she had taken these in a somewhat subdued mood, I got her to promise to apologise to Agnes, and to ask Holy God to make her a good child. There was a large and very moving portrait of the Sacred Heart, facing her over the mantelpiece, and she directed her little prayers to It. When she had finished, she turned to me.

"That's Holy God, Mamma," she asserted gravely.

"Yes dear," I agreed absently, tucking the blankets around her.

"But Mamma, Mary Brown next door, says she has Holy God in her house," she said earnestly.

"That's right," I agreed, lighting the red oil lamp in front of the picture.

"But she's telling fibs," maintained the child confidently.

"How's that?" I replied.

"Well you always said there was only one Holy God, didn't you, Mamma?" she appealed in a rising voice.

"Yes, yes of course I did," I assured her.

She smiled smugly. "There's only one Holy God and we have Him here."

I hid a smile; no way was I going to take on a theological proposition with the young imp, just now, but I filed it away for further discussion.

Again, I emphasised the need for her to mend her ways, and after a kiss and cuddle, I escaped thankfully back to my baking.

As I entered the hall, I saw a glamorous flapper ascend the stairs to Alan Floy's room; there was much laughing and talking as his door banged shut. Agnes appeared at suppertime. She looked pale and woebegone and complained of a headache, so I gave her a cup of tea and an aspirin.

There was no further mention of leaving, and I did not refer to it either. Agnes was competent, and I had no fault to find with her work, so I allowed for the tough time she had been having with the child.

Rosemarie duly apologised to her and they appeared to be on friendly terms. The battles in the bathroom abated, due mainly to bribes of lucky bags and sweets from Agnes.

But unfortunately, the reign of peace did not last, and Rosemarie resorted to her old ways. I had a return to removing bottles and glasses from the bathroom shelves, while Agnes had her hair pulled, the walls daubed in bath salts, and the hated shampoo formed a river to the door.

On one occasion, Ginger happened to amble into the bathroom while a rumpus was in progress, and got a bar of soap, intended for Agnes, full in his furry face. Startled and blinded, he leapt for the toilet, and promptly fell in. Fortunately, the Captain was passing on the landing outside, and hearing the shouts and yowls, rushed in and dragged him out by the tail.

"Poor pussy, poor pussy," lamented Rosemarie, but the cat was beyond sympathy, and shaking his wet fur frantically, shot through the door, and somersaulted down the stairs to the safety of the basement.

When our daughter was in bed, Agnes emerged from the fracas, looking very grim, and would not talk to anyone. This time, I thought dismally, she will surely hand in her notice. While she retired to repair the damage to her clothes and person, I prepared a cup of cocoa, her favourite beverage, and a slice of seed cake as a peace offering and in recognition of her suffering, for which I myself was beginning to feel guilty.

I was surprised when no such notice was forthcoming, for the difficult task of managing Rosemarie did not improve, but took on another turn. Now her behaviour further deteriorated, and it became an onerous task to get her to sleep at night. She slept fitfully, and would often stand up in her cot in the middle of the night, jangling the brass bars agitatedly, and crying for us to take her into our bed.

On one such night, there was a knock on our bedroom door and Adelaide Lister, in a long purple dressing gown, gave me a forbidding look when I went to see what she wanted.

"Mrs. Davis, I will not put up with so much noise, and it's the same every night," she complained.

"I'm very sorry...." I began wearily.

"I shall have to reconsider my tenancy if this continues," she interrupted sharply.

Edward came to my side with the child in his arms. "My wife has apologised and that should be enough for you," he said angrily, closing the door.

I was at my wit's end, as Rosemarie continued her nightly crying, and Adelaide followed up with demands for the quietness we all so dearly longed for.

Hoping that there was a medical solution to the problem, I called in the doctor, but he could find nothing wrong, and concluded it was just a phase she was going through; all we needed was patience! So the verdict seemed to be that we would have to live with the problem until she grew out of it.

It was sometime later that the cause of all the trouble was revealed, and I got the complete picture of what was going on. Agnes had taken it upon herself to find the solution to the dilemma by frightening the "boldness" out of the child.

This she did by telling her that there was a bogey man living nearby, who had heard how bad a child she was. This old man had a sack on his back, and collected bold little girls in it, and took them away at night. They never came home again to their Mammas and Daddas, and no one could save them.

Rosemarie listened avidly, as Agnes delivered these terrifying tales. In the daytime, she behaved much as usual, although subdued, but at night time she seemed to shrink with fear. She would lie very still when put into her cot, the teddy pressed to her breast, a listening look on her face.

We thought she was outgrowing the tantrum stage and were grateful for the respite. Adelaide's nightly grumbles also stopped, and we had comparative peace.

Agnes hummed tunelessly as she worked, and her long face wore a smug smile. In the bathroom, order was restored, as stories of wicked old men, devils and demons, were unfolded during the hair-washing sessions.

But I grew anxious, as the pretty, pink-cheeked, child grew pale and listless, and terrified when it came to bedtime. We had another battle in the kitchen, and Rosemarie had to be carried to bed kicking and screaming. She was no sooner in the cot when she was up, and down the stairs after us. This went on until someone sat in the room with her, and she fell into an exhausted sleep.

I was in a worse predicament now; she had a real aversion to Agnes and I could not discover why.

It was Ida who put me on to what was happening. She had been going up to her flat one evening, and on passing our bedroom door, the threatening tones of Agnes's voice, arrested her attention.

"Go to sleep now. Remember the black demon is waiting outside the window. If you make a sound, he'll hear you and just break in, and nothing will save you."

Ida crept to the partially open door and peered in. Agnes was bending over the child, who was lying in her cot, rigid with fear. Ida was about to intervene, when a shriek from above had her rushing up to their flat, where she found Adelaide had scalded her hand with the electric kettle. She was not badly hurt, but it took some time to dress the burn and calm her down.

Meantime, Agnes sat in the bedroom with Rosemarie until she thought the child was asleep, but when she attempted to go downstairs, the child began to scream when she found herself alone. In a flash she was out of her cot and her shouts for "Mamma, Mamma," brought me flying up the stairs, followed by the Captain who was crossing the hall. Half-heartedly, Agnes lagged behind him.

It took a great deal of persuasion to calm Rosemarie this time, and I was very worried by the way she clung to me, sobbing and shaking. Again, the Captain came to the rescue. He carried her down to the kitchen where he distracted her with funny stories, about a marmalade cat called FiFi, he once knew on a ship .When Edward came in, he found them both fast asleep in the old rocking chair in the living room.

Meantime, Agnes re-emerged from her room to inform me that she could no longer stay in my employ, as the child was too difficult to manage, and she herself was suffering badly with her nerves.

This information was very welcome to me, as I had been toying with the idea of giving her notice myself. I was fed up of her moroseness and perpetual complaints about sitting with Rosemarie, until the frightened child was asleep.

It was not the sort of job she was used to, she added with a superior sniff, which begged the question from me:

"What kind of job were you used to?"

She eyed me coldly, "With ladies, Mrs. Davis, not jump-ups who were never used to domestic helpers."

"Oh, then you'd best be off to one of these ladies," I answered, "because I'm giving you immediate notice now," and I gave her a stiff lecture on her treatment of Rosemarie, for I had gathered a lot of data from Ida, and was beginning to understand the cause of my child's problems.

But Agnes suddenly dropped her cavalier manner, and begged to be allowed to work the week out, pleading she had nowhere to go. Very reluctantly, I agreed, a decision I was bitterly to regret, but I made it a condition that she would have no communication with the child whatsoever, and to this she agreed.

Edward then took over the task of getting his daughter to sleep with singing and stories. When she seemed to be asleep at last, he took up a solitary vigil just inside the bedroom door; the landing light enabling him to read bits of his newspaper as he waited hopefully. If he mistook her quietness for sleep, and moved accordingly, a creek on the stairs would alert her, and it would be "Dadda, Dadda come back," and the whole lengthy business, beginning with song or story, would have to be repeated again. One night the whole thing came to a climax. I had put her to bed and left the bedroom and kitchen doors wide open, so that she could be reassured by hearing us talking and moving about.

The nightlight was burning and I had read her favourite fairy story; at last, I thought she was sleeping peacefully, and I stole softly downstairs. There was complete quiet for a while, and then we heard an occasional whimper.

"Leave her for the moment, and she'll drop off again," advised Edward, as we sat down to a belated meal of grilled rashers and tomatoes. Feeling weary and hungry, I readily agreed, and we thought we had won the day, when a terrified scream came from above. The cup danced in my hands, as we dashed for the stairs.

We pushed in the bedroom door, and I stopped dead. An eerie sensation ran through me, as my shocked eyes fell on the crouching form bending over the cot.

The strange figure wore a tattered black overcoat, a battered hat hid the face, and on its back hung the bulk of a big sack. A piece of scraggy fur was wound around the mouth, and from its depths a voice growled:

"I've come to take you away. You've had too many chances. I'm the demon bogey man, and I've been watching you for a long time. Oh....Oh....Oh!" and too long arms were spread out as if to catch the child.

Neither of them noticed us, mesmerised there in the doorway. Suddenly, Rosemarie jumped up in the cot and with dilated eyes, screamed:

"Mamma! Dadda! save me, save me."

That broke the spell. Edward pushed past me and grabbed the child from the cot. Surprised, the figure fell back, and I still did not recognise who it was in the shadowy light. Then the hat slipped off, and I saw the gaunt face of Agnes. She turned and gave me such a look of hatred, as she rushed from the room, that I would have fallen had I not the support of a chair beside me.

I was roused from my fright by Edward's voice, crooning soothingly to the child, as he took her down to the kitchen.

As I left the room, I was startled to see Agnes standing motionless at the far side of the landing. With an effort, I said with loud authority:

"You'll leave this house first thing in the morning. If I find you here when I come down after nine o'clock, I shall hand you over to the police. And don't you dare ask me for a reference."

I was shivering as I ran recklessly down the stairs after Edward. We stoked up the fire and gave Rosemarie, who was trembling violently and drenched in sweat, a warm mustard bath. All the while we spoke to her in gentle matter-of–fact tones, and by the time she was clad in a fresh nightdress and blanket, she was a lot calmer, only the fitful sob proclaimed her ordeal.

After a mug of hot milk, laced with a shot of whiskey, Edward went through a soothing repertoire of her best loved songs as he rocked her to sleep.

The next morning I was relieved to find that Agnes had gone, and that was the last I ever saw of her. Secure now in the knowledge that she would never again be around in her little world, Rosemarie made a good recovery from her unhappy experience.

Ida came down to apologise for Adelaide's many complaints and took the child in hand, as she loved children and had spent her working life caring for them. Rosemarie joyfully responded to the teaching of simple arts and crafts, and was soon absorbed in making plastercine figures, knitting jumpers for teddy, stringing bead necklaces, painting pictures, furniture –making with matchboxes for a cardboard dolls house, and scrap collecting for sticking in special books.

She grew vey attached to Ida, and it was a moving sight to see the gracious, white-haired lady and the excited child (complete with teddy in a new striped coat and scarf) setting out hand in hand for a ramble around St. Stephen's Green or Herbert Park.

Funnily enough, it was dear Edward who solved the hair-washing quandary. A new catchy song about blowing bubbles broke on to the musical scene, and Edward and daughter would sing it together. Capitalizing on the implication, Edward bought a bubble pipe in Woolworths; he showed her how to use it in the bath when her hair was covered in soapy shampoo....this being the very best time to get the biggest bubbles, Edward assured her, and she took his word for it with no reservations. Now she thought she would never reach the hair-washing stage quickly enough and, suddenly and simply, our problem was solved.

All this is not to say there was a dramatic and lasting change in her exuberant and bossy little character; strong-willed, imaginative and full of energy, I had many a run-in with her, as she fought hard to get her own way whenever she saw a chance of doing so.

Chapter 40

Ida and I were in the kitchen making marmalade. We chatted companionably, as I weighed pounds of Seville oranges, which Aunt Cissy had got in Moore Street.

Ida was putting the sterilised jars in the oven to keep warm when she began talking about her family.

"I worry about Adelaide," she said reflectively. "She misses the family home a great deal, and is always fretting for the old days and a completely different way of life."

"I'm sure she'll settle in eventually," I said briskly, but Ida did not seem to hear. She picked up a tea towel and wiped her hands absently.

"She was the most sensitive of the three of us. Probably it all started when she fell off her pony and broke her leg."

"Poor child," I sympathized, trying to visualise the formidable Adelaide as a vulnerable small girl.

"She was always very conscious of her disability," went on Ida sadly, as she chopped the oranges into the preserving pan and I measured out the sugar.

"Of course, that ugly boot didn't help, especially at balls and parties. She used always wear long dresses to cover it. On one occasion she was coming into the ballroom at home; it was a grand affair, my twenty first birthday party, and somehow, her flimsy dressed got tangled in the boot and she fell awkwardly. One or two girls laughed when they saw she wasn't hurt, and I'm sure they didn't mean it unkindly, but Adelaide was always one to take offence easily at the best of times, and she limped from the room with a face like thunder. I ran after her with the two girls, who were deeply upset themselves at the unexpected turn of events, and were loud in their apologies, but she went into her room and locked the door against us, and no amount of persuasion would bring her back to the party. Of course, it cast a cloud over the celebrations...." Ida paused, staring pensively at the rain beating on the window pane, and the hurt of that long past incident was fresh on her face.

"It would have been the last party for her; she never went again."

There was silence, broken only by Rosemarie's coloured pencils scratching at the table, where she was busily engrossed "making pitches."

"I can't get it right," she wailed in exasperation.

Ida put down the jar she was labelling and went to help her.

"What's that?" she asked the child, pointing to a black splodge on the paper.

Rosemarie gave her a pitying look. "A fly," came the impatient answer, "but I want to make him a bee."

"You can't do that," said Ida reasonably. "A bee is a different insect."

"Oh no it isn't," contradicted our budding entomologist. "A bee is a fly in a fur coat."

It took a lot of explaining on Ida's part to persuade her pupil of the error of this logic, and she remained unconvinced, until Edward confirmed that indeed, two insects were involved in the argument.

Peace restored, Ida and me went back to our marmalade, the lovely tangy smell of which permeated the kitchen. Ida took up her stand by the big saucepan, stirring the bright sticky mass, while I set about cleaning-up operations.

After a while, Ida continued reminiscing, as if she had never been interrupted. "When she was thirty-six, Adelaide met Stephen Laurence at a Church social, and they fell in love. At first, Adelaide would not believe that Stephen was serious about her, on account of her lame leg, you understand.

But Stephen never seemed to notice it....he was always so gentle and patient with her. He had a difficult time convincing her that it didn't matter, and that he would love her just as much if she had only one leg."

Ida's voice faded; she was lost in the past and only her hand moved automatically over the steaming saucepan.

"Adelaide blossomed under his affectionate care, and they got engaged. She even looked different....sort of misty and soft."

"What happened?" I asked, sympathy in my heart, for I sensed a calamity.

"He was killed in the war....just before the armistice."

"Oh how awful," I exclaimed, painfully aware of the inadequacy of the words.

"I'll never forget the day the telegram came from the war office. There was no one at home, except Adelaide....no one else to take it and soften the blow." Ida drew a trembling hand across her tearful eyes as she spoke.

"She was never the same after that. She was ill for months, and over the years she grew a little strange in herself. Sometimes, I'd hear her at night talking, as if someone was with her. She'd wander about the garden at all hours of the night, and her interest became solely centred on her dolls. That's when she began collecting them seriously. There was only my unmarried brother, Thomas, at home, with our elderly Nanny, and a couple of old servants. So I gave up my job at a girl's boarding school, to stay at home with Adelaide."

"Did you find that very hard to do?" I questioned curiously.

"Oh yes indeed, I simply loved the school life; I had so many friends among the girls and staff," she replied earnestly, and I could guess at the wrench that that decision had cost her.

She gazed unseeingly into the saucepan and continued: "It was very difficult to help Adelaide. She was fiercely independent, and when I offered to go out with her, because she never went anywhere, she was very resentful, and accused me of prying and interfering. In the end, I got a job in a local kindergarten, where I was home early and able to keep an eye on her. Adelaide and I had been inseparable as children....there was only us two girls and Tom....and he worked in London and only came down at weekends. But she grew away from me; sometimes she wouldn't speak to me over nothing at all."

She looked at me with bewildered eyes, as if I could throw some light on the mystery, or apportion blame where it was not justified.

"She hated me having a job," Ida took up her story again. "Vulgar, she called it. No lady in the family had ever worked before; it would have to be me, acting like a skivvy for other people's children. But I didn't give up my job," she said with spirit. "I love children; I understand them and I could give them time. Lots of those children were from big families and got no individual attention."

I understood what she meant and thinking of Rosemarie, I said sincerely. "You have a wonderful way with children, Ida, and it would have been a terrible loss if you hadn't kept up working with them."

She looked grateful for my assurance, and I waited with interest for more of her story.

"Anyway, things went on uneventfully for years," she continued, Tom never married. He had a drink problem and was feckless with money. He surrounded himself with a hard-drinking, dare-devil crowd that he considered his friends.

He gambled recklessly and some nights he never came home at all. The estate became run down and neglected; there was no money to pay his debts or keep the place in repair. When I remonstrated with him he became violent, and I was afraid of him. Adelaide hated him; she thought he was making a show of the family, dragging a noble name through the dirt, and for that she wouldn't forgive him. The rows between them were terrifying; she had absolutely no fear of him. Once at dinner she alluded to his "contemptible" friends, and he responded by making jeering remarks about her lame leg.

Instantly, she jumped up and threw the carving knife at him. Thank heaven she missed him, but only by inches. I had to scream for the servants to come and separate them. After that he avoided her, and never sat at table with either of us again."

There was a sob in her voice and I busied myself making a cup of tea to give her time to recover. Slowly she sipped her tea while still stirring the marmalade and resumed her sad story: "Worse was to follow. One winter night, Tom was found stabbed to death on a lonely country road, near our home. There was a lot of dreadful publicity, but no one was ever got for the murder. We drank our tea in silence; Ida struggling with her memories, and my heart aching with compassion for her.

"After Tom's death, the house and estate had to be sold. The place was heavily in debt, and those to whom Tom had lent money simply melted away.

There was nothing but a small annuity, which mother had left to Adelaide and me."

"So you lost your home and everything?" I prompted, reluctantly getting up to test the marmalade.

"Yes," she answered with a sigh. "We saw your advertisement in the evening paper and you were kind enough to take us in. Our needs are simple now, so we can get by alright."

She smiled more easily, as if a weight had been lifted from her heart, and turned her attention to the syrupy blob on the saucer. "I think that's about ready," she said briskly, dipping a spoon in the marmalade and watching it wrinkle to the correct setting point.

"You're right," I agreed, sampling our product with a nod of approval.

Not to be outdone, Rosemarie rushed over for her share, and pronounced it the "best yellow soup" she had ever tasted.

Ida put a couple of jars in a basket for Adelaide and herself, but I noticed she seemed ill at ease and reluctant to go.

There was fear in her voice as at last she plucked up the courage to whisper:

"You won't let Adelaide know that I told you about the family; she'd be wild if she knew I said a word. She'd say I betrayed the family and I'd never hear the end of it." She broke off, unable to go on.

Impulsively, I gave her a hug. "You know I'd never mention it to a soul, Ida. Don't you ever worry about that....ever!"

Chapter 41

A few days later I went up to the ladies' flat with a box of groceries and the rent book. Ida and Rosemarie had ambled off to the Green with a bag of stale bread for the ducks. I knocked on the door and it gave under my hand, but there was no reply. Adelaide had informed me that when they were not in, she always kept the door locked, hinting darkly that "there are those going about who would think nothing of spying on people's privacy, and even rooting through their belongings." Scarlet with rage, I had tartly informed her, that no one of that nature resided in my house, and if she feared she was living among robbers, perhaps she would be happier elsewhere. "Naturally as landlady, I have a duplicate key...." I finished coldly.

"I'm aware of that, Mrs. Davis," she replied icily, "and I was not referring to you..."

"Well thank you for that...." I interrupted, but she ignored me and continued: "There are others in and out of this house.... naturally with strangers you cannot be sure of their contacts."

Grudgingly, I had to concede the point. I was only too well aware of the many flamboyant characters calling on Alan Floy at all hours, but as they made no undue noise, I had avoided a confrontation with him. I guessed she was hitting at Floy's liberated habits. It was not easy to keep track of him, as he came in late and spent the weekends elsewhere, leaving his rent on the hall table with his rent book, which I marked, and he picked up on his return.

Now I knocked more loudly on the ladies' door, but there was no sound from within. Rustling the rent book idly in my hand, I was undecided what to do. Then, conscious of the weight of the box of groceries under my arm, I concluded that, as the door was unlocked, there could be no harm in placing it, and the book, on the table. I swung the door fully back, and stood spellbound on the threshold. The day had turned dark and windy, and rain was trickling against the window; the room was shadowy, and fitfully lit by a glowing fire, but it was the table in the centre of the room that held my attention. It was beautifully laid with exquisite china, and silver baskets of sandwiches and cakes.I felt a chill creep over me, for seated at each place setting was a doll.

In front of me sat the swarthy doll; its head twisted, so that it appeared to be watching me over its shoulder. I stared into its black beady eyes, which in the dim light, seemed to emit a look of brooding malevolence. The open mouth, with its band of pointed teeth, began to waver from its fixed smile into the same leer I had noticed before.

Sweat prickled the back of my neck. I turned abruptly and there was Adelaide, standing on the landing watching me, motionless.

"What are you doing here?" she hissed. "You were not invited to the party."

"I'm sorry," I stuttered hoarsely, trying to keep my voice steady. "I only came up to leave your groceries and the rent book," and I held them out to her.

She snatched them in her black-gloved hands, and clumped heavily past me to the open door, where she glanced around anxiously at all the dolls.

She turned to me, a forbidding figure in black, iron grey hair pulled into a knot at the back of her head, sombre eyes boring into mine. Her voice came low and threatening.

"Reza will tell me if you come in here spying when I am out, remember that. Beware of upsetting her; I'm warning you, be very careful." She pointed to the ugly doll, whose glassy eyes seemed to smoulder in watchful alertness.

Finding the atmosphere overpowering, I stumbled to the top of the stairs, and grasping the banisters, made my way quickly to the kitchen.

For some moments I stood by the fire, trying to control my trembling; the dolls glaring eyes were all around me, and Adelaide's threats rang menacingly in my ears.

As I began to calm down in my familiar surroundings, I gave a shaky laugh.

What kind of a fool was I anyway, afraid of an inanimate doll?

A picture of Adelaide glaring at me darted through my mind, and my immediate reaction was to dash back up the stairs and give her notice, but the thought of facing her cold fury alone, and all those watchful dolls, filled me with an irrational fear. I bolstered up my sagging courage by assuring myself that Adelaide was doing no harm, and upsetting no one else in the house.

And what about gentle Ida, who had done so much for Rosemarie? If Adelaide went, she would have to go too, and arriving at that conclusion, I dropped the idea. Ida had been through enough; it would be a strange repayment for her goodness, if I was to deprive her of her home, just because her sister liked playing with dolls.

Feeling somewhat better, I put the kettle on in readiness for our usual cup of tea, when Ida returned with Rosemarie after their daily airing in the Green.

The kettle was boiling, and the hot scones set on the tray when Ida and the child came in, rosy-cheeked from the cold. Rosemarie was full of indignation; it transpired that one of the larger geese had flown out of the pond, and unceremoniously snatched the bread from her hand, nipping her fingers in the process.

"Rude, rude, Mamma, hobble rude," she squealed in outrage, before turning her attention to the buttery scones and hot milk I set in front of her.

Ida was rather quiet, as she accepted her tea absently, and I wondered if her mind was on the party in the flat. Discretely I edged around it.

"That's a beautiful collection of dolls your sister has," Ida looked startled.

"Yes indeed, but she had a lot more of them," she replied.

"Really?" I prompted, "What happened to them?"

"They got destroyed in a fire," she replied, and I knew she was wrestling with a very unhappy memory.

"Oh what a pity!" I exclaimed, as rows of staring dolls dissolving into ashes, flashed before my fevered imagination.

"It happened after Stephen died," Ida said, "Adelaide used to get up in the middle of the night....she'd say she could hear the dolls calling her and would have to go down to see what they wanted." She stopped and took a long sip of tea, and I thought she was not going to say anymore. I gave the fire a sharp poke, scattering the embers and the sound reawakened her memories.

"She had two collections of dolls," Ida went on, staring at a sudden burst of flame exploding in a shower of sparks. "One was housed in her bedroom and the other downstairs in the old playroom. This particular night she went down, carrying a lighted candle instead of the usual lamp. The dolls were arranged in a shelved alcove, covered by a heavy curtain, and as Adelaide leaned forward to look at them, the soft plush material caught fire. The dolls were reduced to rubble and the room badly damaged."

"And Adelaide?" I asked anxiously.

"Adelaide was severely burned trying to save them. Did you ever see her hands?"

I shook my head; I had only seen her ever wearing black gloves.

"....terribly scarred....she always keeps them covered...." Ida was almost talking to herself.

I tried to change the subject. "That gypsy doll seems to be her favourite," I ventured cautiously. As I spoke Ida gave an audible shudder, and the cup rattled in her hand.

"I hate it; I loathe that doll," she cried with a vehemence I would not have thought her capable of. "I hate it," she repeated, "that thing's evil."

"Why do you say that, Ida?" my heart had quickened its beat, but I tried to think rationally.

She threw a warning look at Rosemarie, but for once, the child was busily absorbed arranging a new box of furniture in her doll's house. Keeping her voice low, Ida continued her story.

"Adelaide was only four or five years old when this old gypsy woman called to our house. Mother was gardening at the time, and Adelaide was playing beside her when the gypsy made the usual demands, and pulled out of her basket yards of lace for mother's inspection. She had an old pram with her, and amongst clothes and ribbons and bits of flashy jewellery, sat that dark, ugly doll. Adelaide was instantly drawn to it, and went straight over to the pram and lifted the doll out, cooing and fussing over it.

Mother ordered her to put it back, but Adelaide started to cry, imploring the gypsy to allow her to have it. The gypsy was willing at a price, but mother, obviously disliking the doll, would not hear of it. In the end, the gypsy ignored my mother and made a present of the doll to Adelaide. Mother, unable to dissuade Adelaide, made the best of the situation and gave the gypsy some money, which she emphasised, she would have given her anyway. In due course, mother hoped that she would tire of the doll, but this never happened; if possible she grew more attached to it and took it everywhere with her."

"It's a strange story," I commented, but why on earth did your sister take such a fancy to that doll; you'd think a child would be frightened of it?"

"Yes, I agree with you there," Ida responded. "That thing gives me the creeps. We had a lot of misfortune down the years after it came into the house, starting with the death of my mother. She could not bear to be in the same room with it. One night not long after, she was coming down the stairs to dinner when she fell badly. By the time the doctor arrived she was dead....a heart attack, he said, but she was only a young woman of thirty-six, who had never been sick in her life. She hesitated and gave me a questioning look. "I could tell you about a strange experience I had, but perhaps you think I'm talking rubbish."

I hastily told her that I thought no such thing and begged her to go on.

Satisfied, she began: "One evening when I was seventeen, I went to a local ball. It was very late when I got home afterwards. The father of a friend had arranged to bring me home, and this he did, dropping me off at our avenue gates. He asked if I would like him to accompany me to the hall door, but he had a carriage full of other young people, so I said there was no need. I waved them on their way with much laughing and joking, and walked slowly up to the house. My mind was on the enjoyable evening I'd had, and I hummed one of the tunes I'd danced to. The night was still and heavy with the scent of the red currant; the trees tall aloof sentinels on either side of my path. I came on to the lawn bordered by flowering shrubs, beyond which the river glittered like a white ribbon in the moonlight.

There was a faint rustling sound, like a withered leaf seized in a sudden breeze; I felt uneasy and quickened my steps. As I hastened on, my eyes fell to the wooden seat on the far side of the river bank. But the seat wasn't empty; Adelaide's gypsy doll was sitting upright on it, gazing straight at me with that evil sort of smile. I stopped in surprise, wondering how the doll had come to be left out....Adelaide was always so careful of it. I must tell her about it when I got in, for nothing would induce me to go next nor near it.

I moved on, still watching the doll; it seemed to shimmer in the mist coming up from the river, and then it started to move! Slowly it got down from the seat and began to glide towards me over the still water. Petrified with fear, I couldn't move, couldn't scream....the doll was gaining....only a few yards from me....it's mouth trembling in such a horrible expression...."

Here she stopped at the fearful recollection. I refilled her cup, my mind grappling at the weird story. After a few sips of the comforting tea, she went on:

"Suddenly I felt the power returning to my legs, and grabbing my long skirt, I bolted for the hall door. When I reached it, I had to search for the key, terrified at what might be behind me. But I couldn't find the key, and overcome with fright and panic, I kicked and hammered at the door, screaming for help. After an age, Nanny opened the door; the candle in her hand shaking, as she was greatly alarmed by the noise.

I was soaked in sweat and it took me some time to regain some vestige of composure. Adelaide, awoken by the commotion, appeared on the stairs complaining about the uproar. I ran over to her and told her the doll was behind me in the garden...."

"Yes," she answered, with the sort of superior look she wore when speaking of her dolls. "You must have seen Reza; she likes to walk in the garden at night."

Then she turned and walked laboriously up the stairs, calling: "I'll just go up and see if she's come in."

I was having a glass of hot brandy with Nanny when Adelaide returned. She sat down opposite me, an old black coat pulled over her nightdress.

"Reza has returned alright," she told me, "except that her dress is wet....it's very damp by the river to-night. I brought it down for you to air in the kitchen, Nanny," and she drew the doll's flowered skirt and blouse from the pocket of her coat.

Ida, her eyes staring blindly, was silent. I busied myself putting coal on the fire and washing up the tea things. I wondered if I should make any reference to the bizarre tea-party going on in their flat.

Ida roused herself and said with a worried frown; "I get so anxious about her, Lynette; she lives in a world of extended childhood. Those dolls are the only reality to her; she cares for them like children. To-day she is giving them a party ...." She buried her face in her hands, and I rushed over to her.

"You mustn't worry so much, Ida dear. She's not doing anyone any harm, and if she finds the dolls a comfort, let her have them."

She raised her head and wiped her eyes with a wispy handkerchief, and I started laying the table for the evening meal.

"Anyway, I'm sure her collection of dolls will turn out to be an investment in the long run," I said briskly. "They must be very valuable indeed."

Ida nodded, glad to put the conversation on a more mundane level. Still with my mind on the dolls, a thought struck me. "I noticed all her dolls are female, Ida, except that sad little soldier one."

"Yes dear," she agreed, "that doll was in Stephen's pocket when he was killed by enemy gunfire just before the armistice in 1918."

I thought of the dark brown stain on the doll, and my heart lurched sickeningly.

"How dreadful," I shuddered.

"He bought that doll in France for her birthday. He wanted to give it to her himself, but as it happened, it came home in a sad little parcel with his few other personal effects. A soldier friend of his brought it to her with a torn fragment of a letter. Maybe, he shouldn't have given it to her...."

Chapter 42

The kitchen door was flung open with a flourish, and Myrabelle skipped in, all twirling skirt and silken legs.

"Darling Lynny," she gushed, pecking my cheek in a friendly kiss, and flinging several parcels on a nearby chair.

"Oh it's lovely to see you, Myrabelle. How are you keeping?"

"Just about surviving," laughed the fair one airily, scooping Rosemarie up in her arms and kissing her soundly.

"The darling child!" she exclaimed. "How she grows! Now what has Aunty Myrabelle for a good little girl?"

The child danced around her, all expectant delight, as Myrabelle took a picture book and a box of paints from her bag.

"Lovely!" chortled the daughter in an ecstasy of happiness.

"A kiss so for your old aunt," demanded the charming Myrabelle. Rosemary hugged her enthusiastically, oblivious of the expensive dress and priceless pearls. Alarmed, I called her off.

"Not to worry," Myrabelle laughed indifferently. "You were always a fuss pot, Lynny. There's plenty more glad rags where they came from."

Edward, just in from work, had witnessed the cheery scene with amusement.

"Have you one for me too, Myrabelle," he joked, putting his arms around her.

Myrabelle responded with a wink at me. "Come on Mr. Davis," she stage-whispered, "quick, while she's not looking," and a laughing peck was exchanged.

I started to get the tea, as we all joked and chatted light heartedly.

Then Myrabelle pointed carelessly at a large Bewley's cake box.

"I timed it well darlings," she drawled, "open that for the tea."

Protesting feebly, I opened the box to expose a gorgeous Austrian Chocolate Torte.

"Yum! Yum!," screamed Rosemarie, making a rush for the table.

I felt happy to see Myrabelle in such good humour. She flirted a little with Edward, played with Rosemarie and insisted on doing the wash-up....to keep her hand in, she said, as the "general" would never let her do it in her own kitchen.

The jibes and barbs she had often given me in the early days of our acquaintance, were a thing of the past. She was full of life and gaiety, and yet inexplicably, I felt a flutter of unease; was there a core of unhappiness at the heart of it all?"Penny for them, Lynny?" her laughing voice roused me from my reverie, as she waved a plate she was drying, dangerously in the air. "You need cheering up, my girl," she grinned. I rescued the plate.

"And how do you suggest I get cheered up?" I asked a little despondently.

"That's an easy one," laughed my bubbly friend. "You have the house organised in great style now. Let's have a party....a house warming party."

Speechless, I stared at her, and Edward said: "I don't know how you'd organise a party in this place....and we have no help either....we felt we needed a little time to recover our sanity, before we chanced another foray on the domestic servant frontier."

"Leave all that to me," said Myrabelle grandly, "We really must celebrate your success with the house."

"It would be expensive," I demurred, thinking of our overdraft.

"Nonsense," laughed the irrepressible one, "It can be done and I'll help out, of course." She held up a commanding hand like a warrior, as I attempted a protest. "It's a great idea and you two need a bit of fun," she insisted beguilingly.

I knew it was less than useless to argue with Myrabelle in full flight. She was already turning over ideas for the party.

"A dance," she decided. "We must have a dance."

"We can't," I managed to get in. "The floor wouldn't stand all that jumping and thumping."

"That's quite a way to describe our potential dancers," she laughed mockingly, "but I see what you mean....coming through the ceiling is not part of the entertainment."

An idea hit her and she grabbed my arm excitedly. "The basement!" she shrieked: "The glorious old basement!"

"You can't have a party in a basement," I scoffed.

Myrabelle ignored me as she strode to the door. "All roads to the basement," she commanded.

Rosemarie leapt up and caught her hand, and we all trooped down the dark wooden stairs, to gauge the possibilities offered by the original kitchen.

It was a very large room with white-washed walls and a stone flagged floor. Two small windows with iron bars looked out on an area several feet below street level. A few broken packing cases leaned dejectedly against an ancient range, which filled an entire wall. Otherwise the room was empty. Edward and I had some ideas for using it, but had never got around to putting any one of them into operation. "That range," groaned Myrabelle. "Something must be done about it." She thought for a moment. "I have it. You could knock a mural out of that fellow, Floy, to drape over it."

"Oh I couldn't," I muttered without conviction, knowing I would have to try if Myrabelle considered it necessary.

"Of course you could," Myrabelle said complacently. "Can't you tell him you want to exhibit it."

But I couldn't," I began again.

"Don't keep saying you couldn't," said Myrabelle impatiently. "You sound like a song caught in the groove of a record. Anyway, Floy will be thrilled to have it on exhibition here....well, sort of exhibition," she amended, as she caught my cynical eye. "It's just great," she enthused, her eyes darting about, "all it needs is a good sweep."

"It's spacious enough," Edward conceded, catching her excitement. "I think we could manage it alright."

Myrabelle went on planning. "This place will do for the dancing....nothing to smash or damage. We can lay a buffet supper in the drawing room. I'll send "the general" with a couple of the maids to organise things. They are doing it all the time for me, so you won't have to worry about a thing."

Myrabelle gave a few dancing steps and was immediately joined by Rosemarie, whose own efforts were wildly enthusiastic.

"I don't know, I haven't danced for years," I told the dance addicts doubtfully.

Edward took my hand and broke into a smart foxtrot, "Of course you can. There! Look at that," and where he danced, I dashed, and with a final twirl, he steadied me on my feet, while observing that I wasn't all that bad and "only needed to polish it up a bit."

"But there are other dances," I wailed, "I can't do the Charleston."

"You can learn, can't you?" said Myrabelle firmly. "Edward can teach you," and as there was no suitable response from that quarter, she went on recklessly. "Sure I'll teach you myself."

I was not convinced that either of them would succeed in making a dancer out of me, but I said no more; if Myrabelle wanted me to dance then however it was accomplished, dance I would.

Undaunted, she went on with her plans, and her enthusiasm and generosity were so infectious that despite my misgivings, I was caught in the elation she generated.

In a last perverse effort to dampen the proceedings, I came up with the oldest cliché of all: "But I haven't a thing to wear."

Myrabelle stopped in mid-sentence and spoke patiently, as if to a downcast child.

"Oh Lynny darling, that isn't an excuse at all. I have loads of dresses and you can take your pick of the lot of them. Yes, I know I'm taller, but your Aunt Cissy is quite capable of shortening one for you. We'll see you're not hanging in rags, my love," Edward grinned, and I knew the battle was lost.

Edward was teasing Myrabelle. "Any old trousers in your cupboard for me?"

Myrabelle pretended to think. "Only a pair of pink satin cami-knickers," she chuckled. "But I'm sure the "general" would spare you a pair of her old flannelette bloomers."

We all went into fits of laughter, and Rosemarie, feeling that she was being overlooked, screamed imperiously; "I want a new dress too, Mamma."

Having agreed to the child's satisfaction of the style and colour of her first party frock, we went on to discuss the appropriate drinks, sandwiches, cakes trifles, and other specialities, which would make a gourmet feast on a couple of large tables, fitted together under a mammoth white cloth.

Humming gaily, Myrabelle turned over various schemes for the entertainment of our guests. Most were outrageous but some might just work.

"That old Captain of yours must come," said Myrabelle, when we reached the stage of selecting the guest list.

"I didn't know he was a friend of yours," Edward chipped in with a wink.

"He's not really," she smiled "but he happened to let me in this evening, and I thought him a charming old boy. I suppose you'll have your ladies?" she inquired saucily of Edward.

"I don't know," I said hesitantly, as a picture of Adelaide swam before me....tall and gaunt, with disapproval of such frivolity in ever line of her pale face and pursed lips.

"Of course, she'll have to be asked," I went on, hoping thereby to forestall her complaints about the inevitable noise.

Myrabelle rattled off a barrage of people she would bring along, most of whom I had never heard of. Edward contributed a few of his colleagues from work, and members of his family. I had only one relative, dear Aunt Cissy, and there was Ida, if she would come.

Myrabelle was looking reflective, and I wondered uneasily what else she was about to suggest. "That creature Floy, will turn up whether you ask him or not; he goes to every do in Dublin that he gets wind of. He's just accepted now as an odd bod; you can't have a party without him. Indeed, you have a lot to learn about society, Lynny darling."

"We don't see much of him at all," Edward said, "but Miss Lister....the contrary one....collared me in the hall last night, and went into a long tirade about the late hours he keeps, and the noisy flappers he brings back to his rooms."

"Well I suppose you could object to the young women's nocturnal visits to your house, and of course, we can only speculate here on the goings on. He's an unpleasant character; keep an eye on him." Myrabelle warned.

"What do you mean," I asked, alarmed.

Myrabelle leaned against the window-sill and lit a cigarette. "Lots of Dublin landladies wouldn't allow him inside their doors," she said, blowing a ring of scented smoke in a halo around her.

"Why ever not?" I demanded uneasily.

"He has a peculiar tendency to leave in a hurry without paying his rent, not to mention enticing a little on the side from any resident females."

"Well he's always paid his rent alright, and there's no one here likely to get herself enticed," I said with relief.

"What about Adelaide Lister?"asked Edward innocently, the incongruous suggestion bringing much merriment.

"What's on the side, Mamma?" shrilled Rosemarie, who, unnoticed by us, was sitting on the floor listening intently.

There was a sudden silence, but Myrabelle rallied quickly.

"It just means having something nice for yourself, like that lovely teddy of yours," she said soothingly, as the child opened her mouth for a fuller explanation.

"Time for bed," I broke in, and I could see by her little disappointed face that she was wishing she had not drawn attention to herself.

Reluctantly, she got to her feet and we left the basement.

Edward went to the drawing room to examine a new gadget he had just purchased called a wireless, and Myrabelle and I headed to the bathroom with a loudly protesting child.

The house became a hive of industry, as the "general" and her minions, descended on it. They turned the place upside down, and I escaped to Aunt Cissy's with Rosemarie, for lunch and tea; with Edward following at the end of the day to take us home.

The "general's" standards were very high and her methods brooked no short cuts. I entered the house one afternoon, after a bout of shopping, to find that lady and one of her subordinates, at daggers drawn. The maid in question had been cleaning the bathroom, when she left a heavy jar of bath salts fall into the washbasin, cracking it badly. As I stood in the doorway, the "general" and maid were facing each other, and I could not get a word in between the cold logic of the one, and the roars of outraged innocence from the other. Eventually, the "general" spotted me during a pause in the battle.

"I'm sorry ma-am for the damage, but this person came to me with such good references; I think she must have written them herself."

"I niver writ dem letters," blustered the guilty one, but the "general" soon silenced her with accusations of other disasters carried out by her in Mrs Dobson's home, which were beyond denial and added up to imminent dismissal.

Furious at another expensive breakage, I rounded on the girl for her carelessness, but she brazenly continued to bluff her way out of the situation.

"It fell of it's own self, "she asserted. "Ya should'na had it there; it were bound to fall in the basin."

The "general" bristled to the attack. "None of your cheek, you," she said icily, drawing herself up to her full five feet.

The girl glared at her. "Anyways, I'm goin.' I'm not standin' here to be insulted. The ting were cracked and I couldna stop the dam jar fallin' in ta it," she shouted defiantly.

The "general" cut in sharply, "Good riddance," she, barked, "there's a bad egg in every dozen."

"Who ya callin'a bad egg ta, ya oul cogger? I'll get me mudder on ta ya."

The general was not intimidated, and for the first time ever allowed her fury full rein. "Get out of my sight, you hussy, before I take the brush to you," and seizing the potential weapon, which happened to be handy, swung the dusty bristles in the direction of the wayward domestic. The girl, surprised by the change in the "general's" usual dignified demeanour, leapt nimbly aside, and screaming abuse went running and tumbling down the stairs.

That left me with the job and expense of finding a plumber to fit a new basin. He duly arrived, puffing and wheezing, and while he hacked out the broken basin, I went down to pay the bread man. When I returned, I was mortified to find Rosemarie drawing the plumber's attention to the toilet bowl.

"That's Mamma's pot," she informed him gravely.

Chapter 43

Next day when I called on Aunt Cissy, I found her opening a dress box, which Myrabelle had sent over for me. I could choose any one I liked, the enclosed note informed me.

We had a great time going through the selection of six gorgeous dresses, and I danced and pirouetted gaily in each, while Aunt Cissy assessed them critically.

But each of us knew at once which was "the one" when she held out a beautiful gown in midnight blue silk, with a three flounce skirt and narrow shoulder straps, over a bodice of several diagonal insertions of matching lace.

"Oh!" I breathed reverently, as the garment fell in shimmering ripples around me. I surveyed myself disbelievingly in the mirror. "It must have cost the earth," I sighed.

"Actually, that's one I made for Myrabelle," Aunt Cissy remarked casually, busy at my feet with a mouthful of pins. "Myrabelle is taller than you; I think one flounce will have to come off."

I did not argue. Aunt Cissy knew her job, and after a quick cup of tea, I left her to get on with the alterations.

When I got home the Captain met me in the hall. He told me that Mrs. Dobson had called and left a message for me.

"What is it, Captain," I asked curiously, as I made for the kitchen to dump the heavy shopping bag.

"Well Mrs. Davis," began the Captain, struggling as usual to light his pipe. "She says you're not to forget to ask that Floy fella to do a picture thing to cover that range in the basement."

I felt a bit annoyed with Myrabelle. How could I ask Floy for one of his "masterpieces" to disguise the old range in the basement?

I thanked the Captain for taking the message, and spent the rest of the day churning over various approaches to the problem of the mural.

That evening, I heard Floy come in at about nine o'clock, and fearing he would be out again before I could catch him (or I lost my nerve) I went up and knocked on his door.

He opened it immediately, dressed in a flashy green dressing gown, lavishly spattered with writhing gold dragons. He must have been expecting someone more exotic, for he looked deflated at the sight of me.

"Ah, the charming landlady," he rallied. "What can I do for you, Mrs. Davis?"

Trying to bolster a confidence I did not feel, and praying for inspiration, I said: "We're having a housewarming party, Mr. Floy, and we'd like very much if you could come; you may bring a friend or two of course...." I added, as a further inducement.

He leaned nonchalantly against the door post, polishing his monocle and regarding me with a conspiratorial smile.

"I understand from Mrs. Dobson, that you are a very good artist, and I was wondering....I mean she was...." I stopped in total confusion.

He placed the monocle carefully into his eye after careful scrutiny, and I struggled on. "Could you let us have one of your pictures to exhibit at the party?"

"Of course, of course," he responded with alacrity. "Anything for Mrs. Dobson.... you too, of course, dear lady," he added as an after- thought. "Now where do you wish to hang it? I'm sure you know that light is a very important factor in the placing of a painting."

I didn't, but in the circumstances I was willing to learn. Maybe there was some special technique I could use to emphasise its artistic qualities, if any, while making full use of its camouflaging capacities.

I felt unable to furnish him with the exact details he seemed to expect, so compromised by saying I wanted a long picture to fit across one of the basement walls, where the dance was to be held. I reckoned his vanity would dictate the magnitude of the mural's proportions.

"A pleasure, dear lady," he fawned. "I'll look through my paintings, and I think you might be lucky," he promised modestly.

Over his shoulder, I saw a lace-trimmed tray in the middle of the table with two crystal glasses on it, and a decanter of whiskey. Light footsteps on the stairs heralded the appearance of a young girl with blackened eyelids, scarlet lips and a short, frothy yellow dress, under a swinging fur coat.

"Theodora, my darling," said Floy caressingly, my presence forgotten.

He held out his arms to her, but she ignored him and looked at me sourly with raised brows. Feeling very much out of place, I hurriedly thanked Floy for the promised painting, and made my escape. The girl's light lisping voice trailed after me; "Very much the efficient landlady, I hope, dearest one, or was she up for a teeny, weeny bit of hanky panky?"

I heard him laugh archly as the door banged, and hot with fury, I raced down the stairs.

Chapter 44

The day of the party dawned cold and windy, but all was festive and warm inside.

The basement was transformed with coloured fairy lights and paper chains. On the window ledge reposed a cluster of shiny green plants and assorted geraniums....all from Myrabelle's conservatory.

"They'll die there," I remarked when she stood back to admire the effect.

"Nonsense, you old fusspot," she laughed. "Those things are used to being shifted about and have seen at a lot of the best doos."

The "general" had nailed Floy's mural across the alcove containing the range, but it did not reach down far enough to obliterate it completely.

Myrabelle stared at it with narrowed eyes. "It's wrong," she said flatly, at which opinion the "general" nodded discreet assent.

I looked uncomprehendingly at the huge sheet of paper, generously daubed with thick splashes of violent red, orange, black and gold glitter. It was grandly described as "A Philosopher Muses At Evening."

"I couldn't agree more," I said, pleased to find that my opinion concurred with Myrabelle's, who understood art to a fair degree, against my dismal ignorance. "It certainly doesn't look like anything in particular; Rosemarie could have done as well, and I wouldn't be under a compliment to Floy for that piece of rubbish." I finished with the authority of a top drawer RHA.

Myrabelle gave me an amused smile. "It's not that sort of wrong. It's just wrongly placed."

"But it's a coloured mess...." I objected, visions of Vermeer, Raphael, Michael-Angelo, and the like, floating across my inner eye.

"It's not that bad, darling girl," she insisted. "It's a new art form called Impressionism."

"Well, I'm not impressed," I said disdainfully.

"You see it's meant to convey a mood...."she broke off at a gasp of disbelief from me.

"Ah well, its art and the likes of us don't question it," she said, giving up on my artistic education. "Anyway, the main thing is that it's a nice long piece of dramatic colour with a specific job to do," she rushed on, as I opened my mouth to argue. "But it must come down."

I shook my head hopelessly, whatever way the mural was placed could never improve its artistic pretensions, and I could make no sense of either Myrabelle or the "Philosopher." "You can't take it down," I told her, noticing several tears in the paper where the "general" had been less than careful. "It's nailed," I pointed out unnecessarily.

"It's got to be un-nailed then," said Myrabelle briskly going to the door and calling for the "general's" help.

The "general" appeared and they both set to work detaching the mural, which looked much worse after their efforts.

"I have an idea," said Myrabelle.

"I was afraid of that," I answered with a genuine tremor.

"You won't be so smart when you see the difference," Myrabelle grinned.

At her direction the mural was lowered to cover the unsightly range completely, and the shelf above it served to hold the top of the mural under a frill of red crepe paper weighed with a row of potted plants. The effect was striking and served as a distraction from what was lacking in the painting.

So long as one just admired it in their ignorance, and kept a respectful distance, the security of the "masterpiece" was tastefully assured.

The drawing room was resplendent with flowers and several magnificent antique lamps, donated by Myrabelle, of course.

"I hope you have them insured," I exclaimed in horror, as I watched her casually extracting them from a capacious shopping bag.

The huge table, made up of several from around the house, was covered with a huge damask banqueting cloth, and groaned under the weight of Shelly china, silver baskets of fruit, plates of assorted sandwiches, bowls of jelly and trifle, and culinary delicacies I didn't recognise. A rich cake and a few other commodities, which she deemed necessary to the well-being of the party, arrived a little later.

"Lord, Myrabelle!" I cried. "Talk of borrowed plumes! You might as well move in here yourself now. Even to the "general"....!"

I eyed that important personage appreciatively, as she bustled about in a white lace-trimmed apron, her massive bust straining against the confines of her black silk dress, which had obviously grown too tight for her.

Her staff of three....Ruth, Lilly and Maud, were also in conventional afternoon attire, their lesser status apparent in the narrow white bands bordering their foreheads. All stood in perfect docility behind the "general" ready to execute her slightest command, at the flick of a finger or rise of an eyebrow.

I hid a smile and went up to dress.

Chapter 45

"You look beautiful, sweet girl," said Edward admiringly, as I twirled provocatively in front of him in the lovely blue dress. Myrabelle had left her make-up bag on my dressing table, warning me not to come down without making use of it.

Daringly, I had applied a film of Icilma Vanishing Cream and a dust of Ponds Rachel face powder, a slick of a lipstick intriguingly called "Dark Mystery," and to finish the picture, a little black kohl pencil on the eyebrows.

I whirled again, just out of Edward's reach, and the flounces of my skirt swirled softly against my silk-stockinged legs. I felt glamorous and desirable, and Edward's eyes confirmed those feelings, as he held me close and nuzzled my neck. Just then Rosemarie dashed in and the romantic moment was rudely shattered.

"Look at me! Look at my new dress," she yelled, jumping about in her pink silk party dress, which was frilled to the waist. With the beloved teddy tucked under her arm, she took a hand of each of us and we all skipped happily down the stairs.

Myrabelle emerged from the living room, which had been turned into a ladies cloak room for the night. She looked superb in black velvet, with silky fringing rippling around the hemline. The top of the bodice shimmered with a diamonte trim, and tiny, shoelace straps, drew attention to her milk-white shoulders. A narrow diamond band encircled her fair bobbed head, and starry clusters glittered in her ears.

"You look lovely, Myrabelle," I told her, as we brushed each other's cheek in loving salute.

"You look pretty gorgeous yourself: Eh, Edward?"

"Devastating," agreed the husband, giving me a squeeze that left me breathless, and endangered the circlet of stars on my forehead. Impulsively, he gave Myrabelle a quick kiss.

"Easy boy," laughed our femme fatale, "if you don't want this face to leave it's mark on you," and she winked saucily at me.

Then the guests started to arrive. Most of them were friends of Myrabelle, but some I remembered, like the effervescent Marie Rose, who had not endeared herself to the Rathgar ladies.

Aunt Cissy arrived in a pretty mushroom pink dress, which took years off her age. With her was Edward's sister, Peggy, in a short pleated dress of yellow taffeta; her eyes sparkling as brightly as the new sapphire and diamond ring on her engagement finger. I knew she was doing a steady line with a young doctor, but not that the relationship had blossomed into an engagement. In no time, she was lost in a crowd of females wanting to wish her happiness and exclaim over the ring.

"Dan will be popping in later," she managed to whisper to me.

Rosemarie went off to find Ida, who made a shy entrance in a flowing old-fashioned dress of black satin, which did nothing for her sallow complexion. She had tried to brighten it up a bit with a narrow gold belt and a bunch of violets, but her winning touch was an exquisite necklace of glowing amethyst, which must have been a cherished heirloom. They worked like magic on every woman in the room, who reverently (and enviously) handled and fussed over them, so that Ida was never without an admiring little crowd all evening.

I saw the Captain in a corner seat; he was surrounded by a knot of giggling flappers, and I could hear his gruff tones whenever there was a lull in the babble of voices, disclaiming vigorously about his years on the high seas.

Adelaide kept to her flat all evening, although I had given her a special invitation in case she felt overlooked.

"She says one of the dolls isn't well and she must stay with it." Ida told me quietly when I got an opportunity of asking if her sister would be down. She looked at me meaningly, and I said no more.

The drawing room was a credit to all the efforts the "general" had lavished on it. The chandelier flashed in the soft glow of Myrabelle's strategically placed lamps, and the huge pier glass reflected the silks, satins and velvets of the guests.

As I stood alone for a moment by the oak cupboard, a sudden rush of deep affection for this gracious old house, assailed me, so that tears burned my eyes. How many families, long gone, had it lovingly sheltered in its two centuries of existence; how many parties like ours had it witnessed?

A light hand caught my arm. It was Myrabelle. "Wake up, Lynny darling, and meet my husband, Alex," and she ushered a tall, impeccably dressed man, with smooth black hair, into my presence.

Good looking, I thought, as he took my hand with formal friendliness, and I noted the classic profile and dashing moustache. His manner was affable and enigmatic, and he joined in the light-hearted conversation with a witty turn of phrase, revealing an unexpected puckish sense of humour.

After a short time, he excused himself to me, saying he was sorry to leave, but he had an urgent appointment. Myrabelle, who was standing nearby, flirting outrageously with a delighted dandy, turned instantly and said with cynical amusement: "Something awfully, awfully, darling?"

"Very awfully, awfully," Alex returned with a brilliant smile.

He turned to go, but was detained by a glamorous young thing, who was sparsely covered in a shimmering sheath of pink and green spangles. After giving her some flattering attention, he walked quickly down the stairs and out to his car.

Myrabelle returned to her dandy and was soon followed everywhere by a flock of male admirers, and for the remainder of the evening, she appeared the most vivacious and hilarious member of the party.

Chapter 46

The "general" and her entourage moved discreetly among the company with trays of sherry, whiskey and port, while Myrabelle's gilded punch bowl supplied the abstainers with a deliciously refreshing fruit cup.

The gramophone manned by Edward, kept up a flow of modern "hits" and many feet tapped in tune to the tantalising rhythms. Sometimes, he mischievously increased the tempo by shifting the indicator to an exhilarating seventy-eight, and the tapping feet, unable to keep up with "The Cuckoo's Gallop," lost control of the beat, and slithered to a halt amid shrieks of laughing confusion.

At a prearranged time the "general" made a majestic entrance with her three serfs, each carrying a silver teapot. They lined up behind the big table and at an eye signal from the "general," began filling cup after cup of Smith's best tea, to the relief and delight of the guests who were parading about with well filled plates.

I moved among the little throngs of guests to make sure no one was forgotten. At the end of the room, I came upon a bunch of middle-aged women who were intently following the movements of a lovely fair-haired girl, dressed in a red clinging dress and feathered boa.

One gimlet-eyed woman in grey lace, who reminded me of a spider in a web, was saying: "That's that Parker girl exhibiting herself again."

Her companion, whose skinny form was wrapped in yards of mustard georgette, answered sharply: "She got that dress in "Zelda's" Second Hand Boutique."

"How do you know?" asked gimlet eyes.

"It was mine," admitted the mustard lady after a pause.

The gimlet eyes widened. "Never," squealed she in horror. "You can't mean you traded it in?"

"Well yes," confessed the mustard one uncomfortably.

Another female, fat and be-spectacled in silver- spangled majenta, sniffed contemptuously. "There's one thing, Shelia girl, you never looked like that in it," she told her acidly.

With a wry smile, I was about to move on, when I felt a hand detaining me. It was Marie Rose, radiant in pink satin, and heavily made up with cupid-bow lips and richly blackened eyes. Shades of "Pola-Negri," I thought, as visions of that exotic vamp of the silver screen, floated across my mind.

Marie Rose, was sitting on the arm of the Captain's chair, one shapely leg crossed engagingly over the other.

"You're looking great," I greeted her, wondering how she was attuning to life with the staid-looking gentleman she had married six months ago.

"I'm feeling great too," she laughed.

"And James?" I ventured.

"Marvellous! He's still treating me like precious porcelain.... something in the old adage about an old man's darling rather than a young man's slave. I'm loving it, and I see that he does too," and her eyes twinkled happily as she exchanged a wave with her husband, who was talking to Edward by the gramophone.

The Captain was waving his brandy glass in one hand, while the other was gainfully employed around the waist of a fluffy redhead in a skimpy green dress, who was perched tipsily on his knee. He was fairly euphoric, and as I chatted with the girls, he broke into a comic song, which soon deadened the light tenor on the gramophone.

"Is it me faskinatin' smile,Or is it the dimples on me dial,Or is it me tiddly bits a lace,That seems to tickle their fancy."

This hilarity was accompanied with much squeezing of the redhead, who responded with screams of delight.

I went over to the table to top up my own plate, and a buxom woman, dignified of mien, sailed by. An important person, she had been introduced to me as the wife of a Government Minister. She was carefully selecting a savoury from a dish of vol-au-vents, but her regal appearance was somewhat diminished by the row of squashed marshmallows on the seat of her black velvet gown. I cringed guiltily, as I remembered spotting Rosemarie counting out a row of marshmallows on a chair....Myrabelle caught my arm. "Let's start the dance now, Lynny," she cried eagerly.

I agreed and asked her to announce it. This she did with her usual grace, adding that those who preferred a more decorous evening could stay where they were. "Only dancers will be safe in the basement," she warned.

There was much laughter and giggles, as a crowd of girls and fellas trooped after Myrabelle and Edward to the nether regions. I followed slowly, having told the "general" to keep a weather eye on the captain and give him no more drink.

"Don't you worry ma-am," she retorted grimly. "I'll see he behaves," and I believed her.

The basement twinkled in the glow of multi-coloured lamps and yards of gold and silver tinsel. An accordion player and his wife with violin, were supplying the music. Myrabelle had heard them playing together in Wicklow street, and considered them too good for merely busking, and had given them the job of performing at all her socials.

They were in the middle of a waltz from the "Merry Widow," when I entered, and couples were swaying dreamily to it.

Edward was looking for me, and seizing my arm, led me expertly among the dancers. To my relief, and disbelief, I found myself dancing easily and not kicking out in all directions as I had feared.

After the waltz came a foxtrot, the tempo growing faster. After one mad whirl, I saw the "general" beckoning to me from the door. With difficulty I made my way to her side.

"Mr. and Mrs. Devlin have just arrived, "she informed me in a stage whisper.

I nodded and followed her up to the drawing room, where little groups lazed and chatted, on chairs, and cushions on the floor.

The Captain snored blissfully in his favourite armchair in the corner, deserted by his sultry admirers. In the centre of the room, a tall military-looking man named Colonel Sydney Blacton, with stiff side whiskers and heavy spectacles, had taken a commanding stance.

In one hand a glass of whiskey shook for emphasis and in the other, a smouldering cigar waved ostentatiously, as in imperious tones he discoursed to a bored-looking couple about his exploits on the Somme.

A few feet away, a dumpy little man with a heavy red face was vainly trying to out -do him in volume....his chosen subject being the merits and demerits of various breeds of gun dogs.

Over by the window, I spied Aunt Clare with Andy, Cissy and Rosemarie.

When Rosemarie saw me she pointed to the street below and screamed excitedly: "Mamma, Mamma, come quick; the Germans are coming."

Baffled, I strode to her side where a good many of the guests had simultaneously rushed.

Down in the street, a funeral was solemnly passing; the heavy black carriage, with ornate glass panels and silver fittings, carried a coffin smothered in flowers. It was drawn by a pair of high-stepping ebony horses with nodding white plumes. Sadly, I noted the white plumes, which indicated the passing of a young person.

Aunt Clare took my hand and smiled gently. "I wonder how that child of yours has come to associate Germans with funerals," she observed, kissing my cheek.

"Heaven knows," I laughed. "I never know what she'll come out with next." "How lovely you have everything," sighed Aunt Cissy, comfortably seating herself by the fire, as the "general" appeared beside me with a very enticing tray for the newcomers, "All borrowed," I grinned, pulling out a small stool for the tray. "Myrabelle arranged it all for me."

Clare smiled sagely as the "general" passed the tea to herself and Andy. An elderly lady joined us, greeting Clare like a long-lost sister, as the sounds of revelry clamoured from the basement.

"Off with you now, "beamed the aunt to me, "and don't be leaving that good looking husband of yours at the mercy of all those flappers, while us old fogies catch up on the years."

"Well if you're alright...." I began politely.

"Hop it," laughed Clare making room on the sofa for her old friend.

Happily I went out and found Rosemarie on the landing looking for Meggy. Luckily, Ida came to the rescue and I left her coaxing the child to go to bed.

I made for the back stairs, idly noting the accumulation of empty tin cans of "My Lady" peaches, on the stone shelf leading down to the cellars. Now what had I hoarded all those for.... some free gift perhaps, or competition?

The music and colour hit me as I pushed in the heavy kitchen door. A bevy of young folk stood along by the wall, clearing the floor for Myrabelle, who was poised for the first notes of the Charleston.

And then she was off, feet twinkling, head bobbing, legs flashing, and fringed skirt swirling to reveal seductive glimpses of lacy blue cami-knickers. She was a superb dancer, grace in every line of her, as toe and music fused in perfect harmony. I suppose she was a challenge to every woman, and yet she had many female friends of all ages. Those who won her friendship prized it highly, and husbands were allowed to partake of it too....within certain supervised limits, of course.

There was a long ripple of clapping when her dance ended, and she was led by the grandiose Colonel Blacton to recover her breath on a seat by the window.

Again the Charleston struck up, and this time everyone was dancing it in a whirl of gaiety. I watched their progress with tapping toes, glad to be outside the reach of flying feet.

But as I hummed the tune and laughed at the antics of the dancers, a hand touched mine and pulled me on to the floor; it was Edward, dancing as wildly as the best of them. In self defence, my feet picked up the steps, gaining in speed and boldness.

When the music stopped, I found my sparkling necklace from Woolworths had broken, and beads were rolling around everywhere. I collapsed with exhaustion and laughter on to the nearest chair, just as a familiar scream issued from the doorway.

"Charleston! I want Charleston," yelled Rosemarie, who had made good her escape from Ida. She ran among the dancers, the battered teddy under her arm, and the pink flannelette nightdress sweeping the floor. Behind her rushed Ida, flustered and calling in vain.

Edward laughingly caught his daughter in his arms, but she quickly indicated that she wanted to get down. He had been dancing the Charleston all week with me, and Rosemarie had loved it. Step by step she had danced it with us, until she was as good as both of us....maybe even better.

Now the two musicians got the message and the tantalizing melody once again hit the old kitchen. Rosemarie, all excitement, dropped the woebegone bear, which was hurriedly rescued by Ida, and bounced straight into the dance.

Trying to calm her, I tucked the nightdress into her knickers, while she wriggled impatiently.

Now there was no holding her, and she made an enchanting little picture as she danced....feet flying, arms waving and legs kicking in perfect time. There was not a smile out of her while she concentrated on every step. The onlookers applauded in unison and loud cheering greeted her last step.

"A born dancer there, Mrs. Davis," commented Marie Rose admiringly.

But not quite satisfied that she had sufficiently demonstrated her prowess, Rosemarie prepared to give a repeat performance. I did not want her over-excited, which tended to make her sick, and whispered to Edward to carry her up to bed.

Of course, this was only achieved after suitable protest by the star and her allies. My face was brick red by the time her sobbing appeal for an encore had failed, and she had kissed all and sundry a reluctant goodnight. Ida's promise of a private feast for herself and teddy, of gin-gin biscuits and lemonade in bed, was the only thing that saved us from a major battle of wills.

After the child and Ida had departed, the dance was resumed with renewed gusto. "Black Bottom," a new dance and considered rather risqué, was danced by Myrabelle and Marie Rose, before we all joined in.

The great kitchen shook to the foxtrot, danced to various current tunes, like "Honeymoon Lane," "The Red Red Robin," "Bye Bye Blackbird," and many more topical numbers.

In the middle of a Franz Lehar waltz, which was deemed "a rest," I happened to glance across at Alan Floy's mural, which was decently expected to be disguising the naked antiquity of our dilapidated old range. I was shocked to see that one of the more enthusiastic male dancers had fallen through it, and it lay in tipsy folds on the floor. A couple of Myrabelle's ornamental flower pots had descended with the impact, but the young man, evidently a bit dazed, climbed up on the range (now exposed in all its shabbiness) where he seated himself comfortably among the drooping greenery, legs dangling nonchalantly over the torn "masterpiece."

I could not control the laugh that rose in my throat, although a hefty bottom dancing by, fair winded me. Then I froze; Alan Floy, more dandified than usual in a black and red tapestry waistcoat, had just come in. His eyes darted straight to the ragged mural, and the young man who had caused its downfall. The expression on Floy's face mingled horror with outrage and sheer disbelief, as he glared at the youth who, oblivious to all but the music, continued tapping his heels with mounting enjoyment, as the pace of the music increased, and the final remains of the masterpiece slid to the floor in a tattered heap.

When I furtively looked towards the door again, Mr. Floy had disappeared.

Someone gave me a push, and to save myself from injury, I turned my attention to the placing of my feet in a pared down version of the "Can-Can", which soon knocked all thoughts of Floy, his mural, and the undignified appearance of the ancient range, right out of my head.

During an interval, we were amused to hear cheering from the street above. Some late revellers, attracted by the music, were clustered around the railings, which bordered the area over the basement at the front of the house. They were singing and shouting drunkenly, until a policeman ordered them to move on. This they did reluctantly, but as soon as he was out of sight, back they came again, and this time with bottles and obscenities. Very soon they were indicating their wish to join out party, in no uncertain manner.

Exchanging dialogue with them through the kitchen window was getting tempestuous when a police lorry halted, and a dissenting bunch of them were hoisted on board to recollect themselves in the "Joy."

The housewarming party (and the place was sure warm after it) went on merrily until the small hours, and ended with a ribald rendition of "Paddy Mc Ginty's Goat" and a wild performance of the "Seige of Ennis."

Everyone was loath to leave, even after an unorthodox breakfast of left- overs from the party, and the whole affair was voted a resounding success.

It was one of the happiest and most memorable occasions of my life. We were alive, young and Oh, so happy. Sadly, the years have taken their toll, and when I look down the stairway of life, my heart is wrenched with the pain of nostalgia for that magical night in the old Georgian house, whose loving walls embraced so much happiness and romance.

Chapter 47

We decided it was time for Rosemarie to go to school. She was becoming a handful of high energy with not enough interests to satisfy her. Ida was great with her and had already introduced a range of games, crafts and early play-school activities to her daily routine. She was so bossy, active and full of mischief that we felt a little discipline, and the company of other children, could be nothing but advantageous.

Only that morning, I had found myself at the receiving end of one of her tantrums in Kellet's Drapery Shop, of George's Street. We had gone there to buy her a new coat for school. At this time, she had acquired a mania for rubber balls, and this included anything bearing the slightest resemblance to one.

The method for cash transactions in the shops was that the assistant would unscrew half of a metal, ball-like container from a wire above her head. Into this she put the money received from the customer, with the bill. She then re- screwed it back into the other half, put it onto the wire contraption, pulled a wooden knob, and the ball shot off to the cashier's office along the wire over head. The cashier opened it, checked the money, and the receipt with change, was returned by the same route to the shop assistant to give to the customer.

Rosemarie watched all this in silent wonder, having expressed herself delighted with the teddy bear coat I had bought her.

Suddenly she caught my arm. "Ballie!" she shrieked, pointing at the flying cash container.

"Yes dear....ballie," I agreed nervously.

Her voice rose. She pointed emphatically at the ball skimming along the wire.

"Buy it now," she shrilled.

"You can't have that; it belongs to the shop," I whispered, scrabbling in my handbag for a piece of "Peggy's leg", hoarded for such an emergency. I held it out to her pleadingly. She grabbed it and flung it on the floor.

I felt my temper rising. "You can't have it then; it belongs to the shop, I told you."

"Ballie," persisted the child, rolling around the floor, arms and legs waving angrily.

"You are not going to get it, so you'd better behave yourself at once," I said firmly, trying to keep my voice down, and giving her a little shake.

By this time we had gained an audience. Some of them tried to help by diverting her attention, others made soothing noises, and quite a few eyed me with down-right disapproval, but Rosemarie was impervious to appeals on all fronts, and yelled louder for the "ballie." But one harassed-looking woman with a cranky-looking child in tow, gave me the best advice and I took it.

I bent down and gave the screaming child a few smart slaps on the bottom. It was not easy to make an impression here, as she was wearing a warm fleecy-lined pair of pulley-ups.

However, this brought an audible murmur of censure on my head from the disapproving brigade, and Rosemarie sensing, this set up a long howl for their sympathy.

Scarlet with rage and humiliation, and trying to hang on to a few shreds of dignity, I hauled her to her feet, and snatching up my parcels, dragged her uncompromisingly out of the shop.

Shopping with her was a nightmare, although she was constantly begging to come to town with me, and Ida was not always in a position to look after her while I went out, so I had reluctantly to take her with me. When I hesitated, reminding her of past escapades, she would put her arms around me and promise to be "terrible good." And I, only too happy to believe her, would go through the whole trauma again.

On another occasion we were in Woolworths....a store that was like an Alladin's cave to her, and to reach the delft section where I wanted to buy a few cups, we had to pass a display of multi-coloured balls. These were built in a huge pyramid to the ceiling.

"Ballie!" she whooped, and before I could stop her, she had plucked a ball from the pile. Helpless and horrified, I watched as millions of balls hopped around us, and on us, from every direction. This caper, Rosemarie considered the best fun yet, and while she bounced around joyfully after them, I leapt about fruitlessly trying to catch them. The usual crowd gathered, some trying to catch the balls themselves, while others watched my antics with wide smiles and the odd cheer; none of them paying any attention to the real culprit.

Eventually, of course, the manager appeared to see for himself the cause of all the hopping balls, and to bring the comedy to an abrupt end. After much apologising to himself and the staff, not to mention some irascible customers, I managed to bundle the child outside, only to find her firmly clutching a ball under each arm. Back I had to go to the shop with a vehemently protesting child, where a grim-faced manager coldly received them with blatant looks of hostility.

Edward thought the incident very funny.

"You'll have to teach her the ten commandments" he laughed.

"Wait till you're caught out," I muttered darkly. "Then we'll see how funny it is."

There was another occurrence I found far from amusing....at least at the time it happened.

One afternoon I opened the hall door to an imperative knock. Facing me was a large disagreeable-looking woman with an equally off-putting child at her side. The woman appeared to expect me to recognise her, but as I hesitated, she frostily informed me that she was Mrs. Royston Chillington. Her daughter, for such was the child, gloried in the unlikely name of Zarina....prefixed by "Miss" in deference to my lower status.

As I still looked puzzled at such an unexpected visit, Mrs. Royston Chillington said arrogantly: "That party you had the other night....I had to leave early for cocktails at the Russell Hotel with the Forde Bentlys. Rather noisy, your party, I prefer dinner parties myself...." she rambled on in the same vein, leaving me to wonder where all this talk about parties was leading. Surely she hadn't called just to tell me she wasn't giving ours her stamp of approval.

I remembered her now, clad in yards of emerald velvet and glittering jewellery, especially the quantity of slave bangles hanging on to her plump, freckled arms. Someone had introduced us, and I could not help noticing how condescending her manner had been.

"Oh yes," I laughed, "wasn't it a great party? Pity you had to leave so early; I never noticed you had left."

She ignored me and invited herself in to discuss a matter of "some importance."

Reluctantly, I opened the door wider to accommodate her fat, ungainly figure in a magnificent silver fox fur coat. The bold-faced child followed and furtively stuck out her tongue at me.

We went up to the drawing room, and Mrs. Royston Chillington planted herself firmly in a rather unsteady armchair....I having hurriedly booted a protesting Ginger out of it. She had one of those full moon faces, which no amount of artifice could flatter, although she had tried with a flaming red lipstick drawn in the popular cupid's bow, and plenty of white face powder. Her mousy hair was dragged back in an uncompromising bun, and was no help in her efforts to achieve a classy look, which was probably the effect she was hoping for.

Miss Zarina was a miniature of herself....all huge hands and powerful fat legs. Despite her size, the child was dressed like a doll in a pretty wooly coat and dainty blue satin dress; the short skirt revealing layers of lace on matching frilly knickers. Her brown hair was bobbed, and greatly resembled an inverted pudding bowl, topped with a large blue bow poised like an avenging butterfly.

I awkwardly tried to make small talk while painfully aware of Zarina's desperate attempts to open a cupboard bursting with clutter, and badly in need of a sorting session. Mercyfully, before she succeeded, Rosemarie bounced in and took her down to the kitchen to show off her toys.

Noticing that my visitor was still wearing her fur coat, I politely offered to relieve her of it. She hesitated before allowing me to lift it carefully off her massive back, and continued to watch me closely, as I laid it across the couch.

Then seating herself heavily in the armchair, which tilted drunkenly on impact, she said gravely: "It's my watch."

"Yes?" I was mystified.

"I'm sure I was wearing it here the other night. I remember taking it off to wind...."

"Oh dear! You've lost it. I'm so sorry...." I commiserated.

She eyed me sharply. "It's much more likely it was stolen."

"Well if you think it was stolen you're in the wrong place; there's no one here who would touch anybody's property." I told her sharply.

She brushed me aside. "It's a valuable gold watch on a diamond bracelet; you must make inquiries urgently about it."

I felt infuriated by her implication. "I will have the house searched in case you dropped it somewhere, but certainly, I found no watch when I was clearing up after the party."

She leaned towards me and said warningly: "That isn't good enough, Mrs. Davis. You will give me a list of everyone present that night," she paused dramatically," if not, I shall be obliged to go to the police. Now the servants....I take it, you have the usual staff?"

I thought of the "general" who had been the real master of ceremonies that night, and a wild desire to laugh suddenly hit me, at the mere idea of conveying such suspicions to that rather intimidating domestic.

I jumped up and told her to go to the police. "I refuse to accuse anyone in my house that night of being a thief."

"Very well, if that is your attitude," she said coldly, reaching out for the fur coat, "but you have not heard the last of this matter."

I tossed my head haughtily with an assurance I was far from feeling. "Don't you try any of your threats on me," I flung at her.

She gave me a look of disgust and marched to the door as majestically as her waddling figure and huge coat would allow.

Meantime in the dining room, Rosemarie was not fairing much better with Miss Zarina.

Ida informed me afterwards, that she had seated the two children at the table, and supplied each with paper and paints; a jar of water for mixing the colours sitting between them. Ida then continued working on her tapestry fire screen with the children in view. After a short time Zarina grew tired of the painting, and got down from the table to investigate other sources of interest. She spied Rosemarie's little armchair and squeezing herself in to it, lay back indolently, twisting the hands of an educational clock until they snapped off.

Rosemarie glanced up and leapt to her feet, shouting furiously: "get off my chair."

"Won't," answered the other obstinately.

"Get up this minute," screamed Rosemarie, rushing over and trying to drag her up by the hair.

Zarina looked scared, but still refused to move. "I want me Mammis," she wailed. "Where's me Mammis?"

"Out of my chair," shouted Rosemarie, grabbing a handful of the blue satin dress.

Ida, thinking it was high time to move in, put down her tapestry, but was just not quick enough to prevent disaster. Rosemarie had caught the jar of coloured water, and emptied the lot over Zarina's head.

Zarina set up a series of piercing screams for "Mammis! Mammis!" while the dirty water streamed down her face and on to the blue satin.

Before Ida could deter her, she was spluttering and bawling her way to the hall, where her mother was in the act of drawing on a pair of kid gloves, and issuing me with a final warning.

"I regret to see you taking this stand," she was saying regally, "but as the article in question is of considerable value, you must accept that I cannot drop the matter, so seeing your attitude...."

Then the roars erupted into the hall, and Mrs Royston Chillington added to the din with a shriek. "What have you done to my child, you wicked woman."

Baffled, I stared at the snivelling child, wrapped in the broad hairy bosom of her mother, while Ida tried to explain, and

Rosemarie stood defiant in the back ground, guilt all over her sulky little face.

"Get away," shrilled the distraught mother, as Ida made futile efforts to mop the child dry. "Don't touch her, I said," and wrenching the hall door open, she half dragged, half carried, her sobbing daughter into the street.

"My goodness," gasped Ida, thankfully shutting the door on the pair, "If there had been a policeman handy, she would have had us taken off to the Joy on the spot."

Some days later I heard from a friend, who was familiar with tales of the rumpus Mrs. Royston Chillington was capable of causing, that the watch had been found.

It turned out that the military man, Colonel Sydney Bacton, who had discoursed so laboriously on his wartime exploits, had found the watch in his motor car, after giving the awful woman a lift home from the party.

Needless to say, we heard no more from the bombastic Mrs. Royston Chillington, not even an apology.

"Dressed up vulgarien," snapped Aunt Cissy with feeling, when I recounted the incident to her. She had been "done" by the same woman on one occasion, when a dress she had made for her, had not given the flattering results anticipated.

"The old battle axe never paid me, and it was one of the most difficult dresses I'd ever made. Your one saw it in a picture of Clara Bow and thought she'd look the same in it...." Aunt Cissy's frown vanished in a fit of laughter.

"But didn't you send her a bill?" I asked naively.

"Bills, more likely," snorted the aunt wiping her eyes. "I sent her one a month for ages, until I realised I was throwing good money after bad in the post. Ah well, I tell you this, girl, I learned and fast."

Chapter 48

"Send her to school," snapped Edward a few days later, after he had been involved in one of Rosemarie's exploits.

It was a Saturday afternoon and he had offered to take her down to the Green to feed the ducks.

They had just reached the corner at the end of Leeson Street where, along the footpath several dealers in stiff white pinafores were standing over barrels piled high with domes of apples, tomatoes, bananas and grapefruit.

With the apples and other fruits our daughter was familiar, but not the grapefruit. No one liked it in our house, so it was never bought.

"Ballie!" screamed Rosemarie in wild excitement."I want a ballie," and not quick enough on the draw, Edward was unable to prevent the inevitable.

With a flying leap, Rosemarie snatched a grapefruit from the centre of the pile, with predictable results. The dealers shouted a string of curses as the yellow fruits rolled madly about in every direction. Being adjacent to the other fruits, the whole display was soon in ruins around the muddy street.

Sweating and furious, Edward bent to gather up the squashed tomatoes and mucky grapefruit. Motor cars banged indignant horns, horses reared and a passing messenger boy swerving dangerously on his bike, started whistling:

"Oh yes, we have no bananas, We have no bananas to-day."

The chorus was readily endorsed by a rollicking crowd of bystanders, while the dealers were ranting about people who couldn't control their brats, would walk all over you if they could get away with it, and who thought they owned the street....

Harassed and bewildered as he tried to get hold of his daughter, who was rampaging happily through the crowd with as many grapefruit as she could hold, Edward tried valiantly to appease the dealers.

"Ah sure, are ya listenin' ta him, Josie," scorned a very large dealer. "Does he think I was born yasterda? Bad cess ta yar cheek."

A gang of ruffians seized the chance of firing the fruit to each other under the pretext of returning it to its owners, until a policeman strolled pompously over and charged the dealers with a breach of the peace. That really enraged them, and while they defended themselves, and berated the copper for his tardy intervention while they, "poor dacent women tryin' ta make an honest livin' were been threatened by robbers and murderers."

In the middle of the melee, Edward seized the opportunity to move unobtrusively home, firmly holding a protesting child, and leaving the combatants to search out some common ground of agreement.

"Get that child to school; get her to school," reiterated Edward, a touch savagely when I opened the door to them. "What happened? What has she been up to now?" I exploded as I took in the appearance of both of them, particularly Rosemarie who was clutching a large grapefruit under one arm, while her father held her firmly by the other.

Both of them were generously spattered with bits of fleshy tomatoes and other unidentified debris. Her state was not surprising, but Edward....!

"Have you been playing with tomatoes too?" I questioned him sweetly.

He did not answer, but marched impatiently into the house, leaving me to deal with the erring child.

Chapter 49

I had already enrolled Rosemarie in Miss Alice Jackson's kindergarten across the street. To our relief she started on Monday, and when the time came to go she was full of enthusiasm. She had a little brown case and jotter with a penny box of crayons, a flask of cocoa and a two-penny packet of "Marie" biscuits.

With her usual winning ways she had recovered her position in Edward's affections, and the episode with the grape-fruits was wiped off her slate. I left her in Miss Jackson's care and away she danced to meet the other children.

When I called over for her at one o'clock she was quite unwilling to leave. Cautiously, I inquired about her behaviour from Alice, and she told me that her main problem was trying to persuade Rosemarie to stay in her place at a long table with the other children.

"She keeps copying me, and when I go around to inspect the work of each child, she follows me, doing the same." Miss Jackson paused, and although her voice was stern, I thought I discerned a twinkle in her eye, as she added: "She even bosses the bigger girls, and advises me on punishment when she considers they have stepped out of line."

Next day, a little before closing time, an older child brought Rosemarie across the street, and left her at the hall door. She was terrified, being too small to reach the knocker, and began screaming and kicking the door until a passer-by knocked, and handed her into me. Miss Jackson, on being told of the incident, admonished the older child for leaving before the door was opened.

However, that day Rosemarie refused to be appeased, she had another problem on her mind. It appeared that she wanted to keep a bead work set belonging to the school, which Miss Jackson had given each pupil that morning.

"I'll get you one just like it," I promised hurriedly, setting her dinner in front of her.

"No," she said firmly. "I want that one."

Next morning, I asked Miss Jackson about that particular bead set. She looked a little annoyed, and told me that there had been an unpleasant scene in class when she had come to collect the set from Rosemarie.

The child had refused to hand it back, and when the teacher made to take it from her, she had flung it on the floor. The beads had been scattered everywhere, and it had taken some time to get the set together again. Two slaps on the hand had been the punishment, and Rosemarie had raised a fearsome uproar in response.

I was scarlet with rage and shame, for Rosemarie had assured me that Miss Jackson had told her "milins of times" that she was the best little girl in the class.

Now she boldly demanded the bead set in front of the teacher, threatening not to go to school anymore if she did not get it. I told her smartly that she could scream all she liked, but there was no bead set until she changed her behaviour.

In the meantime, I could hear Miss Jackson's unattended pupils behind the closed door, beginning to get restless. Unwisely, Miss Jackson offered me the bead set for the child, but I refused on the grounds that if Rosemarie got away with this, she would never learn respect for anyone's property again.

"I'll get it for your birthday," I compromised, "but only if there's a great change in your behaviour before then."

Realising that she had no allies on this one, and was out -manoeuvred, she went reluctantly into the school room, and from then on became a little more manageable. Whenever she was inclined towards rebellion, I only had to wag my finger and say: "All right, no bead set," and she would unwillingly change direction.

Thank heaven for these bead sets, I thought with relief; there was the aura of magic about them as a weapon, for dealing with my little minx.

When the longed-for birthday did eventually dawn, she was duly presented with it, and much loved, it outlived many other expensive toys in her affection.

In spite of the shaky start she grew very attached to Miss Jackson, but then that lady had a fine understanding of children and their little world. It surprised me when she told me about the simple things her pupils prized as rewards for doing their best.

Miss Jackson would select five children at the end of each week who she considered to have made a special effort to be good. A corresponding number of empty face powder boxes, scent bottles, odd beads or empty sewing reels, would be placed on the table, and each child, beginning with the one with the highest marks, could select the object she preferred.

The children looked forward excitedly to this, and when Rosemarie won the distinction of getting into the first five, she delightedly chose a pretty yellow box with white powder puffs all over it, which had once contained the famous Coty face powder. She really enjoyed winning that simple token; it was lovingly taken to bed until it fell to pieces. Luckily, she had graduated to an empty talcum powder tin by then.

The only trouble I had with Rosemarie in the kindergarten after that, was when a little friend of hers named Lisa Barry, gave her a grubby beaded purse in exchange for an old sweet tin.

"Where did you get that from?" I asked as I tidied her school bag and found the purse, which reeked of stale tobacco.

"Lisa Barry gave it to me," replied the child airily.

"Didn't I tell you not to be bringing things home that don't belong to you?" I cried in annoyance. Impulsively I caught the purse and flung it in the fire.

"It's a dirty old thing," I told her, as she set up the usual roar of protest. But seeing me in my no-nonsense mood, she withdrew from the fray, and returned her attention to teaching a mulish Ginger "to give the paw."

A few days later she came in from school with the news that Lisa wanted her purse back. Surprised, I told her she couldn't have it, as she well knew I had put it in the fire. But that was not the end of the matter.

Next day when I was leaving Rosemarie into the kindergarten, Mrs. Barry was waiting for me.

She was an over-blown, discontented-looking woman, with peroxide hair, which bloomed in a halo of frizzy curls around her head. Deeply embarrassed, I listened while she told me dolefully, that the purse was of sentimental value, as it had belonged to her late father. In those circumstances she felt sure that I would understand her desire to have it back. She paused to give me a simpering smile, and before I could reply, she rushed on to explain that Lisa had already been punished for taking it without permission. This piece of information was accompanied with a scowl at the small, cowed child beside her.

Cornered, I did not know what to say.

"I'm so sorry," I mumbled, "but unfortunately it fell into the fire."

"Oh no, it didn't, Mamma," piped up Rosemarie who was listening intently to every word. "You threw it in the fire after tea...." Mrs. Barry's wrinkled face darkened.

"You said 'twas a dirty old thing, Mamma...." Rosemarie was jumping up and down; her voice shrill with excitement.

The urge to shake the little monkey until her teeth rattled nearly overcame me, and I could only feebly mumble, "I'm terribly sorry," and wish the ground would open and swallow me.

Mrs. Barry was not impressed. She pursed her lips and gave me an intimidating stare. "That is just too bad," she said slowly. "I happen to be at the loss of a valuable antique purse, and I would like to know what you intend doing about it."

The solution was obvious. "I will buy you a purse," I said with relief, glad to know there was a way out of the dilemma.

"See that you do then," she said aggressively, turning away.

That afternoon, I went down to Woolworths where the cheapest purse was considerably better than the one I was replacing. Next morning, Mrs. Barry was at the school door to receive it. She scrutinized it carefully, before an icy nod indicated that the purse was accepted and the matter now closed.

Edward gave a great burst of laughter when I regaled him with the story.

"Clever woman," he observed. "She got herself a new purse out of the deal, but my poor wife didn't even get the old sweet tin back."

"Maybe she needed it more than I did," I said crossly, "and there's no way I'm going back into battle with that old targer over a silly sweet tin."

Chapter 50

I had been plagued with a series of heavy colds, and all the effort of keeping such a big house running smoothly, plus the ordinary duties of cooking, cleaning, shopping and of course, keeping one jump ahead of Rosemarie, were taking their toll on my energy.

"We must get another girl to help you," commented Edward worriedly, one night, noticing how tired I was.

After the Agnes affair, I was not enthusiastic, but Edward was adamant. So we answered some advertisements in the "Evening Mail," and a young girl of seventeen from Kerry was selected.

She came to us a week later. Eily Donnelly was shy, rosy-cheeked and, she insisted, "mad about children." She came with glowing references supplied by her Parish Priest and local school teacher. After a cup of tea and a chat....or rather I did the chatting....she seemed too bashful to say more than yes ma-am, and no ma-am....I showed her where everything was kept and the general run of the house, and thankfully took myself off to bed.

In the morning, Edward insisted I have a lie-in, and he would send Eily up later with a cup of tea. I did not need much persuading and turned over gratefully.

I was just dozing off when Edward came rushing in shouting testily: "I don't know what sort of a fool that girl is; she's walking around outside and there's no sign of my breakfast. I'll be late for work...."

Resignedly, I said good-bye to the lie-in and the promised cup of tea, and wrapping my dressing gown around me, headed after Edward for the kitchen to ascertain how our new domestic was faring.

But there was no sign of Eily. Glancing through the open window, I saw Ginger lazily washing his face in the sunshine, and then I spotted Eily. She was walking around the tiny garden, apparently searching for something. Over her arm she carried the white pail I kept for washing the floor.

"Eily!" I called impatiently. "What on earth are you doing? The boss has no breakfast and he'll be late for work."

Eily looked up, red-faced with exertion. "I can't find the well," she complained.

Astonished, I thought I had not heard her aright. "The we.. ll?" I stuttered.

It was Eily's turn to be impatient; she rattled the pail significantly.

"For water!" she exploded, throwing her eyes skywards, and looking appealingly at Edward to enlighten his fool of a wife.

Trying to hide a fit of the giggles, I diligently explained to her the mysteries of indoor plumbing and running water in the city of Dublin.

She came indoors rather doubtfully with the pail, and I showed her how to fill the kettle from the tap, and that marked the beginning of a reign of terror with the water.

Having made the great discovery of water being endlessly available in the house, Eily became obsessed with it. She would wash anything and everything so long as it kept her engaged at the taps; she had no time for any other jobs, except those involving the use of plenty of water. Her hands became like red hams, but she cheerfully rubbed Vaseline into them at night in readiness for another twelve hours at the sink next day.

Apart from the undisputed advantage of having everything in the house in a state of perpetual cleanliness, there was a minus side to the business. Often she forgot to turn off the taps. I thought at first she did not realise that this was a basic requirement, but after many a lecture, she would still "forget."A number of times, I came into the kitchen to find her sweeping water out through the back door.

In order to facilitate the needs of the rest of the household, I had to allocate a certain night for her bath, as she deemed one of vital importance twice daily, and no one could beat her to the bathroom. Once she left the water running in the bath, and we were all walking ankle deep in scented suds on the landing for a couple of days.

After that, Edward took a hand in the matter and threatened her with instant dismissal if it ever occurred again.

Even poor old Ginger was nearly drowned when she flung a bucket of water out of the window, after washing the floor. The animal had been snoozing in the sunshine when the deluge hit him. He leapt up, yowling and bedraggled, and struggling frantically to shake off the water. Evidently deeming the vicinity unsafe, he shot through the hole in the garden door and was not seen again for a couple of weeks. When he did return, he was very wary of Eily and understandably, gave her a wide berth.

Still on her preoccupation with water, another fascination with our "help" was the WC. When she discovered that pulling a chain resulted in a flood of water, there was no discouraging her. Our bedroom was near the bathroom, and we were disturbed at all hours of the night by Eily's nocturnal visits to that apartment, and the inevitable gurgles and swooch as she heaved on the chain.

At least these visits were modified by day with her using the other WC at the end of the garden, or maybe she just considered the rumbling cistern more effective at night.

Of course, our clothes were frequent casualties of this munificent washing spree. Edward's best white shirt rose from the depths of the sink, patched in splodges of purple and red dye from being in close proximity to a heavily patterned Foxford rug.

Even Rosemarie's new teddybear coat did not escape her eager ministrations; it emerged from the tub five inches smaller in every direction, and so matted that an indignant beggar woman refused to accept it.

"I'll tell you this," said Edward grimly one morning, as he held up his once white wooly drawers, one leg of which was a bright scarlet, the other a mottled green, "that girl is crazy; she needs a head-shrinker, and you'd better do something. I think she's planning to drown us all," he prophesised gloomily.

For the umpteenth time, I hastened down to the kitchen to reason, cajole and upbraid our erring domestic. Eily was in her usual position at the sink, humming tunelessly, and scrubbing the drawing room fender. She explained in her shy, plaintive voice, that she was giving it a "rub," as there was nothing else that needed "doing."

I offered a prayer of thanksgiving when I heard this, but my troubles were not over. In search of more washing, Eily decided to call on our boarders for supplies. Fortunately, she began with the good-humoured Captain, who informed me of her plans over a cup of tea one afternoon.

"Up she comes to me room, Missus," he shouted jovially, pouring the marmalade from the jar over his scone," and tolt me that she'd do all me washin' for a small charge. She eyed everythin' in me room, although she didn't get beyont the door mind you, and told me that there were a lot needin' doin.' I tolt her that I alwees does me own landrey, and seen no rason to change me ways now. "Still", he paused, "I might take her up on her offer....a good lookin' young wan like that...." and he broke into fits of rollicking laughter, spluttering and coughing into his tea.

Rather annoyed at the ribald turn of the conversation, I raised my voice to drown his amusement, and pointed out that he was indeed very lucky that he had not allowed her to do any washing for him yet. He sobered up pretty smartly when I enlightened him on what the outcome could be if he did; mentioning delicately, the possibility of shrunken and multi-coloured under wear as a result.

I then went up to alert the other guests of Eily's intentions, and they wisely determined to keep their doors locked against her. Only Floy took a different view. Lounging against the door post in his dragon dressing gown, and smiling sardonically, he murmured, "how kind of the young lady, Mrs. Davis, please send her up, and I'm sure we can come to a mutually satisfying agreement."

I gave him an icy stare and went down to the kitchen, where Eily was washing a pair of bedroom curtains to extinction. Ignoring her efforts, I warned her not to go anywhere near Floy's room on pain of dismissal.

"Yes ma-am," she agreed absently, returning to her labours with renewed vigour.

As an immediate solution for ourselves, I began doing our personal washing in the bathroom; the bigger items I dispatched to the Manor Mill Laundry, leaving Eily with only a few towels to gratify her mania.

I tried hard to distract her with sewing, cooking and knitting lessons, but her enthusiasm for the water only began to wane after she scalded her hand with a kettle of boiling water. To my amazement, the day actually arrived when I was left with all the washing jobs.

Gradually her character took on other aspects; sometimes she was painfully shy and downcast, while at others, surprisingly outspoken, even brazen, and all the shades of evasiveness, cunning and innocence, in between.

At first she would not go out on her day off, preferring to stay in her room "writin' home to me Ma," or "doin' a bit of readin.'" Her reading matter was soley comprised of sexy romances(known further up the social scale as "penny- dreadfulls," but after she became friendly with the maid next door, her taste progressed to the more hectic tales in a magazine called "The Miracle." This she bought every week, and swopped with her pal for its equally exotic counterpart, "The Oracle."

Eventually, Eily and her friend began to investigate the possibility of spending their free time in more exciting pursuits, and to this end they set out on a round of the city's dance halls.

Eily was never one to do things by halves, and she was soon as crazed by dancing as she had formerly been by water. Two or three nights a week, she danced the hours away, coming home with her crony and a string of raffish youths in tow well after midnight. Their ribald language caused much caustic talk among the neighbours.

When I remonstrated with her on the lateness of the hour, she was shyly apologetic, but matters failed to improve, and I was forced to grow stronger in my protests, threatening her with dismissal if she failed to come in at a reasonable hour.

An impasse was reached, and then one particularly late night, I waited in the hall with the intention of dismissing her, but she bounced in and resolved the situation, by giving me her notice before I could reprimand her. By way of excuse she said that her mother was ill and needed her, besides she felt "shockin' homesick."

Apparently, she was not quite "homesick" enough to return to Kerry, for a few weeks later, I saw her in Sackville Street with two other girls. They were standing at Nelson's Pillar, loudly dressed, giggling and shouting. Presently they were joined by a bunch of rowdy-looking fellows, with whom they soon paired off.

Eily did not go back home, as I learned from her mother in an anxious letter asking for news of her daughter. Undoubtedly, the freedom and frivolity of life in the city, proved a permanent cure for her shyness and "shockin' homesickness."

Chapter 51

Again we were looking for another maid. "Why can't we cut the cackle and get a fully trained general this time?" asked Edward in exasperation, as we discussed the relative merits of advertising and domestic servant agencies. "Because we cannot afford one," I said crossly, as I baulked at the prospect of trying to train another raw country girl in the ways of domestic life in the city. We eventually opted for an agency, which promised the ideal girl for every home from a bevy of mother's helps, girls to train, city girls, country girls, cook generals and just plain generals. From among them we chose Lilly Whelan from Mayo. On interview, she assured me that her greatest ambition was to be a competent mother's help and learn all she could about housekeeping. She was a boisterous girl of seventeen, very willing, but awkward and ungainly in everything she did. We were to refer to her afterwards as the "house breaker." She broke nearly everything she handled; she simply could not touch an article without letting it fall. I was unable to keep up fresh supplies to meet the demand in the matter of breakages. I tried stopping the cost of the damage out of her wages, but to no avail; she simply borrowed money from my paying guests, tactfully implying that I was short of cash and could not afford to pay her. I went into the kitchen one morning to find her smoking her favourite woodbines, one plump buttock on either side of Rosemarie's little chair. Before I could protest, the chair collapsed to sounds of splintering wood leaving Lilly sprawled in an undignified heap on top of the wreckage. But the last straw came when she broke half my treasured tea set. I was having Myrabelle, Ida and Alice to tea, and after the meal, at which the precious china had been used, I carried it down to the kitchen, and told Lilly to leave it for me to wash when my guests had left. A little later, myself and the three friends, were stunned by a sudden crash. We bolted for the kitchen from whence the noise had come, and there on the floor, lay most of the tea set in smithereens. Lilly stood by the sink, wringing a dishcloth over the disaster. It transpired that she had washed the china and put it on a tray, which was resting on a small stool beside her. At one point she had carelessly turned around and knocked the whole lot over. I was broken-hearted for the remains of a lovely wedding present and issued the usual notice. Unabashed, Lilly retorted that she was going anyway. "You have too much delft in the bloody house anyway," was her parting shot.

"You don't half pick 'em, sweet girl," was Edward's comment on the situation, as we sat in the dining room after our meal reviewing the last chaotic days of Lilly's reign. Now what, I wondered? Should we try for another general, or car on without the potential upheaval another one of the domestic fraternity would probably cause? "Have another bash," Edward reckoned. "You're bound to get someone suitable this time." Again we took a gamble with the advertisement column of the "Evening Mail," and Eileen Madden from Connemara was the result. Eileen was bouncy, freckled and well developed, or as Myrabelle said dryly, "the full of her blouse." She had flaming red hair, which stood stiffly around her head like a Zulu's, and was altogether a broth of a girl of seventeen summers. She was extremely shy and it took a fair amount of time to elicit more than "yes ma-am, no ma-am," out of her. Mercyfully, she had seen running water and indoor plumbing before, as her married sister in Galway had shown her "all dem latest yokes." She was very good with Rosemarie, and her greatest pleasure, she assured me, was taking the child to St. Stephen's Green every afternoon to feed the ducks. In terms of housework, she left a lot to be desired. "Out of sight, out of mind, was her motto," and dirt was brushed meticulously under carpets, mats and furniture. The beds had their blankets hurriedly pulled up, a fact only revealed by the presence of a cold hot water bottle hitting perishing feet the following night. She dispensed with the formality of laying a table, and after cooking a pot of potatoes, would simply turn them out in the centre of the table, and shout that our meal was ready. Certainly, she was not overjoyed by the presence of water as her predecessor had been. Rather she veered in the opposite direction, and I had to firmly point out its necessity in the interests of hygiene. When washing up she would use a few meagre inches of greasy water, and when I remonstrated with her, she complained that getting her hands wet caused chapping and chipped her nail polish. She was inordinately proud of her hands, which were indeed shapely and soft, if perpetually grubby. She was always rubbing some jelly or cream into them, and I said nothing until I tasted one of these "soothing" concoctions in the food. Then I flared up and told her that she would have to keep her hands clean, and free of nail polish, if she intended keeping her job in my house. Reluctantly, she agreed, but I had to be very vigilant in seeing that she observed a basic standard of cleanliness. Apart from that, she was quick and willing to learn, and this advantage she soon applied to her appearance. The pink rosiness of her cheeks was soon submerged under a heavy coating of cream and suntan powder. As soon as she got her wages she was off down to the cosmetic counter in Woolworth's to sample the delights, and test the promises, of a variety of enticing beauty products. She particularly favoured "Snowfire," which offered "to set hearts on fire," and Rosemarie enjoyed the benefits with a large hoard of little tins. With her flaming hair she fought an ongoing battle. She wanted it fashionably short and sleek, and to achieve this affect would douse it in violet oil, but after a short interval, the hair would surmount this obstacle and stand in triumphant glory all over her head again. Edward remarked that one advantage of the oil, if not the only one, was its pungent capacity to denote her whereabouts at any given time. "You'd smell her a mile off," he scowled. Nothing daunted by the oil's lack of staying power, Eily experimented with generous dabs of Edward's "Brillcream." Alas, its success rate was no higher, and in desperation she got the maid next door to do a thinning job on it, which proved a disastrous mistake, and ended with the two girls not speaking to each other again. She never managed to get it to her satisfaction, and what was left of the firey mop divided into spikes, which stood out in stiff tassels all around her head. Every penny she earned went on clothes and adornment. Her taste, greatly influenced by the "pictures," was flamboyant and daring. I tried to guide her taste along more restrained lines, and she would respectfully agree with my suggestions, but at the first opportunity, back she would come with something audaciously eye-catching and guaranteed to "click" with the fellas. She was especially partial to "diamonds," particularly those available for a few pence in "Woolworth's." Of these she had a collection which was the envy of Rosemarie. The trouble was that Eileen believed in putting the whole lot on together, so that she blithely arrayed herself like a jeweller's shop whenever she went out. But I closed my eyes to her little foibles, reckoning that time and a little persuasion would calm her youthful exuberance. What counted most with me was her kindness to Rosemarie. She never seemed to tire of taking that small person for walks to Herbert Park or Stephen's Green.

Chapter 52

One day they were very late returning from one of those outings. Rosemarie always had her tea with Eileen promptly at half past five, but an hour later, they had still not come home and I began to feel very uneasy.

Edward was working late, so my fear was heightened as the minutes ticked away. I stood anxiously at the hall door from where I could see down the street, to the iron gates of St. Stephen's Green.

At a quarter to seven, I threw on my coat and headed for the Green. I strode through the gates, along the shrub-lined path, searching with darting frightened eyes for Eileen and my daughter. It was not until I had raced over the little hump bridge, and stood by the pond, that I found Rosemarie wandering about on her own.

She was chasing the ducks into the water, her teddy under her arm, and on one such foray, nearly falling into the pond herself after them. I hurried forward, catching her in my arms. She began to cry and I hushed her gently.

"Where's Eileen?" I asked, trying to suppress my anger at finding her alone.

"With Jacko, Mamma," she answered, rubbing her eyes and sobbing afresh.

"Jacko kicked my ballie away; don't like Jacko."

"Who's Jacko?" I wanted to know.

"Eileen's fella. Don't like him Mamma; he wanted my teddy," and her eyes were round with fright.

"Don't you worry, lambkin," I soothed. "You won't have to see this Jacko ever again."

A thought struck me.

"Is this Jacko here every day?"

"Yes, Mamma, and Eileen won't play with me when he comes," and her voice rose to an indignant wail.

I took the child by the hand and we walked around the Green until we came to a more secluded part of it. Drawn by much bawdy shouting and laughing, we suddenly came upon

Eileen engaged in vigorous horse play with a rakish-looking youth.

I stopped. "Eileen," I shouted.

Shocked, she sat up, gaping at me in horror, as she fought to pull her skimpy skirt over her knees.

"How dare you!" I cried in a cold fury. "How dare you neglect my child? Anything could have happened to her while you made a fool of yourself with that ruffian."

The youth got to his feet sheepishly, straightened his vivid green tie and rammed a battered cap on his head.

"I'm sorry, ma-am, we was owney...." he began, but I was not interested in any revelations he was about to make. Ignoring him, I turned on the girl.

"You're not fit to have children in your care, and you will leave my house to-morrow morning, and don't expect a reference either."

At those words, Eileen was cringing and apologising, but I hardened my heart, knowing I could never trust her again. I felt completely overwrought, as horror images flashed across my mind of what could have befallen the child out there on her own.

Eileen ran after me, as I turned on my heel, but I was deaf to her pleas, and marched grimly home with a tired, sobbing child.

Eileen begged again for another chance that evening, but I was adamant that she would go. If she had wrought some damage in the house, I could have forgiven her, but for her negligence of my child there was no reprieve.

When she saw there was no hope of reinstatement, Eileen's spirits made a remarkable recovery.

She left the house late next morning, heavily made-up and wearing a gaudy orange and black striped dress, her person a veritable advertisement for Woolworth's jewellery. The rebellious red hair stood defiantly on her head like a crown in the slanting sunlight.

Further down the street Jacko was waiting, and nonchalantly swinging a battered suitcase, she took his arm and swept audaciously out of our lives.

Chapter 53

I remember it well; it happened on a bitterly cold winter's night coming up to Christmas. Rosemarie was in bed, and Edward out visiting Aunt Clare who was not very well, and I was at home "between maids," at the time.

A bright fire burned comfortably in the drawing room, and after a light tea on a tray, I settled back on the sofa with a magazine, feet relaxing on the tapestry footstool.

After a while, I must have fallen into a doze, for suddenly I was conscious of waking up. The fire had burned down to a dull glow, and I was startled by the slump of its embers. Grey shadows flickered down the walls of the room, and a strange frozen stillness lay over everything. The atmosphere seemed devoid of air, and I felt a leaden tiredness come over me. Only my head moved, apparently without effort on my part, until my eyes focused on the other end of the room.

But nothing there was familiar; the big oak cupboard had vanished, and in its place hung a gilt-framed portrait of an elderly gentleman in a white curling wig, and dark blue eighteenth century costume.

Our modern wall paper had disappeared, replaced by one of red and gold stripes. In one corner where the gramophone should have been, stood an open harpsichord with a stool beside it, on which rested a large workbox with a profusion of silken threads trailing out of it.

The door slid open and a comely young woman with dark hair in curling ringlets, entered in a hazy white dress. She had a winsome little girl by the hand, who was excitedly jumping up and down, as the woman struggled to dress her in the cloudy dress she carried on her arm. Happily she hugged the little one, and I could see the child's teeth shimmer in a loving smile.

All the while, there was no sound, and the scene was bathed in an eerie glow, which seemed to fluctuate with the shadows. The woman stood up, and her pearly necklace swung, glistening softly. She seemed to glide to a gilded looking glass on the wall, patting her hair and drawing a dark cloak around her.

The mood became expectant, almost jubilant, as if the mother and child were preparing for some longed for occasion. Then a feeling of change crept in, and I felt tense with a foreboding of impending disaster.

The drawing room door had been left open, and as the mother drew on a pair of white gloves, the child darted from her and out of the room. Moments later the silence was shattered by a sickening thud, and the woman, clutching her cloak, ran in great agitation after the child. Then the strange scene faded, and gradually, I saw the oak cupboard reappear in its usual place, and our gramophone, once again, where the harpsichord had been; the ordinary night sounds of trams grinding on tracks, and the tolling of a nearby Church bell, drifted through the long windows.

I felt exhausted, but curiously unafraid, as I heard myself sobbing helplessly, for I knew that something terrible had happened to the little girl. I do not know how long I remained in this state, but somehow Edward was there, his arms reassuringly around me.

"Lynn, Lynn, sweet girl. What's the matter?" he asked, his voice seeming to come from a great distance.

"Oh Edward," I moaned, "that poor child...." and with an effort I told him what I had seen.

Edward looked worried, but to my relief, he did not try to jolly me out of my story.

"You must have witnessed some tragic event from the past," he sighed.

He leaned back to look into my face as he said seriously: "You simply must not concentrate so much on things that happened so long ago, Lynn. Those days are gone forever; don't try to call back yesterday."

"But Edward, they are people who lived in this house. I must try and find out what happened to that poor child," I pleaded urgently.

Edward regarded me thoughtfully, and smiled wanly. "You're the limit, Lynn but I'll do what I can."

"Do what?" I said doubtfully.

"Well they were evidently well-to-do people, so a major calamity in their lives would be bound to be recorded. I'll look it up in the library."

"But we don't know the year or even the name of the family," I argued.

"Wrong," replied my clever husband. "If we assume that a tragedy occurred, as you feel it did, I would estimate that to-day, the 23rd of November, is an anniversary of the event. Now we don't know the year, but we can work it out from the style of dress and hair style that the woman was wearing."

I nodded wearily and waited as Edward warmed to his subject. "Do you remember that old book of poetry that Mrs. Gandon gave me?"

I remembered it alright, and Mrs. Gandon telling me that it had belonged to her great grandmother, who had married a lawyer and lived all her life in this house.

"Get it," I said with mounting interest.

Edward rose from my side and went to a drawer in the oak cupboard. He rummaged about and returned with a faded book, it's cover richly embellished with cupid aiming his arrows among the flowers. It was called "A Garland Of Poetry," and on the yellowed fly leaf was a spidery inscription :"Madeline Hooper, Her Book, From Thomas, July 1767." A miniature painting of a young woman in a blue gown, was pasted to the inside cover.... "probably a copy of a larger work", opined Edward.

I examined it carefully.

"That's the lady I saw; she had such pretty ringlets, just like this picture, and the necklace too....looks the same"

"Right," said Edward briskly, replacing the book in the drawer. "The Freeman's Journal" or "The Gentleman's Magazine," should tell us something."

It was some time before Edward was able to carry out his research, and in the interval, there was a sequel to the bizarre events.

A few nights later when I was in bed, I was awoken by an unusual sound. The room was in darkness....the little red lamp in front of the Sacred Heart picture having burned out. I was about to snuggle down again, reassured by Edward's gentle breathing beside me, when I was alerted to sounds coming from downstairs.

I sat up, rubbing my eyes, very much awake now and listening intently. There was no mistaking the sounds of furtive footsteps and whispering voices.

Our bedroom door was open, and a sudden gust of wind swept upstairs with a low moan. "Edward! Edward!" I cried, shaking him.

Edward groaned. "What is it?" he muttered sleepily.

"There's someone downstairs in the hall," I cried in alarm.

"Go to sleep...you've been dreaming," he murmured, turning deeply into the pillow.

I did not answer; all was still around me and maybe I was dreaming. I was just about to settle down again when stealthy footsteps, and muffled voices, drifted up to me.

Very sure of my wakeful state now, I stole out of bed donning my dressing gown and slippers. I crept to the door; the house was in darkness and I could not see where I was going. Only my instinctive knowledge of the layout of the house, brought me safely across the landing to the top of the stairs. Cautiously I tiptoed down to the second landing where I was facing the last flight of stairs to the hall. I stood clinging to the banisters, and that queer suspended state I had felt a few nights earlier, came over me again.

The hall was divided in two by an arch, topped by an elegant fanlight. Beyond this everything was bathed in a strange misty light. Slowly this lifted so that I could identify the open hall door, which revealed a black carriage outside in the street.

Then I saw that there were groups of people in old-fashioned clothes, apparently mourning, and talking in huddled whispers, although there was no sound now in the shadowy hall. A man in a tall hat was carrying a narrow white box, and I knew it was a child's coffin. Following the cortege was a young man, his arms around a weeping woman in heavy black. She turned her head as if to speak to someone, and I recognised her as the lady with the little child in the drawing room. The sad little party drifted through the open hall door, and the scene dwindled away, until only a veil of vapour remained.

I stood like a statue, conscious of sweat on the cold wood under my frozen hand. A bell tolled from a city church, and moonlight shone fitfully through the open hall door.

Although I felt unafraid, I did absorb the emotion of the ghostly scene of long ago, and my heart was full of grief for the untimely death of the little girl.

Slowly I became aware of two men who were advancing up the hall towards me.

"What do you want?" I quavered, desperately trying to steady my voice.

One of the men, middle-aged and authoritative, spoke: "Mrs. Davis? Detective Ron Burke," and he flicked a card at me.

"Yes," I answered, alarmed.

I recognised him now; he lived across the street from us, and I was on nodding terms with himself and his wife.

"It's alright," he assured me. "I saw your hall door open as I was going home. I thought I'd give you a call in case of any trouble."

"Trouble!" I shivered.

"You know, burglars....there's a lot of robbing going on," he explained patiently.

Relieved, I told him there was nothing to report, and thanked him for taking the trouble to let us know our door was open in the middle of the night.

"Some late comer must have been negligent in the matter of security, and I would advise you to make sure the door is well locked, especially at night," he smiled, and touching his forehead where a hat would have sat, bade me good night. He closed the door firmly behind himself and his companion, leaving me wondering who could have left the door unlocked.

I thought of Alan Floy; a bit over the top for drink, or maybe one of his visiting girlfriends?

Feeling exhausted and very cold, I was about to return to bed, when I heard soft footsteps on the landing above. The bathroom door was closing quietly, so I drew swiftly into an alcove and waited breathlessly.

A few seconds later, a young girl in a fur coat, stepped from the stairs into a beam of moonlight. One of Floy's late night ladies!

"Who are you?" I confronted her angrily.

She jumped with fright, and I said more gently: "My hall door was left open, and the police have just called to know if everything is alright. Why didn't you make sure it was closed after you?"

The girl turned a heavily made-up face to me, and I saw she was not as young as I had presumed.

"I didn't leave the door open if that's what you're saying," she responded insolently, "and don't you try accusing me of anything, either."

She swept boldly past me and across the hall in squeaky high heels, but my annoyance changed to amusement, when I heard her stumble over an unsuspecting Ginger, who was wandering around on some nocturnal business of his own. Her language left a lot to be desired, as did Ginger's uninhibited yowls.

Chapter 54

Next morning, Adelaide accosted me, as I was sweeping the hall.

"I really must complain about the noise last night," she began in her cold voice. "I was awakened in the early hours and not for the first time, by people talking and banging doors." She paused, and I attempted to explain about the open hall door, and the call from the detective, but she interrupted impatiently.

"I do not want excuses, Mrs. Davis, but I do want a night's rest in a respectable house, and that's just not what I'm getting."

"What exactly do you mean, Miss Lister?" I asked grimly, edging the brush dangerously around her feet.

"You know right well what I mean," she countered tartly, "or if you don't, it's high time you woke up. That Mr. Floy has a different woman in his room every night. Such behaviour should not be tolerated in a decent house. Don't take me for a fool," she warned. "I know what's going on up there alright."

I felt my eyes widen as I wondered at the nature of the exploits envisaged by this dark, forbidding woman. Randy images she would surely know nothing about, ran wildly through my mind, but as she went on complaining, I had to admit she did have a point.

There was a procession of ladies in nightly attendance on Floy, and I was not so naive as to miss the drift of what she was implying. I had been perturbed by the presence of so many unknown females passing through my house, but I did not relish tackling the problem. But tackle it I must, especially in view of the hall door being left open and the detective's warning.

"You have a responsibility," Adelaide was hitting home, "especially with a young child in the house."

Haughtily she drew the rabbity collar of her shabby coat more closely around her thin neck, and with a virtuous sniff, clumped heavily into the street.

I leaned worriedly on the brush and pondered on how I should deal with Floy and his charming admirers. There must be easier ways of keeping the pot boiling than being a landlady,

I thought wrathfully, as I marched stoically up to Alan Floy's room the following night.

I knew he was in as I had heard him go up the stairs earlier, but he was in no hurry to answer my knock. When he did appear he seemed rather flustered, but I accounted for this by the comic informality of his attire. He was wearing the dragon dressing gown, and around his paunchy middle was stretched a yellow apron, decorated with ducks of different colours. Undoubtedly the property of some hard working flapper, as the apparel was many sizes too small for him.

"My dear Mrs. Davis, what a surprise" he exclaimed, quickly recovering his usual aplomb. He waved a dirty tea towel significantly towards the alcove containing his kitchen equipment. "I'm so sorry to appear like this, but I was just starting the washing up."

"That's quite alright, Mr. Floy," I returned affably, glad to see him at a disadvantage, and a far cry from his customary demeanour. "May I speak to you a minute?"

He regarded me keenly with his little shifty eyes, then reluctantly stood aside. "Of course, dear lady, you are most welcome any time."

The words belied the suspicious look in his eyes. I stepped past him and glanced swiftly around the room, which had deteriorated further since I had last seen it.

Newspapers lay in tattered heaps, tubes of paint half empty, jostled in murky disorder with scraps of canvas and items of food on the table. Unwashed delft lay everywhere; various articles of masculine underwear were draped on any available space, with one or two lacy items, which I knew could not possibly be his. Over all clung a grey cloud of dust.

He did not ask me to sit down, and indeed I could not have done so without damage to my person, or his assets, depending on where I tried to perch. Lazily he leaned against the table and waited for me to open the conversation.

"It's like this, Mr.Floy...." I began bravely.

"Oh yes," he interrupted, staring at me disconcertingly, and beginning to polish his monocle.

"There have been a lot of complaints about the noise your visitors are making at night," I said.

"Is that so, and from whom?"

"The other tenants. Now I must ask you...."

Again he interrupted. "I must say I am unaware of any noise. I am very particular on that point, being an early bird myself, you know. Have to hit the hay early in my line of business."

"May I ask you what your line of business is?" I pursued frostily.

He looked amused and began to swing the monocle on its gold chain.

"My dear Mrs. Davis, didn't I tell you I'm a journalist, but of course, I'm into art in a big way," and he flung the tea towel carelessly across the room. "Anyway, I fail to see what my business activities have to do with your complaints. Noise, you were saying? In here?" and he gazed at me in hurt surprise.

"Oh there's noise alright, and plenty of it. I hear it myself..." I said in rising anger.

"And who is complaining besides yourself?" he cut in insolently.I felt my face reddening, but stood my ground. "Miss Lister, for one."

"The old crabby one with the funny boot?" he sneered. I nodded, ashamed of his disparaging allusion to Adelaide.

"Ah that old bag!" and he threw back his head and laughed mirthlessly.

"Surely you don't act on everything that mad old one says?"

"My actions are not under discussion, Mr. Floy," I reminded him, "but yours are as long as you remain in my house, and I would be obliged, if you did not speak so rudely about an elderly lady, in my presence."

He looked nonplussed, and started struggling to remove the ridiculous apron, but the safety pin holding it together, had become embedded in the cloth and refused to open.

Encouraged by his discomfort, I said calmly: "Mr. Floy, I must emphasise that I do not approve of women coming in and out of my house at all hours of the night."

He smiled, exposing sharp yellow teeth. "You surprise me, dear lady; no women come in here, except my sisters."

"You have rather a lot of sisters," I retorted sarcastically.

"Really?" he laughed. I held his gaze unflinchingly.

"Yes really, my dear Mrs. Davis. We are a large close family, and I have eight sisters. Satisfied?" he smirked.

Feeling at a loss to counter this doubtful explanation, I shifted back to firmer ground. "Anyway, I want no women visitors after twelve o'clock....sisters or not," I stated, stressing the "sisters" boldly.

By this time, he had abandoned the battle with the safety pin, and was eying me with undisguised hostility.

I edged towards the door, saying with as much dignity as I could muster: "I must consider the other people in my house. The same rule applies to everyone, and if it doesn't suit you, you have the option of going elsewhere."

He made no reply, but I could feel his eyes boring into me as I left the room.

"Another bitch," he hissed, banging the door behind me.

Our relationship deteriorated very much after that encounter, and on the rare occasions when I met him in the hall, he barely acknowledged me. But the noise ceased, and whether that was due to a cut back in the number of female visitors, or that they were more discrete, I do not know, for I never saw anyone going up to his room again, and Adelaide cast no further aspersions on his morality.

But for me, there was a much more telling outcome; he no longer left his rent on the hall table, as had been his former habit.

Thinking it was just an oversight on his part, I consoled myself with the thought that I would collect double the following month. But again no rent appeared, and there was no reply when I tried the strategy of knocking on his door at different intervals during the day.

I watched for him anxiously, and I don't know how he got in and out without my seeing him. I slipped notes under his door, which were ignored, and at last the penny dropped. I remembered Myrabelle's caustic remarks about him, and knew I was going to be done! Reflecting on the situation, I realised, with a flutter of fear that I actually knew nothing about Alan Floy, apart from his interest in art, and that seemed to cover a wide range of activities.

One day on getting no reply to my knock, I used my duplicate key and gingerly opened the door of his room. The place was in semi-darkness, and on pulling the curtains aside, the filthy state of the apartment was only too patently obvious.

Dirty delft, mouldy food, empty packets, newspapers, discarded tubes of paint, littered every available space. I looked in the wardrobe; it was empty. The big suitcases that had stood in the corner were gone. Undoubtedly the bird had flown, but when?

I went over to the unmade bed and looked on the bedside table; foolishly thinking he might have left the rent there, but only an ash tray filled with cigarette stubs met my angry gaze.

Needless to say, I never saw Alan Floy again. I had to write him off to lack of experience and my own naivety.

Chapter 55

We had another maid.

Her name was Biddy Murphy and she resided with her husband and ten "childer" in the Liberties.

She had been recommended to us by a neighbour, who was generous in her acclamation of Biddy's domestic prowess. Indeed, she made me feel that I was getting a gem from amongst the servant fraternity. (We later discovered that Biddy had only been employed by her for rough charring jobs.) Because of her many commitments, Biddy could only come to us during the daytime....she went off duty at four o'clock, and that made her a daily general.

Oh yes, the neighbour insisted on Biddy's title of fully-fledged "general."

I felt a sense of pride at the realisation that we had at last reached the eminent position of having an experienced general in our employment. Alas, pride does go before a fall.

Biddy was a red-faced, black-haired, powerfully-built woman in her forties. She wore a strange assortment of second-hand garments, which seemed to flap about her ungainly figure as she plodded about. Huge black boots laced with twine encased her feet, under a black and red flowered skirt too big even for her, which circled out like a huge crinoline whenever she swung around.

In the mornings, she wrapped her portly form in an overall that looked as if it had been cobbled together from an old patchwork quilt. In the afternoons when the washing and scrubbing were over, Biddy liked to mark the occasion by changing into a blue and white striped dress (ex-prison stock and got cheap, she confided proudly) and massive white apron. The last item, she informed me, had once been the property of a flower dealer in Moore Street, but In this case, I was not enlightened as to how she had come by it.

Biddy had a mind of her own, and her opinion as to how things should be done often collided with mine. When such a confrontation took place, or she considered I was getting "silly" and "upitty," she clinched the matter by comparing me unfavourably with her former employer, a Mrs. Symmington-Smyth of Rathgar. Myself, family, house and contents, all suffered the same disparagement at various times, and I grew furious when Biddy prefaced every disapproving remark with, "Mrs. Symmington-Smyth was alwees" used to....." or quoting some snobbish observation relating to her superior social position. Worst of all the said lady "alwees" used the most expensive products in the running of her home, and Biddy expected me to do the same.

"Mrs. Symmington-Smyth wouldn't have that stuff in her house...."with reference to our curtains, carpets or crockery. Rosemarie, she described as a young monkey who had the upper hand in the house. Mrs Symmington-Smyth's child.... "a darlin' little angel, but then it's all in the way she were brought up, and the good drop were in her, a course."

I would try to ignore all this, anxious to get the work done, but sometimes in the middle of a tirade, Biddy would notice my indifference, and leaning on her brush, or whatever happened to be handy, would raise a mighty fist for my attention, and proceed to lecture me on my shortcomings like a dictator, "for yar own good, ya should listen and ya might larn somethin."

One thing, she was very fussy about were her corsets. "Never bees without 'em. Keeps the figure in place," she told me, wagging a hand smartly against her balloon-like bottom. "Kept the rematicks off too," she guffawed.

Sobered after her outburst, she cast a calculating eye over my outline, and evidently, seeing room for improvement, advised me to invest in "a pair" with no delay, adding as further inducement that such an investment was the secret of the "mag-nif-esent" figure of Mrs Symmington-Smyth herself.

I could only agree half-heartedly with her, but I couldn't help wondering how many corsets she wore, as she always referred to the garment in the plural. Despite her partiality for the corsets, she was forever blaming them for every ailment that afflicted her. If her back was stiff, her head aching, or her nose running, it was always a cry of: "These dam corsets is killin'me."

Sometimes, she retired to the bathroom to remove part of the offending hardware incorporated in the corsets. That accomplished, she would be in fine fettle for another burst of activity in which brushes would be swung against walls like battering rams, and dusters flapped dangerously around our meagre reserves of china and glass.

She was a great worker, but all delicate articles had to be removed from her path. Even dusting the furniture was a hazard, as all too often her broken finger nails played havoc with the veneer.

She did a great job on Alan Floy's room; it was clinically clean by the time she was through with it, but here she had a clear sweep with nothing around to damage.

Even though alerted to what her stalwart hands could demolish, I still was not quick enough to safeguard all my property from disaster. Eily had left a legacy of handless cups, which Biddy polished off in record time.

"No use anyway," she said dismissively in her deep rough voice, casually flicking the last of the cups into the dustbin. A cracked plate followed it, after spinning in the air during a drying operation. In fact the cups were the least of the devastation. While dusting a pretty little stool one day, she was astonished "to find its legs in me hand." Edward's shaving mirror followed, although she had "owney been lookin' at the bloomin' thing."

Leaving her mark on the window was even easier....she simply put her hand through a pane as she polished. A nonchalant whack of her duster banished Edward's Great Aunt Ellen's ugly ceramic urn forever, for which I was not ungrateful!

However, a stop had to be put to her gallop; I spelled it out. "Anymore damage and you're out of here," I ended a very edifying lecture, which I hoped would find its target.

She laughed hilariously. "Anymore damage and yar outa here," she mimicked, hands on hips. "Janey! Ya'll have to replace all dem bits an pieces with dacent stuff. I've done ya a favour, clarin' the decks of some proper rubbish. Now Mrs Symmington-Smyth alwees rightly says...."

Amazed at her temerity, I just gaped at her, wondering which one of us was the mistress. "That's enough from you," I managed to say icily. "I did not ask for your opinion of my possessions, and you have done a great deal of damage since you came...."

Biddy was unabashed. "Don't you worry about that now," she said in placatory tones. "Just dock it off me wages."

I had heard that suggestion before and was wary of it. I pointed out that if I was to follow that line of action, she would be getting no money at all for a very long time.

She broke into a fit of either laughter or coughing, I couldn't be sure which, and when she had regained her composure, she said piously: "Sure God is good."

There was no way I could argue with that sentiment, and was left wondering where exactly I stood with Biddy now, and what my chances were of calming her activities, and reducing her propensity for noise and destruction.

There the matter rested, as Rosemarie chose that moment to scream from the kitchen, that Ginger was on the table enjoying the fish I had bought for our dinner.

Chapter 56

Mrs. Symmington-Smyth hated cats, and would not permit any member of the feline fraternity into her house. This information was disclosed by Biddy with all the drama of a startling revelation, after banishing Ginger from the kitchen with the sweeping brush, and much threatening volubility.

I pretended not to notice and continued making pastry for an apple tart.

Very disgruntled, Biddy lit a woodbine and flung the washing into the sink. Liberally she tipped half a packet of washing powder into it, while allowing the hot tap flow freely over the lot. The washboard was then slopped in, and Biddy was ready to apply her considerable strength to the task of rubbing the jumbled laundry against it.

"Biddy" I was forced to admonish, "there's no need to rub the clothes that hard; they'll be all worn out by the time you've finished."

The woodbine, which had been wagging furiously in her mouth with her exertions, was stilled, and placing her steaming red hands on either side of the sink, she eyed me scornfully "Well, all I can say is this, if yar bloomin' clothes be worn out as aisy as that, you'd best hand dem to the next beggar man as comes to the door."

"You wouldn't say that if you had to buy them," I retorted hotly.

"Don't get yar knickers in a twist," she laughed raucously, "Janey I were owney jokin, Course some people can't take a joke. Now take Mrs. Symmington-Smyth....there were a woman with a great bit a fun in her. She...."

The voice boomed on as Biddy returned her attention to the sink, and continued her operations with the same vigour as before.

I must find an excuse to get rid of her, I thought desperately. She's the worst one yet. I went on peeling the apples, but my mind was absorbed in various schemes for the removal of

Biddy's patronage from our home, when I was startled by another rumpus at the sink. Swearing riotously, Biddy rushed forward and grabbed the brush. Ginger had ambled in....I having forgotten to shut the back door after a visit to the dustbin.

Biddy swung the brush wildly at the animal. Terrified, he sprang up on a shelf, knocking over a bag of flour, which promptly burst open on the floor.

"For heaven sake stop, Biddy," I screamed, as Ginger arched his back and, with flaming eyes, spat profusely in her direction.

Scared now, she dropped the brush and fled into the hall, while I was left to entice a belligerent moggy into the garden.

When the cat had fled with much yowling, I called her back and demanded she clean up the mess she had caused.

At first she defended her actions indignantly, eying me challengingly, and blaming the cat for the chaotic state of the kitchen. Although trembling inwardly, I forced myself to hold her stare, and she was the first to lower her eyes. Throwing aside the brush she flounced out for a bucket and cloth.

Gleefully, I felt I had won that round, but what was I to do about her dislike of cats, Ginger in particular? I would not get rid of Ginger for her, I vowed firmly.

As she cleared up the spilled flour, Biddy kept up a diatribe against the "basterin'" cat. "Dirty, unhealthy tings," she snorted to the kitchen in general.

Then turning from the sink she asked: "Aren't ya afraid of findin' that cratur in yar bed?"

I assured her, with a hidden smile, that for as long as I was in this house such a circumstance had never arisen. "We must keep a cat," I said reasonably, "if not, you'd be a lot more frightened of the rats and mice."

She shuddered and exhaled a lungful of smoke. "I don't know as I can stay in dis house," she began doubtfully. "There were never anything like dat in Mrs. Symmington-Smyth's...."

"As regards that, you must please yourself" I rushed in, hoping for imminent notice.

But to my surprise she gave a great bellow of laughter. "I were jus thinkin' of me son Mixer who worked in a glue factory in the Coombe. Did I ever tell ya?"

Mystified, I shook my head, wondering if I was really up to one of her lurid disclosures, but Biddy decided that I was. She lit another woodbine, and rested her large bottom comfortably against the sink. Blowing out a satisfying cloud of smoke she went on with her story.

"Well they kept a big striped cat down thar to scare off the mice and rats, as they was doin' shockin' degradation 'round the place. This particalar day, the ould cat were snoozin' on top of a barrel a glue. Sudden like, this huge rat appears, as big as a dog it were, and the cat leapt for it. The factory were full a sich barrels a glue, and as the cat leapt over them, didn't he land on one with a loose lid, and what dia tink?"

"I can't imagine," I feigned indifference. She threw me a pitying look. "Sure any ejit could guess....the bloomin' cat fell into the barrel a glue. He were owny covered in the stuff and Mixer pulled 'im out. Thought they'd have to deestroy ta animal, they did....and mores the pity dey didn't. One less a ta basterin' 'tings, I says."

"What happened the cat?" I asked cautiously.

"Well when Mixer got 'im out, he just shot off with 'imself. It were next day they heard all the tap tappin' on the iron roof.... and wern't it the oul cat again. Stiff he were, stiff as brass with the glue dried in ta 'im. Such a sight! Mixer had me roarin' with laffin' for a month after," and she promptly broke into hysterics of merriment.

I ignored her hilarious reaction to the cat's plight. "But the poor animal; what became of him," I asked anxiously.

"Never a bother on 'im," chortled Biddy airily, fully restored to good humour again. "Didn't that same cat lick every bit a glue off 'imself, and weren't he as good as new in a few weeks."

Chapter 57

Around this time I decided to give a boost to the home front by investing in a vacuum cleaner.

A young man called, extolling its virtues, which were indeed impressive when compared to the dust and drudgery of mops and brushes. By comparison to its ingenuity, our method of cleaning a carpet, or indeed any flooring, seemed primitive.

We spread damp tea leaves over the floor, left it for a few hours, and brushed them out thoroughly, amid a cloud of dust, and loosening a fair amount of the carpet's pile in the process.

Best of all, the salesman explained, the marvel could be paid for by the month; this in itself was a compelling incentive to buy.

When the young man gave a demonstration of its dexterity in the drawing room, Rosemarie ran in to watch the proceedings, but having never seen one before, she had reservations regarding its intentions, and was wary of it.

She sat on my knee for safety, and every time the salesman brought the hoover near us, she bent down to it crooning, "Nice fella, nice fella," much to the amusement of the young man, who was inclined to exploit the situation to his own advantage.

"Wouldn't the little miss just love to have one of these?" he paused in his labour to ask her. "And look, it's so easy you could use it too. Try it for yourself, little one," he invited.

But Rosemarie was not convinced of its reliability, and burying her head in my chest, she refused to touch it.

At the end of the exhibition I bought the cleaner.

"Do you know anything about electric cleaners?" I foolishly asked Biddy that afternoon.

"Like the back a me hand," boasted the general with her usual audacity. "Mrs. Symmington-Smyth alwees kep two a dem yokes. Wan for the upstairs and wan for dee kitchen. Ya know, she alwees knowed whats what in that kind a ting."

As usual, I ignored the litany of Mrs.Symmington-Smyth's achievements.

"Right then," I said briskly. "Let's make a start."

Biddy bridled at this. "What ails ya now? What's the bloomin' hurry? Ta morra 'll do. I'll be goin' home in a half an hour, a bit earlier in fact."

She went on to explain that this was the day her husband (whom she referred to as a "drunken bowsey") got his wages, and she had to be home ahead of him to "knock the money outa 'im afore he hit Darcy's pub and gallons a porter."

I assured her she could go early anyway, and we would have tonnes of time, as the salesman had said that the rooms could be done in twenty minutes.

Satisfied that she would not be discommoded by the enterprise, Biddy joined in with gusto. Together we adjourned to the drawing room where we eagerly dragged the smaller pieces of furniture, and several ornaments out on the landing.

Biddy elected to "drive" the cleaner, while I went down to the kitchen to put a shepherd's pie in the oven for our evening meal. But getting the thing to start was a lot easier for the salesman than it was for me.

First we had to get all the gadgets attached to each other in the right order. This I only managed after fifteen minutes study of "The Practical Instructions," and many extraordinary suggestions from the redoubtable Biddy.

Still, it would not work. Sweating, I dismantled it and began from the "First Simple Instructions" again. Biddy was beginning to get restless and demanded we abandoned "the yoke" and get the old reliable brush and dustpan (not to mention tealeaves) into action. I disagreed; I was ashamed to admit defeat, especially to Edward when he got home.Fleetingly, I wondered how Mrs. Symmington-Smyth would have coped with the problem, but for once, Biddy made no attempt to enlighten me, and I certainly wouldn't ask.

Biddy stood glumly in the middle of the floor, one hand on her ample hip, the other gripping the hoover as if it were a savage dog trying to escape. Wildly I wrestled with the switches, until suddenly, the wretched thing burst into life, and bounced across the room, with Biddy skipping crazily after it.

"Go on, use it," I shrieked above the blare of the engine, as Biddy fought frantically to disentangle her clumsy figure from the yards of curling cable.

Cursing, I helped her out of it. Immediately she swung the long brush at the walls and the chandelier shook at the assault.

"For heaven's sake, take it easy," I screamed, prancing after her as the brush described a wide arc around the mantelpiece, barely missing the clock and an assortment of ornaments, which I had forgotten to take out of harm's way. "Can't you keep it on the floor," I implored, and the brush descended with a swoop from the ceiling. Fearfully, I wondered if Biddy was controlling the cleaner, or if it had taken possession of her!

Biddy was now scrubbing frenziedly at the carpet. "Lord! I thought; how long can it stand the battering before it disintegrates?"

I watched the cleaner's manoeuvres closely, and noticed that it was not picking up the dust at all. I halted the action, and in desperation, adjusted anything adjustable, finishing with an "expert" pull. Suddenly the noise died; the thing would not work at all. Wildly I pressed any knob I saw, still nothing happened, and in a fit of exasperation, Biddy lifted a booted foot and aimed a kick at the "yoke." Instantly it came to life with a roar, to expire almost immediately in an explosion of sound; while simultaneously the light went out.

There was a scream from Rosemarie who was playing in the kitchen with her friend, Daisy. Biddy was already giving voice in vivid language. "Oh the Lord save me! I can't stand up with me back. Oh me corsets is killin' me alive," she bellowed.

I tried to hang on to my temper, and told her to stay where she was....an admonition which only drove her wilder.

"Looka here, where the hell dia tink I can go with me back?"

I ignored her and attempted to negotiate the muddle on the landing. Ida appeared on the stairs above, a lighted candle in her hand, and peered down fearfully at me.

Simultaneously, the Captain was in the hall demanding to know "what the blazes is goin' on?"

Just then, Edward's key turned in the lock of the hall door and I groped my way gingerly down the stairs, rubbing my elbow where it had made hard contact with one of the landing tables.

There was a scuffle behind me, and I jumped aside as Biddy galloped past with the candle she had snatched from Ida, shaking perilously in her hand. She had forgotten the state of her back and the restrictions of her corsets as she listed her grievances. "Janey! It's a nice state a tings that I bees reduced to slavin' in a mad house. Mrs. Symmington-Smyth would never have wan a dem yokes....that drunken bowsey 'ill have all me money spent....that young Mickey 'ill burn me house down if he finds the matches...."

The tirade was interrupted as a terrified Ginger streaked in front of her, and she narrowly missed crashing into the hall stand.

"Blast that basterin' cat," was her parting shot when she hauled the door open and gained the safety of the street.

Meantime, Edward's efforts to reach the kitchen were less successful. I gauged this when I heard him shout, as he fell over Rosemarie's blackboard, which she had left with her usual carelessness, just inside the door.

To save himself from falling, he grabbed the clothesline I had slung across the room for indoor drying, and the whole wash came down on top of him. Somehow, a print of a seascape, hanging nearby, became dislodged and landed on his chest with the cord around his neck.

All this was revealed when the Captain appeared in the doorway with a ship's lantern, which he kept in working order in his room, because " dem new-fangled electricts don't alwees work."

How handy his caution proved, and what a God-send that old lantern was to us now.

But as its light fell on my husband, I could not suppress the giggles while he struggled to his feet; a striped sock around his neck, a towel on his head and the picture swinging from his chest. "I see nothing whatever to laugh at, and I'm pretty sure you're responsible for all this," he said wrathfully.

As the truth of this shot home, I sobered up, and went to a drawer in search of a candle.

The Captain, ever alert, called: "If you're lookin' for a candle, Missus, travel no further; I have one here," and he drew a small candle from his pocket.

"Came prepared," he beamed, handing the lighted candle to Edward. The pair of them then retired to the cellars to examine the state of the fuses.

Unfortunately, it was not as simple as that. Whatever I had done to the cleaner, I had not only blown our lights, but everyone on the street as well.

In the way of men, Edward was inclined to put the blame for the whole business on me. "You should have consulted me before buying the thing in the first place...."

"But you agreed to it when I told you the woman next door had one. You always say the dust makes you sneeze." I protested.

"Yes," the husband argued doggedly, "but you shouldn't have tried to put it going until I had examined it first."

I felt furious at his assumption that I could not be expected to understand the mechanics of a simple domestic appliance.

"OK then," I said huffily. "You go and get it working, as you're so superior and clever."

Edward said nothing to that, but he went straight up to the drawing room, where the cleaner lay innocently awaiting his masterly powers of resuscitation.

To my chagrin, he had the whole thing set up and working in a few minutes.

"Easy," he laughed boyishly, "that is, sweet girl, when you know how."

He gave me a hug and planted a kiss on my lips, but rather spoiled the affect, by patting me condescendingly on the head.

Chapter 58

The next day the hoover was pressed into action. I was extra busy, as the bold Biddy had not shown up at all, and I wondered if she would ever deem it safe to return to us.

Rosemarie, and her equally mischievous friend, Daisy, retired to the living room after school, to play hoovers. I could hear the racket in the kitchen, as they made booming noises purporting to resemble the cleaner. Relieved that they were happily occupied, I returned to a bout of washing.

A while later, I was alarmed by a crash, and grabbing a towel raced up to the dining room. There I beheld a room that looked as if a bag of soot had been thrown over it. The crash was the result of a wallop to the Venetian lamp, which now lay in fragments on the floor. The room smelled like something out of the Arabian nights, due I found later, to the purloining of cinnamon and mixed spices from the store cupboard.... "to make dirt," a tearful Rosemarie later confessed.

"To make dirt," was successfully achieved here; the dark powders covered everything, and the exotic perfume was to pervade the place for weeks.

Daisy had obviously been playing the part of the cleaner salesman. She bashfully stood in the middle of the mess with Edward's hat falling over one eye, squinting nervously up at me, as I scolded her on her lack of respect for other people's property.

Rosemarie was standing uneasily beside her, draped in one of Biddy's massive aprons, with a duster tied around her head. But my hackles really rose when I discovered her new red raincoat, tied over a yard brush to make a hoover.

I was still reprimanding them furiously, and trying my hardest not to take a hand to both of them, when there was a whoop behind me, and a familiar Dublin accent gave an astonished shriek:

"Janey ma-am! What a mess dem young divils 'ave made. Ya'll never see this place clane again. No dacent childer 'ud ever do dee likes in their own home. Course it's all in the upbringin', as Mrs. Symmington-Smyth alwees says...."

I turned on her angrily. "I don't give a dam what Mrs. Symmington-Smyth says. And you can see about cleaning it up. I presume you've condescended to return to your job?"

That whipped the smile off her face, I noted, with a certain spiteful satisfaction. "You can use the hoover now...."and I held up a restraining hand, as she opened her mouth to protest. "It's perfectly alright," I assured her; "the boss showed me some little thing I'd just overlooked," I lied airily.

I packed the children into Mrs. Brown's next door, after a hurried consultation with that lady. Then I took out the hoover and smugly got it working, but if I thought Biddy was going to let me off the job of using it, I was very much mistaken. No way would she be left alone with "the yoke," which brought clear reminding of her previous antics with it. I was finally forced to accept defeat and "drive" the thing myself, while she stood well back at the door, making suggestions and shouting orders.

"Oh what wonderful pot-pourri you have," exclaimed Myrabelle on her next visit, but Edward's friend held a different opinion.

"What's that atrocious smell?" he asked in a stage whisper next time he came to tea.

Chapter 59

Biddy continued to rampage through our home. I tried to curb her exuberance, as I dreaded the business of bringing another untried stranger into the house.

"I know Biddy," I defended her to Edward, "She's honest, good-natured and not afraid of tackling the rougher jobs."

In between those virtues, well.... Of course, Edward kept out of her way, and left all dealings with her to me. "Your department, sweet girl," was all I could get out of him, when I asked his opinion on some of our general's more controversial approaches to domestic science. Faced with a verbal collision with her, he ducked out on any pretext, and left the problems entirely up to me.

I wrestled endlessly with various modes of subduing our formidable Biddy, but trying to make her fit our notions of restraint, was an unrewarding exercise.

The last straw came when I gave a little dinner party for two of Edward's colleagues, and their wives.

I roasted a pair of plump chickens for the occasion, but when they came out of the oven, the legs were still pale and in need of further cooking. After laying the table and putting the finishing touches to the menu, I instructed Biddy to remove the legs from the chickens, and put them in the oven for a little longer.

We were rather grandly sipping a glass of sherry in the drawing room with our guests, who were rather straight-laced and middle-aged, when the door flew open and Biddy plodded in.

She was clad in a skimpy, lace-edged apron over a dress of red and white stripes. In deference to her role of parlour maid, she had wrapped a wide strip of lace around her head. Despite it being secured with safety pins, this innovative head dress kept slipping absurdly over one eye.

"Will I put yar legs in the oven now?" She yelled in my direction.

I made eye-contorting signals to her for silence, but with poor results. She caught my eye alright, but misinterpreted the message. "The chickens....the chickens legs a course," she bellowed impatiently, and gave a shriek of laughter at what she considered my foolishness.

I felt my face burn, as I noticed our guests, caught between curiosity and a mannerly attempt to ignore her presence. But Biddy was not to be diverted.

"I never seen chickens legs cooked twice in all me life," she informed the assembly. "Mrs. Symmington-Smyth alees gave hers to ta cat....ta chickens, I mane," and she exploded again at her own joke .

Edward was talking over-loudly to our guests, but I knew they had taken the situation well in.

"That will do, Biddy, thank you," I said, giving her an ominous stare.

Biddy gave a loud snort, and picking up a tray, flounced to the door, kicking it open with a massive boot.

"Ya best look to dem chickens yarself. I knows nothin' about all this cookin' a chickens legs," was her parting advice, as she tramped triumphantly down the stairs.

Trembling with rage and embarrassment, I escaped to the kitchen at the first opportunity, where I found four over roasted chickens legs in a too-hot oven.

Relations deteriorated between Biddy and me after that party, and I seriously toyed with the idea of letting her go. Again, I was subdued by the prospect of looking for yet another general; swayed by the old adage that the divil you knew was still better than the one you didn't.

However, the decision seemed to be taken out of my hands when I found my crystal salad bowl, a much loved wedding present, in smithereens in the dustbin. Now I realised the time had come for a parting of the ways.

Buoyed up with rage at the discovery, I went in search of her. Finding her was no problem, as her activities were invariably accompanied by powerful renditions of Irish ballads. When I came upon her, she was vigorously engaged in cleaning the bath, to a somewhat personalised version of "Wrap The Green Flag 'Round Me, Boys."

"Biddy!" I shouted.

"Biddy!" I screeched again in a desperate effort to beat the chorus. So absorbed was she that she got quite a fright when I eventually got through to her.

"Janey, ma-am, ya near put the heart cross ways in me," she said, struggling to her feet. "It's the oul back....not what it were anymore, and these dam corsets is near killin' me."

She was on her feet now and I gave it to her straight.

"I've just discovered the latest piece of damage you've done. Yes I've found my crystal salad bowl in the bin....and you wouldn't even tell me you'd broken it. Now I've been more than fair with you, but I'm at the end of my patience and I'm giving you a week's notice."

With a dripping cloth in one hand and a packet of Vim in the other, she drew herself up majestically. She gave me a menacing look. "Yar not firin' me 'cause a dat oul bowl in the bin? Janey! it were chipped anyway."

"It was not," I contradicted her sharply, "and the way it is at present, I simply can't afford you any longer."

She gave a disparaging sniff. "What are ya fussin' about? There's nothin' a rale value in dis place. Now take Mrs. Symmington-Smyth, she had carpet on the stairs and a full set a china for the kitchen."

"That's not the point," I argued hotly, "and I'm sick to the teeth of that Symmington woman; if it was such a wonderful place why didn't you stay there and give us all a rest?"

"Well now, seein' as yar so curious, I'll tell ya why I were forced to leave the best job I ever had; wan a me childer were taken sick and I had to give in me notice to look after her. Mrs Symmington-Smyth were heart- broken...."

"I'm sure she had more than her heart broken," I cut in cynically. "Anyway, I have a list of articles broken by you, and I will deduct them from your wages as agreed."

"Don't ya dare cut me wages, ya ould skinflint. I have ten childer...." and she went on to expound on life in two tenement rooms, with a drunken bowsey for a husband, and nothing coming in but "the mane wages" I gave her.

I knew I had lost the battle against the sheer power of her voice, and the length of her defence. I could not get a word in, until she was forced to draw breath. Then I reminded her that she had been shown kindness in my house. I had given her outgrown clothes of Rosemarie's, which were in very good condition for her children, and the many parcels of food I had placed in her basket, when she had pleaded that the "childer" were on the verge of starvation, due to the misdeeds of her husband.

But Biddy was not interested in the good deeds of yesterday, and to end the futile argument, I agreed to take nothing off her wages, "but only for the children's sake," I warned, in a last effort to get the better of her.

Biddy gave a derisive grunt. "Looka here now, I'm goin.' Ya can keep yar notice ta polish yar floors. I has me reference from Mrs. Symmington-Smyth, and that'll get me a job anywhere, dia hear?"

To this piece of bravado I said nothing, for my attention was focused on the work waiting to be finished in the bathroom. The bath was only half cleaned, the wash basin sported its weekly collection of pink tooth paste spots, and the floor was awash with puddles, especially around Biddy's portly form.

I longed for the courage to whip the dripping floor cloth out of her hand and squeeze it dry, but Biddy's look forbade any such liberty.

Horrified, at the thought of having to take over from her, for I particularly disliked cleaning the bathroom, I heard myself plead cravenly, "this place is in a mess; won't you finish it before you go?"

Biddy aimed the floor cloth, followed by the Vim, in the direction of the bath with deadly accuracy, and began to wrestle with the strings, of what she described, as her charring apron.

Probably thinking I had loss my wits, she laughed uproariously. "Not bloody likely. Ya can do yar own dirty work, me fine lady, till ya find another egit to do it for ya. As Mrs. Symmington-Smyth alees says, ya can't make a silk purse outa a sow's ear." And without a backward glance she stormed out.

I followed slowly, as her heavy boots took the stairs at a gallop. Silently I settled my account with her, and I knew she had gone when the house shook, at the resounding crash of the hall door behind her.

We did not get a general, trained or untrained, for a long time after that experience. Indeed we had to spend whatever money we could spare repairing the damage wrought by previous holders of the title.

It was Myrabelle who eventually got us our domestic treasure. Her own competent general had an eighteen year old niece, named Jane, who was about to start out in life as an untrained general. Would I be willing to give her a start, Myrabelle twinkled coyly? Would I!! If she was remotely like her aunt, I was home and dry at last.

Jane was plump, pink-cheeked and pretty. She had lovely dark hair to her waist, which she wore in two rich coils over her ears. She was endlessly good-humoured, resourceful and kind, and Rosemarie loved her from the start.

Until she left us to get married, and there was not a dry eye when she did, I had one of the best appointed domestic routines in the country.

Chapter 60

It began as a lovely sunny day.

In the early morning, I sipped my cup of tea in our minute back garden. It was a dear little place to dream awhile, and watch the bees hum lazily from flower to flower. The only sounds were the clip-clop of the milkman's horse, the occasional jangle of an early tram, the sharp whistle of the postman, and the deep boom of the Cathedral bell from St. Patrick's.

Edward was a born gardener. He had got a load of earth to raise the level of the ground, bordering the path at the side of the house. This produced a nice patch for growing things, particularly as it was sheltered by an old granite wall, which separated our house from the one next door.

Edward had been successful with a wide selection of old fashioned flowers, notably marigolds, lupins, summer stock, lobelia, pinks, candytuft, and the magical night scented stock of the gorgeous evening perfume.

There was a big clump of scarlet dahlias in a sunny corner, which exploded in colour year after year, and were originally planted by Mrs. Gandon, when she first came to the house, at least it was probably its descendant. Sometimes, in the drowsy twilight, I felt the presence of a tall lady in poke bonnet and silken gown, bending over the lush petals with a reviving jug of water. Against the wall leaned two pink hollyhocks, and a thriving jasmine clung tenaciously to the glinting stone in a profusion of starry blossoms.

I smiled, thinking of Rosemarie playing here on her own, or with a little playmate from the kindergarten, but I thought with less pleasure of some of her escapades.

Only last week, the starchy Miss Grandville from next door, had marched in to complain that someone was firing stones over the wall, and cracked the glass of her little greenhouse. On investigation, that "someone" had turned out to be our Rosemarie, who insisted that the stones had been thrown back at her.

"That lady was playing ballie with me," she accused our crotchety neighbour, who managed to extract compensation for several panes of broken glass on the strength of it.

Another day, I was disturbed by the wild miowing of a cat in the garden, and there was my daughter with Ginger by the tail, whirling him around for all she was worth.

"What do you think you're doing," I yelled in horror. Rosemarie dropped the animal, who scampered madly away through a hole in the garden door.

Aiming a smack at her bottom, I demanded: "How could you treat poor Ginger like that?"

"I was only giving him a swing, Mamma," she pleaded tearfully.

I sighed now as my eyes fell on her "piece" of garden, the sight of which never failed to annoy her father who felt it could be more gainfully used for more flowers. It was usually filled with stones, tins and puddles of muck, which the child used in the manner of a sand-pit, making castles and mud pies.

Edward used many ploys to move her out of occupation, but she firmly resisted his every effort. The worst part for me, was trying to keep her away from the water, which she wanted for pies and other noxious mixtures.

Her latest creation was to be a pond similar, if not in size, to the one in the Green. If she achieved this, she calculated on bringing home "a few ducks from the Green; only little ones," she added hurriedly, as I opened my mouth to protest.

"There are too many ducks down there, Mamma, and one big duck is always following me. I think she wants to give me a few of hers."

The construction of her pond was hindered by the water seeping out of it, and my unwillingness to keep up the plentiful supply she demanded. A trail of water, widening all over the kitchen floor, put an end to my patience, and it was with great difficulty that I got herself, and her bucket, outside the back door.

She roared mournfully for some time, but I wisely took no notice. Eventually, she realised that I was not to be shifted, and quietening somewhat, drifted over to her "piece" where, I surmised, she was planning her next move.

I hummed to myself in some relief, as I cleaned out the dresser and re-arranged our limited supply of crockery and groceries, on newly-papered shelves.

Suddenly, the peace was shattered by a man's angry shout, and Rosemarie's indignant protests. Rushing to the door from whence the commotion ensued, I swiftly opened it to find myself face to face with the cranky Mr. Lamb, who occupied the house at the end of our garden.

There was a sullen scowl on his wrinkled face as he confronted me, holding my daughter by the collar of her coat. She was crying loudly and dripping in dark sludgy water.

Mr. Lamb was cross-eyed, so I wasn't so sure whether he was addressing me, or some unknown entity at the back of my head.

"You should be lookin' after this kid of yours," he growled. "She could 'ave been drowned."

"What on earth's happened," I gasped.

"What's happened?" he mimicked, "Well I'll tell ya, quick too. This young divil was bucketing water outa me trough when she fell in."

"Oh lord!" I groaned.

"That's all verra fine, but me hosses could find thereselves without water," he grumbled.

"The child could have been drowned, you said," I reminded him tartly. "And a lot you care, complaining about your horses," and I pulled the sobbing Rosemarie into my arms.

The mis-named Mr. Lamb threw his arms about in wild gestures. "I can't spend the day in me garden mindin' yar kid. It's a disgraceful situation when parents want other hard workin' people to look after their kids. Disgraceful, I call it. Don't bloomin' care, they don't," he ended spitefully.

The child shivered, and I was about to turn away when a thought struck me. "How did you get into Mr. Lamb's yard?" I demanded of her, as our garden door, which leads to the laneway shared by us and several other houses, is always kept locked.

She pointed dumbly to the bottom of the door, which revealed a gaping hole in the rotten wood. I knew Ginger used it by way of an escape route, but I never guessed that Rosemarie could wriggle through it.

"You wouldn't give me water anyway," she sobbed defensively in an effort to put the blame for her misdemeanour squarely on my shoulders.

"That's all very fine...." and Mr. Lamb went into another spasm of rage.... "but yad better keep that young wan under control. I mightn't be so handy the next time to rescue her."

He paused and eyed me severely. "I can't have kids walkin' all over me garden. If there's any more if it now, I'll have the law on ya."

I gaped at him. Mr. Lamb's "garden" was a place of utter dilapidation. It was always referred to by the neighbours as "the yard." It housed a stable of cart horses, and also doubled as a coal yard, for Mr. Lamb had a thriving business supplying huxters shops and casual customers, with small amounts of firewood and coal. He was also known to dabble in second-hand clothes, vegetables, paraffin oil, and bits of furniture in the last stages of disrepair.

The wall dividing it from the lane had long since fallen down, and Mr. Lamb had not deemed its replacement necessary.

He had recently branched out into pig farming, and was seen regularly collecting swill from the houses around. The fact of this enterprise was confirmed by the piggy odours which had begun to overpower the sweetness of our little garden.

"Garden!" I exploded. "It's a long time since that dump was a garden. That lane is a health hazard for anyone using it, or indeed living near it. You have no right to have your animals wandering all over it, and the place is never cleaned."

"Don't ya give me imprince," he roared, wagging a filthy fist in my face. "Ya think ya own the house...." and he threw an angry arm in the direction of my domain.

"How do you know I don't?" I retorted, and that's none of your business, but you think you own the lane...."

Rosemarie gave a bored wail as Mr. Lamb turned purple and shouted: "That's all verra fine, but ya wait 'till next time...."

I turned my back on him, and hustled the child none too gently inside, kicking the door behind me.

Chapter 61

After a warm bath which once again revealed the pink and white prettiness of my daughter, Rosemarie was dancing about in a clean cotton dress and blue sunbonnet. Ida was taking her for a walk in Herbert Park as a change from the Green.

Edward had bought her a doll's pram for her birthday, and had proudly borne it from shop to home across the back of his bicycle. It had cost a pricy 12/6 and was the apple of her eye.

We went up to the hall, and there the child happily arranged her teddy in the pram, among a couple of miniature rugs I had knitted from scraps of wool.

Ida came down the stairs in her coat, all ready for the trip to the park, and Rosemarie rushed to meet her.

They were just about to leave when Adelaide appeared at the top of the stairs; she was carrying the dark gypsy doll in her arms.

"Rosemarie," she called sharply, and as the child and Ida turned in surprise, she limped laboriously down the stairs and over to the doll's pram.

"You may take Reza out in the pram to-day," she informed an uneasy Rosemarie. "Reza wants to see the park," and she cast aside the little rugs, and pulled the teddy out of the pram, letting it fall to the floor.

"No," shrieked the child, snatching up the beloved teddy.

"Don't want hobble doll," and she made to throw it out of the pram.

Adelaide pushed the doll back amongst the rugs.

"You wicked, ungrateful child," she hissed with blazing eyes. "You take Reza and be very careful with her. Don't you dare touch her. I'll arrange her in the pram," and she began tucking the rugs around the doll.

Rosemarie continued to shout, "don't want hobble doll" and I was about to intervene, when Ida went to the pram and gently removed the doll.

"Not to-day, Adelaide. Reza would rather not go out to-day; she would find the sun too hot, and this pram is much too small for her....see she can't lie down in it."

Adelaide clutched the doll, and went to reinstall it in the pram. I put out a hand to restrain her, but hesitated, as I felt it was better to leave Ida manoeuvre the situation in her own way.

Ida again intervened, and suddenly they were both struggling with the doll. I cannot say exactly how it happened, but there was a horrified scream from Adelaide as the doll crashed to the tiled floor; its waxen head disintegrating in a shower of shattered pieces. There was an appalled silence, and we all stood in frozen apprehension. Cautiously, I raised my head as Adelaide retrieved the broken doll and was staring at it vacantly, the limp body seeming to twitch weirdly in her trembling hands.

Ida looked pale and shocked, as she stared aghast at her sister; only Rosemarie moved serenely, sitting the teddy in the pram, happy that the usurper had been ousted.

I broke the silence. "I'm so sorry, Miss Lister, but I'm sure you can have the doll repaired."

At my words, Adelaide seemed to emerge from a trance. "You can't have her repaired, you stupid woman. Can't you see she's dead," she cried venomously.

"I'll never forget this for you," she went on, with burning eyes. "Only for you, this wouldn't have happened to my poor Reza."

I stared at her blankly, frightened by the unreasonable accusation, which I knew it would be useless to refute.

Ida put an arm about her sister's shoulders. "You know that's not true, Adelaide dear." she said soothingly. "Mrs. Davis had nothing to do with the breaking of your doll."

Adelaide shook her sister's arm away, and regarded me with malevolent eyes. "She is to blame. She should have punished that wicked child for her ingratitude," and she took a menacing step towards Rosemarie.

The child was instantly on her guard, and rushed over to me. I put my arms protectively around her. "Don't be afraid,"

I said gently, "no one will hurt you," and I managed to hold Adelaide's hard stare.

She turned to Ida. "Go upstairs and bring down my jewel box," she commanded.

Ida looked at me and hesitated, but I nodded, and without another word, she went swiftly up the stairs.

Adelaide was muttering incoherently as she stared at the tattered doll, and I wondered if I should escape to the kitchen, or wait for Ida to return. I was still trying to make up my mind, when Ida returned, carrying a beautiful oblong box of filigree silver. Adelaide snatched it, and commenced to pick up the broken pieced of the doll, piling them into the box.

We watched her silently after an offer to help was firmly repulsed. When all the fragments were gathered in the box, Adelaide rose stiffly to her feet and, with the jewel box safely under her arm, limped disconsolately up to her flat.

After a pause Ida followed her.

"I'll just make sure she's alright," she whispered to me.

She returned shortly, saying that Adelaide had locked herself in and refused to open the door.

"I'll take Rosemarie out....give her time to cool down," she said, nodding towards the stairs and straightening her hat.

"Well if you're sure," I said uneasily.

Rashly I heard myself offering to look in on Adelaide, and take her up a cup of tea. I don't know what made me say it, for the last thing I wanted was a tete-a- tete with Adelaide Lister.

Ida thanked me gratefully and helped Rosemarie out with her pram.

Later, I went up to the flat and knocked timidly on the door; there was no reply.

"Miss Lister," I called softly, resisting the temptation to turn the door knob to see if it was locked.

I was just about to leave when her harsh voice reached me. "Go away. What do you want?"

"Would you like a cup of tea, Miss Lister?" I replied bravely.

Her voice came back sourly. "I don't want tea. If I want tea I can afford to make it myself."

Without another word I went downstairs, glad I had not to face the ordeal of talking to her.

Next day, Ida slipped into the kitchen to tell me that herself, and Adelaide were going away for a few days. "We are going to a cousin in Rathfarnham," she told me, and I noticed how strained she looked as I sat her down for a cup of tea.

After a few sips, she said with an effort: "Adelaide has laid out the doll in the jewel box and she wants to bury it in some country spot."

I stared at her in surprise. "You mean she takes it all that seriously....believes that the doll really died?"

"Was killed," said Ida tiredly. "It's all very real to her; no question about it. That doll is as real to her as we are....maybe more so."

Trying to be practical, I offered the opinion that if the thing was buried, perhaps Adelaide would get it out of her mind. I hoped the cousin would be understanding, and the whole unpleasant business quickly forgotten. The sisters duly left for their cousin's country house. Ida holding a tapestry bag of their immediate necessities, Adelaide, grim-faced, with the jewel box pressed to her breast.

Ida waved as they were driven away, but Adelaide never looked in my direction, nor uttered a word when I bade her a pleasant journey.

With their departure, ordinary every-day life was resumed, and the vagaries of Adelaide, receded to the back of my mind.

Chapter 62

Myrabelle paid me an unexpected visit. She looked pale and listless, and I said concernedly: "You seem a bit down in yourself."

She followed me down to the kitchen, and parked herself despondently on the arm of a chair. "I've had a dose of 'flu, and I suppose I'm a bit run down," she answered tiredly. She lit a cigarette and I noticed how her fingers shook as she applied a light.

She did not seem to want to pursue the subject, for she got up and went to the backdoor calling for Rosemarie. The child was messing about in her piece of garden, but she rushed in delightedly.

Myrabelle smiled wanly at my grubby urchin and hugged her warmly.

"Look what your Aunty Myrabelle has for you," she said, handing her a brown-paper parcel.

Rosemarie soon had the paper off, and exclaimed rapturously: "Oh, a gramophone! Oh Aunty Myrabelle, a gramophone just like Dadda's!"

Admonishing Myrabelle for spoiling the child, I rose to make a cup of tea, leaving both of them examining the new toy.

But Myrabelle raised a detaining hand. "Not for me Lynny, and thanks all the same. I only dropped in to see how you are and give Rosemarie a belated birthday present."

Dismissing my thanks for Rosemarie's gift, she rose to go, fastening her soft wooly coat, and kissing me briefly. Then she hugged the bemused child and walked quickly to the hall. There she paused, and I felt she was going to say something, but changing her mind, she went down the stone steps to the street, leaving me vaguely puzzled and uneasy.

Rosemarie soon dispelled all gloomy thoughts. It took her only a short time to get the gramophone going; Myrabelle had included in the gift a little stack of records, and these were played and replayed endlessly. It was a lovely, yellow-coloured instrument....the real thing in miniature, and it played all the small records perfectly.

The only headache for me was the repetition of the same tunes over and over again, and when I protested, Rosemarie soon solved that problem in her own inimitable way; she simply borrowed Edward's smallest records. Anything bigger would overbalance on the tiny turntable, and be liable to crack, so she thought if she kept the sound low, we would not notice what she played.

These miniature records were sold in Woolworth's at a half-penny each, and we often spent a happy hour on a Saturday afternoon, going through the latest offerings, while the shop gramophone belted out new, and not so new, favourites. Alternatively, Peggy Dell enthralled us with her playing of many catchy tunes on the piano, and always had a good crowd around her to take up the chorus.

How I loved "Ramona," "Spanish Rose," "Sonny Boy,""Bye Bye Blackbird," catchy bits from the operas, and many others of that era. This was the age of the black singers, "Layton & Johnson", who romanticised with such tear-jerkers as "In The Evening," and "My Darling Chikeeta."

There were comic records for the more ribald minded, excerpts from great classical singers, and music hall hits like "Sweet Adeline" and "Two Little Girls In Blue." Edward had a preference for "Darling I Am Growing Old," which he warbled continuously.

Infuriated, I would snap deflateingly, "It's ok; I have noticed," or even less romantically: "Not again, for heavens sake."

And the standard answer to that was always, "oh yes, there was a time when you couldn't get enough of me!"

For myself, I adored Percy French, and if Edward wanted to be specially loving, or make amends after a row, he would confidently return, ensuring his reinstatement in my wifely affections, with a recording of "Ballyjamesduff," "Phil The Fluter," or whichever one was lacking in my collection.

As I say, we loved them all and bought them all, or at least a sizeable amount.

After Mass on a Sunday morning, Edward, Rosemarie and I (with one eye on the cooking dinner) would adjourn to the drawing room, where we played the records, and Edward sang to his own accompaniment on the violin. He had a fine tenor voice, and it was the unanimous opinion among our friends that he could have made a good living from it. But he had no ambitions along those lines, and was simply happy to sing for family and friends when pressed to do so.

Rosemarie also loved to sing and dance; she particularly enjoyed a ditty called "Me And Jane In a Plane." This was one of those she "borrowed," and it was played so often that it became very scratchy. This drove me frantic when it got stuck in a groove and Rosemarie, fleetingly interested in something else, would forget to turn it off. She left this grating symbol on most of our small records, so we always knew which ones she had taken. Fortunately, the standard size record was too big for her turntable, but such obvious unsuitability did not deter her from finding this out for herself. The result was inevitable....the record overbalanced and cracked.

Usually we never recovered the remains of the ones she broke; sometimes they were unearthed in the oddest places.... the coal hole, the old basement range, or under the bath.

Once she hid the fractured "Red Red Robin," behind a picture on the landing, and frightened the life out of me on my way to bed, when the two halves of it slid noisily to the floor.

Chapter 63

Adelaide and Ida returned a few days later.

I was in the hall dusting when they came in. Adelaide looked haggard and absent-minded, never acknowledged me, and Ida only nodded and smiled wearily.

It was the following afternoon when I learned how they had got on at the cousin's. Ida had come down for a chat, and I asked how Adelaide was.

"She's kind of more remote than she was before that dreadful doll was broken," she replied worriedly."Relations between herself and our cousin were very strained, and it was only too obvious that Sarah was greatly relieved when Adelaide told her we were leaving."

"The doll?" I asked quickly. "What did she do with the doll?"

"I'm not sure," Ida frowned. "She went out into Sarah's garden in the middle of the night with the box, and I haven't seen it since. I was afraid of mentioning it in case it upset her."

A feeling of apprehension swept through me. "What are you going to do, Ida? I mean, it's very difficult for you trying to look after her."

Ida paused, a frightened look on her face. "I don't rightly know what to do. It's useless trying to talk to her. I'm afraid...." and her voice trailed dismally away.

"Yes?" I prompted gently.

"Well, she'll probably get more strange," she said helplessly.

We fell silent; both dwelling on the terrifying implications of that word "strange."

We jumped when Rosemarie bounced in, and Ida roused herself.

"I'd best go up and prepare the evening meal," she sighed.

Next morning, I was searching in the linen drawer for a clean tablecloth, when my fingers closed over something smooth and hairy with jagged edges.

Drawing it out, I recoiled in horror when I found a fragment of Adelaide's broken doll in my hand. One black eye remained in the piece, and it stared back at me with eerie intensity. Above it, a shock of coarse black hair entwined around my fingers.

I stifled a scream and dropped it back into the drawer, forgetting the tablecloth in my fright. I guessed of course, that Adelaide had put it there, but why?

I determinedly put it out of my mind, but a similar incident occurred about a week later. I opened Rosemarie's clothes cupboard, and on top of a pile of vests, was an arm of the gypsy doll. That night while Rosemarie was having her bath, I went into the bedroom to prepare her cot and there, on the pillow, was another part of the doll's face; it's weird black eye glaring up at me.

Feeling really worried now, I debated whether to go up and confront Adelaide, or not. Frightening me was one thing, but suppose the child had opened that drawer, or pulled the blankets back from the pillow....? My heart missed a beat at the thought.

When I asked Edward's advice, he said he thought it would be useless to accuse Adelaide, as she would most probably deny placing the broken pieces of the doll among our possessions. There was also the possibility of her becoming very unpredictable in her unstable condition.

I decided to leave things be for the present; after all, practically speaking, there could not be many more pieces of the doll left. Surely, Adelaide would tire of trying to intimidate me when she found I was ignoring her, but I would need to remain vigilant. I would have to be the one to find anymore pieces and destroy them.

Shortly after that, we were in bed one night, when I was awakened by a disturbance downstairs. I heard the drawing room clock chime twice and I listened intently. Then the sound of music drifted in a lonely wail through the darkness.

Without waking Edward I got out of bed, snatched my dressing gown, and cautiously opened the door. The music was a lot clearer now, and I recognised it as an excerpt from Greig's "Pier Gynt," a record I had recently bought for Edward.

The music was coming from the direction of the dining room; I reached the first landing where the moonlight filtered through the red and blue glass of the bathroom door, and reflected the colours in elongated shadows on the floor.

Who could be playing music at this hour? Suddenly there was a crash and the music stopped abruptly, while at the same time, Rosemarie gave a terrified scream; she was prone to nightmares since the day that Adelaide had tried to force her to accept the gypsy doll.

I rushed back to the bedroom to comfort her, but Edward was crooning to her, and she was almost asleep again.

"Where have you been Lynn ?" he whispered.

I did not want to say anything in case Rosemarie could hear me, so I said as calmly as I could: "Oh, just to the bathroom."

Rosemarie stirred and began to sob that the "hobble" doll was coming to get her.

I told Edward to go to sleep, as he had an early start in the morning, and tucking the child up cosily I began to tell her a favourite fairy story.

Eventually she dropped off to sleep, and I stole down the stairs intent on finding the cause of the noise. I was on the landing when I heard stealthy footsteps coming from the kitchen, across the hall and up the first flight of stairs. I had only a moment to hide behind a tall screen, before a small figure stepped into a beam of moonlight, and I saw that it was Ida.

As quickly as she had come, she was gone soundlessly up to her flat. I crept out from behind the screen, and peering furtively about in the dim light, descended to the dining room.

At first I could see nothing as the room was in total darkness. Then the light snapped on, and I found myself staring into the pale face of Adelaide Lister. She was fully dressed, even to her drab outdoor coat with the rabbity fur collar.

I felt faint with fright and near to blind panic.

"I'm looking for Reza," said Adelaide in a flat empty voice, and I realised I was facing a woman who was no longer sane. She looked so tall and formidable; what would she say if I said something to anger her? I decided my best course was to try and go along with her in as normal a manner as possible.

"I haven't seen Reza either, Miss Lister, perhaps she has returned to bed."

She paused and looked at me closely.

"Someone murdered Reza. Did you know that? Oh, yes and they have to be punished."

I shivered, unnerved by her piercing black gaze and menacing stance. Desperately, I wondered how I could get past her, and up to the safety of Edward and our bedroom.

"Can I do anything for you? Let me help you up to bed, or maybe, make you a cup of tea," I offered, trying to control the tremor in my voice.

She made no reply; her dark hooded eyes boring into mine.

"Perhaps you have a headache....?" I said feebly.

She muttered something, and turning slowly, crossed the hall and ascended the stairs, her injured foot clumping heavily in the silence.

Then I heard Ida from the upper landing: "Where have you been, Adelaide?" she cried; her voice shrill with anxiety. "I've been all over the house searching for you."

Adelaide gave a harsh laugh. "Gave you a fright, did I? Serve you right. I knew you were sneaking around spying on me, but I was hiding...."

"You shouldn't have done that," Ida interrupted her accusingly. "I heard a crash and thought you'd fallen...."

The voices faded and the door closed softly.

Feeling I'd had enough for one night, I switched off the light and throwing caution to the wind, ran blindly back to the bedroom. There, I lay awake until morning, wondering what was to be done about Adelaide.

Chapter 64

Next morning when we were having our breakfast the peace was shattered by a shriek from Rosemarie, who had wandered off to the dining room after her meal.

Spilling my tea, I ran out to find her, closely followed by Edward.

We did not need to ask what was wrong, for on the floor lay the treasured little gramophone reduced to a twisted pile of battered metal. A few feet away, the "Pier Gynt" record was splintered beyond recall.

Someone had taken a heavy implement and brought it down hard on the toy, which explained the crash both Ida and I had heard in the night.

Rosemarie's sobs grew louder, as she held up pieces of the ruined toy to me pleadingly.

"Who could have done such a thing?" demanded Edward in a cold fury.

I could not speak; only clasp the sobbing child lovingly in my arms. I thought of Adelaide, wandering about in the dark, and her obsession with the broken doll, and I felt a terrifying anxiety. Had Adelaide, unbalanced and in search of the lost Reza, found revenge in destroying the child's favourite toy?

When Ida came down to collect the post, she put her head around the door to ask what was the matter with Rosemarie. Miserably I showed her the wrecked toy, and she admitted it could only be the work of Adelaide. Sadly she said that she was not really surprised, as in her younger days, if anyone upset her sister, she would await an opportunity to destroy some cherished article belonging to the person she believed had offended her.

"It's no use trying to reason with her, either; she'll deny everything, and by the time she's finished abusing you, you'll wish you'd never said anything," sighed the long suffering Ida hopelessly.

Fear shot through me, as I tried to grapple with the problem of Adelaide. She would definitely have to go; the situation was fraught with danger, especially now she was convinced that Rosemarie was responsible for the destruction of her doll.

Yes, Ida and I would need to talk seriously, but not at this hour of the morning when we were all tired and bewildered. It was difficult to pacify Rosemarie, and impossible to explain the wanton destruction of her beloved toy.

"I will make good the damage," promised Ida with tears in her eyes. "Don't cry child. I'll make sure you get another exactly the same."

Rosemarie ran to her and put her arms around the little lady. "Don't be sad, Aunty Ida," she consoled her, and with inspiration added, "Santa will bring me another one for Christmas."

Ida hugged the child. "You won't have to wait that long, my pretty one," she said. "You and I are going to the shops after dinner to buy a new one, and we'll have a sweet cake and lemonade in Bewley's afterwards."

Rosemarie's tears dried rapidly, as she danced around at the unexpected solution to the debacle. Happiness once again restored, thanks to Ida's loving handling of a nasty situation.

The following night at about eight o'clock, the Adelaide predicament reached a dramatic climax. I had seen nothing of Ida since the previous day when she came home with Rosemarie after the shopping expedition.

Rosemarie had been in high spirits on their return, and she exhibited her new gramophone joyfully to everyone, but Ida seemed tense and worried behind the cheerful show she put up in front of the child.

I felt distressed at allowing her to bear the expense of replacing the toy. After all, she had been in no way responsible for the damage, but no matter how I argued, she would not hear of me even sharing the cost. Forcing a smile she had added:

"Well I bought a present for myself too," and she unwrapped a canvas depicting an old country cottage, set in a profusion of flowers.

"Gorgeous!" I murmured, in awe of the prospective work involved in bringing the scene to life.

"Keep me busy for some time," she observed, letting her hand slip through the medley of silken threads needed for the tapestry.

Later as Edward and I were having supper in the dining room we suddenly heard a great deal of commotion coming from overhead. Sudden screams rent the air, and I felt the hairs rise on the back of my neck.

Shocked and shaking we dashed into the hall, where a bewildered Captain was gaping upwards, pipe sagging from his lips. From the top of the stairs, Ida came rushing down, a lurid red streak running down the side of her face.

"Oh my God!" I thought, "Adelaide."

Edward caught her as she stumbled on the last step and brought her over to me. Just then Adelaide appeared, glowering down on us from the first landing.

She was shouting wildly and brandishing a heavy poker in a black -gloved hand: her whole aspect grotesque and dishevelled. I had never seen her other than fully and neatly dressed, but now she was clad in a yellow nightshirt, which reached to her bare calves, and her skinny legs were thrust into clumsy unbuttoned boots. Her voice rose in a spate of incoherent threats, and the poker shook in her hand with deadly ferocity.

Edward pushed Ida and me into the dining room, and I had the helpless feeling of being trapped in a nightmare.

"Rosemarie," I shrieked in an agony of terror, as I remembered the child asleep in the bedroom.

"She'll be alright. Take a grip of yourself, Lynn, for all our sakes," Edward insisted, and firmly disentangled my clutching fingers from his arm.

He went back to the hall, locking the door on us. Ida was crying openly and wringing her hands helplessly, the blood from the cut on her head seeping into the shoulder of her dressing gown in a vivid patch.

Trying to suppress my panic, I set about dressing the wound with whatever I could find. As I worked, my ears strained to the agitation in the hall. Then there came a heavy thud which transcended the other sounds....and silence.

I rushed to the door and hammered on the panels. "Edward! Edward!" I screamed, totally blinded by fear. "Are you and Rosemarie alright?"

After an age, I heard his voice above a babble of voices. "I'm alright Lynn. Keep calm and stop shouting."

Reassured, I went over to Ida. As we stood at the window, the wailing of an ambulance filled the room as it pulled up swiftly to the door. Two men leapt out carrying a stretcher, and I could hear their voices brisk and efficient in the hall. Minutes later they returned to the ambulance with the prone figure of Adelaide; in seconds they were gone.

Ida was weeping bitterly as her sister was taken away, and I was doing my utmost to try to console her, when the door was unlocked, and Edward came in with Dr. Hall from down the street. While he attended Ida, I followed Edward into the hall.

"Rosemarie....is she alright?" I began fearfully.

Edward put his arms around me and said soothingly, "of course she is....slept through it all."

"Thank God," I cried feelingly. "And Adelaide....what happened?"

Edward's voice was low and strained. "She tripped and fell down the stairs. When I went over to her she was unconscious with her legs twisted badly under her...."

He stopped and I looked at him inquiringly. "It was a mercy, I suppose, for the Lord knows what damage she could have done with that poker, and the state she was in."

I shuddered as Edward continued. "The Captain went for Dr. Hall. He examined her and said her two legs were broken....he got the ambulance...."

He stared at my white face. "You mustn't worry, Lynn. She was acting strangely for a while now, and was a danger to herself and all of us."

Later on, when Ida had partially recovered from a severe headache and shock symptoms, told me what had led up to the traumatic event.

It appeared that over the past week, Adelaide had become progressively more obsessive about finding Reza, maintaining that she had seen the gypsy doll sitting by the fire, or looking through the window of their flat.

Just this evening, after a visit to a local shop, Adelaide told Ida, that when she returned, Reza was standing at the door waiting for her. Adelaide had held out her arms and called to the doll, but it always evaded her when she tried to take it in her arms. Later she complained that the doll was missing, and must have been stolen by some evil-doer, who would pay dearly for such a wicked deed.

Ida had not been well all day and had not left the flat, mainly because she was alarmed by her sister's eccentric behaviour, and was afraid of leaving her alone. Earlier, Ida had found her throwing some of her more valuable dolls out of their cabinet, and beating them in an effort to elicit information from them concerning the missing Reza. After tea, which Adelaide refused, she grew very agitated and began flinging clothes and household items around the flat in a demented search for the missing doll. Ida had tried to calm her, reminding her gently, that Reza was buried in Rathfarnham, but Adelaide, growing more angry, grabbed the poker and struck her on the side of the head. Terrified, as she sought to escape from her sister's rage, Ida managed to get through the door and down the stairs.

The rest of the sad story we knew and it's tragic ending. Adelaide did not recover in hospital: she was certified insane and confined to an asylum. Six months later she was dead.

I had never liked the hard, autocratic woman, but I could only feel compassion when I recalled the early catastrophe in her life, coupled to a feverish imagination and mental instability, which had warped her mind.

Maybe, I mused dolefully, I too could have turned out like her if anything had happened to Edward....there but for the grace of God....

Adelaide's dolls were sold to a collector, along with a few pieces of her jewellery, and the money made a nice little nest egg for Ida. After spending some time alone in the flat, she vacated it, saying it was too big for her needs, but I suspect she could not bear to go on living in it because of its unhappy associations. Jane and I removed all her possessions from it to the room once occupied by the flamboyant Alan Floy, and there she settled down peacefully.

Adelaide's ancient garments went to the ragman. I had offered them to a lady beggar, who informed me she was in a bad way for "an oul coat, dress or skirt," but she was deeply offended when offered this collection.

"I wouldn't be got dead in dem tings," she said in disgust, casting aside a heavy crepe dress, which might have been à la mode forty years ago. "Janey ma-am, I'm not that desperate," she commented indignantly with a curl of her lips, when I suggested she tried on the fawn coat with the rabbity collar.

Chapter 65

I was tidying a pile of coats in the hall when Captain Rodgers came in, an old carpet bag tied with string in one hand, and the disreputable parrot cage in the other. He looked preoccupied and disgruntled, and did not appear to notice me.

"Good evening, Captain," I greeted him brightly.

"'Evening Missus," he answered without his usual gusto.

"How did you find your friend Joe?" I pursued, for I knew he had been staying a few days with an old seafaring friend.

"Game ball, game ball," he replied gruffly.

"That's good," I paused. "Anything the matter Captain?" I noticed he was speaking in a funny muffled tone.

He hesitated, and then seeming to make up his mind, dumped his bag and cage on the floor to the angry shriek of the parrot.

"Yea, I enjoyed the visit with Joe, but owny up to a point. Now Joe's a dacent oul mate if ever thar were wan....served in The Nina with me long ago, but he got 'imself a right oul egit of a dog....a flaming' great ting....a mastieve or somethin' he called it."

"You're never serious?" I encouraged, leaning against the hallstand, and wondering where the "oul egit of a dog" was leading.

"Well ya see when I got up this mornin', me teeth were missin'" he tapped his mouth meaningly, and I viewed a wide expanse of gummy jaws.

"Ya know, Joe allows dis oul dog to trapse around ta house, day and night. Anyways, me teeth were missin,' an I alwees leaves 'em beside me bed for mornin'. Now why, I ask ya, should I suddenly depart from me usual practice, and put 'em somewhere else?"

He gazed at me challengingly, but I could not offer any solution to his question, and thought it wiser to remain silent.

Kicking his accoutrements on the floor, which brought a resounding screech from the parrot, he absently drew out his pipe, and banged it against a china vase on a side table.

"Anyways, neither of us could find dem anywhere," he continued gloomily, and I can't smoke me bloody pipe eather.... savin' yar presence, Missus....in case I swally it....no grip, ya know, "and he pocketed the pipe in disgust.

The parrot squawked, and could be heard busily trying to peck the hated red rag off his cage.

"So you looked everywhere and couldn't find them?" I probed.

"Ex-ac-alee," the captain agreed.

"We went all over the bit of a garden, and were lookin' in the dustbin, when Joe spots the oul dog rootin' about. The next ting, he were off across the garden with me teeth in his gob, and Joe tearin' after 'im."

The Captain stopped with such a look of outrage on his face, that I ached with the pain of trying to conceal my laughter.

"Then," he resumed peevishly, "Joe ketches up with ta fool of a dog and starts wraslin' with 'im, tryin' to shake me teeth outa the animal's jaws, and the oul dog tinks it's some sort of a game, and drops me teeth in the muck in two fecking pieces.... of little use ta man nor dog. There I am now with nare a tooth in me head...." and swearing vengeance on the "egit of a dog," he picked up his baggage and marched indignantly to his room, but the parrot had the last word. As the the rag succumbed to a final peck, he emerged in all his scruffy finery, screaming," missin' teeth, missin' teeth. Ha! Ha! Ha!"

Chapter 66

The Listers flat had been unoccupied for several weeks, and I felt it was high time it was pressed into service again. I answered an advertisement in the "Mail," and that was how Mr. and Mrs. Samuel Vector came to take their short abode with us.

He was a small, fussy man who sported gold-rimmed spectacles: the same costly metal sparkling in his teeth whenever he opened his mouth.

She was plump and soft with a dazzling mound of platinum blonde hair.

Bleach, I thought sceptically, and this suspicion was confirmed, when the evidence showed up in the dust bin in the form of empty bottles marked "Peroxide."

She spoke in a gentle shy voice, as she explained that they would be only taking the flat for about six weeks while the builders were finishing their new house in Clonskeagh.

They owned a grocery shop in Thomas Street and sold everything from a "knife to a needle," he related to me boastfully.

"Self -made, I am," he informed me pompously, tapping the heavy gold watch, anchored to his waistcoat by a double gold chain. "Me father was the same before me. I never went beyont fourth book at school, and me father hardly went at all. Hard work is me motto. Get on with the work if you want to get on. I always say that, and I have the results of it here," and he rattled his breast pocket significantly which, I presumed, indicated his wallet. "I'm what you might call very well got in the trade," he stated dogmatically, pushing back his opulent leather coat, and sticking his thumbs under a pair of red braces.

I listened, helpless to stem the tide of his oratory, as he enlightened me on the methods he used to "gain business."

In my ignorance, I did not think them very acceptable, but he laughed mirthlessly at my reservations, and countenanced no argument with his opinions .

"Correct me if I'm wrong, Nonie," he alluded to his wife magnanimously at intervals, knowing he would receive the same hackneyed support of "just as you say Sam," to his every pronouncement. At last I managed to guide him tactfully up the stairs to the flat, she trailing behind to look at our pictures and ornaments en route. When we stood in the neat little flat, he looked about indifferently, but she seemed very taken with it, reminding me wistfully of my own happiness when Edward and I first rented it. After deferring respectfully to him, and obtaining his apathetic agreement, Nonie told me they would take the flat. She was really a nice person although completely dominated by her overbearing husband. We finalized the arrangements for their early occupation and I offered them a cup of tea.

She looked eager to accept, but he moving impatiently from foot to foot, said he had an important appointment and was in a hurry. I did not miss the look of disappointment that flashed across her face, but she acquiesced to his wishes without a word. No need to look for the boss in that outfit, I thought grimly.

Awkwardly, I tried to fill the embarrassing pause "That's a lovely costume you're wearing, Mrs. Ventor," I lied, and swept my eyes admiringly over her scarlet outfit, fat legs and shapeless red shoes. A pull-on purple hat, stabbed with feathers and cocooned in spotted black veiling, clung with fascinating tenacity to her blonde head. The ensemble, possibly quite expensive, but badly chosen, did nothing to flatter her ungainly figure, and the gaudy colours made her look old and washed out.

Her face brightened and she smiled gratefully.

"Do you really like it?" she responded diffidently, and glancing at her tetchy husband, added apologetically: "Sam loves to see me dressed up, you know."

Sam looked at her indifferently, and evidently thinking that his own finery was entitled to some admiring recognition, held out his coat to me.

"Feel that," he commanded. "Bet you've never been that close to a real leather coat. Cost me a fortune, it did," he said with pride.

"It's lovely, Mr Ventor," I said without enthusiasm, making no attempt to "feel" its grandeur.

He smirked at his wife who was watching him respectfully. "You know, I have her spoiled," he said playfully, winking at me. "Before I married her, I had a watch and chain, now I'm watched and chained," and he burst in to paroxysms of ribald laughter.

In a few days they took up residence, but I never got pally with them, as they kept very much to themselves.

The Captain made various attempt at friendly overtures, but Sam Vector firmly discouraged him with a formal "good morning," or "good evening," and Nonie never appeared without her husband.

All the Captain managed to discover about them was that they were "clane mad on motorin' cars."

"How did you manage to find that out?" I asked curiously.

The Captain banged his pipe off the mantelpiece and fingered tobacco carefully into it, before he answered: "I seen dem goin' off every evenin' in their toweresin' car."

"What sort of a car if that?" I said in surprise.

Ida who was embroidering quietly by the window, chipped in, "he means a touring car."

The Captain gave her a look of exasperation. "Toweresin," he contradicted with grand finality.

Chapter 67

I had not seen Myrabelle for weeks and had assumed she had gone abroad on holidays. Rumours about the Dobson's marital problems had been circulating for months, and I knew that all was not well with the marriage.

I had been rather naively shocked on hearing two women discussing them on a tram one day. A fussy looking woman of uncertain vintage was saying to her companion: "I hear that Alex Dobson has a nice little pad for his flapper in Harcourt Street....randy old devil."

"I heard that before," scoffed her companion tartly. "That uppish wife of his leads him quite a merry dance. I believe she cooked her goose when she took up with that rancher from Canada."Her voice dropped and she leaned confidentially towards her friend, who reacted to her disclosures with much shaking of the feathers in her hat.

The pair got off at the next stop, still nodding, speculating and trying to out-do each other in wild innuendos.

I was baking a cherry cake one afternoon when a sharp knocking on the hall door had me flying to answer it.

Aunt Cissy was standing on the step, pale and agitated. She slipped past me without a word until we reached the kitchen.

"It's Myrabelle," she gasped. "I've just heard from Mrs. Russell that she's seriously ill with pneumonia."

"Oh lord!" I cried in shock, "how bad is she?"

"Very bad indeed," said Aunt Cissy, "They don't expect her to pull through."

I felt sick at the news. I could not visualise the world without Myrabelle's sparkling presence, her generosity and gaiety. I was appalled at the thought that she might die....Tears stung my eyes.

"I must go and see her," I said in bewilderment, fumbling with the strings of my apron.

Aunt Cissy pushed me into a chair. "You can't. No one is allowed to see her."

I paid no heed, but rallied a little. "She's young and strong.... she can have the best of care."

"That's right and we must pray, hard," the aunt agreed soothingly.

She eyed me keenly and busied herself with that cure all, the tea pot.

"How on earth did she get pneumonia?" I asked when the hot tea had revived me a little.

Aunt Cissy stirred her tea thoughtfully. "That's the strange thing about it. Mrs. Russell told me that Myrabelle had been found wandering about Stephen's Green last Saturday. You remember what a terribly cold, wet day it was. She was soaked to the skin when the park attendant found her huddled on a bench at closing time. Apparently they could get no sense out of her; she was coughing and weeping and in a bad way....the keeper brought her home in a taxi."

I remembered the last time Myrabelle had paid me a visit. She had come with the gramophone for Rosemarie and had only stayed a few minutes.

"She didn't seem like herself at all; she seemed worried, and I didn't get the chance to ask her anything; you know how it is, you're afraid of being nosey." I ventured uneasily.

"No," Aunt Cissy replied. "She didn't look well for some time now. I noticed she showed no interest in a new evening gown I was making for her. It's been finished for weeks, and she never came to collect it. Usually she's all sparkle when it comes to new gowns," she frowned as I refilled her cup. "She's not been happy and with all the rumours flying about...."

"These rumours going the rounds; is there any truth in them?"I interrupted.

Aunt Cissy looked regretfully at me. "I'm afraid so. It is truc; Alex Dobson does have a mistress and a child."

"A child!" I was astonished

Aunt Cissy gave me a whimsical nod. "It is possible to have a child with a mistress, you know."

"I'm not that green," I retorted, "but the child; is it a boy or a girl?"

"A girl of about three years," she answered.

I thought how hard that revelation must have been for Myrabelle who so loved children, and had none of her own.

"They seemed so well-matched," I mused, remembering the charming and handsome Alex at our party, "but then again you never can tell how any marriage is going to work out."

"That's true," summed up the aunt despondently. "Very little is as it seems."

I called every evening for four days to Myrabelle's home before a grim-faced "general" informed me that she was out of danger.

"But no one is allowed to visit her yet, we so very nearly lost her," and the blank inscrutable mask slipped from her face and she looked vulnerable and afraid.

On one of those anxious days when I called to her home I saw Alex Dobson wandering about in the garden. He looked pale and remote and to have aged since I last saw him. I wondered about the mess their lives were in, and how he felt while his wife fought for her life. He did not appear to notice me as I hurried towards the hall door, or if he did, he showed no desire to talk to me. On my next visit I was admitted to the house by a pretty woman in her middle forties. She had a heart-shaped face, deep blue eyes, and although her hair was white it fell to her shoulders in soft waves.

"I'm Kitty Bannon," she introduced herself with a wide smile, "and I know you're Lynn Davis."

I looked surprised and she said in a stage whisper: "The general" keeps me informed."

She ushered me into Myrabelle's blue sitting room, with its chintzy curtains and pink chaise longue.

" How is Myrabelle to-day?" I inquired eagerly, but I knew by the woman's manner that the news was good.

"The crisis is over and the doctor says she'll be alright now, but of course, we have to be very careful yet. Yesterday we thought she wouldn't pull through...." She stopped and her bright eyes dimmed at the memory. Then she drew herself up and said cheerfully, "I know you're longing to see her so we'll go up shortly."

The "general" entered silently; she gave me a welcoming smile and placed a tray of afternoon tea on the walnut table in front of Kitty and me.

While she poured out, Kitty told me a bit about herself. She hailed from Kilkenny, but had come to Dublin in her mid teens to take care of Myrabelle, then just eighteen months old.

After nearly twenty years of caring devotedly for her, she had returned home and married a childhood sweetheart. Sadly, she had no children, "but I have got Myrabelle, and she's as precious to me as if she were my own."

I looked at Kitty with new interest, here was the beloved Dee, of whom Myrabelle had often spoken with glowing affection.

"So you are Dee; I've heard of you so often. I'm very happy to meet you at last."

Kitty smiled. "That's me alright, and I have heard many times of you too, and I was so happy to know she had found sincere friendship in you and your husband."

"Tell me about Myrabelle," I begged.

Kitty paused, and there was no sound but the feeble fluttering of a Red Admiral butterfly against the window pane. I watched him idly, thinking he must have been awakened by the counterfeit sunshine, mistaking it for the golden opulence of summer.

Kitty was talking, her eyes unseeing, her memory rolling back over the years. "Myrabelle's mother died when she was only a few months old, and I came in answer to an advertisement to take care of her. We took to each other like ducks to water and I stayed with her until she was twenty-one." Kitty's voice dropped and her face clouded. "My parting from her caused a lot of misery to both of us, and was due to the high-handed action of her father."

There was a discreet knock on the door, followed by the starchy reappearance of the "general."

"Mrs. Dobson would like you both to go up and see her now," she informed us solemnly.

We rose at once and I followed Kitty up the broad staircase to a beautiful pink and gold bedroom, where Myrabelle was propped against a mound of lacy pillows on a huge bed. A uniformed nurse warned us not to tire her patient, and left the room.

I was shocked at how changed Myrabelle was. Her eyes were dark pools in a white strained face, and the bones of her neck were sharply etched against her wooly bed jacket.

"Lynny darling, so nice to see you," she greeted me weakly as I bent to kiss her.

"Oh, Myrabelle whatever happened you at all?" I stammered with a lump in my throat.

"Don't be so dramatic, Lynny, but heaven knows you were always a desperate fuss pot," she said with a touch of her old bracing spirit. "I see you've met Dee," she went on, as I fumbled at the laden bedside table to make room for the special bottle of perfume I had brought her.

Kitty added a bunch of grapes as she too kissed Myrabelle, admonishing her to keep warm and tell us when she felt tired. She put a chair by the bed for me and left us "to natter awhile."

Myrabelle wanted all the news, especially the latest about "your charming and terrible child."

I told her of the trauma we had been through with Adelaide Lister, and rounded my tale off on a lighter note with the incident of the Captain's teeth, stolen, buried and halved by "an egit of a dog."

She laughed so much that I feared it might harm her, but after a while, I noticed she was losing concentration and growing tired.

I was wondering what to do when the nurse bustled back, and told me her patient needed to rest now. Hurriedly I found my bag, and after promising Myrabelle I would return on the morrow, made my way to the kitchen for a few words with the "general" and Kitty; after which I departed for home and my family's tea.

I went to see her every afternoon, until she was fit enough to sit by the fire for extended periods. She specially asked to have

Rosemarie visit, and the child responded with joyful enthusiasm. So well did they get on that Myrabelle wanted me to bring her every day.

I readily agreed, although warning her to tell me whenever the child's exuberance became too much. Watching them together, Rosemarie so unusually gentle, the woman so tenderly understanding of her wayward little friend, it again struck me, that a child would bring a lot of joy and fulfilment into Myrabelle's life.

Chapter 68

Meantime Kitty and I became close friends, and often she would drop down to visit me of an evening while Myrabelle slept. This was very welcome to me when Ida was out visiting and Edward working late.

On one such wet dreary evening, Myrabelle's chauffeur drove Kitty down to see me. After a satisfying meal and Rosemarie safely in bed, the chat came around to Myrabelle.

"Why do her friends say that life has been hard on her?" I ventured when I had stoked the drawing room fire for the evening. "She seems to me to have everything to make her happy....looks, wealth, and she must have loved Alex Dobson when she married him."

I trailed off, afraid I might appear critical or inquisitive to Kitty.

Kitty, stretching her feet comfortably on the footstool, did not seem to view my remarks in that light. The fire spluttered in a shower of blue and red sparks as she said mildly: "Well, I'll tell you her story and you can judge for yourself.

She was only twenty years of age when she was awarded top place in her pianoforte finals...."

"I never guessed she played the piano," I interrupted in surprise.

"Oh yes, and brilliantly," replied Kitty. "She was well on the road to becoming an outstanding concert pianist, when herself and her father fell out over her first serious boyfriend. The difference has never been resolved between them, and Myrabelle suddenly stopped her musical studies. Erton Thompson, her father, was a clever, but difficult man. By profession he's a merchant banker and a wizard at amassing money. He adored his first wife, Melissa, Myrabelle's mother, who was only twenty-five when she was drowned in a boating accident. After her death, he became morose and seemed to have little interest in anything but the challenge of making money.

"He was very possessive of Myrabelle, making sure her friends were of the "right" family, her school exclusive, and her entertainment high-brow concerts which would be in line with her musical potential. Never would she be allowed to go to a musical comedy or pantomime.

"Maybe this was alright for a child, although I doubt it, but as Myrabelle grew up she became suffocated and bored. How she longed for a little freedom. Luckily, her father spent frequent periods away from home and on these occasions she played truant, and took herself off with her friends to lighter shows and films.

"Erton Thompson's home in Dalkey is magnificent; the gardens are spectacular and there is at least half an acre of hot houses. But at heart Myrabelle is a simple soul. One of her favourite pastimes is gardening, and she preferred to cultivate her own cottage flowers, in a secluded corner at the back of the house, in contrast to the formal beds and unusual foreign plants which were her father's choice.

"Some say she was the apple of his eye, for he never tired of boasting about her, and her musical abilities. She would have to play a difficult piece for his important friends when he was entertaining, whether she wanted to or not.

Often she was embarrassed by his praise and complained to me that he was crediting her with more virtues and talents than could reasonably be found in any one person.

He re-married six years after Mellisa's death, and his second wife was a sophisticated social- climber named Olive Deering. She had been his secretary for years, and often stepped in as hostess at some of his bigger functions. To sum up, he needed a mistress for his several homes, and she wanted to be the victor over the many beautiful women who coveted the status of being Mrs. Erton Thompson.

Perhaps Olive hoped to win his affections when she married him, and I know she tried pretty hard to find a place in his heart, but after years of cold indifference, she accepted defeat and just carried on with the duties of being the hostess who presided at the best parties, and paraded the most elegant clothes.

She never bothered with Myrabelle; maids and nannies were paid for that, and she was a firm believer in the adage that children should be seen and not heard."

Kitty fell silent as she gazed back pensively over the lost years.

"Little Myrabelle grew up happy enough", she resumed with a sigh, " and I did all in my power to make her life loving and secure. But the day came all too soon when everything changed for both of us. I remember it well....a hot golden day in midsummer, just three days after her twenty-first birthday. She was busy in her part of the garden when Olive came out of the house with a young man from a firm of auctioneers. He had come to advise Olive on the sale of some houses that Erton Thompson was selling. Although Myrabelle was quite near them, Olive made no effort to introduce the pair, nor would she have dreamed of doing so....he being so far beneath them in the social rating.

Anyway, that appears to have been no great drawback to either of them for, according to Myrabelle, they fell in love at first sight.

He called to the house on a few subsequent occasions, ostensibly to see Olive on business, when I'm pretty sure he had a shrewd idea she'd be out. However, with a bit of connivance from me, the affair prospered, Myrabelle blossomed, and for the first time ever, had the time of her life.

Her father had given her a small motor car for her birthday, and they used to drive out to the country, or out to the seaside, whenever John....that was the young man's name....had the time off from work.

This went on for weeks until one chilly autumn evening, Olive came home unexpectedly, and found them dancing to the gramophone in the sitting room.

As I need hardly say, the two young things were flustered, and after Olive had recovered from the shock of finding, what she described as an ordinary working man in her house, there was a right rumpus.

The young man was ordered from the house, and warned not to set foot there again, or his employer would be informed of his "unprofessional" conduct.

Myrabelle had to endure a lecture in front of him concerning her "unladylike" behaviour in allowing a "common tout" access to her friendship, which should be reserved for her "betters," or "equals," only.

Of course, Myrabelle fought back, reminding her stepmother of her own poor rating in her husband's affections, shafts that were too near the bone, to put it mildly. Things were said which would have been better left unsaid, but there you are, Myrabelle had been insulted and provoked, and Olive should not have been such a high-handed snob.

You know, John was really an attractive and nicely mannered young fellow, and from what I've seen of Myrabelle's so called equals of the male sex, she couldn't have done better than John, especially as they were so happy together.

Anyway, when her father came home, he was soon acquainted with the "disgraceful" behaviour of his daughter, and bitterly opposed the friendship.

He expressly forbade her to see John again, and when she refused to do his bidding, he did an unforgiveable thing on the girl. He knew how attached she was to me, so he used that against her. He told her that as "Miss Myrabelle" had such an independent mind, and was hell-bent on following it, she should be left to her own devices. Unless she agreed to carry out his directions, I would be given notice to leave the house.

When he sent for me to come to his study next morning, he accused me of encouraging his daughter to mix with unsuitable company and brazenly disobey her father. I tried to reason with him, and told him how absurd it was to coerce his daughter in such a way at her age, and that I would never try to influence her to choose me against the man she loved. Myrabelle in tears pleaded with him to let me stay, but seeing his advantage, he was adamant, and just walked out of the room. The next day he called me to his study and told me that, as there was no change in her attitude, my services were no longer required.

Can you imagine my feelings, and after nearly twenty one years of mothering his child! Dismissed out of hand like a common servant who had woefully neglected her duties.

Well, I had to go and it broke my heart to leave her there alone, without a friend. After that, Myrabelle fought a losing battle. She was more attached than ever to John, but there was so much against them that disaster was inevitable.

As they could no longer meet at her home, John took her to his. He lived in a poorish, but respectable part of Dublin with his mother, who had been widowed when he was four years old. They had seen better times, but with the father's early death money was scarce, and Mrs. Kendle had to go out cleaning to keep herself and her child.

Her health had deteriorated over the years, and when John started work, it was the first reprieve she had from the worries of where the next meal was coming from, or whether she had sufficient to pay the rent and buy a bag of coal.

As far as the mother was concerned, Myrabelle belonged to another world, which could never be reconciled with John's. She was deeply suspicious of the girl, convinced she was only playing with her son's affections, and would cast him aside when the novelty wore off. She told Myrabelle that she would never be able to descend from her fine mansion to a house such as theirs, and that was all John would be able to provide eventually. As for the prospect of her being ever capable of running any home without "an army of servants....!"and Mrs. Kendle just laughed in her face. Myrabelle, finding opposition on both fronts, grew to dread the visits, and John himself must have been torn apart between them.

Meanwhile, Myrabelle's father was getting fed up of trying to wear Myrabelle down, so he went to see Mrs. Kendle and told her in no uncertain terms, that a match between his daughter and her son, was out of the question. With this she fully agreed, but for a different reason which she calmly outlined to him, but he had no time for her opinion, and beginning to lose his temper, he threatened that if she did not use her influence to keep her son away from his daughter, he would see that John lost his job and never got another.

Naturally, the woman was frightened at the prospect of a re-occurrence of the hard struggle she had endured before John had found employment in a firm he was happy in, and which held out a promising future for him. So she felt she had no option but to try and persuade the young couple to break off the relationship.

Later when the lovers met, Myrabelle found John very depressed and worried by his mother's efforts to convince him to follow the wishes of her father. After much discussion, she suggested they should elope and once married, her father would never be able to interfere in their lives. She had been left a good allowance from her mother, and this her father could not touch.

But John was cautious. He said he would not live on his wife's money and argued that her father would surely change his mind when he realized they were serious about each other, and would do nothing behind his back.

Myrabelle was insistent that her father would never come around. I suppose John was tired and worried, for he retaliated by accusing her of showing very little understanding of the situation....how could she, he asked, when she had lived in luxury all her life, and was used to getting everything she wanted, immediately she wanted it. This was a gross exaggeration, of course, but I could see shades of the mother's influence here."

She stopped, and I observed that possibly John was afraid if he married her, people would surmise that he had done so for her money.

Kitty stared mournfully into the fire, and I rose to put some logs on it; flames exploding in a sudden flare of sparks, subsiding to a crimson glow.

"What happened then?"I asked anxiously. Kitty roused herself and slowly took up her story.

"The argument blew into a terrible row and he got up and just walked out.

For them it was the end; they never saw each other again."

"Oh how sad!" I exclaimed, shocked by the finality of her words. "Whatever happened after that?"

"Myrabelle was heartbroken at John's desertion; she went on hoping for months that he'd come back. She blamed her father for it all, and made up her mind to get away from him and have a life of her own. She was at her lowest ebb when she met Alex Dobson, by chance, in Grafton Street, one day. They had known each other since childhood, and had met on many social occasions over the years. But Erton Thompson and Ronald Dobson, also a well- respected merchant banker, had been involved in a lawsuit about land some years earlier. Erton Thompson had won, but bad blood existed between them right up to the death of Mr Dobson.

His son, Alex, inherited the business and turned out to be even more brilliant than his father in the handling of money. In several financial transactions he out-witted Erton Thompson, who had emerged from each conflict a little more bitter, and a great deal more jealous of his younger rival.

He continually warned Myrabelle that Alex was "a bad lot," and she should be wary of him, but Myrabelle had no romantic interest in Alex and the pair just enjoyed a light-hearted friendship over the years. In fact, I often thought they were more than a little fond of each other, and a friend once told me that she had overheard Alex say he intended to marry Myrabelle, one day, whether her father liked it or not.

Now on that fateful afternoon when Alex met her in Grafton Street, he saw how upset she was, and immediately dropped a business appointment and took her out to tea. Eventually, finding him kindly and sympathetic, she poured out the whole story to him.

Alex was charming and easy going, and not given to thinking very far ahead....quite the opposite to Alex the banker, and before the evening was out, he half-jokingly, half seriously, offered to elope with her himself.

At first she was shocked by the suggestion, but still hurting from her row with John, her disappointment in getting no communication from him, she sort of agreed. Desperately, she had waited for John to write and make-up, even come around to her solution of their problem, but the months wore on, and no word had came from him, and her father was quick to remind her that if John had been sincere, he would have made some effort to see her again.

Erton Thompson was pleased that his strategy had worked, and tried to regain her affections by buying her expensive presents, and providing her with luxury holidays to the places of her choosing.

But Myrabelle remained deeply unhappy and resentful, and refuted all his efforts at reconciliation.

Again she met Alex casually at her friend's home. She was wandering around the garden when he found her. As always, they were soon chatting easily, and in the middle of some idle banter Alex suddenly said:

"Marry me, Myrabelle, let's start again and forget our problems."

"And that's just what they did without telling anyone, except myself."

I looked at her wide-eyed. "You mean they just ran off and got married?" Kitty gazed at me solemnly: "Exactly that."

I stared at the strange pictures in the fire, trying to apply Kitty's story to the bright extrovert Myrabelle I knew. Kitty mistook my preoccupation for tiredness.

"I'm so sorry I've tired you. I know I'm a bit long-winded...."

"Oh no, Kitty dear. It's all so interesting....poor Myrabelle. I'd never have guessed....." I answered anxiously.

"I know you've probably heard all sorts of things about Dobson," Kitty said sadly, "but really he did all he could to make her happy. They went on a six-month cruise after the wedding, and there was nothing he wouldn't do for her.

Myrabelle told me she tried hard to make a go of the marriage, and indeed she said that things were going well between them until they came home. They were back a few weeks in Alex's lovely home in Terenure, when one morning Myrabelle opened the newspaper to find a photograph of John staring back at her. He had been knocked down by a runaway horse and dray in Sackville Street, the previous evening, while going home from work. He had died on his way to hospital.

I was staying with her at the time, and I'll never forget how badly she took the news. She was utterly distraught and there was no consoling her; she blamed herself for his death, and this had disastrous results on her health.

She insisted on visiting his grave every day. I tried to dissuade her, but she had all the obstinacy of her father. I went with her to the churchyard on a freezing cold day, and stayed at a distance while she laid a rose on his grave.

She spent so long there that I had to forcibly lead her away, and as a consequence, she caught a heavy chest cold, which clung to her for months. By the end of that time, she was just a shadow of her old self; all that youthful gaiety was gone.

Her next ordeal was to visit John's mother; she wanted to talk about him and make sure Mrs. Kendle was not living in want. Myrabelle told me that Mrs. Kendle received her very coldly, and barely allowed her inside the door. No doubt, she was a very hard woman, and never relented in her dislike of Myrabelle. She told the girl it was a bad day that her son had laid eyes on her, and she placed all the blame for his tragic death on her.

"I warned him he was a fool to bother with you," she said bitterly, "but against my wishes, he wrote to you many times, and called to your home where he was turned away like a common tramp, but you, Miss high-and-mighty, wouldn't deign to send him a reply."

Myrabelle was shocked to learn that John had written to her; she had certainly never got the letters, or been informed of his visits. But no amount of assurances would convince the woman that Myrabelle was speaking the truth.

There was no point of agreement between them, and she was warned never to darken the door again.

"You're just suffering from remorse now and trying to salve your conscience," was her parting shot as she banged the door in Myrabelle's face.

But Myrabelle still worried about her, and racked her brains to find a way of insuring that John's mother would never be burdened with financial want. At length, she hit on the idea of persuading John's old firm to fix her up with a weekly pension, which she would secretly finance.

At least now, the poor woman will have sufficient money to live comfortably to the end of her days," Kitty finished softly.

After a long pause, I asked her if Myrabelle had ever felt like making it up with her father.

Kitty made a wry face. "No, and it wouldn't be any use her trying. He would never forgive her for marrying Alex Dobson."

"He seems a most unloving and unreasonable type," I observed.

Kitty nodded thoughtfully. "Hardly has a heart at all, but I made sure he knew exactly how bad things were with his only child. It took Myrabelle months to recover, if indeed she ever has. Anyway, he never came to see her, or send a message, and it's been the same this time....no word whatever."

"And Alex," I pressed, "how did he react to all this?"

"Well," said Kitty bleakly. "The whole thing put an intolerable strain on their marriage; she grew very irritable, and he being closest to her got the worst of her temper. The marriage floundered, and they each went their own way while maintaining an outward semblance of unity. Strangely enough there was always a strong basic friendliness between them, despite their apparent indifference to each other. Yes, even when Alex took a mistress, and she embarked on a couple of flighty affairs, he was always very proud of her, and loved seeing her in beautiful clothes when they appeared together at the best society doo's.

But as time went on, Alex's mistress became more demanding, especially after the birth of their little girl. This situation brought them into greater conflict, and it looks like the end of the marriage now," sighed Kitty, wiping a tear from her cheek. "Alex has told her that he wants to leave her to live with his mistress and child."

Silence fell between us, broken only by the occasional honk of a motor car, the tapping of the rain against the window pane, and a man's urgent shouts of "Stop Press," in the distance.

I laid my hand on Kitty's arm, "Don't worry too much. God's help is nearer than the door, as we say in the country, and I still believe in miracles."

The French clock struck eleven silvery chimes, and a sharp knocking on the hall door made me jump. Kitty went to the window and gazed down into the street. "That's the car for me," she said, and I helped her into her coat.

Chapter 69

It was a cold, wet November evening, and the light from the street lamps reflected their many colours in the pools of water on the pavement.

I was on my way to see Myrabelle and having a bit of a headache, I decided to walk, instead of taking the tram.

It was a route I enjoyed....up to the picturesque Leeson street Bridge, along by the Grand Canal, left turn and into Rathmines and straight on for Terenure.

As I huddled in a doorway to avoid a sudden shower, I spied an attractive array of fruit and vegetables in the window of a huxter's shop.

I entered its cavern-like gloom, and was immediately assailed by a conglomeration of pungent odours....turpentine, cabbage, candle grease, soap, and the nostalgic scent of turf smouldering from a fire in an inner room. Over all, the mighty smells of paraffin oil and Jeyes Fluid fought for supremacy.

Intrigued by the variety of articles for sale, I bent to examine a stack of odd cups, bundles of yard brushes, piles of chamber pots demurely decorated with wreaths of pink roses and, with Rosemary in mind, a galvanised bucket of multi-coloured balls.

Straightening up, I was nearly knocked unconscious by a string of dusty saucepans swinging from the ceiling. Reeling in an aura of stars and flashing lights, I played for time to recover by dabbling my hands through a basket of cabbages in various stages of decline.

A sudden commotion caught my attention, and thinking my brain had been fatally damaged when it had come in contact with the saucepans, I squealed with terror when the massive head of a huge animal glared at me with blood-shot eyes from the shop's doorway, it's breath sending out clouds of steam, like smoke from a dragon, into the frosty air.

I was about to give vent to my panic in a series of wild screams when the monster raised its head and gave a powerful bellow. Something clicked in my mind, and my country origins recognised nothing more dangerous than a humble bovine intruder....possibly every bit as addled as myself.

Slowly I became aware of another customer nearby, who took the bellow as a signal to leap up on the counter; no mean feat this, for the woman was enormously fat, red-faced and clutching a brace of cauliflowers. A large woollen shawl threatened her safety, as she fought to retain her balance amongst sacks of potatoes and jars of discoloured sweets.

There was a flash of red drawers when her huge feet, in hob-nailed boots, dashed frenziedly from one end of the counter to the other.

"Looka! Looka!" she shrieked. "Get that baste outa here. Bad cess ta yas, will yous get it outa here afore it tramples me ta death?"

I caught her fear and with much less agility than she had shown, scrambled over the counter and into the arms of the wiry little shopkeeper. He was dancing about, swinging his arms and yelling ineffectually in the direction of the cow, "Shoo!Shoo!"

The animal chose either to misunderstand or ignore him, for she continued unabashed to gallop down the shop. Then she turned with difficulty, knocking potatoes and assorted vegetables to the floor with her hefty rear. After another bellow she dropped her "card" in the middle of the floor, and swishing her tail nonchalantly, brushed aside a bowl of eggs and a chip of tomatoes, and ambled serenely out of the shop.

Deeming it safe, I cautiously raised my head above an ancient armchair of second-hand books, as the other woman was being assisted from the heights of the counter by the unfortunate proprietor.

Once safely on her feet the portly woman, breathing wrathfully, rounded on him and abused him thoroughly for "allowin' wild bastes inta his bit of a shop to frighten the daylights outa a dacent body. Cowardly divil yar, and ya won't see me in yar oul shop again."

Skirting the mess, I crept to the door, but was electrified by the woman's screech behind me.

"Come here, young wan. Yar not goin' ta let 'im away with it, are ya?"

I regret to say that my courage deserted me, and I shot through the door, stumbling into the herd of passing cattle.

Chapter 70

When I reached Myrabelle's she was sitting by the fire flicking through a magazine. I was delighted to see how improved she was looking. A touch of pink warmed her cheeks, her eyes had an impish sparkle, and her fair hair bounced prettily about her head.

"You are looking well again," I said, kissing her cheek. "In fact like a very elegant pussy cat who has eaten all the cream."

I stopped, puzzled by some intangible difference in her.

"Maybe that's not such a bad comparison, Lynny darling," and she grinned roguishly like a young girl. "Sit yourself down and I'll tell you all about it, but first some tea. Even as I speak, I hear the gentle thread of the "general" arriving with refreshments."

She was right, and after the usual discreet tap on the door, the "general" stood majestically before us with a laden tray.

I sighed blissfully, and after an exchange of pleasantries, the "general" handed us our tea, and placed dainty plates of sandwiches and little iced cakes, within easy reach.

Myrabelle drew her pink velvet dressing gown around her and snuggled comfortably into her cushions.

"That was a bad fright you gave us," I commented referring to her illness.

"Why on earth were you walking around Stephen's Green on such a very cold wet day?"

Myrabelle hesitated before she said baldly: "I was so depressed, I just wanted to die."

Amazed, I stared at her "But why?"

The cup shook in her hand and I was afraid she was going to drop it. She remained silent for so long that I feared I had upset her. Then she said slowly,

"Well, I suppose you've heard all the rumours about Alex?"

I nodded, and to hide my embarrassment, murmured something banal.

Myrabelle did not seem to notice. "We had a fierce row on that Friday night," she resumed, "and he told me that he had made up his mind to go and live with his mistress and their child. He was leaving me for good."

She paused, kicking off her furry mules, and traced a purple flower on the fireside rug with a pink toe. "I didn't know why it should matter so much to me," and tears glinted on her lashes, "we hadn't lived as man and wife since John died, but the thought of him not being there anymore, hurt like hell. All my life I had been fond of Alex and he had been unfailingly good to me. If I hadn't met John....anyway, it was my fault that Alex went elsewhere."

Her voice dropped and I stretched out my hand to her.

"Don't go on when it hurts like that," I pleaded.

But she looked impatient and blew her nose on a wisp of lace. "I want to talk, Lynny; it's all been bottled up too long."

I took a sip of tea and reached for an iced cake, as Myrabelle took up her story again.

"Alex went to the guest room and packed his bags; all that night I couldn't sleep. I had plenty of time now to think and take stock of my life. I heard Alex leave our home early in the morning, and when the "general" brought me my breakfast as usual, I told her I was going out after lunch to have my hair done. I don't know how much she knows or guesses, but I have no fear of gossip there. Anyway, I had no clear idea of where I was going; all I knew was that I wanted to get away from the house. It felt so desolate without Alex....I never felt so lonely in my life.

It was a terribly bad day, as you know....raining cats and dogs, but I just threw on a light coat and walked from here down to the Green. All the while the problems were churning around in my mind, my head was throbbing and I seemed to be walking around in circles for hours.

For a finish, I didn't know where I was. A park attendant found me sitting on a bench in the pouring rain when the Green was closing. He got my address from a letter in my pocket and brought me home in a taxi. You know the rest, Lynny. I nearly kicked the bucket good and proper," and she grinned saucily with one of her sudden swings of mood.

I wondered breathlessly what was coming next....good news surely to match that sunny smile.

"Well, Alex came home," she went on, "someone rang him at the office to tell him how ill I was. He was terribly worried and stayed by my bedside all through the bad times, as if it were vital to him that I should recover."

She leaned over and put her empty cup on the tray, and snapping open her bag, extracted her cigarette case, then with a shrug of mock despair replaced it again.

"I've been ordered not to by the doc." she laughed, as I waited anxiously for the rest of the story.

"When I was well enough, we had a talk", she continued happily, "at least Alex did most of the talking, and he told me that he did not really want to live with Greta; that he had never actually loved her, but she had been pretty and willing, and offered distraction from the muddle here. I'm lucky really, Lynny, for in spite of it all, and I was no saint either, he said he never stopped loving me, and hoped that one day, I'd forget the past and be able to forgive him. He only went to Greta in the bleak times when hope seemed gone and he wanted to forget."

"And so, Myrabelle, how do you feel?" I asked. "Have you been able to forgive and forget?"

She looked at me with a touch of sadness as she said: "I believed there was no room for anyone in my heart except John, and he'll keep his place there always, but I know now that hearts are bigger than I thought. There's room, loads of it, for Alex too."

I breathed such a loud sigh of relief, that Myrabelle giggled teasingly. "Still the incurable romantic! I think some of your notions have rubbed off on me, you know."

Chapter 71

Christmas was only a few weeks away and Ida was in the kitchen helping me with the pudding. The tangy smell of spice hung on the air as I weighed the sugar, fruit and suet.

"Have you got Rosemarie's presents yet," Ida asked, tumbling the fruit into the mixing bowl.

"I have indeed," I answered complacently. "I've been collecting bits and pieces for her over the last month, and they're safely hidden from her itchy little fingers."

There was a knock on the door, followed by the Captain with two letters in his hand.

"For you, missus," and he held them out to me.

"Put them on the shelf there," I replied absently, and continued measuring out generous amounts of treacle.... "must not forget plenty of that, Edward loves lashings of it."

"I'm making a cup of tea," Ida broke in on my concentration. "You'll have a cup with us, Captain?"

"Well begob, that's right good a ya," he responded eagerly, pulling out a chair for himself at the cluttered table. "These smells here reminds me of me mother. Now she were a woman as enjoyed Christmas. Takes me back, it does," he sighed nostalgically.

When tea was ready we sat down, glad of the break. Ida produced an Oxford Lunch from Roberts, and there was much joking and laughing as the Captain regaled us with tales of his childhood.

He accepted a second cup of tea, and after putting six spoons of sugar into it, went on to tell us: "I remember now right well the Christmas when I were ten year old and Santy gave me a toy pistol....at that time the same man give no more than an orange or an apple in the stockin,' with mebby a six penny piece if the family were anyway flush. Anyways, at the time I had a great pal in our local copper....a young fella he were who enjoyed a bit of fun with the next. I were in the habit of creepin' up behind 'im an shoutin' "Stick 'em up! Stick 'em up!" and he alwees responds be throwin' he's arms in the air and lookin' scared. Well on this per-tic-u-lar day, I spies yar man paradin' about the Coombe. He's back were toward me, and I falleyed stealthily behind 'im until I judged the right moment."Stick' em up! Stick 'em up!" I yelled.

"The words weren't outa me mouth when he spins around , and begob, I'll never forget the fright I got....it weren't me pal at all, but a new copper, a mean lookin' fella with a face like thunder. He made a grab at me, sayin' I'd go ta jail for interferin' with the law, and all the time nare a smile outa 'im. I didn't wait to explain, but ran like the hammers a hell home."

The Captain sighed heavily and lavishly buttered a slice of cake.

"But it were oney when I got home and were safely in our kitchen, that I missed me little pistol. I had dropped it in me fright and me heart were broken. I retraced me steps a few times, but I couldn't find it anywhere."

"Sarves ya right," was all I git from the mother when she wormed the story outa me. A few skelps followed on the backside from me father for makin' a nuisance of meself with the law, and misusing' me Christmas present."

The Captain drained his cup noisily, licked his fingers, and applied the cover from the parrot's cage to his lips, before divulging the rest of his misadventure.

"However, this new copper had a young son who were put in me class in the skule, and didn't he turn up with a pistol exactly the same as mine. He were the envy of every kid in the skule, and boasted that he's father had given it to 'im for Christmas. I had me auspicions a course, that his da had picked mine up and made 'im a present of it, but there was dam all I could do....savin' yar presence, ladies....as I were in mortal dread of bringin' meself to the notice of he's oul fella."

The Captain gave a disgusted snort and reached into his pocket for his pipe.

I snatched my bowl out of his reach just as he was about to give his customary bang of the pipe, and laughing merrily, Ida and I returned to the job of steaming the pudding.

Chapter 72

Later that evening I remembered my letters and settling down by the kitchen fire and a last cup of tea, I opened the nice thick one from Mam. The family were all well, and up to their eyes in Christmas preparations. There was great excitement over Dora's engagement to Dikie Murphy, and Nell was doing "quite a line" with the local vet. Dora hoped to have her wedding in the following June and of course, the three of us were expected to attend.Rosemarie would be thrilled when she heard she was going to be a flower girl, and Aunt Cissy would be in charge of the wedding dress and trousseau. Mam, already fussing about "The Cake", asked me to try and find her a special new cookery book called "The American Bride Cake," and Dora wanted a publication named "All The Bride Needs To Know."

Dora herself would be coming up "towards the end of Jan," and Mam warned that I could expect a "spree of shopping." Dora would also appreciate the "sophisticated" advice, which she believed, I had automatically acquired from living in a city "like Dublin."

I smiled indulgently, remembering Dora's opinion of Dikie Murphy, but with love in the air one could expect anything, and as Aunt Cissy said later, Dora had certainly met her match in the bold Dickie.

The other letter I idly turned over in my hand. It was very official looking and addressed to Edward. Maybe he had won some competition, I thought hopefully, for he was always entering for something or other. Perhaps, and here I felt a pang of excitement, someone had left him a fortune! I rattled the envelope and held it fruitlessly up to the light. Could it contain an offer of promotion for Edward, or, and my hopes plunged fearfully earthwards, as I remembered the bills! That was it, a bill, and I speculated with some trepidation on the modest number of tradesmen who may have become impatient or distrustful of our ability to meet our financial commitments.

Ah well, better leave it for Edward, and I was about to put it back on the shelf when I stopped. Why not open it? The envelope was typed and therefore, I reasoned, not private. Edward had always told me to open any letters that came for him, and there was something compelling about this one which did not admit of delay.

Getting a table knife, I slit the envelope and extracted a stiff sheet of expensive paper. It was from the firm of solicitors who were acting for the Pembroke estate. I knew they were the landlords of our house, and much of the Georgian property around our area. I felt a flutter of unease as I sat down to see what they were writing to us about. The letter was short and formal and I had to reread it, with pounding heart, before I could take in what it said.

It wished to inform Mr. Edward Davis, that the tenancy of the house occupied by him in Lower Leeson Street, would shortly expire and he was being given six months notice to find alternative accommodation and vacate the premises....

I sat there in the dining room for a long time with the letter in my hand. We were now nearly five years in the house....five wonderfully happy years and I looked upon it as our own. Certainly, I had never visualised that a day would dawn when someone could tell us we would be governed by a short tenancy, a definite expiry date, and most intimidating of all, a document called "A Legal Agreement."

Foolishly, I had assumed we would just carry on living happily in this dear old house forever. Ida came in with Rosemarie and roused me anxiously. Dumbly I gave her the letter and she read it quickly.

Perhaps she was more in touch with reality than I was, for after an exclamation of surprise, she spoke crisply of the new houses being built in the suburbs, which she lauded as being airy and compact for a young family.

"The city is becoming too congested and unhealthy with so much traffic, and that's going to get a lot worse," she prophesied while unbuttoning Rosemarie's black boots with the long button hook.

Some remote spot in my brain agreed that she could be right, but the blind misery in my heart was a denial of it. I simply could not imagine life outside these beloved walls, and the thought of living elsewhere was unbearable. Only Ida's understanding kindness, and Rosemarie's anxious cries of "what's wrong, mamma, what's wrong?" coupled with two strong cups of tea, raised me a little from the depths of depression.

"Where's Roesmarie?" Ida asked suddenly.

I put down my cup hastily, knowing from past experience that the child's quietness indicated her absorption in some forbidden activity. I hastened down to the back door, calling her, but there was no reply. I was just about to close the door when I spotted Ginger crouched on an old mat in the garden enjoying a small cooked chicken. I went over to him and he stopped gnawing to eye me belligerently.

"Wish I'd seen it first, old boy," I muttered enviously, wondering who the unsuspecting donor was. Maybe, there would be reprisals when the theft was discovered. Hurriedly I went in and closed the door.

As I rejoined Ida, Rosemarie skipped in from the hall brandishing a large Christmas stocking.

"Look!" she yelled triumphantly, "what Santa had hidden in the shoe cupboard for me."

Chapter 73

I felt restless and sleep eluded me. Just overtired, I told myself, listening to the gentle breathing of Edward and the child.

The opportunity of telling Edward about the letter had not presented itself, as it was very late when he arrived home from the annual Christmas dinner for the library staff. I felt that the letter would upset him and take from his evening's enjoyment, so I pretended to be asleep when he came softly into our bedroom.

Better leave it until tomorrow evening, I thought. Things were too hectic in the morning for the in-depth discussion such a disclosure would bring.

The red lamp glowed softly in front of the Sacred Heart picture, which had been a wedding present from a friendly nun in the Convent where I had gone to school. I tried to see the gilt clock beside it, but just then, two silvery chimes from the drawing room clock broke the heavy silence.

Right, I was not going to lie awake all night fretting. I would go down to the kitchen for a cup of tea and an aspirin.

I crept out of bed and into my dressing gown and slippers. The door creaked when I opened it, but only Edward stirred slightly and sank deeper into the eiderdown.

I gained the landing and lit the candle we kept there for emergencies; I did not want to disturb the house by switching on any lights. The candle flared and settled to a steady flame, throwing leaping shadows against the walls as I tiptoed down the stairs.

I reached the kitchen and pushing open the door, stood transfixed on the threshold. The room was in darkness except for a band of moonlight which illuminated a hunched figure sitting by the empty fireplace. It was a woman, I noted, with some relief, the silvery light glinting on the brown hair and the pale, almost translucent, feminine hands.

There was no sound, but I knew she was crying. Her face was hidden in her hands, and her shoulders were heaving against a dark garment, which completely enveloped her figure.

"Who are you?" I heard myself ask in a voice I did not recognise. "What is the matter?"

The girl took her hands from her face and raised her head. Tearfully she gazed at me and I was shocked to find myself gazing into my own face.

I stood motionless as the figure rose from the chair. Dimly I was aware of a door opening nearby, and the hall and passage were flooded with light. The ghostly vision seemed to melt away, leaving only a grey mist where it had been.

There was a flapping of slippers behind me, and I whirled around to find the Captain watching me with startled eyes. He was clad in an old striped dressing gown with a red flannelette nightcap pulled over his ears and the ship's lantern swinging uneasily in his hand.

"Oh it's yarself, missus," he said in a quavering tone of relief. "I heard a voice and I sez to meself, begob someone's broken in and I'll give 'em a hidin'," and he held up the walking stick clutched in his hand.

I leaned weakly against the wall, and the Captain moved over to me, his good-natured face wrinkled with worry.

"Are ya alrite....turned faint or somethin'?"

"Yes, yes, I'm alright, thank you Captain," I replied with an effort, feeling the perspiration cold on the back of my neck.

The Captain grunted, and told me to get up to bed before I got my death of cold.

Galvanised into action at the thought of finding myself alone in the kitchen, I got myself up the stairs as fast as I could, leaving Captain Rodgers to put off the lights.

Chapter 74

I worried about the letter all next day, and when Edward came home I could not wait until after our meal to tell him about it.

"Read this," I demanded, flourishing the missive in front of him before he could take his coat off.

"Can't it wait for heaven's sake?" he asked crossly. "Is it good, bad or indifferent?"

"Just read it," I implored. "It's very important."

He snatched the letter and read it in a few seconds.

"Well?" I almost shouted.

Edward threw the letter on the table.

"Well what?" he countered, pulling up his chair to the table by the fire.

"It says we have to leave," I almost wept.

"I can see that," his tone was dismissive as he changed into his slippers. "Didn't we know that all along? The lease had only a few years to run after the death of Mrs. Gandon. Now where's the food; I'm famished."

Trembling with the effort of trying to control my frustration, I took the shepherd's pie from the oven and set it noisily in front of him.

He took a few hungry mouthfuls and grinned with satisfaction. "My girl can certainly cook."

I made no response and he leaned towards me saying: "Eat up there yourself, sweet girl," and as I made no attempt to follow his example, he put down his knife and fork in exasperation and asked: "What on earth are you in a state about, Lynn? I thought you realised that in a short time we'd have to start looking for a house of our own. I wouldn't want to spend my life here, even if I could. No garden, no place for Rosemarie to play unless Ida or Jane can take her to the parks. It's just not suitable for a family anymore. Besides all the traffic, and the air is foggy and dirty from all the smoking chimneys ...."

Common sense told me he was right, but since when did common sense have anything to do with it, I thought angrily.

All the practical explanations in the world were no balm to the feelings I had for this house, and it had for me. I felt both deserted and deserting.

"I want to stay here, Edward," I cried urgently. "Write to them and tell them we don't want to go....won't go. They can't make us....can't we have a new lease or something?"

Edward curbed his impatience and spoke placateingly, as if he were dealing with an unreasonable child. "I know you love this house, Lynn, but you must accept it's a part of our life that's almost over. You can't bring back yesterday, as I'm always telling you; you must move on."

We argued far into the night, me pleading to stay, and he growing steadily more annoyed at what he termed my obstinacy. In the end he stormed off to bed leaving me alone where, totally uncaring of my ghostly visitant of the previous night, I wept softly by the dying fireside.

The great bells of St. Patrick's Cathedral were booming three o'clock, when I was roused from a troubled doze by sounds, like creaking footsteps, coming along the hall and down towards the kitchen.

Every nerve alert now, I moved my cramped legs and listened intently. Moonlight shone through the uncurtained window, slanting a silvery spray on the door leading to the hall. Then I froze in an agony of fright, as the door knob turned slowly.... often the door stuck and this happened now....prolonging the suspense.

Then it swung back soundlessly, and my over-charged nerves relaxed in a low moan, for Edward was standing there in the shadowy light. He rushed towards me and gathered me close.

"I tried not to frighten you," he whispered anxiously, "but when you didn't come to bed....I'm sorry, sweet girl....Look, as it means so much to you, I'll write to the solicitors and ask them for a new lease."

I was too relieved and exhausted to say anything. I held him tightly, grateful for his understanding, whatever the outcome.

When I was settled in bed, Edward poured me a stiff whiskey in my tooth mug, which happened to be the only available container; I would not hear of him going downstairs again on any pretext.

By this time, Rosemarie was awake and hanging over the bars of her cot watching us curiously. Edward tried to persuade her to settle down.

"No," she said firmly. "I want a mug of that stuff like Mamma."

"Then you can't have it," Edward said unwisely. "That stuff's only for big mammas."

There was the usual howl of protest and the rosebud lips turned down mutinously.

"Just one sip then," I cut in hoping to quieten her so we could all get some sleep, "but you won't really like it."

"Taste....weeny taste," she begged, rising to her feet and rattling the cot vigorously.

"I don't think we should give her whiskey," said Edward doubtfully.

In spite of my weariness I laughed. "You don't think she'll get hooked on the stuff at four years of age and get drunk on a few drops of whiskey," I challenged.

"Whiskery! Whiskery!" screamed the child, loudly enough to waken the house.

"A sip will do her no harm; it'll calm her down," I said desperate to stop the uproar, and snatching the mug with a few drops of the whiskey in it, I held it firmly to her lips.

There was a splutter as she coughed and spat it out until tiredness overcame her, and grabbing the teddy, she sank into a peaceful sleep.

"And that experience will probably make her a teetotaller for life," grinned Edward switching off the lamp.

Chapter 75

Edward wrote the letter as promised to the solicitors, and with this accomplished, I felt our tenancy of the house was assured; the granting of a new lease a mere matter of form. After all, we had six months notice and a lot could change in that time. In my ignorance, I believed that everything could be resolved by Edward signing a new lease.

The excitement of Christmas was upon us with all the extra work it entailed, so the problem of the house receded to the back of my mind.

Now it was Christmas Eve and our plans were going smoothly for the big day. The turkey had arrived from home, and was stuffed and ready for the oven. The best piece of ham from Wicklow would soon be boiling nicely and emitting it's own particular aroma, reminding me so nostalgically of home.

The dining room and drawing room were gaily festooned with tinsel and red, orange and green paper chains, made by Edward from crepe paper strips, pasted together in rings.

Ida and Rosemarie were busily engaged dressing a little spruce tree, dragged by Aunt Cissy from Moore Street, and which would later be a glory of colourful lighted candles. Mince pies reposed on the kitchen dresser next to the traditional Christmas Cake, painstakingly baked and decorated by Ida and me. A large chocolate roll, slightly messy and complete with holly and robin motif, awaited the "chop" for tea. This was Rosemarie's first proud culinary effort, assisted by Ida.

Jane had gone home to spend the festival with her family, after a mighty onslaught on everything sweepable, washable, and dustable!

Our child had written endless letters to Santa Clause, which she refused to trust to the local post offices, so a visit to the GPO was a must anytime we went to town.

We had taken her to meet Santa in three or four stores, but the last one in Pims of George's Street, had been fraught with disaster.

Ida and I with a wildly excited child, had been wandering through the glittering magic of fairyland in that store, and were coming out of the witch's tunnel to meet Santa. He was an elderly- looking man, seated on a most unrealistic, cow-like reindeer.

Starry-eyed children surrounded him, but with a delighted shout, Rosemarie pushed past them and climbed confidently on to the great man's knee. After giving him a generous list of her Christmas expectations, Santa held out three small parcels to her. One for herself, and the other two for the mammy and aunty. Rosemary quickly stripped the paper from her gift and regarded a book of nursery rhymes rather dubiously.

Ida's packet revealed three bars of Jasmine- scented soap and mine a green tooth mug.

"Nice for your Mamma's tooth brush," Santa observed chattily, taking in the displeased look on the child's face as she carelessly flicked through the pages of her book. She pushed the hair back from her face and gave him a scornful look.

"Mamma puts whiskery in her tooth mug," she told him patronisingly, and paused before making her next revelation, "and she gives me whiskery too."

I felt my face redden as a titter went up, and I became the focus of speculative interest for several mothers listening intently; their stares implying that here was one of those fast types, bandying whiskey about like snuff at a wake.

But Rosemarie diverted their attention from me; her eye had been caught by the flowing beard hanging a little crookedly around Santa's chin. Apparently it had become loosened from its elasticised moorings and Rosemarie, adjusting it roughly, found it came away in her hand. Amazed, she stared from it to the pimply youth whom she had taken for dear old Santa.

Again, the mothers turned in silent reproach to me, and one or two gave angry voice to their disapproval. Rosemarie was staring hard at the embarrassed Santa, but finding her voice fast, she cried disgustedly:

"You're not Santa Clause; you're only let-on. I'm going to tell the big man in the shop about you...."

By this time, Ida and I had had enough of Rosemarie's mortifying behaviour, and we rushed over and half-dragged, half carried a furiously protesting child out of the doubtful enchantment of fairyland.

When we stopped to assess the situation, we found ourselves in the splendour of the evening gown department. Ida set the child unsteadily on her feet, and we were bewildered to find her still clutching Santa's beard.

Before we could get it from her, she had darted over to a long mirror, and was holding it critically under her chin. A sedate looking floor walker glided over to us, and Ida falteringly explained what had happened in "fairyland."

Fortunately, the man had a sense of humour and took the whole thing in good part, but his benevolence was stretched to breaking point by the time he had rescued the bushy beard for the distracted Santa Clause.

Chapter 76

I was aroused from my day dreams by a knock on the hall door. Myrabelle's chauffeur stood on the doorstep with a note for me. I read it quickly; Myrabelle wanted to see me.

"I know you're wicked busy, Lynny darling, but I specially want to see you. Jacke will bring you up and back. Just an hour, please Lynny."

There was no denying her appeal, so I told Ida and she said of course I must go and not to hurry home. "I'll see to Edward and Rosemarie," she promised.

"Oh I'll be home for tea, and I'll call on Aunt Cissy and bring her back with me," I assured her, powdering my nose and slipping into the new blue wool coat, with the fox fur collar, that was Edward's Christmas present to me.

Myrabelle opened the door herself and I noticed an air of suppressed nervous excitement about her.

"I'm delighted you could come, Lynny. I've something special to tell you," and she kissed my cheek and took my coat. After admiring its cut and smartness, she handed it to the "general's" trainee, a timid-looking girl named Violet. Filled with curiosity, I followed Myrabelle into her beautifully decorated drawing room.

A huge Christmas tree filled one corner. It was covered with unlit candles and balls of iridescent glass shimmering in the firelight.

"I see you approve," Myrabelle said with a happy smile at my rapt expression.

My eye was held by a mound of parcels beneath the tree, and particularly a handsome doll's pram with a lavishly dressed doll, residing grandly amongst its lacy pillows. Myrabelle caught my surprise.

"That's what I want to tell you about," she whispered, drawing me over to a chair by the fire, as the "general" entered with a tray.

"Oh but she hasn't half done us proud!" I exclaimed, when hot mince pies, delicate vol-au-vents, and thick slices of rich plumy cake, met my hungry gaze.

Myrabelle poured tea from a silver teapot, and with a cup in one hand and a plate of cream-topped mince pies in the other, I settled down to enjoy my unexpected break.

"The doll's pram is for Alex's little girl, Rose-Ann; she's coming here for Christmas," Myrabelle began, gazing pensively into the fire. "As you know, Alex and I have straightened things out between us and everything is going so well. He didn't want to go back to Greta, but he worried about the kindest way of telling her. However, while he was still worrying about the best way to tell her of his decision to come back to me, Greta confessed that she had met someone else....an Australian rancher, and she wanted to marry him and go back with him to his own country. The snag was he didn't want the child, so she asked Alex if he would like to adopt her. He, of course, was only too delighted at the prospect, as he adores the little one, but he was desperately worried at what my reaction would be....he didn't want to foist another woman's child on me. He thought of asking his sister in Longford if she would take care of Rose-Ann, but she already has a large family of her own."

Myrabelle paused and a tender smile hovered about her lips.

"And?" I prompted, "Oh do please go on, Myrabelle."

"Well," she exploded joyfully, "I was over the moon at the chance to have a little child of my own to love, so I suggested we both adopt her."

"Oh Myrabelle," I breathed. "A Christmas baby!" Then a thought struck me.

"Please don't think I'm trying to cast a damper, but will the child make strange?"

I could not go on. Miserably I felt I should have kept my misgivings to myself.

Would she understand, or be offended that her friend was the one to cast a shadow on her happiness?

But Myrabelle only smiled and met my gaze serenely. "I know what you mean, Lynny; will the child miss her mother and reject me? I don't feel that she will. She is only three years old and saw very little of her mother, anyway. Greta was into interior design in a big way and left the care of her daughter to various nannies. It's Alex for whom the child holds a deep attachment, as he has always made it a priority to see her very regularly."

"I'm so happy for you, Myrabelle," I said firmly. "There is no doubt but that the little girl will find every happiness with you and Alex. When is she coming?"

"Any time now," she replied wringing her hands nervously; the serenity of a few moments earlier, suddenly dispelled.

"Oh Lynny, I'm really a bit uneasy....well terrified, actually; suppose the child doesn't like me. After all, she's never even seen me," and the bright eyes clouded apprehensively.

"Don't be daft," I answered briskly, stifling my doubts in the knowledge that what she needed most now was encouragement.

"You're a very nice, kind and generous person; Rose-Ann is a lucky child."

"I wasn't always what you'd call kind and generous," mused Myrabelle wistfully. "I'm afraid all my troubles made me difficult and jealous. I found the going hard when I saw other people happy. You remember how nasty I was to you in the beginning?"

I put my hand over hers. "Don't think about that ever again, dear Myrabelle," I begged. "You've had a lot of disappointments in your life, and I wouldn't be much of a friend if I didn't understand what that can do, even to the nicest people. Probably, I would have reacted in the same way myself if it had happened to me....possibly I'd be the hell of a lot worse," I responded emphatically.

Just then a car pulled up on the drive. "That must be them," she cried with flushed cheeks.

I jumped up to leave, but she caught my arm. "Oh please don't go, Lynny, I want you to stay with me....for moral support. I mean....supposing she really doesn't take to me!"

Voices sounded from the hall, and we crept to the door and listened breathlessly....a man's voice, a child's treble and the "general's," crisp and reassuring tones.

Myrabelle's hand trembled on my arm, and we moved away from the door as it opened to reveal a happy and beaming Alex. He was holding a pretty little girl by the hand; she was dressed in a white teddy bear coat and red pully-ups. Her pale face was surrounded by a mop of fair curls and the blue eyes were large and frightened. She bore a great resemblance to Alex, and her delicate colouring could have made her Myrabelle's daughter. Endearingly, in her free hand she clutched a bedraggled yellow duck.

No one moved, and it seemed as if we were all frozen in a timeless painting.

Then Myrabelle bent down opening her arms to the child, and the spell was broken. The little girl instantly left her father's side and rushed into the loving embrace.

Holding her close, Myrabelle gazed with shining eyes over the soft curls, at her husband. Wordlessly she held out a hand to him and he went to her side, putting his arms around the two of them. Tears misted the scene and my heart ached with joy, for I knew they were all safe at last in each other's love.

I wept openly, and the highly charged atmosphere was only lightened when the "general" pushed a trolley of glasses and a bucket of champagne, into the room.

Alex was the first to speak. "Bubbly all around," he ordered gaily, pulling the cork expertly from the magnum bottle. Rose-Ann chuckled in surprise as a golden spray shot towards the ceiling. The "general" walked quietly to the door.

"Not so fast, Marlana," Alex halted her, and I gulped in amazement as the "general's" glamorous name was revealed.

"Alex is the only one who dares call our "general" by her name," giggled Myrabelle to me.

For once, the "general" looked disconcerted, but Alex moved swiftly towards her, and putting a friendly arm around her starchy person, led her over to us.

"You must drink to our happiness," he informed her with a grin. "You're a valued member of this family too, so come on, you too Lynny, to us all together," and he handed each of us a crystal glass of the golden libation.

The "general" was giggling girlishly at the end of her second glass of champagne when Myrabelle brought the little girl over to her. In a few minutes, the shy child and intimidating "general," were engrossed in examining the doll's frothy underwear, and settling it to sleep in the new pram.

Myrabelle seated herself on the couch, her long legs tucked under her, the smart shoes kicked into a corner. Alex, all smiles, sat beside her, his arm around her shoulders.

I sighed contentedly and gave a sudden hiccup.

"All's well that ends well, and may the best horse jump the ditch," I misquoted merrily, fairly tipsy from the excellent champagne.

"Watch it," laughed Myrabelle. "I'd best send you home before Edward comes looking for you, and finds you three sheets to the wind, with a glass in your hand."

Hilarious now, we wished each other a merry Christmas and success to temperance. Laughingly we exchanged kisses under the mistletoe, even the "general" coyly submitting to a brush from Alex's tickly moustache.

I need not have worried about Rose-Ann settling in; she lay sleeping peacefully in Myrabelle's arms and would not be parted from her.

Before I left, Myrabelle and I exchanged presents. I had bought her a beautiful porcelain vase, depicting Japanese ladies enjoying life with some frolicsome males, in a highly ornamental eastern garden. I had come upon it in a dirty old bucket, amid chipped china and ancient kitchen ware. The lot had fallen cheaply to me at a local auction, and it was only after washing the vase carefully in "Princess Flakes," that the exquisite design and delicate tints, were revealed in all their glory.

Indeed, I had not wanted to part with it, but at my wit's end to get something beautiful and unusual for Myrabelle's gift, and knowing how much she would appreciate it, it seemed the perfect answer.

"It's a wonderful piece," Myrabelle enthused, holding it at arm's length to catch the light. "I don't know how you can bring yourself to part with it; are you sure, Lynny?"

"I'm sure alright," I said firmly. "It's safer with you than me. If Rosemarie got hold of it she'd most likely swap it with one of her school pals, for a jam jar."

I turned my attention to Myrbelle's present to me, and stripping aside swathes of tissue, I found a blue nightdress of finest georgette, very seductive and diaphanous. A petticoat, French knickers, and matching bed jacket, completed the set.

"Oh they're gorgeous!" I sighed, but hesitated slightly over the nightdress. "I can't wear this," I demurred. "It would expose too much of me; besides I'd be perished."

Myrabelle shook with laughter, and the child woke to stare at her inquiringly.

"Lynny, you really are the end. Aren't you lucky to have so much to expose? Surely it isn't a problem," she chortled.

I blushed hotly and folded the nightdress in its bed of tissue.

"Haven't you a fine handsome husband to keep you warm in it?" put in Alex jovially.

"Don't answer that," grinned Myrabelle. "I was rather thinking along the lines of someone else's husband."

I bandied their jokes good humouredly as Myrabelle produced a delightful doll's house for Rosemarie, which, according to Alex, would guarantee hours of peace for me.

For Edward there were two bottles of the best Sherry from Smith's on the Green, which I reciprocated with a box of cigars from Edward to Alex.

Ida was not forgotten either. Her parcel later disclosed a set of exotic cushion covers to embroider, complete with hanks of colourful threads.

As I left, I slipped a box containing a pair of leather, fur-lined gloves into the "general's" hand. She looked surprised as pink-cheeked with pleasure, she thanked me, and observed: "Oh you shouldn't, Mrs. Davis. I'll be a right swank in these and get a head full of notions," and with a sprightly twirl showing a glimpse of sensible brown bloomers, she headed for the kitchen, completely forgetting to see me out.

Chapter 77

Christmas 1929 was a very happy one for us all.

Although Rosemarie's faith had been badly shaken in the reality of Santa Clause by the revelation in Pim's, she still looked forward to his visit on Christmas Eve. Needless to say, she did her level best to stay awake and catch him out, and we had to wait until nearly morning to deliver the goods, by which time she was dozing, half sitting up, still holding on to the bars of the cot.

When I awoke next morning, it was to find her sifting through Santa's offerings and carefully discarding anything that could be described as practical.

We went in a happy party to the Gaiety on St. Stephen's Day; Alex, Myrabelle, Rose-Ann, Aunt Cissy, Rosemarie, Edward and I. The pantomime was "Robinson Crusoe" and what I remember most about that was the alluring new hat I was wearing for the occasion.

It was in soft pink felt with long scarves of silk ninon, which were wound around the neck, and left to flutter beguilingly at the back. Unfortunately, a small child behind me found these scarves far more entertaining than the doings of Crusoe and his friends, with the result that they were soon reduced to sticky, chocolate-stained rags, and far more embarrassing than beguiling when I got outside.

Myrabelle and Alex treated us all to another pantomime in the Olympia; this time it was a dazzling production of "Cinderella."

I was hatless and carefree....at least until Rosemarie found it necessary to give Rose-Ann her version of the story in a voice that reverberated around the theatre.

There was much clucking of tongues and urgent admonitions to "Sheeeeeeeeeeeech," before I managed to persuade her to keep the telling until afterwards.

Peace reigned again, and I settled down to enjoy the show with my hand in Edward's. There was a sparkling dance sequence on stage when Rosemarie signalled that she wanted to tell me something. Thinking it but a mundane request for "Miggy," I held out my hand to her.

But Rosemarie had other ideas; she wanted to join the dancers on the stage.

"I know that song, Mamma, and you and me have done that dance at home; you can come up there with me too," she ended generously.

It took a daunting amount of whispered persuasion and many disapproving hisses from the immediate audience to quieten her, and even then I did not fully succeed.

"Why not, Mamma?" she demanded rebelliously, pounding my knees with her hands.

But Myrabelle saved the day. She beckoned and Rosemarie made her way hurriedly to her side. There was much whispering between them, a large pink marshmallow changed hands, and Rosemarie caught my eye and smiled smugly. For the rest of the show she remained quietly and happily with Myrabelle.

I stole a look at Rose-Ann seated on Alex's knee, her eyes round with wonder as she followed every movement on the stage.

"A wee angel," I sighed, and smiled wryly at my unpredictable little terror.

Chapter 78

The New Year came, and I still refused to consider the possibility that it could be our last in this lovely old house.

A week later the solicitors wrote. I got the letter when I was polishing the hall. Shaking with nerves, I took the stiff, official envelope into the dining room to read.

It was expectedly terse and to the point. Yes we could have a new lease, but this could not be arranged until the Pembroke engineers had completed an inspection of the house....

But all I really absorbed were the words, "you could have a new lease."

Any further implications were way beyond my comprehension. When I told Edward later he was wary; he wondered why the granting of the lease should depend upon an inspection of the house.

In due course we found out.

An engineer duly arrived and spent the morning going over the house. His findings were that the house was in a very bad state of disrepair; ceilings were about to descend on our unsuspecting heads, dry rot was rampant, floor boards needed replacing....the list was formidable.

And that was only the inside.

By the time he had reamed off a list of repairs required for the outside, which would run into hundreds of pounds to be borne by us, I knew with a sinking heart, that we had lost the battle to stay in Leeson Street.

"We could never afford to carry out all the work we would automatically take on with a new tenancy," said Edward gently when we discussed the situation over a belated lunch.

"It would break us, for they'll make us do it to their specifications," said Edward with a worried frown.

Dispassionately, I forced myself to contemplate the situation; I accepted that the amount of repairs necessary for the house were immense. There were sprawling patches of damp in nearly every room, which had in some degenerated into dry rot.

Woodworm had invaded the furniture and window frames; its pitted tracks were everywhere.

In the stillness of an evening rats could be heard gnawing beneath the floor boards of the breakfast room, due to its close proximity to Mr. Lamb's malodorous stables next door. A pervasive smell of mould hung in the basement, a part of the house no longer suited to its original purpose, and the only time we had used it was on the memorable night of our party.

I swallowed hard, and in the face of Edward's reasoning, I had no option but to concur with the realities as bravely as I could.

"Dearest Edward," I whispered, and put my cold hand over his, "I know you did your best to consider me, even against your better judgement, but it's out of our hands now. I realise we could never take on the huge expenses that staying here would involve us in."

I jumped up quickly and furtively brushed away a tear.

"Let's go and look at some new houses. I should like to live by the sea. I saw in the papers that lots of new houses are going up in Clontarf...." I babbled on, afraid to stop in case I cried forever.

Chapter 79

A few days later all my hard won-resolutions went topsy- turvy.

Our Solicitors wrote again to inform us that the house was going up for auction, and supplied us with dates and a venue for a meeting should we be interested in making an offer for the property.

A great surge of hope flooded my being; the list of repairs we should have to expedite were forgotten by me, and I begged Edward to make a reasonable offer for the house. Edward disagreed, but I became so distressed at his refusal that he relented, and promised to advise our solicitors to act on our behalf.

"But you know we have very little money, and we'll be faced with all those repairs....the Pembroke lease is very strict and can compel us to follow their instructions to the letter," he demurred.

"You can get a mortgage....there are banks and building societies, and I can continue with the lettings...." I countered wildly.

Edward shook his head despondently, but agreed to do what he could.

"Do anything....try everything," I implored.

Edward finished his breakfast and left for work, and I tried to compose my racing thoughts, and divert my nervous energy, into the ordinary domestic routine.

When Edward returned at tea time, I could hardly wait to ask how he had fared in his efforts to raise the money. The news was good; subject to its rules and regulations, and seeing that Edward had a good and permanent job, one of the main banks was prepared to give us a loan. I was jubilant.

"But don't forget," Edward cautioned, "what we borrow, we must pay back with interest."

That evening, Edward wrote to Norris Grimes of "Jacob Grimes, Grimes and Reynolds," instructing them to act for us in making a bid for the house, and naming the maximum price we were prepared to pay.

I posted the precious letter, going specially down to the GPO to do so.

The date of the auction came and went; I was sick with anxiety to know how we had fared.

But we heard nothing, and I hovered around the hall door every morning, unable to have my breakfast until I saw the postman pass by with nothing for us.

At last, Edward and I decided to call on Norris Grimes of "Jacob Grimes, Grimes and Reynolds," to find out why we had heard nothing from them.

The result was astounding. The solicitor had made no bid for the house on our behalf, and it was sold over our heads at a price a little lower than the one we had been prepared to offer. Mr. Grimes, huge of girth, pompous and disdainful, informed us coldly that he had got no "mandate" from us "to tender for the dwelling house in Lower Leeson Street," and he summoned several equally disagreeable looking members of his staff to back his assertions.

What could we do? We knew nothing of the law, except as something to be avoided. The thought of challenging the intimidating Norris Grimes, Jacob Grimes, anonymous Grimes or possibly terrifying Reynolds, never crossed our minds. All we could think of as we left their imposing offices was the question, why had they not done as we had instructed them? And to that conundrum we never got an answer.

When we were safely outside in the street, I burst into helpless tears, but Edward sounded relieved as he mused: "It's strange about that letter they said they never got. Knowing you, there's no doubting that they did, but thank heaven, you took sole charge of it. If it had been left to me, nothing would have convinced you but that I hadn't posted it."

And guiltily, I knew he was right.

Chapter 80

We bought a newly built, four bed- roomed house in Clontarf, standing on half an acre of garden. There was a magnificent view of the sea, flanked by the Dublin mountains, from the front bedroom.

It seemed like doll's house after our mansion in Leeson Street, but it was compact, in a nice airy locality, and with Church, shops and schools at an agreeable distance. The rather daunting price of £850 had the fifty pounds knocked off after a haggle with the builder.

From then on it was all hard work, and for this, I was grateful; I did not want any free time in which to think or speculate.

The tenants had been given notice. Mr. and Mrs. Ventor had gone to their new home in Sandymount, and the dear old Captain had found safe harbourage with a mate from his seafaring days in Howth. Ida would, of course, come with us, as would Jane who was leaving in a year or so to marry a nice young bricklayer to whom she had got engaged at Christmas.

It was the evening before our departure. Most of our furniture had gone on ahead, or rather, the few necessary items which had escaped the auctioneer's hammer, as much of our stuff was too big for the box-like rooms of the new house. Lace curtains were stripped from the windows, floor coverings rolled up, and the pictures and pier glass removed from the walls, leaving behind only the wraith-like imprint of their presence.

I went sadly from room to room, murmuring goodbye to each, and dropping many tears on the way. To-day I could cry my heart out, but to- morrow I must try and pretend, for my family's sake that I was happy to exchange it all for a modern villa in suburbia. A box-like house, cold and impersonal, which had never been privy to the hopes, foibles and contradictions of a family. How could such a place compare with this old house from whose walls memories of a motley humanity still emanated, where a shadow might flit around a corner, old silks rustle in the hall, or a sudden ghostly whisper catch the ear?

I stood by the mantelpiece in the empty drawing room for the last time. Moonlight spilled through the long Georgian windows to lie in a silvery pool on the bare floor.

In the darkened street, a late tram trundled past, and in response, a shadow ran along the wall, momentarily revealing the gilded cornice of the ceiling. Footsteps echoed forlornly on the pavement below and were lost in the distance. One might hear a pin drop, a hall door banged across the street, and the urgent clip-clop of Mr. Lamb's horse and cart, returning from a swill- collecting expedition, only emphasised the heavy stillness.

The chandelier tinkled eerily, as if an unseen hand had lingered on its crystal drops, and yet that could not be, for early this morning, Edward had carefully packed each sparkling piece.

I closed my eyes and the gentle Mrs. Gandon was there beside me; her distinctive Eau-de-Cologne suffusing the air, and proclaiming her unbroken link with the room she had loved best in the house.

Was this enchantment mine as well, or would the house someday, forego its hold on me? At last I went wearily to bed, and after much restless tossing, fell into an uneasy doze.

Sometime later, I was disturbed by a distant sound; I listened fearfully and the sobbing and sighing of a woman's voice penetrated my senses. I lay rigid, fully awake as the crying grew closer, my heartbeats exploding in my ears.

"Edward," I moaned, but tired out from all the upheaval, he slept on.

The bitter weeping was now outside our bedroom door, and I felt I could bear it no longer, but must open the door to whoever was there in such distress.

I stole to the door and the sobbing ebbed, as if its source was drifting away. I hesitated and then pulled it open. The landing was shrouded in darkness and there was no sign of anyone. I let out a long shuddering breath, and the thought grew in my mind, that the house was crying because it did not want me to leave it.

I closed the door and crept silently back to bed, but my uneasy sleep was beset by nightmare images; I found myself alone in a foggy street, peopled by spectre-like figures. The buildings rose close and high in towering peaks, some had gaping holes where windows might have been, but all appeared to be centuries old. Then I was in a doorway waiting for a tram, and although I could see no one, the air was full of murmuring voices. Suddenly, there was a crash and the buildings were falling out of the sky. Terrified, my heart jumped and then plummeted sickeningly, and I sat up in bed drenched in sweat. I turned to Edward, but he wasn't there, and succumbing to a few drops of "whiskery" from the tooth mug, I fell into an exhausted sleep.

Chapter 81

I awoke on this eventful morning to the cheery call of newsboys, the ringing of Church bells and the clangour of trams and carts. The milkman's can rattled against the polished churn, his gruff "yup" and "hike" a signal for the horse's guidance. The coalman's bell mingled with the postman's whistling, while either, or both, banged loudly on the hall door.

These were the sounds I had awoken to for the last five years, but were hearing now for the last time, and what would replace them out in the wilds of suburbia? Sadly I wiped away a tear as I remembered the weird experience of the previous night. Was the house really grieving for me and saying a last farewell?

I looked around the bedroom; it was empty. Edward and Rosemarie were up. I listened, and could catch snatches of her childish treble downstairs, raised in some urgent demand, and hoped she was not being too rough on Ida.

I dozed a little and sleepily turned to find Ida by the bedside with a tray of tea, poached eggs on toast, and a little mound of potato cakes.

I feebly protested while she helped me into a sitting position, and adjusted the pillows comfortably behind me. I could hear Rosemarie running through the empty rooms, her feet echoing on the bare boards.

Ida chatted cheerfully, as I tried to eat the breakfast she had so lovingly prepared for me, fully understanding how low my spirits were and what a wrench the loss of the house was causing me. I was just finishing my cup of tea when there was a shout from Edward from the floor above.

I sprang out of bed and rushed upstairs with Ida close on my heels.

There we stood appalled.

The landing ceiling lay in clumps of broken plaster on the floor in front of us, and through the open door of the adjoining bedroom, I could see that the ceiling there had suffered the same fate.

I looked upwards at the rotted rafters, some suspended drunkenly, others crumbled away. Here and there thin pencils of light filtered through where slates were broken. Occasional thuds disturbed the silence, as lumps of plaster fell dismally around us. A large spider scurried for shelter, and a sudden shaft of sunlight illuminated a spiral of swirling dust.

I turned and caught Ida's eye; only yesterday she had vacated that room as the furniture had all been removed, and she had spent the night on a couch in the dining room.

"That accounts for the crash last night," said Edward grimly, emerging from the damaged bedroom and rubbing his dusty hands together.

"What crash?" asked Ida in surprise.

"Didn't you hear it then?" I was amazed,

But it transpired that she had heard nothing....she had peacefully slept through it all.

And what of my nightmare? Had it been a premonition, some sort of warning, or had the actual crash been inexplicably fused with my fevered dream.

Rosemarie ran up and caught my hand. Speechless for once, she stared open- mouthed at the desolation around her.

We went gloomily downstairs to make our final preparations, grateful that no one had been hurt when the ceiling had crashed without warning. My mind raced; supposing it had been the ceiling in our room or below in the dining room....! I felt sick at the thought, and some realisation dawned on me of the great disturbance in store for the house if it were to survive. Undoubtedly, we would have to go; we could not remain while such massive repairs were in progress.

Chapter 82

Jane was already installed in the new house. She had gone ahead to take in the furniture, light the fires, prepare a meal, and generally bring some order into the chaos of moving.

Ginger had vanished a few days earlier, probably fed up with all the disturbance, and would surely manage to insinuate himself comfortably in another household. Certainly, he had made it clear that he was not moving out to Clontarf; he was a city puss, born and bred. As a token of my best wishes for him, I left him a saucer of milk and a generous supply of the biscuits he favoured....cafe noir.

At last all was done, and Edward pulled the hall door behind us giving me the key. Rosemarie and Ida went ahead while I lingered on the granite step, and clung to the railings overlooking the basement. How often had I strapped Rosemarie's pram to them in the sunshine.

I felt Edward gently loosen my grip and guide me to the street below. Everything was so ordinary and that hurt. Did no one, with their closed inscrutable faces, out of all those passing by, hurrying to work, dallying to the shops, even polishing the brasses on their hall doors, feel a pang for me?

"Come on, sweet girl," Edward's voice was urging me as his arm tightened around my waist and he led me down to our own little motor car. Ida and Rosemarie were safely ensconced in the back of the car, the child looking subdued as she sucked her thumb, and hugged the once beautiful doll that Myrabelle had given her, but now its fair curls were askew, and its painted features smeared from too much washing.

Edward started the car and I saw the house swim by in a mist of tears; it looked so serene on this lovely sunny morning. For the last time, its loving ambience enfolded me as it had first done five years ago. The years might roll away, but nostalgia would keep tender for always my memories of it. All future happiness would be measured against those halcyon days when it was ours.

I sighed, the car accelerated, gathered speed, and the medley of street sounds took up the refrain in my heart.... "Come back....come back....come back yesterday."

The End